The GHOST of KHARTOUM

The Thomas Scoundrel Novels

Vol.1
Scoundrel in the Thick

Vol.2
Passage to Moorea

Vol.3
The Ghost of Khartoum

The GHOST of KHARTOUM

Vol.3

The Life & Times

of

Colonel Thomas Edward Scoundrel, USA, Ret.

B.R. O'HAGAN

PEDEE CREEK PRESS

PEDEE CREEK PRESS

The Ghost of Khartoum is a work of historical fiction. Apart from the well known actual people, events, and locales that figure in the narrative, all names, characters, places, and incidents are the products of the author's imagination or are used fictitiously. Any resemblance to current events or locales, or to living persons, is entirely coincidental.

Printed in the United States of America

ISBN: 978-1-7342263-5-5

For inquiries about volume orders please contact:

info@brohagan.com

Cover Illustration

Thomas Scoundrel in the Sahara

by B.R.O'Hagan

For Gary Hartzell. Cherished friend, teacher, and indestructible wit. Drinks at the Algonquin are on me.

CHAT NOIR #84 Boulevard de Rochechouar
Montemartre

14 April .84

Thomas, my dear new friend, how very American it was of your army to hang so wonderfully barbaric a name as le Scélérat- The Scoundrel- around your neck. Watching Toulouse wheel away from the table in laughter only to fall into the ample bosom of that angelic dancer as she struggled to maintain her composure and remember her steps on stage, was a true highlight of the evening for me. I leave for the south of France tomorrow to paint the harvest, & will think of you making your way to Istanbul via le Express d'Orient. I have no doubt you will make a grand adventure of your travels. Return to us soon to share your tales, and I will prevail upon you to sit for your portrait.

Vincent

~PROLOGUE~

Winter, 1417 B.C.
Tasekhet-ma'at

Amunet ran like the wind through the winding limestone canyons his people called *'The Great and Majestic Necropolis of the Millions of Years of the Pharaoh, Life, Strength, Health in The West of Thebes.'* The tomb entrances, outbuildings, and workers' village he passed beneath the star-swept desert sky were located on the holy ground west of the mighty *Iteru,* the great river whose yearly floods deposited millions of tons of rich black soil along its banks. This isolated valley, the eternal place of rest for the all-powerful rulers of the upper and lower kingdoms of Kemet, was beloved of the gods and protected against bandits by cadres of Pharaoh's best soldiers and hundreds of priests who were skilled not only in worship rituals, but also in the more temporal and practical use of spears and swords.

At 14, Amunet was not only the chief builder's favorite messenger, but also the fastest and strongest runner among the thousands of diggers, stone cutters, artists, slaves, cooks, and other craftsmen who lived in the village of Deir el-Medina and spent their lives cutting deep into the limestone and marl rock in the twisting valleys to fashion tombs designed to last for eternity.

During a typical ten-hour workday the boy would be assigned to an assistant builder or architect and charged with transmitting their verbal instructions to workers inside and outside of the tomb complex. His message delivery had to be precise; if he left a single word out of the builder's instructions, or if he added a single word, it could result in a wall not being properly raised, a corridor not being accurately angled, or a cornerstone being set off balance. In such events, workers could be maimed or killed by falling rock or, worse, many days —even weeks—of work could have to be completely redone. The dead and badly injured were easy to replace after their mangled bodies were tossed into the open pits that littered tomb construction sites. But the work took priority over everything, including human life. Such was the decree of mighty Amenhotep, whose name was never to be spoken aloud by low caste peasants like Amunet lest their tongues be cut out and tossed to the jackals.

The inside of a tomb was a warren of passages, staircases, chambers large and small, and countless vestibules that sometimes led in the proper direction, and other times led to deep shafts cut into the bowels of the earth for unsuspecting robbers to fall to their deaths. Theft and desecration of a royal tomb meant death for the live miscreant and eternal damnation of his soul.

It had been both a surprise and an honor for the boy to be summoned to the tent of the chief builder tonight. He had prostrated himself upon the sandy floor, and when commanded to stand he listened carefully to each word of the lengthy message the builder shared, and then repeated it back verbatim. When the builder was satisfied that he had memorized the message perfectly, he was taken outside the tent and given a bowl of soup and a piece of warm bread to strengthen him for the marathon ahead.

He finished his meal and was astonished when a guard handed him a pair of newly woven sandals.

"Now, boy," said the guard, "you will take the message to Pharaoh. He is encamped not far from the banks of *Iteru* where he has come to inspect progress on his tomb."

The boy was overcome with fear. Pharaoh? What could possibly be so important that a runner was being sent in the night to the tents of His Majestic Presence? Would not a chariot get there faster? Then he realized that in the darkness a chariot would have to slowly and carefully pick its way around the rocks and potholes that littered the miles of trails one had to follow to get out of the valley and onto the plain that ran along the great river. Sending a runner made sense.

"Do not stop along the way," the guard added in a gruff tone. "Even should your legs turn to lead or your heart burst in your chest, you will run. No lion will overtake you; no bandit will block you. Is this understood?"

The boy's eyes shone with pride. He stood tall and returned the guard's gaze with a look of fierce determination.

"And how will I find Pharaoh's encampment?" he asked.

The guard smiled. "His retinue stretches for more than a mile along the river plain and will be illuminated by the light of a thousand torches. Run east out of the valley and away from the foothills and follow the smell of water. When you think you see the fire of heaven itself, you have found Him."

Two hours later the boy emerged out of the final mountain ravine and onto the shrub-covered plain that swept down to the river. He had stumbled several times onto sharp rock piles in the darkness, and both his knees were bloodied. He stopped for a moment and drank deeply from the small goatskin water pouch tied at his waist and then pressed on. The bushes and grasses grew thicker as he went, and at times he had to push his way through low walls of matted plant debris. His lungs ached more than his legs did, and he began to feel a throbbing pain at the base of his spine, but he was not deterred. He kept up a smooth rhythmic stride when he hit open spaces and gritted his teeth and bowed his head when he had to make his way through spiny-branched thickets that tore through his tunic and left deep scratches across his chest, abdomen, and sides.

Once he felt the presence of a wild beast, and sensed the animal was tracking him. That only spurred him to run harder, and to dismiss the pain coursing through his body. The stars whirled across the bowl of the sky above him, and together with a sliver of yellow moon gave off just enough light to make out shapes a few feet ahead.

Then he tripped over a branch, rolled down a hill, and smashed his head on a rock. He pulled himself to his knees, dizzy and nauseous. Blood flowed down from his forehead, and he had to wipe it from his eyes with the hem of his tunic. How long had he been running? Three hours? Four? He forced himself to stand and take a deep breath. He had to find the strength to keep going.

He turned around to make out the path on the other side of the hill and was astonished to see a dull yellow glow on the eastern horizon.

Sunrise was hours away, and on the opposite side of the world. The light could only be from the massed torches at Pharaoh's camp.

He took a final sip of water, splashed some on his face, and tossed the empty goatskin aside. His destination was finally in sight, about an hour's run from where he stood. His fear subsided, his pain diminished, and his heart felt it could run through this night and into forever.

He encountered the first sentries a few hundred yards from the long line of tents that stretched across the strip of land along the river that his people called 'the cultivation.' A narrow path wound to the top of a low rise, where two men in leather head coverings crossed their spears and called him to a halt.

"What, now, boy," said one of the men. "Do you not know that travel here is forbidden while the Majestic One is in residence? Turn, and go back to your village."

Amunet bent at his waist, placed his hands on his knees, and took a deep breath. Then he stood and said, "I bear a message for Pharaoh and have been commanded by the Chief Builder to deliver it to His Majesty and no one else."

"You have reached the camp of His Majesty's High Priest. Who shall I announce?"

"Amunet, the Builder's personal messenger," said the boy.

"Will he know that name?" the second guard asked.

The boy shook his head. "He will not. But he has seen my face many times when he has come to view the progress on Pharaoh's resting place."

The guards exchanged a glance. If they took the boy to the Priest's tent and asked the noble one if he recognized the messenger, the Priest would be the one to decide if the boy should be allowed to be taken before Pharaoh. They would not bear any blame if this was some kind of ruse.

"This way," the first guard finally said.

Amunet followed the guard as he wove through the torch-lit camp. The deeper into the rows of tents they went, the more soldiers they encountered. Many of them were seated in small circles on the ground playing dice or rolling marbles and moving lion-shaped figures across Mehan boards decorated with snake symbols. When they stopped in front of a tent that was considerably larger than any others they had passed, Amunet saw four guards standing beside a line of brightly colored pennants.

"Wait here," he was told.

Ten minutes later two soldiers in officers' tunics came outside, followed by the High Priest.

"This is the boy?" asked one of the officers.

"It is," Amunet's guard replied.

It was not cold, but Amunet felt his teeth begin to chatter, and his knees went weak.

"Do you know this boy, Lord?" an officer asked the High Priest.

The Priest nodded. "I see him often at the tomb. He is the builder's messenger."

"And would one such as he be entrusted to carry a message meant only for His Majestic Presence?"

The priest thought for a moment. Despite his power, prestige, and status at court, he faced the same dilemma as Amunet's guard: take the boy before Pharaoh and risk being humiliated, or deny the boy's request and possibly face Pharaoh's wrath.

"Do you swear before the gods that you have been charged to deliver this message to Pharaoh?' he asked Amunet.

"I swear," the boy replied with his head held high.

"And should you have come here for the purpose of some deception; do you understand that your punishment would be death?"

Amunet looked at the expressions on the faces of the High Priest's guards; they would have no qualms about enforcing the penalty if called upon. "I understand," he replied.

The priest turned to one of the officers. "Go to His Majesty's chambers and ask if he wishes to allow a messenger from the Chief Builder into his presence."

The officer nodded and walked towards a cluster of large tents. Dozens of embroidered purple and turquoise pennants and six war chariots encircled the largest tent, where Amunet estimated there were at least 50 soldiers armed with swords and spears standing watch.

"Clean him up and give him a fresh tunic," the Priest said to Amunet's guard. They he turned and went back into his tent.

An hour later four soldiers arrived to collect Amunet. They wore red-striped headgear, their breastplates were woven with several thicknesses of linseed strips, and each carried a bronze sickle-sword in one hand and a wood shield reinforced with leather in the other.

The soldier who had accompanied him from outside the camp lay his hand on the boy's shoulder. "Be brave," he whispered.

The escort surrounded Amunet for the walk to Pharaoh's tent, where they handed him off to a senior officer dressed in a knee-length leather tunic reinforced with rows of small bronze pieces and a multi-color belt fashioned from semiprecious stones mined in the Upper Kingdom.

"Do not speak unless invited," the gray-haired soldier said as they walked between a row of torches. "Do not turn your back on Pharaoh, and do not sit in his presence. If you need to cough or break wind, do it before we enter."

Amunet felt bile rising in his throat, and he struggled to hold off the urge to vomit. His head was spinning; he, the son of a simple village baker, was about to be ushered into the presence of a god. It was an honor–and a terror–too great to contemplate.

A soldier pulled back the tent flap, and they walked across a thick animal-hide carpet towards a cluster of wood and canvas chairs upon which three men and two women were seated in a semicircle. The tent was larger than the grandest room inside Pharaoh's tomb complex. Incense and spice perfused the air, and magnificent illustrations of lions, crocodiles, great birds, and oxen adorned tapestries that were hung along the walls above ornate tabled laden with fruits, breads, rare delicacies, and flagons of beer and wine.

The boy did not need to be told which of the people was Amenhotep. Pharaoh was famous for his great physical strength, and tales of him shooting an arrow through a brass ring at 100 yards and beating 200 soldiers in a single-man boat-rowing contest, were frequently told around the cook fire in Amunet's home.

No one took note of his entry. They continued their lively conversation, sipping wine, nibbling on fruit, and laughing at one another's witty remarks. Then, after several minutes passed one of the women nodded in the officer's direction. He placed his hand in the small of Amunet's back and gave him a gentle push. The boy stepped into the circle and then, as he had been instructed, went down to his knees, bowed his head, and held his hands at his side.

"And so our Builder deigns us worthy of receiving a message so important that it could not wait until daybreak," a man's voice said. "From the looks of the child I would say that the journey from our valley tonight was not without some danger. Raise your head, boy, that I may take stock of you."

Amunet slowly raised his head and looked at Pharaoh. He was surprised to note that that his fear had evaporated, replaced now by curiosity. Pharaoh was not a tall man, but his bare arms under his sleeveless tunic were heavily muscled. He wore golden bracelets on each wrist, and his eyes were outlined with a vivid green shade of *kohl*, a cream made from fats, galena, and malachite that was favored by the nobility and merchant classes alike. He wore a smooth, flowing robe of scarlet, and in one hand he held a jewel-encrusted goblet.

Pharaoh leaned forward. "You bear a message for me from our Builder?"

"I do, Lord," Amunet replied in a clear voice.

Pharaoh held up his goblet for a servant to fill. Then he settled back in his chair and said, "You may grace us now with the message from our Chief Builder."

The boy cleared his throat and stood up.

"Oh, Majestic Presence," he began, "the Chief Builder conveys his greeting, and beseeches your Lord to give ear to the words I am about to speak. Four days ago your artists began to apply paint to the walls of your resting quarters," the boy began. "The craftsmen first applied a thin coat of plaster, and when it was dry the next day the artists began to sketch the scenes your Majesty selected for each of the four walls. When the sketches were complete the next morning they began to apply paint, and by nightfall the room was completed."

"Go on," said Pharaoh, "thus far this sounds like an ordinary day."

"The Chief Builder and architect inspected the room late that night and pronounced it complete. I myself carried the message to the camp, and notified everyone that we would begin working on a new antechamber the next morning."

"I am guessing that work did not begin, for some unforeseen reason," Pharaoh said.

"It did not, Lord. I was summoned into the newly completed chamber at sunrise the next day. The Builder and the Architect were both there, along with the Master Painter who supervises the artists and the Captain of the tomb guards."

"Had the paint already faded?" laughed one of the guests, which made Pharaoh smile.

The boy shook his head solemnly. Thinking back on the moment he stepped into the chamber yesterday morning sent chills up his spine. To make the scene even more difficult to bear was that someone had forgotten to put salt into the torch oil to prevent it from smoking. Even with the smoke, though, he was convinced that what he saw was nothing less than the miraculous intervention of one of the gods.

"What had happened?" Pharaoh asked.

"After the artists completed their work the night before, someone came into the chamber and covered over a large section of one wall with fresh plaster and then painted a new scene, one that had not been authorized."

"A new scene overnight?" Pharaoh asked. "But doesn't the plaster have to dry for a full day or night before it can take paint, and doesn't it take a crew of several people?"

Amunet nodded his head. "Yes, Lord, that was half of the mystery."

"Half?" asked another of the guests. "It's not enough that someone committed a sacrilege against His Majesty? There is more?"

Amenhotep looked thoughtful. He took a drink of wine and looked at the messenger. "That is because it was not simply that someone painted over fresh artwork, is it boy. It's what they painted. Is that not so?"

Amunet lowered his head. "It is as you say, Lord."

The mid-day sun arced above the furrowed brown hills whose long, winding valleys had been chosen more than a century ago to become the home for the tombs of Kemet's leaders. Far from the prying eyes of the citizens of Thebes, and most importantly, far from the traditional sites that were scoured by thieves in search of burial treasure, the hills and valleys that spilled down to a narrow plain on the western shore of the great river satisfied both the religious and security requirements for constructing holy places of rest that would be safe for eternity.

Half of Amenhotep's palace guard had journeyed through the night from his camp to the tomb site, and the other half accompanied Pharaoh and his party in war chariots soon after sunrise. Amunet's heart swelled with pride when he was ordered to clamber up alongside a grizzled soldier on one of the last chariots in the long line that was soon sweeping across the plain and up into the rocky valley. The fact that his chariot was awash in the dust of the lead riders for the entire two-hour journey did not dispel the boy's enthusiasm. A smile creased his face as he planted his feet on the woven leather floorboard and gripped the edge of the engraved acacia wood frame, and it never wavered as they snaked along the heavily rutted path.

By the time Amunet's driver wheeled his horse to a halt near the entrance to the tomb complex, Pharaoh had already alighted and was talking with the Chief Builder beside a shaded table piled high with refreshments.

Amunet waited as the Chief Builder and High Priest organized the small group who would enter the tomb to examine the paintings that had so mysteriously appeared in the 'Hall in Which One Rests,' the royal burial chamber located deep within the tomb complex. The boy was surprised when an assistant to the Chief Builder asked him to join the party at the limestone steps called the 'Passage of the Way of Shu,' after the god of air.

"This invitation is the reward for your heroic race out of the valley and onto the cultivation last night," the assistant explained to the startled boy. "I was taken into the tomb this morning and have seen the monstrous destruction Great Pharaoh is about to confront. I caution you, boy, though you will be shocked at the sight, do not cry out, or speak, or in any way make a show of your discomfort. The High Priest believes that *Apopis*, or some other demon of chaos, has been at work in the tomb, and therefore only Pharaoh himself can call upon the Divine Ra to drive this evil from the tomb. Do you understand?"

Amunet fell into line as the group began the descent down a long stairwell and came to a halt in a chamber that was decorated with 37 small statues of the gods who were extolled in the Solar Litany. They continued to the 'Hall of Hindering,' a large room designed to stop both flood waters and thieves once the tomb was complete and went down more stairs and through four more chambers before they reached the burial chamber.

The High Priest brought them to a halt when they came to the steep ramp leading down into the resting chamber. Amunet knew the room well; he had delivered messages to the workers inside its spacious stone walls dozens of times over the past several months. It was enormous in comparison to other rooms inside the tomb, and its size was only magnified by the presence of eight imposing pillars that had been carved upriver and transported to the valley on barges.

The priest raised his hand for silence, and then chanted a prayer normally used for soldiers about to go into battle. Despite the warmth in the corridor from the torches and the press of bodies, Amunet suddenly felt chilled. The priest stepped forward and pulled aside a heavy curtain that had been placed only this morning, and stepped aside as first Pharaoh, and then his party, set foot inside the royal burial chamber.

When Amunet went down the steps leading into the main chamber and the vestibules leading off to other chambers, everything at first seemed normal. The vaulted ceiling was covered with paintings of everyday life along the great river, vividly colored protective deities looked down at the massive stone sarcophagus that dominated the center of the chamber, and the cabinets and shelves carved out of solid rock had just been painted in preparation to receive the treasures that would accompany Pharaoh to the afterlife upon his death.

Then he noticed that Pharaoh was rooted to the ground a few feet from the wall opposite his sarcophagus. His priests and advisors were clustered around him in a tight circle, so Amunet had to climb up onto a step to see what was going on.

The wall in front of Pharaoh had been painted with a spectacularly colored panorama of the Beautiful Feast of the Valley, replete with nobles, priests, demi-gods, and soldiers bearing baskets laden with bread, fruits, fish, and small, woven reed boats that symbolized the harvest act itself.

At least that described the wall as it looked yesterday. An astonishing transformation had taken place overnight, an audacious and amazing sleight of hand that the gods themselves would have a difficult time explaining.

He gazed over the heads of the crowd, taking note that everyone, from Pharaoh to his bodyguards, was transfixed by the fantastic images on the wall. No one moved, no one spoke. Then the High Priest cleared his throat and began "Mighty One…" only to be cut off by a curt shake of the head from Amenhotep.

Then Mighty Pharaoh slowly backed up to the middle of the chamber and leaned against the stone sarcophagus in which his physical body would spend eternity. When one of the torches sputtered and died a servant rushed forward with a lit reed to bring it back to life, but no one else moved or spoke.

Finally, Pharaoh stepped forward, turned, and addressed the chamber. "How many of you were here after the paintings were first complete, but before the new painting was added?"

"I am the only one who saw the completed work before its desecration," said the Chief Builder.

"No one else, are you certain?" Pharaoh continued.

The Chief Builder stared at the floor for a moment. "Only I, Majestic One, and perhaps my messenger, who I would have sent out to see that the workers returned the next morning."

"And is your messenger with us now?" Ahmenhotep asked.

Amunet spoke without permission, which was a serious breach of protocol. "I am here, Lord," he said in a calm, quiet voice.

Pharaoh looked across the chamber. "Join me," he said.

All eyes were fixed upon Amunet as he walked across to Pharaoh. His Majestic Presence looked at the boy as if he were sizing up a new horse or spear and then motioned for Amunet to step over to the newly painted wall beside him.

The boy had been in several tombs, and he sometimes sat and watched the artists as they carefully and precisely applied paint with thin horsehair brushes inside the outlines that had been drawn onto the fresh plaster with charcoal. The canon of practice that guided their hands had been handed down for hundreds of years. No deviations from the rules were permitted; faces were to be painted just so, bodies were to be turned perpendicular to the head at exact angles, and the final geometry of each section was plotted and applied within a narrow and unchanging set of principles. The mural in front of them now violated every one of those ancient laws.

Amenhotep turned to the boy. The low caste messenger was the only person in the room who did not have a host of political or religious motivations to mask his feelings about the scene painted on the wall. A Pharaoh might be an all-powerful ruler whose judgment could never be questioned, but he was not immune to the constant intrigue and struggles for influence that swirled around him at court. The fact that he did not turn to the Chief Priest or any of his ministers to ask for their opinion would cause great consternation, but what Amenhotep desired at this moment was unvarnished honesty, and that, he knew, would never come from people whose entire lives revolved around keeping their ruler happy.

"Take a moment to regard the painting, boy," Pharaoh said, "and then tell me what you see."

There was a buzz around the chamber as the self-important courtiers realized that their collective wisdom in such matters were being dismissed in favor of the feelings of a peasant boy. It was unthinkable.

Amunet had no awareness of the hornet's nest his mere presence had stirred up among Kemet's most powerful nobles, but it would not have mattered had they told him. The portraits on the wall had taken complete hold of him.

He took one step back and motioned for a servant to hand him a torch. As Pharaoh looked on with a bemused expression, Amunet paced back and forth before finally handing the torch back and going silent. The images on the wall were so foreign to his experience that he was struggling to summon up words to describe them.

The painting featured two life-size figures of a man and a woman. Beyond that obvious fact, nothing about the images was traditional or even recognizable. The figures faced forward and had been painted so realistically that they looked as if they could step out of the stone and into the room. Their faces–especially their eyes–had been drawn in precise life-like detail. The pupils and irises were distinct, and each hair in the eyebrows appeared to have been drawn individually. The man's eyes were forest green, the woman's were robin egg blue. They were relaxed and smiling, as if greeting an old friend, and Amunet noticed that neither was missing any teeth, another anomaly in a nation where everyone–even Pharaoh–was missing at least one or two.

The man had wavy brown hair that came to his collar, and the woman's thick, dark hair fell in waves to the top of her breasts and was shaped in an unusual style. He was built like a warrior, with broad shoulders, a narrow waist, and long legs, while her ample bosom and shapely hips had been drawn so honestly that it sent a tingle through his groin.

Neither of the figures wore the simple, wrap-around tunic favored by both men and women in Kemet. The man's partial tunic went to his waist and was tucked into some kind of cotton leggings. The upper part was fronted with a row of beads or fasteners, and the wide leather belt encircling his waist featured an oval shaped brass ring whose purpose Amunet could not discern. The woman was wearing a similar kind of top that was gathered into a flowing skirt much like those worn by many women at court. They were not wearing open-toed sandals; instead, their feet were sheathed in dark leather coverings with laces threaded through small eyelets.

There was a leather pouch affixed to the belt on the man's right hip in which a bright metal object with a dark round handle was visible. For her part, the woman held a stack of papyrus sheets in her left hand and some kind of stylus in her right.

Behind the couple was a representation of the scene outside the tomb, but in place of the orderly construction and freshly hewn stone structures that Pharaoh's party had walked through just a few minutes earlier, this painted valley was a jumble of fallen statues, crumbling tomb entrances and mounds of debris that looked as if they had been taken out of the tombs and scattered thoughtlessly around the landscape.

No one inside the chamber had spoken for five minutes. Pharaoh let the boy conclude his inspection and when Amunet finally turned away from the painting, he asked, "What are your thoughts, messenger?"

Before the boy could answer the Chief Priest proclaimed, "This is a sacrilege, Mighty One, an affront to you and the gods. It must be torn out immediately."

Voices around the room joined in, "Yes, tear out the entire wall," someone said. "Find the villains who committed this unspeakable treason and throw them to the crocodiles," another called out.

Pharaoh raised his hand for silence. "Do you concur with my advisors?" he asked Amunet in a quiet voice. "Shall we destroy the painting?"

The boy shook his head. He had never been more certain of anything in his life than what he was about to tell Pharaoh. "It is a gift from the gods, Lord. I would not let its unusual appearance diminish that fact. They wanted you to see this. They want this painting to watch over you for eternity."

Amenhotep placed a hand on the boy's shoulder, which caused gasps to break out around the chamber. Such familiarity between a Pharaoh and peasant was unheard of.

Pharaoh paid no mind. "You are wise beyond your years. You shall come to my palace and become my personal messenger."

Amunet's heart swelled with pride, but he had one more thing to share with his new lord. "If you please my Lord, there is one other aspect to the painting."

Amenhotep's eyebrows went up, and the room grew quiet again.

The boy went to his knees in front of the painting. "Here, Majesty, next to the man's foot. The cartouche and the inscription below it are quite small, but they must be important."

Pharaoh squatted down next to the boy. Like the others in the room, he had not noticed the small painted oval and the text beneath it. He turned his head and said "Priest, attend us, and make what you can of this."

Amenhotep and the boy stood up and the Chief Priest knelt with a small torch in one hand. When he got to his feet a moment later there was a quizzical expression on his face.

"Tell me, Priest, what meaning does the cartouche and text below it convey?" asked Pharaoh.

Everyone in the chamber leaned forward and strained to hear the priest's words.

"The inscription is a calculation of the passage of time," said the priest. "Many, many passages of the periods of the Inundation, Emergence, and Harvest."

"Totaling how many years in all?" asked Pharaoh.

The Chief Priest performed a calculation in his head. "3,301, Lord."

"Years that have passed us?"

The priest gathered his thoughts. "No, Lord," he said in a whispery voice. "Years that have yet to come."

Pharaoh was pensive. "And what of the cartouche above the text?"

"It may be intended as a puzzle, or worse yet, a joke," the priest began. "It is a single word, but one that can have several meanings…"

"And those meanings refer to what?" asked an impatient Amenhotep.

The priest's voice trembled. "It speaks of a man of questionable-repute, one who cannot be trusted in certain situations, especially in matters of the heart."

Pharaoh scowled. He was used to having his questions answered with greater clarity. "This man," he said, "you would say he is…"

The priest looked down.

"Lord, this man would be known as a …"

"…Scoundrel!"
"Querida! Come back to my bed, this minute!"

~ONE~

(3,301 Years Later)
Cuernavaca, Mexico, March 1884

Colonel Thomas Edward Scoundrel, retired American army officer, hero of the Battle of Pebble Creek Ridge in the final weeks of the Civil War, recipient of the Congressional Medal of Honor, former San Francisco journalist and Hawaiian sugar plantation owner, sighed and stepped away from the flower-covered bedroom balcony.

In the courtyard below, a tiled fountain perched on the crowns of three leaping dolphins splashed softly, while the scent of baking bread and fresh coffee drifted from the hacienda's kitchen to gently stir the house awake.

He was dressed only in loose-fitting white linen trousers and huarache sandals–both borrowed from the wardrobe of Don Enfante, husband of the most impatient Doña Maria Alcazar Enfante. Don Enfante himself was seldom in Cuernavaca; the aristocratic Tucateco was far too busy expanding his agave rope-fiber plantations and endless fields of sugarcane to satisfy the world's booming sweet tooth. He had grown fabulously wealthy by pressing the native Mayans into backbreaking labor for pitiful wages. And with the Don away, La Doña had time to play.

And that's what I've become, Thomas thought, setting his coffee on a wrought-iron table as he stepped back into the high-ceilinged bedroom. *A plaything.*

One glance at Doña Maria–propped against lace-fringed pillows – reminded him why it had been so easy to follow her trail of seduction. She lay naked in careful repose, her arms behind her head, lifting her ample breasts toward the cotton canopy above. Turned slightly, she offered an unguarded view of her hips, thighs, and the exquisite triangle between her legs. The look in her eye was pure challenge: try though you may, this is the one thing you cannot resist.

Thomas recalled Goya's Nude Maja, which hung in the National Palace in Mexico City. Doña Maria had crafted herself into a living reproduction of the painting, down to the hair, the half-smile, and the perfect positioning of her body. He had no illusions it was coincidence. She had surely studied the masterpiece and, in matters of love, she spared no effort in rendering her lovers helpless beneath her artful web.

Grinning inwardly, Thomas stepped across the room to the massive bed. As he slipped off his sandals and pulled down the linen trousers, he promised himself a good hard knock upside the head.

Later.

Rosalillia had endured enough. Thomas had been absent-mindedly stirring his soup for several minutes, answering only in mumbles when she or Diego spoke. She shot her husband a look. He nodded.

"Tómas!" Diego barked. "*Escúchame...*"

His sharp tone snapped Thomas out of his reverie. "Yes, of course. Sorry."

"If the lunch displeases you, we can ask the chef to prepare something else," Diego added. "Though you seem to find the Zinfandel sufficiently amusing."

Thomas glanced at his empty glass and gave them a sheepish smile. He realized he hadn't spoken since they'd sat at the long oak table near the fireplace.

"Apologies," he said. "Too much on my mind."

Rosalillia laughed and sputtered into her wine. Four months pregnant and more radiant than ever, she was well aware of Thomas's escapades with Doña Enfante.

"She speaks for me," Diego added. "The problem, *mi amigote,* is not too much on your mind. The opposite–not enough."

Thomas poured another glass before replying. "I can go anywhere and be insulted. I don't have to take it—"

"Oh, but you do," Rosalillia interrupted, "because we're your family, and we love you enough to tell you the truth."

Diego said nothing; his wife had it well in hand.

Thomas leaned on his elbow, chin in hand. She was right. Restlessness gnawed at him.

Three months after returning from rescuing Rosalillia from kidnappers in Colorado, he had been summoned to Mexico City by President Manuel González Flores and given command of a 100-man cavalry troop–the finest trackers and fighters in the Mexican army. His orders: hunt down and capture or kill the Apache shaman and war chief Geronimo, who had been raiding villages, robbing freight wagons, and torching fields across Sonora before slipping north into Arizona Territory.

Eager to return to the field, Thomas led his men to the Arizona border, where they fought a series of skirmishes. Though they never cornered Geronimo himself, they killed two dozen warriors, scattered their horses, and destroyed hidden caches of ammunition and food.

With the first winter snows piling in the Sonoran mountains, Thomas gave up the chase and returned to Mexico City. President Flores awarded him Mexico's highest military honor in gratitude for degrading Geronimo's force.

Now, he had settled back into quiet life in Cuernavaca with Diego and Rosalillia–riding through flower-covered hills, playing cards in gentlemen's clubs, and pursuing beautiful women. Especially married ones. They were, he had learned, the most willing–and most appreciative.

"You're right, my dear Lillia," Thomas said at last. "I feel like I can't move forward or backward…"

"Up and down, however, does not seem to be a problem," Diego chuckled, "or so I hear from Señora Enfante's friends."

Rosalillia blushed and feigned outrage, though she clearly enjoyed the joke.

Thomas laughed, drained his glass, and pushed back from the table.

"I've got to do something. Anything. I can't go on like this."

Diego reached for a cigar, but Rosalillia's sharp glance made him reconsider.

"Ah," he sighed. "Babies change everything."

"For the better, darling. For the better," Rosalillia assured him.

"Tomás, sit," Diego said. "I've been meaning to talk with you."

"You need purpose again," Diego continued. "We need you to find something meaningful."

"Before we start arguing?" Thomas asked.

"Before we come to blows."

"And what exactly do you suggest?"

"You enjoyed writing for the San Francisco Chronicle, no?"

"More than anything else I've done."

"Then write to your editor, Andrew Whitton. Ask for your job back. You parted on good terms?"

"The best."

"Sit. Write. We'll have it sent out by special post. Whitton will have it in weeks."

"My old job," Thomas mused softly.

"And your restaurants, gambling–"

"And women who speak the King's English," Rosalillia added with a laugh.

"That too," Diego agreed. "What do you say, Tomás?"

Thomas didn't need time to decide. He slapped the table. "Damned if that isn't the best idea I've heard in months."

He rose, but paused at the door.

"When's the next post?"

~TWO~

Thomas squinted against the midday sun and watched Esteban work the young Morgan in the corral behind Diego and Rosalillia's stable. The silver-haired, weathered vaquero was the finest horseman and trainer Thomas had ever seen. Esteban could drop his twisted leather hide and horsehair lasso over a bull's horns from twenty yards or loop it around the leg of a galloping animal with precision. The former Mexican cavalry officer was a master of *colea de toros*, the furious horseback race where a rider caught the tail of a running bull, whipped it under a hind leg, and slammed the beast to its back.

Today, the small, heavily muscled Morgan was graduating from a training bosal noseband and hackamore to a lighter rig with a metal bit. By next week, it would be a perfect mount for a gentleman or officer, and Esteban would move on to his next trainee.

It was warm for April, and Thomas was about to head up to the house for a glass of water when a barefoot boy burst out of the garden gate and ran to his side. The boy handed him a manila envelope stamped *Postal Urgente*, accepted a peppermint candy with a grin, and trotted back toward the main house.

Thomas waved to Esteban, then made his way through the flowered garden to the patio behind the villa. He poured himself a glass of cool water from a stoneware jug on the sideboard and settled into a chair near the fountain. Turning the envelope in his hands, he noted the first of the three postmarks—San Francisco, dated four weeks earlier. Only a month to travel 2,300 miles. The Mexican government's aggressive railroad expansion was paying dividends, he thought.

He tore open the envelope and withdrew four pages covered in the neat scrawl he recognized instantly as his old editor, Andrew Whitton. Ten years earlier, Thomas had been the *Chronicle's* most popular reporter, writing under the moniker T.E.S. Bayside to conceal his true identity as a decorated hero of the Civil War. His features on crime and corruption had made his weekly column a must-read among San Francisco's wealthy and powerful.

But he had pushed too far when he published a scathing exposé on Colin P. Stafford, one of the richest, most ruthless men in California. Within hours of the article hitting the streets, Thomas became a marked man. Stafford's killers had hunted him across Hawaii, Tahiti, Moorea, and finally back to the United States–where assassins and renegade Tahitian warriors pursued him from coast to coast.

He pushed the memories aside. San Francisco and Moorea–especially Moorea–would always be both the best and worst chapters of his life. He found himself almost hoping that Whitton would not offer him his old job. It took only a moment to realize he was going to get half his wish.

After updating Thomas on old friends, including the Kwans, who still ran his favorite restaurant, Whitton surprised him with unexpected news:

"...because I will be 70 next year, and that's too damn old to do this job properly," his friend wrote. "I'm selling out to my nephew and taking my wife on a long trip to the East.

But as for a job for you, by God your timing couldn't be better. What do you know about the Orient Express, the luxury train that runs from Paris to Constantinople? They started service last year, and damned if every blue blood in Europe and the States isn't booking passage just to say they've done it. I hear the train serves the finest food and wine imaginable. I've been wanting to hire a travel writer for a while now–our readers love tales of far-off places. This train's the perfect way to kick off the new series.

How about it, Thomas? Are you game? You'd file reports from each major city along the route, give my readers a feel for the adventure. I'll pay you a flat salary, plus all travel expenses, and arrange an international letter of credit to handle any surprises. My bank has partners in Paris, Strasbourg, and Vienna—though not Constantinople, unfortunately. Abdul Hamid II keeps defaulting on Ottoman loans, and they've cut him out of the system. So you'll be mostly on your own once you reach the end of the line.

I'm confident you'll take the job because, hell, why not? It's got Thomas Scoundrel written all over it.

My bank will wire Mexico City—you'll be funded by the time this letter reaches Cuernavaca. Skedaddle over to Vera Cruz and catch the next steamer to France. And about France: your old friend Émile Aubert is here in Paris for a gallery show. Just arrived from Tahiti. I'll let him know you're coming—might as well take in the sights while waiting for your train.

Your letter made my day, my friend. Hell, it made my month. Write me from Vera Cruz with your schedule for France.

Yours in gratitude,
Andrew Whitton

Thomas was humming as he folded the letter and headed up the bougainvillea-draped stairs to join Diego and Rosalillia for lunch.

Whitton was right: why the hell wouldn't he take the job?

~THREE~

Port of Vera Cruz, Mexico, April 1884

The porter wiped his sleeve across his forehead and adjusted his broad-brimmed straw hat. The tropical downpour that swept through that morning promised an early rainy season, and the broiling sun and humidity left him drenched as he loaded bags onto the wide plank leading into the *SS City of Paris* steamship's cavernous hold.

He watched with some amusement as the first-class passengers disembarked from their coaches and gathered in small clusters, fanning themselves, loosening collars, grumbling about the heat. Boarding would begin in a few minutes, and until then, the wealthy Europeans and Americans were left to broil beside the dockworkers. The porter smiled at the thought.

One Americano stood apart, however. He didn't join the others queueing near the boarding ramp. Instead, he remained off to the side, seemingly in no hurry to reach his cool stateroom, where champagne, cold beer, and fresh fruit would be waiting. Odd enough by itself, but other details made the tall, broad-shouldered man with thick brown hair and green eyes stand out. Unlike his fellow passengers, whose trunks, hatboxes, and oversized suitcases were being hauled onboard by porters, this American had only a small suitcase and a slim leather valise beside him. He hadn't called for assistance, clearly intending to carry them himself.

The man caught the porter's glance and offered an easy, wide smile. The señoritas would think him a handsome devil ,thought the porter. He gestured toward the man's bags, offering his services, but the American shook his head politely. Then he removed his light linen jacket. Heat or not, a gentleman was expected to dress properly–which was one reason the porter never fancied such a life for himself. "As if that should be a worry," his wife often reminded him.

A bell rang, and the line of first-class passengers began shuffling up the gangway, each couple or individual escorted by a valet who would tend to their needs for the eight-day crossing. The porter nodded once more at the American—and that's when he noticed the revolver. A Colt Single Action Army, most likely .45 caliber, resting comfortably in a well-worn holster. Not illegal, nor uncommon, but most gentlemen carried smaller pistols suited for dandy showpieces or the occasional duel. The .45 was for killing. This caballero has a story to tell, the porter thought.

Nearly 800 steerage passengers had already boarded. Once first-class was settled with flutes of champagne in hand, the City of Paris would steam out into the Gulf.

On the second morning out of Vera Cruz, the City of Paris anchored briefly in Havana harbor to take on a dozen Cuban and American passengers. Then her 560-foot hull pressed eastward through the Straits of Florida, engines humming at full capacity. At twenty knots, her 18,000-horsepower triple-expansion engines carried her swiftly into the open North Atlantic.

Thomas was just settling into his table in the walnut-paneled first-class dining room, studying the wine list, when a compact man of about sixty approached. He had thick, graying hair and a full beard still touched with red. Piercing blue eyes. A glass of whiskey in one hand and a freshly lit cigar in the other.

"Colonel Thomas Scoundrel?" he asked, his voice crisp with a New England accent.

Thomas had intended a solitary evening. Roasted lamb was on the menu, and he planned to enjoy it in the company of a superb Bordeaux. His reply was brief: "Yes."

"My apologies for the interruption, sir." The man turned to leave.

But there was something in the man's bearing—a world-weary melancholy Thomas recognized instantly. It made him pause.

"Please," Thomas said. "I didn't catch your name."

The man set his glass on the table and extended his hand. "Melville. Herman Melville. The poet Walt Whitman is, I believe, our mutual friend. As is Jules Verne, whom I'm visiting in Nantes."

Thomas blinked in recognition. "Of course, I know your work. Will you join me for dinner?"

Melville smiled faintly. "I didn't think you were in the mood for company."

"And I didn't realize one of my favorite authors was aboard," Thomas replied. "Please, sit."

Melville settled in as a waiter hurried to set another place."And where does this voyage lead you?" he asked, sipping his whiskey.

"Paris. From there, via the Orient Express to Constantinople."

"Holiday?"

"I'll be writing travel reports for the San Francisco Chronicle."

Melville raised his glass. "A writer! Excellent news."

"Not in your class, Mr. ..."

"Please–Herman."

"I had some experience with the paper in my twenties, but that feels like another lifetime."

"Ten years–a lifetime?" Melville smiled thinly. "I've labored nineteen years as a customs officer in New York. Believe me—it feels more like eternity."

He sighed deeply. "An eternity."

The waiter arrived with the Hermosa Vineyards Zinfandel Thomas had ordered.

"Will you join me?" Thomas offered.

Melville took a sip and nodded. "A fine little wine. Thank you."

"Walt is well?"

"Since his stroke, his health is delicate. But he carries on, stubborn as ever, tending his garden at Stafford Farm in Laurel Springs. He refuses to contemplate the inevitable."

"May that be a hundred years from now–for us both," said Thomas.

The two men clinked glasses.

The waiter returned.

"Gentlemen, may I take your orders?"

"Have you a recommendation?" asked Melville.

"Honestly, sirs, as fine as the other entrées on our menu may be, I would be criminally remiss in my professional duties if I did not insist that you have the leg of lamb."

Melville winked at Thomas before asking the waiter, "And how is the lamb prepared?"

Their server placed his hands on his hips and leaned forward. "We begin with a semi-boneless leg of fresh spring lamb, which is slow roasted over coals while a rosemary-garlic sauce is ladled on until it forms a perfect crust."

"Semi-boneless?" asked Thomas. "I'm not sure I have heard of that."

"Ah," the waiter replied. "Our chef, who is Italian by birth, removes the shank and blade bones but leaves the leg bone in the roast."

"For appearances sake?" Melville asked.

"Oh, no, sir," insisted the waiter. "Keeping the bone in adds an unsurpassed richness to the flavor, and from a practical standpoint it makes the meat easier to carve than a fully bone-in leg."

"The lamb it is, then," said Melville.

"Make it two," added Thomas.

The waiter poured more zinfandel into their glasses. "And, if I may, while this zinfandel is a perfectly acceptable accompaniment to the lamb, may I suggest perhaps going with a classic Bordeaux?"

With a nod of approval, the waiter described the full menu to come—consommé, pan-roasted asparagus with brown butter and lemon, herbed tomatoes, crisp potato wedges, and a surprise for dessert.

The first-class dining room was awash in spirited conversation and frequent laughter and the violin trio was taking a short break when Thomas and Melville finished their lamb and asked for another bottle of the extraordinary Château Montrose their waiter had recommended. It was a blend of Cabernet Sauvignon and Merlot, rounded off with a touch of Petit Verdot, and its bouquet of flowers, fruit, and spices was unlike anything the men had experienced.

The secret, their waiter told them, was a combination of the unique terroir, soil that consisted of deep gravel over clay, and "forgive my being crude, but the estate produces its own compost with a mix of cow manure, mulched vine shoots and grape stalks." He shrugged. "Such is the essence of a true *Grand Cru Classé*."

Thomas could only shake his head. "Manure."

Melville, whose face had grown ruddy from the wine, raised his glass.

"To the selfless and magical contribution that fine French *merde* has made to our feast, my dear Colonel Scoundrel."

Over the next several days, they settled into a comfortable rhythm: coffee in the First-Class library at two, dinner at seven. Melville was flattered by Thomas' familiarity with his South Seas books and fascinated by the truth behind Thomas' heroics at Pebble Creek Ridge.

"So, you are saying that the god-awful painting of the battle that hangs in every saloon in the nation isn't a truthful telling of the story?" Melville chuckled over brandy on their second night out of Havana. "It is certainly a heroic vision, my friend; you in the center of the battlefield waving the flag against the crystal blue morning sky; your magnificent stallion rearing back on his hind legs as the Confederate soldiers bubble around you like a swarm of angry wasps. It's something I would expect to see in the marble halls on Mt. Olympus itself. Is any of the artist's representation true?"

Thomas tossed back his brandy and smiled.

"Strangely enough, a good deal of the painting is accurate. The sky was blue, the Reb riders did encircle me completely, and my horse, Cornwall, did rear back when he took a bullet in his hindquarter. But the portrayal of dozens of dead Rebs all around me is a complete fiction; I was trying to get the hell off that ridge, not singlehandedly defeat an entire regiment of seasoned fighters."

'You were wounded," Melville said in a low voice as the waiter refilled their glasses.

"In my back, abdomen and leg. I was three weeks in hospital outside Washington, D.C."

"Which is where you met Walt Whitman?"

"He was my night nurse. He would sit beside my bed reading his poems, and sometimes he even wrote as I slept."

Melville raised his glass: "To Walt."

Thomas raised his glass, and then said, "May I ask a question about your books?"

Melville nodded.

"I know that you were roundly condemned by critics who suggested you had embellished your experiences in the islands. The whaling adventure, your captivity, and battle for survival. How did you deal with that?"

The author grinned. "By closing my eyes and remembering every blasted second of it, my friend, from the spray of salt air to the lushness of the vegetation, and even though I did not go into a lot of detail, the perfect curves of the native women."

Thomas stared at the tabletop for a moment, lost in his own memories of his life on the shore of the turquoise lagoon on Moorea.

Melville watched his friend's expression change. "But you know the truth of island life as well as any man, Thomas. Walt told me about Keani, and about your trip to New York City to introduce Émile Aubert's paintings to the world. I am so very sorry about your wife."

Twelve years had passed since Thomas sailed for Tahiti and Moorea beyond. Twelve years since he had been pursued across the American continent by a band of South Seas warriors and an Irish assassin. And 12 years since he last held his beloved Tahitian bride.

Melville knew what he was thinking.

"For what it's worth, Thomas, and I say this as one who has walked this earth for nearly twice as many years as you…it doesn't get easier. It doesn't fade. The only thing that changes is the ways you find to deal with the…"

He picked his next word carefully. "Pain."

Neither man spoke until the waiter appeared with two crystal dessert bowls filled with Italian panna cotta, a silky, eggless custard thickened with a touch of gelatin and topped with blackberries, blueberries and a single bright red raspberry. Then the waiter poured two cups of coffee and set an unopened bottle of fine brandy in the middle of the table.

"It seems he has divined our true intentions," Melville said with a sly smile.

"Well, he's not wrong," Thomas answered as he used his pen knife to cut the wrapping from around the bottle top.

When their glasses were topped off and Melville lit a fresh cigar, they picked up the conversation.

"Someday, Thomas, you must write your personal memoirs. I can think of any number of publishers who would pick them up," Melville said.

"My story will die with me," Thomas replied in a matter-of-fact tone. "And when my last friend has died, that will be the end of the Thomas Scoundrel story."

Melville looked pensive. Then he threw back his head, laughed, and said, "Except for that damn painting!"

Thomas could not help but join his friend in laughter.

"Very well, I will be remembered for the wrong reasons, while you will be remembered for each of the books you have written. That will be a fine legacy."

"They won't remember all of them, Thomas, kind as it is of you to say. My best and finest work was lampooned by the critics and ignored by the public. It barely saw the light of day."

"Really? That's hard to believe. What was the title?"

"*Moby-Dick; or, The Whale,*" replied the author. "I wrote it 31 years ago, and everything I know, everything I believe, everything I am certain of, and everything I fear, is written in those pages. With my blood."

Thomas refilled their brandy and looked into his friend's eyes. "You shall have at least one more reader, Herman," he said. "When we land in Le Havre, I will seek out a book shop and buy a copy."

Melville stood and laid his hand on Thomas' shoulder. "I will save you the trip; I have a few copies in my stateroom and will bring one to you."

Then he scooped up his brandy glass and cigar and headed for the door, tipping slightly to the left and right as he navigated the busy dining room, more from the wine and brandy than from the sea, Thomas thought.

On the fifth morning out of Vera Cruz, the City of Paris steamed into the leading edge of a great storm sweeping across the North Atlantic. A steward clad in a waterproof oilskin coat and hat came to Thomas' stateroom just before lunch to tell him that all passengers must remain in their rooms until the Captain felt it was safe to walk about. Meals would be delivered to the room, and the steward assured him that his dinner would be accompanied by wines selected personally by the head waiter.

He resigned himself to the news and settled into a leather armchair with a pot of coffee and a plate of fresh-baked croissants. He turned up the lamp on the side table, opened *Moby Dick*, and, as the giant ship plowed into the gale and began to roll left and right, he started to read. He was reading when the steward wheeled in a cart with a lunch of stew and salad four hours later, and still reading when his dinner was delivered.

It was after midnight when he reached the end of the book.

"And I only am escaped alone to tell thee," Ishmael said after being rescued by the whaling ship Rachel.

As the ship canted left to right in the troughs formed between the huge waves boiling around it, Thomas closed the book, blew out the lamp, and sat quietly in the dark.

~FOUR~

Café Le Chat Noir, Paris, April 1884

Thomas gathered his bottle of wine and glass from the small table inside *Le Chat Noir's* main lounge and stepped into the cool, clear night. A waiter led him to a table beside the low wrought-iron fence separating the popular café from the cobblestoned Rue Victor-Massé, where he sat beneath the amber glow of a gas streetlamp to await the two artists Émile Aubert had written about.

"To know where art is going, you must meet these gentlemen," Aubert had telegrammed from San Francisco, where the *Chronicle* was sponsoring his latest one-man show. "After a year in the cultural backwaters of Mexico, you'll be dropping into the crucible of the arts revolution that's tearing down the last of the old European Academy. My friends are in the front line of the revolt, and meeting them will help you understand why we 'barbarians'–as the old guard call us–are winning.

Sois bien, Émile.

P.S. They will be *cassé*–that is, broke–and will look to you to fund the evening's entertainments."

How like Émile, Thomas thought with a smile. Still, if his friends had even a fraction of Aubert's charm, the expense of a few bottles of wine would be well worth the evening.

An hour passed, and the men had not arrived. Thomas was ready to leave. It was nearly 10 PM, few people wandered the tree-lined boulevard, and the list of items he needed to purchase for his journey aboard the Orient Express was growing longer. He was signaling his waiter for the bill when two men rounded the corner and paused briefly beneath a streetlamp as one struck a match to light a cigar.

The man lighting the match was almost clownishly short, his legs far too abbreviated for his elongated torso. He wore a black dress coat and bowler hat over boy's trousers, his meticulously trimmed moustache and horn-rimmed glasses giving him a professorial air. His companion was of average height and slim build, wearing a rumpled workman's jacket and shirt over denim trousers and weathered shoes. As they neared the gate, Thomas noticed dabs of dried paint spattered across the taller man's clothing. Aubert's friends had arrived.

The hostess led the artists to Thomas' table and made the introductions. Indicating the shorter man, she said, "Colonel Thomas Scoundrel, I have the pleasure of introducing Comte Henry Marie Raymond de Toulouse-Lautrec-Monfa, and Vincent Willem Van Gogh, two of our most..." She paused, clearing her throat, "...celebrated artists."

"And notorious raconteurs," added Lautrec with a grin and a half bow.

The dwarfish man extended his hand. "Please, call me Henri."

The other man, Van Gogh, appeared ill at ease. He shifted from one foot to another before extending his hand.

"Vincent," was all he said.

Thomas motioned for them to sit. When he told the waiter to bring drinks for the three of them—and to put it all on his bill—Vincent and Henri shared relieved smiles.

"*Merci*, Colonel Scoundrel," said Vincent as he slid into his chair. "Your generosity has turned what would have been a very short visit into something more civilized."

"In short, Colonel," added Lautrec in halting English, "we are, sadly and temporarily, a bit light in the wallet."

The look on the waiter's face suggested this was not the first time he'd heard that line from these two.

"Call me Thomas," he said. "And if you don't mind, shall we speak in French this evening?"

The waiter impatiently tapped his pencil on his tray.

"Gentlemen?"

"What is your pleasure?" Thomas asked.

Lautrec answered first. "*Vin ordinaire*, if you please. A bottle."

The waiter raised his eyebrows and gave Thomas a look: do you know what you're getting yourself into? Thomas simply nodded. He turned to Vincent.

"Absinthe... perhaps a half bottle?" Van Gogh said, keeping his gaze on Thomas.

"And I'll have more of the Bordeaux I enjoyed with dinner," Thomas added.

As the waiter scribbled their orders and turned to leave, Thomas asked, "Have you gentlemen eaten? Please, be my guests."

Lautrec slapped Vincent heartily on the back. "You see? I knew Émile would not send us to dine with a miser."

"Dinner it shall be," Vincent said quietly.

Before the waiter departed, Van Gogh reminded him to bring four cubes of sugar and a spoon with his absinthe.

Seeing Thomas' puzzled expression, Vincent explained, "Absinthe is too powerful to drink straight. The wormwood and botanicals would overwhelm you. You'll see."

The waiter opened the double doors leading inside, releasing the sounds of a piano, accordion, cello, and dozens of lively conversations.

A few moments later, the wine bottles arrived. A short, thick green bottle was placed before Van Gogh. He poured a small amount into his glass, balanced a slotted silver spoon across the rim, and set a sugar cube on the spoon. Slowly, he dripped cold water onto the sugar. As the sweetened water streamed into the absinthe, it clouded into a milky swirl. Lifting the spoon away, Vincent raised the glass to eye level.

"Perfect."

He slid the glass to Thomas. "Taste... but slowly."

Thomas took a careful sip. The thick liquor tasted of black licorice, and by the time it settled in his stomach, he felt as if he'd consumed two glasses of strong red wine.

"Did you know the proper citizens of Paris call those of us who frequent this place *les hydropathes*? They say we fear water and drink only wine," said Lautrec.

"And they are correct," he added, emptying his glass.

For the first time that evening, Thomas saw Van Gogh smile.

The one-legged prostitute sighed and raised her head off the red-fringed pillow on the divan in Lautrec's Montmartre studio.
The diminutive artist had been working at his easel for nearly two hours, applying bursts of color and shading to capture the contours of her nude body while the spring light streamed through the upper windows. From a low stool in the corner, Van Gogh sketched furiously with charcoal, focusing not on her flesh, but on her nature—expressed in bold strokes of black and gray.

And there, thought Thomas as he sipped his third coffee of the day, lay the contrast between the men and their art. Lautrec, the sensualist, drawing with effortless precision. Van Gogh, the agonized theorist, wringing paint and charcoal into emotion.

"Henri," the model whined, "we've been at this for hours. If you were a customer, I'd have finished you long ago."

"If I were a customer, you wouldn't be served tea, soup, and brandy," Lautrec replied. "Now crook your left arm, just so, and be quiet."

Before moving into position, the woman reached down to scratch herself absentmindedly. Days ago, the intimate motion might have embarrassed Thomas. But after time spent with Lautrec, Van Gogh, and their models, such pretenses had long faded.

The gesture reminded him of the highlight of their first night at *Le Chat Noir*.

They had just finished bowls of spring lamb stew, fresh bread, and strawberries when Thomas asked how the café came to be named after a black cat.

Lautrec set down his wine, walked to the club doors, and called to a dark-haired young woman. She joined them at the table, accepting a glass of wine from Lautrec.

"My American friend wishes to know how *Le Chat Noir* got its name," Henri said. "I thought you should tell him."

"And why me?" she teased, before giggling.

"Yes, my lovely," Lautrec smiled. "I couldn't very well ask a blonde or a redhead, now, could I?"

The young woman turned to Thomas, clearly enjoying the moment. "As with many establishments, our name was inspired by a very important place–a destination, you might say, that is warm and most welcoming."

"I certainly would agree," said Lautrec.

"Without question," added Van Gogh.

Thomas was puzzled. What did 'black cat' have to do with a destination? An island? A forest?

She giggled and stood before him. Lifting her dress and petticoat above her waist, she pulled down her drawers, took Thomas' hand, and softly pressed it against the triangle of black hair between her legs.

"Welcome, Colonel, to the black cat," she whispered sweetly.

Then she let go, readjusted her clothing, and returned to her seat as Van Gogh and Lautrec roared with laughter.

"This café was named after a…?" sputtered Thomas.

"Is there, in all the world, a warmer or more welcoming place, *mon ami*?" laughed Lautrec.

On his fourth day in Paris, Thomas met Van Gogh at dawn at Gare du Nord for a short journey south. Disembarking in a quiet farming village, they packed Vincent's easel and paints along a rutted wagon path for two miles, finally reaching a field where laborers harvested early spring wheat.

Vincent set up quickly, eager to catch the morning light. By the laborers' casual glances, Thomas could tell the Dutchman was a familiar presence. Wandering a half mile to a low hill covered in oak and shrub, Thomas surveyed the patchwork farmland and villages, finally falling asleep under a tree until midday.

He returned as Van Gogh opened his knapsack and laid out lunch: baked potatoes, local cheese, a bottle of wine. A young girl brought them each a fat red apple.

Vincent seldom spoke, so when he finally did, Thomas was caught off guard.

"I believe you've been studying me," the artist said evenly. It was an observation, not a criticism.

"Does it seem that way to you?" Thomas answered.

The truth was, he found Van Gogh endlessly fascinating—passionate, intense, monstrously talented. That the man had never sold a single painting at thirty-one astonished him.

He tossed a pebble into the stream and took another sip of wine. The laborers were returning to the fields after their own lunch. Van Gogh sat quietly, awaiting a reply.

"In some ways, we're alike," Thomas began.

"Alike? Do you paint?"

"I don't know one end of a brush from the other," Thomas chuckled.

"Then I don't understand."

Thomas had spoken of this only once before—twelve years earlier, with Keani. Yet here, on a mossy creek bank in the French countryside, he felt unexpectedly comfortable.

"We both carry a tendency toward melancholy," he said. "It rises and falls unbidden, unaffected by reason. I've come to think of it as some primitive defense mechanism buried deep in the brain."

"Les ténèbres," Van Gogh whispered.

"I'm sorry?"

"The darkness, Thomas. Blacker than any color. Deeper than any ocean. Seductive and suffocating. My constant companion."

Thomas studied Vincent's pale blue eyes, seeing infinite layers of sadness."How is it,"he asked softly, "that you create paintings of such extraordinary vibrancy–canvases bursting with life–while wrapped so tightly in darkness's embrace?"

Van Gogh chuckled.

"God has a sense of humor, *mon ami.* In the morning, I paint the sun in its radiant joy. In the afternoon, my charcoal draws me into hell."

Thomas went quiet. Then he placed a hand on Vincent's shoulder.

"My advice to you, dear Vincent, is to throw your charcoals away."

Vincent smiled. They sat in silence as the water flowed past, toward eternity.

~FIVE~

The Valley of the Kings, March 1884

Ahmad bin Abdullah bin Fahal swung out of his saddle and stepped onto the crunchy limestone shards that littered the valley floor, forming a natural pathway between the low brown hills to the west and the stubby rock outcroppings to the east. Piles of debris cluttered the landscape: worthless remnants left behind by tomb robbers, household garbage hauled by barge from the Nile, mounds of desiccated camel droppings, and the remains of recent campfires abandoned by European archaeologists.

There were no foreign excavations here at present–a situation Ahmad knew he was largely responsible for. The war he waged against the Egyptians and British had set the region aflame. The closer he came to capturing Khartoum, the fewer Europeans he encountered in the region. Now that his Ansar army of 40,000 warriors–armed only with swords and spears–had annihilated General William Hicks's 8,000-man Anglo-Egyptian force at the Battle of Shaykan, the British government was finally taking him seriously. They had reappointed General Charles Gordon as governor of the Sudan and charged him with evacuating all foreigners, including Egyptian troops and officials.

Ahmad turned to his young aide-de-camp.

"Is the old man here?" he asked.

"He is, Mahdi," the aide replied.

Ahmad appreciated hearing the title aloud. Three years earlier, he had proclaimed himself the Mahdi, the prophesied redeemer destined to rid the world of evil and injustice. Revered as a descendant of both Jesus and the Prophet, his elevated status made anonymous travel difficult. He would not have risked the six-day journey here if the situation were not so extraordinary.

When the old man's message reached him in his desert camp, Ahmad immediately set out for Luxor with six of his most trusted officers. Disguised as a merchant, he sailed upriver in a small felucca, slipping past prying eyes.

Hassan, his senior lieutenant, approached with a goatskin filled with water. Ahmad sat on a rock, poured some over his head, and took a long drink.

"This old man," Hassan said. "You trust him."

It was not a question.

"I have met many Sufi mystics who claim visions," Ahmad replied. "But this one is different. He foretold my birth, the hunting accident that nearly killed me as a child, my father's death, and our victory at Shaykan."

"And your ascension as Mahdi?"

"Especially that."

"And now?"

"The old man claims that inside the tomb lies a vision of my death."

Three soldiers dismounted and joined them near a cluster of boulders. A trail led from where they stood toward the open rock entrance of one of the valley's many plundered tombs. As they watched, a very old man in a simple white robe emerged from the shadows, leaning heavily on a cane.

Ahmad snapped his fingers, and two of his men rushed forward to assist the mystic. When seated and refreshed, Ahmad began his questioning.

"Is the mystery you speak of inside that tomb?"

"Oh no, Mahdi," the old man wheezed. "I would never reveal its true entrance to any wandering eyes who might happen into the valley."

"My aide tells me there is no one within a two-hour ride," Ahmad said. "Only the laborers you requested. They are being watched."

A scattering of clouds drifted across the opal sky, cooling the air.

"Take comfort, my sons," Ahmad said. "Now you have only cobras, lions, and fat-tailed scorpions to fear."

"Fat-tailed?" a young soldier asked nervously.

One of the others grinned and drew his finger across his neck. "One bite gives you one hour to live, little one. Just enough time to unsheathe your tiny sword for one final stroke before you find yourself knocking at paradise's gate."

The others chuckled at the crude humor, though each glanced carefully at the ground.

"Tell me again, old man–how you came to witness this wonder?"

"A boy came to my tent nine days ago with a fantastic tale. His village lies nearby, and he tends a flock of goats. One wandered off. His father warned him not to return without it. So he searched everywhere, even into several open tombs, but found nothing. Finally, he climbed up there–" the old man pointed to a rocky ledge one hundred feet above them– "and sat to cry, dreading his father's punishment."

"And then?"

"Then the first miracle. As he sat weeping, he heard the faintest bleating–so soft he thought it might be wind sweeping across the shale."

The old man pointed again. "He followed the sound to a loose pile of rubble. As he dug, part of the ground gave way. Sunlight illuminated a stone chamber where he saw the kid perched atop a painted stone box. All around were statues, gilt wooden chests, even a golden throne."

"And afterward?"

"He rescued the goat and scrambled home."

"Whom did he tell?"

"His parents, Mahdi. His father –a coarse man who sells dried camel dung for fuel–did not believe the tale and beat the boy for his trouble. That is when he came to me."

"No one else knows?"

"No, Mahdi. Of that I am certain."

"We will deal with the family later," Ahmad said quietly, glancing at Hassan, who nodded grimly.

They climbed together to the rocky shelf. Ahmad knelt with a lantern, peering into the chamber packed with funerary treasures.

"There is a golden chariot in the corner," he noted. "Describe what lies beyond."

"There are three passageways," the old man said. "I followed the one directly ahead. After clearing some rubble, I entered a second chamber—twice as large as this one—with a magnificent gilt sarcophagus at its center, surrounded by six towering statues of the ancient gods. The craftsmanship is—"

"—what we would expect for a great pharaoh," Ahmad interrupted. "Is the wall painting you described in that chamber?"

"It is."

"And you are certain it foretells my death?"

The old man hesitated. The Mahdi's favor was no protection from his wrath. But his visions compelled him to speak. "The moment and the place, my lord."

Ahmad ordered the ladder lowered. His men entered first; he followed. The lamplight illuminated treasures beyond imagining.

For a moment they stood silently, overwhelmed.

Hassan finally whispered, "This is a king's fortune, Mahdi. The man who owns it would be the richest in Egypt–perhaps the world."

Ahmad smiled faintly. And more than that, he thought.

"Bring the laborers," he said.

The two village men were lowered into the chamber. They followed as Ahmad led the party down the corridor. As foretold, the wall paintings were vibrant, as if newly painted. Soon they reached a rockfall blocking further passage.

At Ahmad's nod, the laborers cleared enough rubble for him to enter the great chamber beyond. As Ahmad stepped inside, he nodded once more at Hassan. The lieutenant motioned for the laborers to follow him into an alcove –where, a moment later, their throats were swiftly cut.

The Mahdi stood alone, lantern raised. The sarcophagus gleamed beneath his feet. Gilt statues towered around him. Tables groaned beneath golden bowls, polished soapstone, amulets, pearl-threaded necklaces, and alabaster urns holding a pharaoh's preserved organs. The walls depicted idyllic scenes of Nile life. Overhead, a vivid ceiling displayed the sun setting in the west.

Ahmad summoned his officers and the old mystic to join him before the far wall. Together, they lifted their lanterns — and froze.

"Lord..." Hassan whispered.

Ahmad signaled for silence, stepping back to take in the entire mural. Then he beckoned Hassan and the old man to his side.

"This makes no sense," Ahmad said quietly.

"No earthly sense, Lord," the old man agreed.

"And you're certain this is thousands of years old?"

"There is no doubt. I've accompanied the British into tombs. The pigments and techniques match exactly."

"But not–" Ahmad pointed to the two central figures–"like these."

Hassan stepped closer. "They are clearly European. And their clothing..."

"Is modern," Ahmad finished. "And that"–he pointed to the man's holstered weapon–"is a Colt single-action army revolver. .45 caliber."

"She is beautiful," Hassan said, studying the auburn-haired, blue-eyed woman beside the tall man. "And he looks dangerous."

Ahmad took another step back. "Do you see the greater impossibility?"

"The setting," one officer said. "It is this valley, exactly as it looks today."

"Exactly," Ahmad replied. "But that is not how the valley would have appeared three thousand years ago. How could the artist have known?"

He turned to the old man. "And yet you say this vision foretells my death. Show me."

Themystic led them to the far corner. Raising his lantern, he illuminated a grisly scene that stole Ahmad's breath.

A man — Ahmad's age and likeness — dressed in royal purple and yellow robes, had been impaled against a rough wooden post, a spear driven through his belly. His head arched back in agony, his mouth open as if whispering a final prayer.

The officers stared in stunned horror. The resemblance was unmistakable.

The dying man pinned beneath the desert sun was their Mahdi.

~SIX~

Andrew Whitton's letter to Thomas outlining his assignment had been clear. The editor of the *San Francisco Chronicle* wanted his readers to experience the opulence, comfort, and mystery of the Orient Express as if they themselves were making the 1,700-mile journey from Paris to Constantinople.

"Tell them about the sleeping cars and dining cars, the food and wine, your fellow passengers, and the countryside you cross along the way," Whitton wrote. "And help them understand how the *Compagnie Internationale des Wagons-Lits* can justify charging 560 gold francs per person for a one-way ticket."

That last part–the price–intrigued Thomas most. It was a quarter of the average Frenchman's annual salary. Even the concierge at his hotel had given his heavily waxed moustache an extra twirl when Thomas asked for a cab to Gare de l'Est to purchase his ticket.

"Five hundred sixty, Colonel? Sérieux? That is an extraordinary sum for a one-week train excursion."

"I'm afraid I am serious," Thomas replied. "And that price does not include meals or wine."

The concierge shook his head and snapped his fingers for the bellboy to summon a cab. "May I assist you further this morning?"

"Yes, you may. I'd also like to visit a local hunting supply shop — somewhere I can purchase ammunition, a good knife, and a new holster."

"If I may ask," the concierge said, jotting down the address while struggling to contain his curiosity, "are you venturing into uncivilized territory?"

"In my world," Thomas smiled, "every place is uncivilized. Or becomes that way not long after I arrive."

Gare de l'Est faced the Boulevard de Strasbourg, part of the north-south axis of Paris built by Georges-Eugène Haussmann, the architect tasked with transforming Paris from a tangled warren of medieval alleys into a cosmopolitan city of parks, boulevards, fountains, and elegant facades.

Thomas arrived three hours before departure. He strolled the enormous steel-vaulted station, watching as trains pulled in, discharged their swarms of hurried commuters, then eased back out for refueling and turning before re-coupling with fresh carriages.

There was no mistaking his train. From its gleaming black engine to the line of cars painted deep blue, fire-engine red, or dark forest green, the Orient Express stood apart from every other train in the station. From his earlier meeting with a company representative, Thomas knew there were four sleeping cars carrying fifty-six passengers, a restaurant car serving thirty at each dinner seating, two baggage cars, and a coal car completing the lineup.

The Express would depart at 12:30, make the 350-mile run to Strasbourg, and lay over for the night before continuing east to Vienna, then south through Budapest and Bucharest before its final descent to Constantinople on the Bosporus. Normally a three-and-a-half day journey, this trip would run five days to accommodate overnight stops in Strasbourg and Bucharest.

In his leather valise beside his travel suitcase were four leather-bound notebooks–200 blank pages each–enough, he hoped, to record his observations for the Chronicle. Also packed: his Colt revolver, five boxes of ammunition, toilet items, field binoculars, a *General History of the Ottoman Empire*, and *Moby-Dick*. His first reading of Melville's epic had been the most transcendent — and challenging — literary experience of his life. With luck, he might travel west to Nantes after the journey, where Melville was still visiting Jules Verne. His list of questions for the Yankee author was growing by the page.

At 7 PM, Thomas made his way from his stateroom along the narrow walnut-paneled corridor to the dining car. In his black jacket and tie, he noted how many of his fellow passengers appeared dressed for the opera: tuxedos, evening gowns, furs, and glittering diamonds lined the narrow space. A hostess escorted him to the table that would be his for the entire trip and introduced him to Albert, the short, balding, and portly waiter assigned to him.

Thomas settled in and surveyed the décor. The dining car's hand-carved walnut panels were offset by stained-glass partitions between tables, offering a touch of privacy. Lead-crystal candle chandeliers bathed the room in a warm glow. Each table featured fresh-cut flowers floating in emerald liquid; the hand-painted bone china and polished silver were perfectly laid.

"May I bring the Colonel our wine list?" asked Albert, as the hostess filled his Baccarat water goblet and placed warm bread with herbed butter on the table.

Thomas nodded. The waiter slipped the dinner menu in front of him and went to retrieve the wine list. As the train raced through the French countryside, distant village lights flickered past the window. Thomas scanned the list and requested a half-bottle of Moët & Chandon *Brut Impérial* while considering his meal.

A few minutes later, as he savored the lively champagne — its chardonnay, pinot noir, and pinot meunier grapes giving it bright fruit and energy –Albert returned.

"Is the Moët to your liking, sir?"

"It has always been one of my favorites," Thomas replied. "The other being Veuve Clicquot."

"Each with its own charm," Albert said. "But only the Moët is reputed to have changed world history."

Thomas raised his eyebrows. The dining car buzzed with activity, but Albert seemed in no hurry.

"You are a military man, Colonel?"

Thomas nodded.

"Then I believe you will enjoy the story. Napoleon Bonaparte first met Jean-Rémy Moët in 1782 while Moët was traveling to sell his champagne. The emperor fell in love with it, and they became lifelong friends. Before every campaign, Napoleon would stop at Moët's estate to purchase several dozen cases of *Brut Impérial*, which he claimed was the only refreshment that could restore him after a hard day's fighting."

Albert poured the last of the champagne into Thomas's flute and continued.

"Alas, one day Napoleon departed for battle without replenishing his stock. He went into battle thirsty, unable to sleep, exhausted, and demoralized. And thus, my dear Colonel, was defeated at…"

Thomas chuckled. "Waterloo?"

Albert beamed.

"On the backs of such small events, history is made, *mon* Colonel. Now, shall we place your dinner order?"

"One question first," Thomas said. "After Napoleon's abdication, many of his friends were ruined. How did Moët survive?"

Albert glanced around to ensure he wasn't needed elsewhere.

"Ah, but that is the best part. When the Russian army occupied Champagne after Napoleon's fall, they looted the cellars, seizing over 600,000 bottles from Moët's stores."

"That's a staggering amount."

"But Moët didn't complain. Instead, he said: 'The soldiers who ruin me today will make my fortune tomorrow. Let them drink their fill — they'll be hooked for life and become my best salesmen back in Russia.' And so it was."

Thomas smiled. The prospect of dining alone for five nights aboard the train had concerned him; Albert's stories promised to remedy that.

"And now, monsieur –for dinner?"

"The turbot sounds perfect," Thomas replied. "Perhaps a dry Riesling from Alsace with it?"

Albert once again glanced around discreetly. "Colonel, you appear to be a gentleman who appreciates fine food and wine."

"You have me there."

"Please keep this between us, but… the reason for our overnight stop in Strasbourg is that our chef broke his leg last night while–ah–while leaping from a second-story window."

Thomas grinned. "When the husband returned home unexpectedly?"

Albert dipped his head in respect.

"Monsieur is a man of the world."

"And with no chef...?"

"The dishwashers must prepare tonight's meal."

"And so, what can I order that won't kill me?"

"Even a dishwasher cannot ruin a roast," Albert said. "A simple roast, garden salad — which I will prepare myself — fresh bread, yesterday's apple tart, and a nice Bordeaux. Our chef in Strasbourg is one of the finest in France. I promise: the remainder of your journey will not leave you hungry."

With his wine glass refilled, Thomas opened his book on the Ottoman Empire as Albert departed to confer with the dishwashers. The journey, he thought, was off to an interesting–if not entirely predictable–start.

~SEVEN~

Outside Munich, Germany

When he saw how crowded the dining car was, Thomas nearly turned back to his stateroom to order dinner in. Albert, spotting him from the rear of the car, squeezed his considerable girth down the narrow aisle between the two rows of tables and caught him just as he reached the door to the adjoining club car.

"Colonel, please," Albert puffed, tapping Thomas on the shoulder. "You do not want to miss tonight's meal. It will be *exquis* — a dinner for the ages."

"Merci, Albert, but the quarters are a bit close for my liking, and I didn't see a single empty table."

Now it was the waiter's turn to grin. "Ah, but I have made arrangements for you — arrangements I promise, on a fine bottle of champagne, you'll thank me for the moment you sit down."

"Is this a bet?"

Albert nodded.

"One I assure you I will win, Colonel. It does, however, require that you share your table with another passenger."

Thomas was about to decline when the train rounded a curve at speed, forcing him to reach for the handhold by the door.

"*S'il te plait,* Colonel. You know I wouldn't seat you with some sweaty salesman or blabbering politician. Trust me."

Thomas sighed. He was hungry and bored besides. No decent card games had materialized for the remainder of the trip, and Albert's promise of a grand meal was persuasive. He nodded.

"A bottle of champagne on you if this doesn't work out, is that right?"

Albert beamed.

"And it shall be your beloved Veuve Clicquot, even if I must scour every shop in Vienna to find it!"

Thomas followed him to the last table in the car, where a magnificent framed Lalique glass panel — a mermaid rising from the sea — separated the dining area from the bar and kitchen. The candle lamp above the table cast a warm glow on the fine china, crystal, and a small bouquet of wildflowers. Across from him, a woman sat with her head buried in a book.

Albert cleared his throat. "Mademoiselle Heléne Bovet," he announced. "May I present Colonel Thomas Scoundrel. And I thank you for generously sharing your table this evening."

Mlle Bovet did not lift her head. She simply waved toward the chair opposite and kept reading.

Albert winked at Thomas, handed him the wine list, and turned to tend to another table.

Thomas sat as a busboy spread a linen napkin on his lap and poured water.

"Thank you," he said. "The dining car was half empty last night. We must have picked up quite a few passengers in Strasbourg."

"Mmm," the woman murmured, eyes still fixed on her book.

Albert soon appeared with a half bottle of champagne, poured Thomas a glass, and placed the bottle in a small ice bucket.

Resigned to a quiet meal, Thomas opened his Ottoman history. But then he caught the title of the book she was reading: *The Malay Archipelago*, by Alfred Russel Wallace.

"Forgive my interruption," he said. "You're reading one of my favorite books."

"You've read Wallace?" she murmured, with a tone of polite skepticism.

"Both volumes," Thomas replied. "I read them on a voyage from San Francisco to Hawai'i, where I had the pleasure of discussing Wallace's work at length with both Thomas Boswell and Prince Akoni, who's an ocean biologist and specimen collector."

He knew name-dropping was unnecessary, but her dismissive tone had stung.

At last, Heléne raised her head. Her sea-blue, almond-shaped eyes studied his face, as if deciding whether to engage. Her auburn hair fell loose across her shoulders –unfashionably–catching the candlelight. A sprinkling of freckles spoke of many hours in the sun. Her lips, naturally red, framed a delicate dimpled chin. The symmetry of her features held him for a moment, as though he were gazing at the work of a master artist.

Heléne broke the spell. "I know Boswell's work," she said. "I have an illustrated copy of his *Plantes à fleurs de Tahiti*. Extraordinary. His sketches are unrivaled."

Encouraged, Thomas sipped his champagne and took a chance.

"I was with him for six months when he began that work."

"On Tahiti?"

"At first. Then he joined me on Moorea, where he continued after I left."

She closed her book and leaned back slightly — Thomas noticed that no food had yet been served at her place setting. Could he hope they might dine together? It had been over two weeks since he'd had a truly enjoyable meal companion — not since he and Herman Melville parted company in Le Havre. Lautrec and Van Gogh had offered plenty of drink and philosophy, but not much in the way of civilized dining.

The train hit a rough patch, and for a moment the clatter of the wheels drowned out all conversation.

When the track smoothed again, Albert reappeared beside them, grinning like the Cheshire Cat.

"And would Mademoiselle care to place her order?"

She nodded and requested the broiled brook trout with green beans and almonds, and roasted butternut squash. Albert approved and recommended a dry Alsace Riesling to accompany it before turning to Thomas.

"You haven't given me a menu, Albert."

"Ah, but by now you trust my judgment, Colonel."

"Shall we wager another bottle of champagne?" Thomas smiled.

"I'll gladly make that a case, Colonel — so certain am I of our chef's talents." With that, Albert vanished toward the kitchen.

Heléne raised an eyebrow. "Wagering with the waitstaff? That's not quite cricket, Colonel."

"I've learned one thing in a thousand restaurant visits — and at sea," he replied. "If you want the best meal and experience a kitchen can deliver, your waiter is your greatest ally. They alone decide how pleasant your evening will be."

"Just them?" she teased, with the barest hint of a smile.

Thomas took the bait.

"Of course, one's dining companion is no less important."

"A very diplomatic save, Colonel Scoundrel," she giggled softly.

Over the next two hours, they talked easily — of travel, books, and the history of the lands the Orient Express was crossing. Though Thomas offered to speak in her native French, Heléne insisted on practicing her English. Her delivery was nearly flawless, but as the wine flowed, she occasionally slipped into French. Thomas found it utterly charming.

Albert had not exaggerated the chef's skills. Thomas opened with a foie gras terrine with pear, cinnamon, and Sauternes — which the waiter proudly explained had taken three days to prepare. The main course was porcini-crusted beef tenderloin, seared rare with truffle butter sauce, accompanied by a twelve-year-old Louis Jadot *Clos des Ursules*. The seasoned beef and firm, earthy red wine achieved a flavor combination unlike any he had ever known. Heléne had to cup her hand to suppress a laugh at his expression as he took his first bite.

When she finished her trout and excused herself to the first-class lounge, Albert slipped in."Everything to your satisfaction, Colonel?"

"There was no chance you'd lose the bet, Albert. Superb."

Albert winked conspiratorially as he poured two coffees. "I did briefly consider opening with oysters and lemon for you both, but once I saw you begin to talk, I realized no such inspiration was needed."

"You're a cad, Albert," Thomas growled –but he smiled.

"Perhaps, sir –but I believe I've won our wager."

When Heléne returned, Albert brought two dishes of lemon sorbet topped with pine liqueur and dark chocolate, then discreetly left them alone.

Thomas noticed that the wine had deepened the flush in her cheeks –a natural effect heightened by her auburn hair and blue eyes.

"I've explained my work for the Chronicle," he said as they sipped coffee over the steady clack of the rails. "But I've yet to ask what brings you to Constantinople."

"You mean why I booked the trip alone? Sans husband or suitable chaperone?"

Her reply caught him off guard. He hadn't considered she might be married. He dipped his head, embarrassed by his own question.

She noticed. "The answers are: no, I'm not married, and I'm thirty-one. My husband died three years ago in Athens while arranging shipment of Greek statues for one of his London clients. He developed a fever and died within a week."

"I'm very sorry," Thomas said quietly.

"And you, Colonel?" she asked. "Is there a Mrs. Colonel awaiting you behind a rose-covered fence somewhere?"

When Thomas lifted his eyes to meet hers, it was her turn to feel a moment's regret for asking.

"My wife died twelve years ago in a diving accident near Moorea, in Tahiti," he said. "I've had no real home since. I spent much of the past year commanding a company of Mexican cavalry chasing Apache warriors through northern Mexico. It's been years since I had anything like a house."

"Twelve years," she murmured. "You were just a boy."

"I was twenty-three."

Heléne poured the last of the Clos des Ursules into their glasses and raised hers gently.

"To their memories," she said softly, as their glasses touched.

~EIGHT~

Vienna

It was unseasonably warm for early May, and Thomas welcomed the cool Vienna wind, the Lüfter, pouring down out of the Alps and the Carpathians that afternoon. He had been walking the Ringstraße boulevard that encircled the historical center of the city for two hours, enjoying the clean lines and orderliness of the architectural design in the state buildings, and the many parks, fountains, monuments, and public spaces. He counted dozens of coffee shops and pastry sellers as he followed along the Danube River; most were crowded with people enjoying what Heléne had called *Lebenkunst,* the distinctly Viennese art of living that celebrated food, music, and the arts every day.

The Orient Express had arrived yesterday afternoon, and its passengers were informed that it would be staying for two nights, not one as originally planned. They were welcome to sleep and dine on the train as it waited in the yards, of course, but most of the passengers chose to check into hotels for the two nights. Thomas took a room next to hers at a small hotel at Steindlgasse 4, next to a 400-year-old restaurant called the *Gösser Bierklinik.*

"You will thank me for this," she told him when they arrived by carriage from the train station. Her recommendation proved out that evening when she went to meet a friend for dinner, leaving him to dine alone in the tall ceilinged, dark-paneled restaurant with stained glass windows depicting medieval battle scenes. His meal of boiled beef Viennese style with creamed spinach and roasted potatoes with apple horseradish cream was a surprising blend of tastes and textures that he did not expect to find in this part of the world.

Even more uncharacteristically, he had allowed his waiter to select the wine. Normally he would study a restaurant's list carefully, weighing each choice, but Vienna's mix of old world and exotic had put him in a more adventurous mood.

His waiter sported a huge, white handlebar moustache over a brown leather vest, and around his neck he wore a tastevin, a shallow silver metal cup that was faceted and convex so that he could judge the color and clarity of a wine in a candle-lit cellar.

"It is a new varietal, Colonel, known as *Müller-Thurgau*," the waiter said when they were talking about the perfect wine to accompany Thomas' dinner. "It is a marriage of Riesling with Madeleine Royale and was created by an Austrian named Hermann Müller only two years ago. I recommend it with your soup and salad."

"And with my beef?"

"Ah, for that course we shall open a *Spätburgunder*–which translates to 'late Burgundy.' It has notes of dark cherry, redcurrant, blackcurrant, and other brambly fruits…you will not be disappointed."

He hadn't been. The *Müller-Thurgau* was a touch sweet for his usual taste but balanced and well-suited to the opening courses. The red was excellent–complex, spicy, with great depth.

He was thinking of those wines now as he rounded the corner toward his hotel and spotted Heléne already seated in the outdoor café where they'd arranged to meet. The afternoon sun was slipping low, and the gas streetlights flickered to life, casting an amber glow on the rain-washed cobblestones and gilding the buildings for these brief few minutes of magic light.

She waved as he approached. Each wrought-iron table was topped with a small umbrella and vase of fresh flowers. Behind them, tall windows revealed the restaurant filling quickly for the evening.

Heléne wore a brown suede jacket, a man's tie over a high-collared white shirt, a felt fedora angled forward. A riding skirt swept down over ankle boots. The word fetching sprang to Thomas's mind–but as her eyes brightened at his approach, the word seemed entirely inadequate. She was simply beautiful.

Their waiter approached as he sat, and Heléne ordered coffee and Sachertorte for two.

"People are making a lot of food and wine choices for me lately," he said with a smile.

"And has that not worked out?"

"On the contrary…I am discovering a whole new world and enjoying it. But, what is Sacher…."

"…torte," she finished. "It is chocolate cake made of two layers that are filled with apricot jam and topped with a layer of chocolate icing. Your heart will thank you."

"And my stomach will groan," he chuckled.

"Later we will walk to the park outside Hofburg Palace. It will take an hour and a half to walk around the plazas and fountains."

"By which time we will be ready for dinner?"

"By which time I will have told you my story, and I will be asking for yours."

Thomas pursed his lips.

"That may take a while longer."

She smiled. "Then we will make sure to take our dinner in the most leisurely fashion possible."

The sun had nearly set by the time they reached the park across from the sprawling Hofburg Palace, and Heléne took Thomas' arm as they walked to help ward off the chill. The new electric lights were being installed in the park and around the fountain complex, and their pale incandescent beams heightened shadows and reached deep into the trees and bushes that dotted the area.

"I am told that the lights are ruining the love lives of thousands of Viennese couples," Heléne said with a sly smile. "Especially those who should really not be cavorting anywhere, especially in public."

"In the bushes, under the trees?" Thomas replied with a grin. "Is that even civilized?"

"No, but until a few months ago a randy pair could slip away from the gas street lights, duck into a copse of fern only feet from the footpath and be wrapped in complete darkness when they…." Her voice trailed off. "And now, this," she said, waving towards a string of electric lights illuminating every corner of the once popular trysting spaces.

"So much for progress, I suppose."

The sound of water splashing in the fountain nearest them had an almost musical quality, and a moment later the afternoon breeze went still and Heléne scooted a bit down the bench.

"On our first night on the train you asked what I was doing on this trip," she began. "I did not answer because I did not know you, or trust you, and before I go on, I need to be certain."

She looked deep into Thomas' eyes, but he remained silent. This was her story, and he wanted her to feel comfortable before telling it.

Tears welled in her eyes, but she held them back, and when she began to speak her voice was so low that he had to lean forward to hear.

"There are men," she began, "powerful men with connections everywhere, like the tentacles of an octopus. They are looking for me, and when they find me…"

Thomas kept his voice calm and asked, "When they find you?"

She lowered her head for a moment, and then raised it and looked into his eyes again. "They are going to ask me a single question. If I do not answer, or if they believe I am being untruthful…they will kill me."

Thomas felt a chill go up his spine that did not come from the night air. All around them the citizens of a happy city were enjoying their strolls through the park, sipping coffee at small tables, and listening to a string trio performing in front of one of the electrically lit fountains. Without thinking he felt for the handle of the Colt revolver in his holster.

"Are you certain you want to have this conversation here, now?" he asked.

She nodded and clasped her hands in her lap.

"Why are men looking for you, Heléne? Who are they?"

A hint of a smile crossed her face, which Thomas figured was a small sign of relief that she could finally share this story with someone. He signaled to a coffee vendor who was passing with his cart and purchased two small cups of very strong coffee. The vendor pointed to a table where they could leave their cups when they were finished and went along his way.

"My father is Édouard Bovet, a well-known and highly respected archaeologist, Egyptologist, and author," she began. "His book on procedures for digging out and evaluating ancient sites in Egypt, particularly in the area known as the Valley of the Kings, where dozens–if not hundreds–of burial tombs of the pharaohs are still undiscovered, set the scientific standard for exploration."

"I have read about that place since I was a boy," Thomas said. "It's fascinating."

"Yes," she replied, "and mysterious, and dangerous."

A hundred questions leapt into his mind, but Thomas restrained his curiosity and remained silent.

"He is a fellow of both the French *Société de Géographie* and the Royal Geographical Society of Great Britain, and he has made an even dozen expeditions of exploration to Egypt," she continued, "and since my husband's death three years ago I have been his research assistant."

Which explains her outdoor complexion, thought Thomas.

"Where is your father now?" he asked.

Heléne rested her coffee cup on the bench. "I don't know, Thomas. No one knows. He has just disappeared."

"In Egypt?"

"Perhaps. In truth he could be almost anywhere."

"I don't understand," he said. "Men are chasing you, and your father has vanished."

"Into the sands of the desert, for all I know," she answered.

"But why?"

Heléne finished her coffee and took both of their cups to the table across the path. It was completely dark now, the string trio was packing up, and there were only a few people still strolling the paths in and among the fountains and ponds. When she came back to the bench she settled in close beside Thomas. That pleased him because he was certain she had been carrying this burden by herself for some while.

"You are safe with me, Heléne," Thomas said gently. "No one will harm you while I am here."

Her eyes closed, and she leaned against his shoulder for a moment.

"The short version is this: several scientific societies, private investors, and a major bank funded his latest expedition. Four months ago, he left for the Valley of the Kings. Except for one letter, he hasn't been heard from since. But now, valuable artifacts from Egypt are appearing across London and Paris. No one can trace their source."

"Is that unusual in your business?" Thomas asked.

"The only way to certify that the objects they are buying are authentic is to verify the credibility of the supplier. The market is filled with fakes and forgeries."

"So, someone is making thousands of dollars."

"No, many hundreds of thousands," Heléne interjected.

"A fortune, then," Thomas continued. "And at the same time your father has dropped off the face of the earth. Putting one and one together, you are suggesting that a lot of people believe your father is the mysterious supplier?"

"Bravo, Thomas," Heléne said with a soft smile. "But not just a lot of people. Everyone believes it, from the halls of government to the offices of the financiers who made his trip possible."

"But has a crime been committed?"

"Perhaps not. But my father's reputation has been destroyed, his estate is being taken to court to recoup investors' money, and he and I both are being pursued."

"By the authorities?"

"No, much worse. You see, there is an enormous black market for Egyptian artifacts that has been around for 100 years. Every member of the monied classes wants to have genuine soapstone carvings or jewelry or statues that came from a pharaoh's tomb. Right now, small lacquered and gilded side tables are all the rage. Who wants to lay their hat on a simple oak table?"

Her question triggered a memory that made Thomas smile. Heléne raised her eyebrows. "Something I said?"

"In the winter of '77 I was called back to service with the Army during the Sioux Wars. I spent two weeks in a canvas campaign tent on the Plains with Bill Cody during the worst blizzard in a century. Our side table was an upturned Sioux battle shield. Not quite the height of society fashion."

"Wait 2,000 years or so," she said with a chuckle, "It could become quite valuable."

She put his arm through his and went on with her story. "One of the most powerful and insidious figures in the antiquities black market is Henri Lavalle, a foul, corpulent beast who operates out of the southern port city of Marseille. It is said that not a single Egyptian artifact, legal or illegal, comes into France or England without him knowing, and getting a piece of the sale. He bribes customs officials, policemen, and even judges."

"You have met him?"

"Sadly, yes. My husband had no choice but to pay duties to Lavalle as a price for doing business. Just being in his presence made my skin crawl."

The breeze picked and Heléne began to shiver. Thomas removed his jacket and wrapped it around her shoulders.

"There is a café just over there," he said, pointing to a building a hundred yards from their bench. "Let's go inside and get something to eat."

A few minutes later they were seated at a quiet corner table in the warmly lit café enjoying steaming bowls of a goulash of beef, peppers, root vegetables and paprika, with slices of fresh sourdough bread and a local burgundy.

"Lavalle was neither a supporter or investor in my father's recent expedition," Heléne said. "But he knew that there was a good chance my father would make a significant discovery, and that meant opportunity for him. When the general secretary of the *Société de Géographie* received a letter from my father claiming that he was about to make entry into the most treasure-filled tomb yet excavated in the Valley of the Kings, word of the discovery made it to Lavalle."

"And he salivated at the thought," Thomas said.

She sipped her wine and said, "Oh, yes. He couldn't wait to feast his eyes on the gold and jewels and other funerary treasure."

"But then your father disappeared?"

"Immediately after his letter arrived and caused such a stir."

"And now a new slew of treasures is appearing on the continent," said Thomas.

"Providing Lavalle with some money, but not enough," added Heléne. "He wants more."

"They always do."

"Lavalle assumes I know where my father is, and where the treasures are located. He sent a personal emissary to my home with an offer: tell him where to find Édourd, or the treasure, and he would cut me in for a piece of the profits. Refuse, and he would kill me, and then find my father and kill him also."

"You went to the authorities?"

"Who, at the request of the Société, the investors, and the bank, also want to find him. They will be of no help."

Thomas pushed his bowl aside and refilled their wine glasses. "So, you packed your bags and joined the Express in Strasbourg. But, to go where…to do what?"

Heléne sighed and stared into the candle lamp on the table.

"Until today I wasn't sure. I knew if I got to Constantinople I would have several choices; stay there and meet with some of my father's colleagues to get information, organize my own expedition and sail for Alexandria, or just hide."

"Hide? For how long?"

A tear rolled down Heléne's cheek. "I don't know, Thomas, I don't know. I've never had anyone threaten to kill me before."

He reached across the table and placed his hand on hers.

"Unfortunately, I have had that dubious pleasure many times, and from some very serious people." He smiled. "But, here I am."

She reached for a handkerchief and dabbed at her eyes. "You are a hard man to kill?"

"Apparently so," he chuckled, "but that hasn't stopped a long line of *hombres malos* from trying."

"Hombres?"

He grinned. "It means 'bad men' in Spanish."

"But why, Thomas? Why would anyone want you dead?"

"Long story."

"We still have three days on the train…Is that enough?"

"It might be, but first, you said that you are no longer confused about what to do next. What changed your mind?"

Heléne shifted in her chair before raising her glass to her lips and draining the last of the burgundy. Her tears were gone, and flecks of sea-foam green sparkled in her eyes.

She tilted her head, graced him with a warm smile, and said,

"You did."

~NINE~

Constantinople

Burak Özdemir was the largest man Thomas had ever encountered. The Turkish antiquities dealer—whose name, Heléne told him, translated as pure iron—stood well over six feet tall and easily weighed 380 pounds. But unlike iron, everything about him was soft and round, from the tasseled fez perched on his head to the upturned toes of his polished boots. At the moment, all of it glistened with sweat, despite the best efforts of the large ceiling fan whirring overhead.

As Özdemir lifted the silver teapot to refill their curved tulip-shaped glasses, Thomas couldn't help noticing the man's fingers — swollen and glistening, like fat breakfast sausages that had burst on a skillet. His thick black moustache, flecked with grey, drooped heavily, and the buttons on his waistcoat strained precariously.

Thomas caught Heléne's eye and fought to suppress a smile when the Turk struggled to turn in his swivel chair to reach a folder on a side table. With the folder opened on his cluttered walnut desk, Özdemir cleared his throat and began to read aloud through the list of items gathered during expeditions around Luxor that he had brokered for Heléne's father in the past year.

"Carved soapstone scarabs, 300," he began in a voice that Thomas found to be almost comically high-pitched. "Green jaspar scarabs, 150. Amethyst, 76. Lotus motif metal decorations in blue and gold, large, 12. Alabaster jars, 231, gilt wooden side tables, 87..."

As the dealer droned on and Heléne took careful notes, Thomas looked out the window behind the dealer's desk to two of the most stunning structures he had ever visited; the Hagia Sophia mosque and the nearby Blue Mosque. He could just make out a few ships sailing the Sea of Marmara beyond the mosques to the south, while out the east window on the other side of the office he could see even more vessels transiting the narrow Bosporus Strait that joined Marmara and the Black Sea and separated parts of Asian Turkey from European Turkey. The history and geography of this small land mass was captivating, and nothing he had read in preparation for the trip or heard from Heléne did justice to the exotic, almost other-worldly feel he experienced from the moment they disembarked the Orient Express and hailed a carriage to their hotel.

Their journey here from Vienna had taken three days. While Heléne pored through her father's journals for any clue to his fate, Thomas labored on his first Orient Express article for The Chronicle. Evenings were spent together in the dining car, where Albert guided them on yet more culinary adventures. Afterward they lingered in the club car, sipping sherry or brandy as Thomas, for the first time, told the full story of his life.

From his accidental heroics at the end of the Civil War that made him a revered household name to his service in the Sioux Wars, his brief stint as a reporter in San Francisco, his life with Keani on Moorea, introducing the impressionist painter Émile Aubert to the world in New York and his search for Rosalilia Verján after she was kidnapped and taken to Colorado, he told his story plainly and without embellishment.

To his surprise, he was even comfortable talking about the only two women he had ever loved; Angela, the military hospital nurse who cared for him after Pebble Creek Ridge, and Keani, the beautiful mute Tahitian woman he married and lived with on the island of Moorea. He had only talked about her death with a few people in the past 10 years, and yet he found it easy to tell Heléne the story in the warmth of the softly lit coach as the train gently rocked along the tracks. And when he spoke of Keani's death on the reef, Heléne quietly took his hand.

They visited late into the night. Yet when Heléne excused herself to return to her stateroom, there was never any hint of invitation or expectation — something unusual for Thomas. He could not recall the last time he'd spent hours talking with such a beautiful woman without slipping into the familiar dance of flirtation that often led to far more.

But perhaps that was the reason: Heléne was brilliant, curious, and well-read. Her wit was quick and precise, like a gifted fencing master. She listened with genuine empathy. And when she laughed, her eyes danced. He was enchanted–and content simply to enjoy her company, perhaps for the first time in his adult life, without imagining her beneath his sheets.

Their routine continued as the Express followed the Danube to Budapest and out onto the vast expanse of sunflower and wheat farms and grasslands known as the Great Hungarian Plain. When they crossed into Serbia, the tracks wound through forested hills and followed the meandering course of the Sava and Morava rivers, dotted with thickly wooded valleys, small rural towns and the domed spires of Orthodox churches. Continuing south and east the train snaked through narrow gorges and tunnels as it ascended into the Balkan Mountains of Bulgaria before descending out onto Turkey's vast Thracian Plain. When the distant hills of the Marmara region became visible, it was not long before the silhouette of Constantinople's domes and minarets became visible.

His first impression of the crowded historical city was of the mix of smells: the scent of the ocean, the baskets of spices overflowing in the city's open-air markets, fresh-baked bread being pulled from outdoor brick ovens, and the savory aroma of kabobs cooking on dozens of wood-fired grills in the city's central souk marketplace.

Özdemir's voice interrupted his reverie.

"Another tea, Colonel? Or perhaps coffee?"

Thomas shook his head, and nodded to Heléne, who was putting her small notebook back into her travel satchel.

"This has been a very instructive meeting, Mr. Özdemir, thank you."

As they stood to leave, the fleshy antiquities dealer leaned back in his chair and swatted at a fly buzzing around a grease stain on his tie.

He said, "A word of caution to you, Mademoiselle Bovet. Rumors swarm in this city like this damn fellow…" he brushed at the persistent fly. "Everyone in the Egypt trade knows the story about your father's disappearance. They believe he discovered the tomb and fortune of Pharoah Amenhotep, and they also believe he has spirited the treasure away somewhere in Sudan until he can find a way to sell it quietly."

"What do you believe?" Heléne asked.

Özdemir leaned forward with his hands on the desk. "What I believe is of no importance; if your father really has discovered the treasure of Amenhotep he will come to me at some point to broker the sales. There is no one else he trusts. No, my dear, it is not I who you should be concerned about. By now every one of my competitors—the honest and the dishonest—know that you and Colonel Scoundrel are in Constantinople, and they know why. No doubt they believe you may know how to find your father…"

The tone in the dealer's voice suggested to Thomas that he might be of the same opinion.

"I do not," Heléne answered firmly.

"Of course not. Of course not," Özdemir murmured. "Still — if you travel to Egypt, remember: the desert is vast and merciless. Many thousands have vanished into its sands over the centuries. Our business is... brutally competitive. There are those who would not hesitate to use less-than-pleasant methods in pursuit of such a fortune." He folded his hands over his belly. "A word to the wise."

Thomas stepped to Heléne's side, deliberately pulling back his jacket so Özdemir could see his hand resting on the Colt's grip.

"Then pass along one more rumor for your competitors, Özdemir," he said coolly. "Mademoiselle Bovet will not be making this journey alone."

Startled, Heléne clapped a hand over her mouth, wide-eyed. She had neither asked nor expected him to volunteer. She looked up at him, silently mouthing: Are you sure?

He gave a brief nod, then turned back to Özdemir, took Heléne's arm, and led her out.

The antiquities dealer watched them go, smiling faintly. Who will notice two more sets of bones bleaching under the Sahara sun? he thought.

~TEN~

Hotel Grand Imperial, Constantinople

The concierge behind the marble and gilt counter twisted the ends of his waxed handlebar moustache as he skimmed a newspaper. It was dusk, and gas lamps glowed to life across the busy, palatial lobby. Thomas had grown fond of the five-story Grand, which matched the great hotels of New York City in both elegance and modern appointments. There was a steam-powered elevator, hot water and flush toilets, and three Italian-tiled fountains where a quartet of musicians played each evening while servers offered complimentary champagne to the guests.

"May I be of assistance, Colonel?" the concierge asked as Thomas approached.

"I've enjoyed your restaurant the past two nights," he said, "but tonight my companion and I are looking for something a bit more adventurous. What can you recommend?"

"Would monsieur prefer something in the European tradition—Italian, perhaps, or French—or something local?"

"Local," Thomas replied. "I've heard much about Turkish cuisine, but so far, I've only sampled a bit of Iskender lamb kebab on pipe bread."

The concierge smiled, nodding. "Was it served with tomato sauce, melted butter, yogurt, grilled tomatoes, and green peppers?"

"Exactly."

"And the flavors were to your liking?"

"They were."

"Then I shall recommend AnTalia, not far from here. They prepare our traditional dishes masterfully. Please do tell them I sent you."

Which will pay for your next dinner there, Thomas thought with a half-smile.

All eyes were on Heléne as she walked across the crowded restaurant on Thomas' arm. Her low cut, form-fitting red velveteen gown was complemented by a single green emerald on a silver chain that swooped down to the top of her creamy décolletage, and her deep auburn hair tumbled to the center of her back.

When they were seated at a corner table and the waiter shuffled off to get the bottle of Veuve Clicquot champagne he had requested the maître d' to have sent as quickly as possible, Thomas experienced a brief instant of doubt; without thinking it through or consulting Andrew Whitton at the *Chronicle*–or for that matter, his own common sense–he had committed that morning to tossing aside his travel assignment to throw in with Heléne Bovet on a quest to find her father in one of the most dangerous and foreboding places on earth. From its hellish landscapes and searing heat to the legions of bandits, antiquities con men, and raging disease to the minor issue of there being a war brewing between Mahdist soldiers and forces under the command of British General Charles Gordon, he also knew that travel to Egypt and Sudan by Europeans and Americans was being actively discouraged by their governments.

Added to that, he had to acknowledge, was his growing enchantment with Heléne, who, as he smiled at her over the golden flame of a small candle, looked more spectacular than ever.

When the champagne arrived, she smiled and reached across the linen to take his hand. That simple touch stiffened his resolve.

"Thank you again, Thomas, for the extraordinarily kind gesture you made today in Burak Özdemir's office," she said as he poured more Cliquot into her Baccarat flute. "But, as wonderful as your offer to come along with me to Egypt is, I need to tell you that I really can make the journey without more help. I will have a trusted guide with me, and…" she reached into the leather satchel that was always at her side, swiftly withdrew a small caliber revolver just long enough for him to see it, and then tucked it back away. "I know how to protect myself."

Their waiter arrived with two ivory-and-gold porcelain bowls. "Ezogelin corba," he said, "to prepare your palates for the evening. It is made with red lentils, sweet-hot tomato paste, grated fresh tomatoes and onions, and a sprinkling of dried mint and chili flakes."

"Isn't a consommé better for cleansing the palate?" Thomas asked, "or a light sorbet?"

"Not tonight, Colonel," the waiter replied. "Tonight, you will dine like an Ottoman emperor."

Thomas raised his eyebrows and smiled at Heléne as the waiter scurried off to get them a basket of fresh bread.

"That was not a gesture I made today, Heléne," he said after taking a sip of the flavorful champagne. "It was a commitment. I have wanted to see Egypt and the tombs of the pharaohs since I was a boy, and in any event, I am certain that my editor at the Chronicle will be delighted to have both a series of articles about the Orient Express as well as one about the search for one of the world's most famous archeologists. And he will cover my expenses."

Heléne leaned forward and looked into his eyes. It was all he could do not to let his eyes linger below her necklace, but a man could only deny nature for so long. Heléne took her time sitting back up, so it was clear to him that she hadn't minded him taking the liberty.

"I told you in Vienna that no harm would come to you while you were with me," he said.

Heléne smiled and nodded, her eyes sparkling.

"I have lived with war and death and all kinds of danger for many years. Some would even say that I attract chaos. But I know how to deal with evil men, Heléne, and, with all due respect to the little pop gun in your satchel, I know how to fight."

She lifted his hand and kissed his palm lightly. "And do you also know how to love, my dear Thomas?"

He hesitated, caught off guard, but the waiter's return rescued him.

"With mademoiselle's permission," Thomas said, "we'll leave tonight's menu entirely to you."

The waiter beamed. Customers seldom entrusted him with their complete dining experience.

"I promise you will not be disappointed," he said as he whisked away to begin their orders, leaving Thomas to get past his stammering and answer Heléne's question.

"Do you mind if I answer your question with dessert?" he finally asked.

"Why Colonel Scoundrel," Heléne replied in feigned disbelief, "I do believe that I have embarrassed you." She lifted her flute and drained the glass, but her eyes never left his.

Their waiter had not been joking when he said they were going to dine like the Ottoman emperors. Dinner began with a selection of appetizers that included *saksuka,* a warm mix of eggplant, zucchini, garlic, tomatoes and chili, along with a simple *kisir* salad of bulgur wheat, tomato, garlic, parsley and mint. They were accompanied by a plate of *yapraak dolma,* grape vine leaves rolled and filled with seasoned rice. When the waiter returned with a plate *ingeol kofte,* grilled meatballs with breadcrumbs and onions served on a round of warm bread, Thomas raised his hands in mock surrender.

"These are just the appetizers?" he asked.

The waiter only smiled as he opened a bottle of French Bordeaux. As much as the Colonel and his guest had asked to remain local with their dinner choices, no wine would do justice to the meal the way the '83 Château Mouton-Rothschild he selected from the cellar himself could do.

A half hour later the waiter and an assistant rolled a wheeled cart up beside their table. On top of the cart was a wooden platter on which sat a one-gallon terra-cotta clay jug with a handle and spout. Heléne shot a questioning glance at Thomas.

"Wine from the countryside?" she asked.

"Dinner from heaven," the waiter replied with a wink. He refilled their crystal goblets with the Rothschild, stood behind the clay jug, and picked up a small hammer.

"You have our attention," said Thomas.

"This pottery holds your dinner," said the waiter. "It is called *testi kabob.* Earlier today it was filled with savory beef, tomatoes, bell pepper, garlic, seasonings, and a knob of butter. The opening was sealed with a peeled slice of potato and then placed into a wood burning oven for three hours."

"But how…" Heléne began.

"Like this," said the waiter. He slipped on a glove, lifted the heated jug a few inches above the wood platter and gave it one sharp hammer rap just below the spout. The entire top came off in one piece, and when the waiter tilted the jug downwards, the meat and vegetable mixture poured easily out onto the platter for the waiter to serve up on a bed of greens and cucumbers.

The mix of flavors and textures was superb; so good that Thomas momentarily forgot being knocked off balance when Heléne kissed his hand and asked if he knew how to love. His forgetfulness vanished when their table was cleared, and the waiter set two small, dark coffees on the table along with a half bottle of cognac and a plate of local sweets. He knew in his heart where this evening was leading, but he was in no hurry to get there.

When the carriage dropped them off at the Grand, Thomas and Heléne rode the elevator to their adjoining rooms on the third floor. She hadn't said a word as they rode from the restaurant. She didn't have to. She rested her head on his shoulder as they trotted along the cobbled avenue and kept her hand in his. The night air was soft and warm, with the barest hint of a breeze off the Bosporus and the cloudless sky was laced with ribbons of stars and lit by a steel-gray moon.

When the elevator door closed and the steam lift began to rise, Heléne turned and kissed him full on the lips. Before he could respond they arrived at their floor and the door cranked open. They walked down the hall to her room, and he waited in quiet anticipation while she fished her key from her bag.

When the door was open a few inches she lay one hand lightly behind his neck and whispered,

"Come with me, darling."

Then, suddenly, the door was yanked wide from inside. Two figures lunged out of the dim light. Without hesitation he pushed Heléne aside and grabbed the first man by the lapels of his jacket. As he did, he saw the flash of metal from the second man's dagger.

The first man was small and wiry, and Thomas was able to swing him around and slam him face first into the door jam. He heard the man's nose crunch and felt hot blood gush onto his jacket. The second man, who was much taller and bulkier than his associate, began slashing at Thomas as he advanced. Thomas raised his right foot and smashed it onto the jaw of the man he had just rammed into the door, and then twisted his body to the side to make it more difficult for the knife wielding attacker to find his mark.

The big man realized he was facing an experienced fighter and backed off just long enough for Thomas to peel off his dinner jacket and wrap it around his left arm. He stepped towards the big man, holding his covered arm at eye height. The man roared, and pushed towards him, slashing up and down with the blade. His first swing missed, but the second time the blade arced toward Thomas, he felt the edge bite through the jacket and into his arm. He stepped back and launched a forward kick deep into the man's solar plexus. He heard the air rush out of the man's lungs and watched him stumble back to the edge of the bed where he almost fell backwards before righting himself and coming at Thomas again.

'Not quite the adventure I had planned for that bed tonight,' Thomas thought as he readied himself to parry another knife blow. Then, in no more than a heartbeat, the small man got up off the floor and rushed over to the open window that overlooked the boulevard three stories below. He disappeared into the curtains just as the big man began his next swing with the dagger.

A shot rang out.

The big man jerked and turned as Heléne stood near the bed, her revolver smoking, readying a second shot.

In that instant, Thomas drew his Colt, cocked, and fired. The slug slammed into the man's lower back as he dove for the window, sending him tumbling into space.

Thomas finally took a breath and looked around to make sure they were alone. Then he turned up the gas wall lamp and looked over at Heléne. She was frozen in place, her head lowered to her chest, her arms drooping at her side. She was sobbing when he took her in his arms and held her tight.

The room was a shambles—drawers overturned, clothing flung across the bed, every possession ransacked. They hadn't come to steal. They were searching for something.

A moment later they heard boot steps thundering down the corridor and the hotel detective and two strong porters flew into the room with pistols drawn.

Heléne lifted her tear-streaked face to Thomas, seeing the blood on his arm. "You're hurt," she whispered, then crumpled onto the edge of the bed. "Oh, Thomas… what have I done to you?"

Thomas cradled her against his chest and gently rocked her in his arms as the detective began barking orders behind them. He nodded to the man to let him know they were fine, and then watched as the detective went to the window and looked down at the broken, twisted body of the big man splayed across the metal wheel of a parked carriage on the boulevard below,

"I told you," Thomas murmured softly, "wherever I go, chaos appears."

His voice had changed. Heléne recognized it now: not the voice of a lover—but the voice of a soldier stepping into command.

Thomas kissed her gently and rose to talk with the detective.

'And this chaos is only beginning,' he thought.

~ELEVEN~

Aboard the S.S. Alexandria, Mediterranean Sea

On their second night at sea, Heléne came to his stateroom. They had dined under a canvas awning on the foredeck of the 103-foot paddle wheel steamer, the last of the elegant old-world vessels in the Oriental and Peninsular Line. With a crew of 25 and 75 passengers, the teak-decked steamer slipped easily out of the Sea of Marmara, through the turquoise waters of the Aegean, and around the Greek isles before turning across the Mediterranean's Levantine Basin towards Egypt.

The sea that evening was a shimmering sheet of blue-green glass. They were seated at a small table below the pilot house and served a savory cognac and garlic infused bouillabaisse Provençal made with fresh-caught fish, sea urchins, and velvet crab, which were served on a platter next to the broth.

The attack at the Grand Hotel had cast a pall over their budding intimacy. Thomas required stitches for the wound on his forearm and Heléne spent two days replacing her ruined clothing and personal items while he drafted a long article about the Orient Express for Andrew Whitton at the *Chronicle*. Once satisfied with his work he delivered it to the American consulate, requesting it be sent via the diplomatic pouch to Washington, where a friend would forward it to San Francisco. There were some benefits to being a full colonel.

Since departing Constantinople, they'd kept mostly to themselves—breakfasting alone in their cabins, reading in deck chairs by day, and quietly observing the jagged coastlines that marked their passage across the cobalt sea.

When dinner ended, Heléne simply squeezed his hand and left for her room without saying a word. Thomas asked for a brandy and stood at the rail with a brandy as the orange wheel of the sun dipped below the Pillars of Hercules and was swallowed up by the Atlantic.

It was unlike him to brood. He rarely hesitated when making decisions, especially ones that placed him in danger. Yet this time was different. Heléne did not fully grasp the peril ahead. She was a scholar. He was a soldier. She read of battle in dusty books; he had lived inside war's bloody chaos since enlisting at 17. She was revulsed by the slimy antiquities dealer, Henri Lavalle, who controlled the European import of Egyptian treasures from his mansion in Marseilles, while Thomas had seen how easily a man like Lavalle could unleash death with a mere nod.

There was no doubt in his mind: the men who ransacked Heléne's room had come on Lavalle's orders–and more would follow.

When the stars sharpened across the North African sky, he asked the steward for another brandy, then made his way to his cabin. He still had work to do before Alexandria, beginning with cleaning his Colt.

An hour later as the ship plowed through the warm, wine dark sea, he was leaning over to turn down the bedside lamp when the soft scent of gardenia drifted through the open window. Then a light knock came at his door.

He opened it to find Heléne standing beneath the glow of the moon, her figure outlined in silver. She stepped inside, fell into his arms, and kissed him as he closed the door behind them.

When she leaned her head back, he saw she had been crying. Unsure what to say, he pulled a chair over from the corner and sat down; if she wanted to talk, he would listen. But Heléne had something else in mind; an impish smile crossed her face, and she looked deep into his eyes before slowly unbuttoning her blouse and loosening the fasteners on the side of her long cotton skirt.

A moment later all her clothing lay in a heap on the floor and then, in the soft orange light of the wall lamp, she pulled her auburn hair behind her shoulders so that Thomas could take in the curves of her hips and the fullness of her breasts. Then, wordlessly, she went to the bed and slipped beneath the coverlet.

He hesitated. He had spent 10 days in the company of this intelligent, charming, beautiful woman, and he had given the possibility of this moment a great deal of thought. He wanted her as much as she desired him, and yet there was something else at play here, something he did not understand. Of course, he was Thomas Scoundrel, and the habits of a lifetime cannot simply be switched off, and so he pushed the thought from his mind and undressed.

When he pulled close against her body, Heléne responded with the most tender passion he had ever experienced. It was so different from anything he had felt before that he laid his head back against the pillow and searched her face.

"My timing may be terrible," he said tenderly, "but I think that you would like to talk before…

"Oh, Thomas, Thomas," she answered through a new wave of tears. She kissed him and said,

"Honestly, my darling, I did not come here to talk…and yet…"

Her voice trailed off.

"And yet?"

She put one hand behind his head and caressed his neck. "I am so frightened for the both of us. I cannot escape the feeling that we are going to die out on the desert. The feeling haunts me night and day."

Thomas raised his head up.

"I have not come along on this excursion to see us become food for the desert jackals, Heléne. I will protect you–I will protect us both. We will find your father, and we will get the two of you back to France, where I promise…," he stopped long enough to lean down and kiss her breasts, "we will enjoy much more of this without fear."

"And I want that so very much," she replied. " But there is more, Thomas, much more than Lavalle or the people seeking to bring ruin upon my father. So much more…"

"Tell me."

"You will think me mad. In truth, I have been worried for months that I am slowly going insane."

"Because of this business with your father?"

"Because…" she hesitated. "Because of the dreams."

Thomas reached for the nightshirt the steward had laid out.

"Put this on," he said gently, handing it to her.

Then he climbed out of bed and slipped on a shirt. He led her over to a chair and retrieved a bottle of brandy from his bag.

"Sorry, only one glass. We'll have to share."

Heléne giggled as she pulled his nightshirt down.

"We were about to share much more, my sweet."

"And we will, I promise. But now, tell me about these dreams, and why they have put such a fright into you."

She took the glass of brandy. "I will, and then you will also probably think me mad."

The brass bell outside the pilot's cabin rang four times and the sound of water splashing around the bow as the ship cut through the water drifted through the curtains of the small window and into the cabin.

"The night we met on the Orient Express," she began in a low voice. "When I looked up from my book and saw you for the first time I nearly fainted."

"Should I say that is a common experience when women first meet me?" Thomas replied with a grin.

"Shush…." she said with a playful slap on his leg.

"I didn't faint because you are handsome, though you are."

That statement earned a light kiss from Thomas.

"It's because I had seen you before, many times."

He looked puzzled.

"The painting? The one of me at Pebble Creek Ridge?"

"No, Thomas, I have never seen the painting. That is not where I saw you—where I still see you."

"In your dreams."

It was a statement, not a question.

"And here is where you will begin to think me mad," she said. "I began having the dream about six months ago. It is always the same. You and I and Samhi–he is my Bedouin guide–are inside the burial chamber of the tomb of Pharoah Amenhotep II, in the Valley of the Kings near Luxor. We are holding torches as we enter the room that holds his sarcophagus. It is overflowing with treasure, Thomas, which is proof that we are the first people to enter the chamber in nearly 3,000 years."

"You mean you have never been inside?"

"No one has. We don't even know the tomb's location. My father spent years pouring through ancient texts and studying the hieroglyphs in other tombs dating from around the same era for any clue of Amenhotep's whereabouts."

"Clues he wrote down in his journals, the ones you keep close by in your satchel."

"Yes, and probably the reason Henri Lavalle has sent men after me. He believes he can find something in those journals that my father could not."

Thomas poured more brandy.

"And you are certain it is me in your dreams? Not someone who might look something like me, or even, forgive me for saying this, perhaps your late husband?"

"You look nothing like him. He was short and dark, you are tall and fair, and, oh Thomas, how I just want to make love to you and hide away from all this insanity."

He chuckled. She looked stunning in the moon light, and his nightshirt did little to hide the smooth lines of her legs, or the contours of her breasts straining against the thin fabric.

"I won't pretend to understand the provenance of dreams, Heléne," he said after a moment, "be they gifts from heaven or curses from hell. My good friend, the poet Walt Whitman, wrote, '*I dream in my dreams all the dreams of the other dreamers. And I become the other dreamers.*' I was intrigued when I first read that line, but I did not give it much thought at the time."

"And now?"

"Now I think there is a deeper meaning in what he says, one that I will think on."

"You don't think I have gone mad?" she asked.

He stood and led her to the bed.

"Leave that on," he said, pointing to the nightshirt. When she was under the covers he continued.

"When I was younger, I spent six months recovering in New Orleans from wounds that I received in a duel."

Heléne's eyebrows shot up.

"We'll talk about that some other time," he added. "I was cared for by a Jesuit priest who opened the world of history and literature and art for me. We talked about every aspect of what he called 'the life of the mind,' the only kind of life that he said was fit to live. I remember him once saying that sanity is quite rare; every man and woman who possess even a modicum of intelligence also possess a modicum of madness."

When he got into bed, she turned on her side to face towards him, her eyes heavy with sleep.

"So…what will we do now, my darling Thomas?" she whispered.

He kissed her softly on the forehead.

"Now, we sleep."

~TWELVE~

Khartoum, May 1884

Major General Charles George Gordon stirred his tea and stepped to the edge of the stone parapet wall that circled his fortress headquarters above the meeting point of the Blue and White Niles. Khartoum had been blockaded by the Mahdi's forces since March, and though the telegraph lines still functioned, he knew it was only a matter of time before the city was fully cut off from the world.

Gordon had sealed his own fate when he disobeyed the Prime Minister's orders to merely survey conditions in Sudan and oversee the evacuation of British citizens, soldiers, diplomats, and loyal Egyptian and Sudanese troops. Now, his only hope of survival rested on a British relief force sailing upriver to destroy the Mahdi's army.

He sipped his tea, reflecting on the grim situation. The city's defenses had been strengthened as best they could; even the paddlewheel steamers ferrying people and supplies had been retrofitted with armor plating and guns. But the Turkish, Arab, Sudanese, and Egyptian troops under his command were a poorly trained, mutinous lot. Only the Black Sudanese regiments, many of them former slaves, offered truly reliable fighting strength. Having fought much of his career against the slave trade, Gordon felt a special kinship with those who had once been sold in open-air markets and later escaped to fight for their freedom.

He harbored no illusions about what would happen if Gladstone's government failed to send aid. Just last November, twenty thousand of the Mahdi's dervishes had annihilated the eight-thousand-man Egyptian army of Gordon's friend Colonel William Hicks at Shaykan. Gordon had walked the two-mile perimeter of the battlefield a week after the slaughter: eleven thousand dead lay scattered beneath the desert sun, swollen and mutilated, the air heavy with the stench of rotting flesh. Many had been shot, hacked, stabbed, or burned alive;

survivors were hunted down and butchered where they fled through the thorny scrub. Spears had been driven into the fallen to ensure no one would rise again. The dervishes had stripped the corpses of weapons, food, water, and clothing. Gordon ordered the bodies burned. As flames roared, thousands of vultures lifted into the sky, darkening the sun.

And now a new complication had arrived. This morning's dispatch from Cairo reported that the American Civil War hero Colonel Thomas Scoundrel was en route from Constantinople with Heléne Bovet to mount an expedition in search of her father, the archaeologist Edouard Bovet, who had vanished months earlier near Khartoum. Gordon knew Edouard Bovet. Rumors swirled that the professor had become entangled in the black-market trade of stolen Egyptian antiquities. Such dealings were hardly new—the looting of Egypt's treasures had flourished for over two millennia—but Bovet, as Gordon knew him, seemed an unlikely criminal.

Under other circumstances, it might have been a minor distraction. But the arrival of a famous American colonel during an active regional war threatened to stir diplomatic havoc at precisely the moment Gordon needed no further complications.

Damn the Bovets. And damn this Scoundrel, he thought as he set down his teacup. With luck, the desert would swallow them long before they reached Khartoum—and he could strike their names from his growing list of troubles.

In fact, the desert had already swallowed one of Gordon's problems.

Professor Edouard Bovet paced the rocky, sand-strewn compound near Wad Madani, eighty-five miles from where Gordon sipped his tea. The bleak scattering of huts and goat pens on the west bank of the Blue Nile had been his prison for nearly four months. His only companions were a herder, the man's wife, their four strapping sons, and two other prisoners who, like Bovet, had run afoul of Bedouin chieftains and been cast into this desolate exile.

Escape was not impossible—but wildly improbable. One of the sons was always watching, and the barren wilderness of rock, hill, and rubble stretched unbroken for miles in every direction beneath the scorching sun. Scorpions, hyenas, and a dwindling pride of Barbary lions claimed dominion here. With no water, no food, no shelter, any escape attempt would end quickly in death.

Two possibilities remained: either he would waste away and be tossed into the canyons–or his captors would eventually summon him to face interrogation once more.

Henri Lavalle. Always it came back to the corpulent antiquities broker in Marseilles. Edouard had done business with Lavalle for fifteen years—not out of choice, but necessity. No one working in Egypt's antiquities trade avoided him. Every stone scarab, alabaster jar, sarcophagus, gilt table, monumental column, or linen-wrapped mummy that left Egypt was subject to Lavalle's monstrous protection rackets. Pay, or see your shipment lost, your bones broken, or worse. Customs officials, freight brokers, ship captains, and politicians all sat comfortably in Lavalle's greasy pockets.

Four months earlier, Lavalle's emissaries had come to Edouard with the same message repeated throughout the Egyptian archaeological world: rumors were swirling that Bovet had found riches beyond imagining inside the tomb of Pharaoh Amenhotep. Lavalle, of course, wished to ensure he received his customary share of any treasure extracted from the ancient chambers.

The search for Amenhotep's tomb had been Edouard's life's work. For years he scoured libraries, museums, universities, and geographical societies across Europe and North Africa for clues. Was it hidden in the Valley of the Kings? Perhaps. He had collected tantalizing fragments of evidence–but only excavation would yield certainty.

Looking out across the bleak rubble-strewn horizon, Bovet fought back despair. At least, he thought, his maps, notes, and journals remained safe in Heléne's hands in Paris.

As long as Lavalle never discovered the existence of those journals, his daughter would remain safe.

Ahmad bin Abdullah bin Fahal stood alone before God in the stillness of the star-swept, jet-black night and listened to the desert sing. Alone on the ridge, under the vast black sky, the Mahdi drank in the quiet songs of the dunes. As a boy, the great ridges and valleys of the erg had first sung to him, and over the years he had learned to read their melodies—the humming whispers of the crescent barchans, transverse dunes, and long seifs. The Saharan landscape, shaped by centuries of shifting haboob winds, formed an intricate, living architecture that far surpassed any work of stone or steel crafted by Western hands.

He knew how to find rainwater inside the mountains of sand called draa, where seeps and springs flowed from the escarpments, and navigating only by smell he could follow the networks of wadis, lakes, and pools that traversed the continent from east to west. The West saw the desert as death. Ahmad saw life. Even in this endless emptiness flourished oryx and sand fox, jackals and hyenas, gazelle and mongoose, desert owls and larks, fan-tailed ravens wheeling through the dawn.

No, Al-Sahra al Kubra, the father of all deserts was not devoid of life; it was the very fount of life. He had walked in London and Paris, Rome and New York. He had seen the West's grand bridges and palaces—but even their greatest marvels seemed feeble beside the desert's sculpted cathedrals of sand, hundreds of miles long, built not by man but by the patient breath of the wind.

Two hours away, six thousand of his AnsŌr warriors camped under the stars, their fires burning like scattered coals against the horizon. One word from their Mahdi, and they would hurl themselves into battle against any odds. They had done so before. They would do so again.

And yet, on this night, as he prepared himself for purification prayers, he struggled to still his mind. Hatred, ambition, anger—these emotions were constant companions. But lately something new had wormed its way into him: fear.

Not fear of battle, disease, or old age—but of a vision that had haunted his dreams since his visit to the Valley of the Kings. The painting. The fantastical 3,000-year-old mural that depicted, in agonizing detail, the moment of his death.

Overhead, an owl whispered past. Ahmad lifted his gaze to Antares, the bright red heart of Scorpius, his birth sign—a familiar sentinel hanging in the black bowl of heaven.

He drank in the celestial light a moment longer. Then, swinging up into his saddle, he turned his horse toward camp. As the hooves carried him through the night, the desert sang once more—and with its ancient song, his fear dissolved into the eternal sands.

~THIRTEEN~

Alexandria, Egypt

Heléne could not help but chuckle at Thomas' discomfort. This was the second late afternoon stroll they had taken along Alexandria's bustling seafront since their arrival yesterday, but as of today Thomas had not been able to find a way to put the city into a perspective that made sense to him.

"New York City has over a million inhabitants to Alexandria's 200,000," he said as they passed rows of commercial stalls spread along the stone wall that separated the road from the turquoise blue bay, "and yet somehow this city seems far busier and more crowded. I don't understand."

"It does seem that way later in the day and into the evening," Heléne answered, "but only when the breezes flow in from the Mediterranean and begin to cool things down. That's when the shops and stalls open, and the food vendors begin baking and preparing the salads and lamb and chicken. Two hours ago, the quays and paths were deserted. Now…" she swept her arm in the direction of the city's main square, "everyone in the city is right here."

It was the 'everyone' part that had rattled Thomas the first time they walked through the city. The narrow streets were packed with the most unusual assortment of peoples he had ever experienced; nomadic Bedouins from the country's vast interior clad in flowing robes and turban-like headdresses with brightly colored and embroidered waist cloths mingled with women wearing dark black robes and head coverings that provided only a narrow slit to see out of. There were dark-skinned Nubians in soft-colored single piece robes with voluminous long sleeves, Berbers in bright red, green and purple robes with matching head coverings, Greeks in baggy trousers and linen shirts, and everywhere, in startling contrast to the dozens of traditional costumes from 100 different cultures, there were also men and women whose clothing would fit in with what the merchants and tradesmen in London or Paris were wearing.

The air vibrated with the cacophony of more languages and dialects than his ears could make sense of, until they all seemed to meld together into a single incomprehensible stew. What amazed him was the way that no one seemed to be the least disconcerted when engaging with a person speaking a language they did not understand. This was especially true with people haggling over prices at the stalls selling spices, fabrics, dried fruits and nuts, teas and coffees, rice, sweets, and cooked and raw lamb, chicken, and fish. Heléne pointed out that everyone used hand and face gestures to communicate their wishes during the buying process and watching thousands of wildly gesticulating hands and arms in constant motion as they walked through the markets and squares only heightened Thomas' sense that he was on a different planet.

The most remarkable thing about the Alexandrians he passed, however, was their good humor. Smiles, backslaps, and full-throated laughter were everywhere.

"Everyone seems so happy," he said. "I haven't seen anything like this in any other big city I have visited."

"This is more than a marketplace." Heléne replied as she took his arm and navigated across the way to a stall displaying brightly colored silk scarves. "It is the town square, the hub of social life, a place for friends and lovers to meet for meals and gossip."

Thomas was about to answer when a swarthy man wearing a dour expression over a traditional Egyptian robe shouldered him hard as he brushed past. Thomas instinctively felt for the handle of the revolver under his light jacket and said to Heléne, "That is the third time today someone has done that. Am I offending people somehow?"

Heléne finished speaking with the scarf vendor and set down the bright orange silk she'd been examining. "They think you're British or French," she said softly. "Few Americans travel to Egypt, and fewer still come to Alexandria."

"So, they assume I was part of the bombardment."

"It has only been two years, Thomas. And when a flotilla of nine British and French iron-clads lays waste to an entire section of your city…" she pointed to the south where the shattered walls of dozens of buildings stood silent and empty, "you do not forgive your enemies lightly."

"And now Great Britan occupies Egypt," he said, "and I look enough like a European that people feel comfortable taking out their anger on me."

Heléne giggled "Oh, Thomas, my darling…that wasn't anger. It was merely a political statement. Anger would have been delivered at the point of a very sharp dagger." With that she paid for her scarf and took his arm for the walk back to their residence.

When Heléne told Thomas they would be staying with her father's Bedouin guide rather than a European hotel, he had pictured dirt floors, tents, or straw pallets. Surely Alexandria offered a proper hotel? But Heléne laughed off his objections and arranged a carriage as soon as they disembarked.

Their driver wound through a maze of narrow, cobbled streets until they arrived at a tall, whitewashed wall with a heavy wooden gate. There were no house numbers here, no street signs. Before Thomas could ask how the driver even knew where to go, Heléne rapped the oversized brass knocker.

The gate swung open. A grinning boy of about ten greeted them and led the way inside.

They stepped into an expansive garden paved in brick, overflowing with flowering vines, willows, terra cotta planters spilling over with blooms, and a three-tiered Moorish-tiled fountain where small birds dipped and splashed. At the far end stood a handsome three-story house: white plaster walls, green-trimmed windows, wrought-iron balconies, and a red-tile roof.

The boy raced ahead of them into the house, and a moment later a stocky man of medium height wearing a full-length pale blue caftan and leather sandals stepped out the door to greet them. Samhi had a close-cropped gray beard and hair, and his deeply tanned face was weathered from years spent guiding archeological expeditions up the Nile from Cairo to Khartoum.

His broad face beamed at the sight of Heléne, and the two embraced like long lost family members. Then he pulled away and took Thomas' hand in an iron grip. "*Ahlan wa sahlan*; welcome to my home, Colonel Thomas," he said. "My family are honored to have a man of your fame share our table."

Thomas nodded, and then raised his eyebrows to Heléne. She shook her head…she had no idea how Samhi had heard of him.

"The honor is mine, Samhi Al-Katib," Thomas replied. "Thank you for accommodating us on such short notice."

Samhi put a hand on Thomas' shoulder. "Heléne and her father are family, which makes you family, as well." Then he put his other hand on Heléne's shoulder and guided them towards the door. "My sons will take your things to your rooms. Please, refresh yourselves, and then join us on the roof for dinner."

Thomas followed Samhi into the house and up a flight of stairs and down a long corridor decorated with oil paintings of the Sahara and the Nile. He was pleased to see that his room was next to Heléne's and even happier when he saw that there was a connecting door between the rooms.

"Our rooms are on the floor above, so it will be very quiet here for you both," Samhi said as his sons brought their bags into the rooms. Thomas exchanged a glance with Heléne as she stepped into her room; if Samhi had meant anything scandalous with his remark about it being 'quiet' for them, his tone did not give anything away.

When Samhi left, Thomas swung open the French doors and stepped out of the high-ceilinged bedroom onto the balcony. He breathed in the soft sea air and looked over the garden to the green-blue waters of the Mediterranean a quarter mile from the Bedouin guide's home.

A half hour later he had washed and changed into a fresh, open-collared linen shirt. He made his way up to the roof-top dining area and was surprised to see a formally set table beneath the shade of a cotton awning supported by tent poles. The roof was encircled by a three-foot brick wall embedded with hundreds of multi-colored glass shards, no doubt to discourage anyone from climbing over from below. A servant followed him through the doors and began laying platters of fruit, fresh baked pita bread, smoked fish, savory rice, lamb kebobs, and grape leaves stuffed with chicken. The platters went on the table beside small dishes of foie gras, tureens of soup, and plates of domiati cheese.

Samhi introduced Thomas to his wife, Marwa, and handed him a crystal stem filled with ice-cold champagne. "Moët & Chandon Brut Impérial," he said. "I am told you prefer Veuve Clicquot, but unfortunately my wine purveyor in the city carries a limited inventory of champagnes. And with the war disrupting so much trade, one must make do…"

"This is excellent," Thomas replied after taking a sip. "The setting even more so."

Samhi gestured across the city. "Two thousand years ago, you would be gazing at the Great Lighthouse. The tallest structure on earth for centuries. And there, beyond, stood the fabled Library of Alexandria."

Heléne arrived at that moment and accepted a glass of champagne from Marwa. "Once a guide, always a guide," she said to Thomas before giving Samhi a peck on the cheek. "Although I'm not sure I would trust him getting me across any town that wasn't built at least 1,000 years ago."

"No town worth visiting is any younger than that," Samhi answered with a grin. "But let us sit."

He refilled their glasses and asked the servant to open another bottle.

"I have so many questions," said Thomas. "This city is overwhelming."

"Yes?" Samhi asked.

"For example, and forgive me if this is an intemperate question, but how is it that you and your wife can drink wine? Isn't it forbidden by your Holy Book?"

"Ah, yes, for many it is considered haram, or forbidden," Samhi answered. "But, my friends, I tell you that the Prophet himself could not have foretold the invention of something this extraordinary…," he held his flute up to the sky and gave it a swish to set the bubbles in motion, "anymore than your Bible foretold the invention of locomotives or hot air balloons."

Thomas had to smile. "Are you suggesting that a holy dispensation can be made in this case because you are drinking only the very best wines?"

Samhi winked at Heléne. "Forgiveness in the face of the divine is a gift from God," he said as he picked up the newly opened bottle and topped off their glasses. "And this, my friends," he said as he took another drink, "is divinity in liquid form."

A cool breeze floated in from the bay, and the scent of orange blossom, spice, and marketplace cooking fires drifted over them. Samhi's youngest children scrambled around the roof garden, under the table and even between Thomas' legs playing tag until Marwa scooted them back downstairs, where their oldest sister would feed them. Then, as Samhi busied himself opening bottles of Château Palmer Bordeaux and a dry white Spanish Rioja from Marqués de Riscal, she described the ingredients and flavors of each of the dishes that covered the long wooden table, and suggested Thomas and Heléne try a bite of each.

When Thomas selected fish and chicken stuffed grape leaves for his first course Samhi poured a goblet of the Rioja for him before pouring a crystal glass of the Bordeaux for Heléne to accompany her lamb kebobs. She raised her glass to Thomas, and then looked down at the scarf around her neck as if to ask if he approved. She was wearing a simple white cotton dress gathered at the waist and embroidered with orange and blue flowers that complemented the scarf she bought earlier in the day. He was enchanted by her lustrous hair and shining eyes, and the way the wine moistened her full red lips made him long to spirit her away from the table to his room above the flower-filled garden.

Heléne returned his gaze, and as the chatter and laughter that had been ringing out around the table quieted, Marwa shared a knowing glance with her husband. She suppressed a giggle at the thought that the door between her guest's rooms would surely be opening wide sometime tonight.

Samhi was not immune to the atmospherics of the moment, either. He had felt a fatherly concern for Heléne since she was a child, and it was heartening to see that she had found someone to care for after her husband's death. Even so, he also felt an obligation on her father's behalf to see just what kind of man this Colonel Scoundrel was.

He cleared his throat and reached for the Rioja, which momentarily stilled the silent communication being shared by the young couple.

"It will take four or five days to get outfitted for the trip to Cairo and beyond," he said. "We have much to plan for, and even more to discuss. Heléne, I would like to read through your father's journals. And Colonel Scoundrel, we must map out our journey to the Valley of the Kings. Edouard is not there, of course, but I daresay there will be someone who knows where he went, and with the war between the Mahdists and the British and Egyptian army growing more intense each week in the east, our ability to travel wherever the clues may point will be severely restricted."

"How far is it to Cairo?" Thomas asked.

"A hundred and fifty miles by train. And then 400 miles upriver to Luxor, which is a five-day journey by boat."

Heléne's demeanor changed as they began talking about the search for her father. "If the journals lead us to Khartoum?" she asked.

"God willing, they will not," Samhi answered. "It's not just that the 1,300-mile trip will take two weeks…I am told there are frequent skirmishes between British patrols and the *AnsŌr*, and that the city will soon come under a complete blockade."

"*AnsŌr*?" asked Thomas. "Who are they?"

"The word means 'helpers,' "Samhi said. "Westerners call them dervishes or *Beja*."

He described the massacre at Shaykan—the overwhelming victory of the Mahdi's forces over Hicks' modern army. Thomas listened in silence, his mind already calculating what they might face ahead.

Finally, Heléne spoke softly. "Do you believe my father may have been taken captive by the Mahdi?"

Samhi laced his fingers and rested his chin on his hands but said nothing.

It was after midnight when Thomas finally closed his book on Flinders Petrie's explorations around the Valley of the Kings and stepped out onto the balcony. The moonlight shimmered across the bay, painting the gardens silver.

Thomas undressed and turned down the bedside lamp, but he could not sleep. His mind raced with thoughts about the expedition ahead, and about the danger he might be exposing Heléne to by taking her so close to an active war. There were the articles for the *San Francisco Chronicle* to complete and mail, too, and gear to purchase for the trip. How did one prepare for a trip up the Nile to search for 3,000-year-old royal tombs? He knew nothing of the geography, local language, or customs, or even who he should be wary of encountering. Tales of roving packs of murderous bandits who plied their trade along the Nile and around the cities and archeological dig sites of Egypt were legion.

He would need more ammunition for his Colt, a new long knife, and if Samhi could find an outfitter that sold repeating rifles, so much the better. He wished he had brought along his favorite Winchester Model 1876 carbine with the half-round, half-octagonal barrel, pistol grip, sling swivels, and shotgun butt. As for travel, would he be expected to ride a camel? He had seen many around the city but could not imagine loping across the dunes on one of those ungainly beasts. Could he find a suitable Egyptian Arabian or Baladi horse, and Western-style saddle and tack? Had he brought along enough money, and if he needed more, how would he be able to access the credit line Andrew Whitton had set up for him at European banks?

He turned to his side and threw back the light bed coverlet. Samhi had seen him off after dinner with a bottle of fine cognac. He would turn the lamp up and find something else to read.

As he swung his legs off the bed, he heard a gentle knocking on the door that connected his room to Heléne's. Before he could speak the door opened and she stepped into the room.

He was startled. The evening had begun with the kind of flirtation that might have led to the bedroom, but their conversation about her father had clearly put a damper on that possibility.

Heléne closed the door and held a finger up in front of her lips to remind him to speak quietly lest they were heard by their hosts in bedroom above Thomas stood still, entranced by her beauty but at the same time uncertain what he should do now–if anything. But he had to say something.

"I did not expect to see you tonight," he whispered.

She smiled. "I know. But, my dearest Thomas, when will things ever be just right for us to be together? Believe me, when we make camp in the Valley of the Kings there will not be time for this...."

She reached up and untied the stays at the top of her light nightgown. It slipped to the floor in a heap, and she stood before him completely nude in the soft light of the moon and the bedside lamp. Her body was an extraordinary symphony of curves and shadows, from her full creamy breasts to the beckoning slopes of her thighs.

"I thought you might just want to talk again like we did..." he stammered.

She glided toward him, pressed her lips to his, and reached behind him, pulling down his pajama bottoms.

Then, guiding his hands gently to her breasts, she whispered, "Oh, Thomas... don't you think we've talked quite enough?"

~FOURTEEN~

Samhi poured their glasses full of sweet green mint tea to accompany the scrambled eggs, tomatoes, cheese, and warm bread that Marwa had just delivered to the small iron table tucked into a quiet corner of the sunlit garden.

The Bedouin guide was still quietly taking the measure of his guest. He was not yet ready to share everything he knew about Professor Bovet's search for the treasure of Amenhotep. If Bovet had truly deciphered the location of the pharaoh's tomb, the riches it contained—rumored to be greater than any discovered to date—would be irresistible bait for the army of fortune hunters that haunted the Cairo and Luxor hotels, always seeking ways to worm into expeditions as they prepared to head upriver.

Samhi had encountered a dozen such European confidence men over the years—posing as museum agents, investors, private collectors, or gallery buyers. Polite, educated, impeccably mannered gentlemen who fit easily into sophisticated conversation at hotel bars—yet one slip around these men could bring a raiding party down on any treasure caravan leaving a dig.

Colonel Scoundrel might not be one of them. But Samhi would take no chances. '*Fi sabil allah, for the love of God*,' he thought, even the American's name roused suspicion.

He had spent much of the night scouring Bovet's journals. They spoke of a life-sized chariot cast in pure gold, mounds of silver from Mesopotamia and Crete, stone coffers brimming with rubies and jewels, hundreds of fine ornaments, dozens of gold-encrusted boxes—beyond imagining. If Henri Lavalle suspected any of this, it was no wonder his men had followed Heléne. Still, a man like Lavalle wouldn't tolerate competition. And Samhi wasn't sure what to make of Scoundrel just yet.

The American was—what was the word? Ah, yes—a cowboy. A man who acted alone and answered to no one.

Across the table, Thomas finished his breakfast and thanked Marwa. Then he turned to Samhi.

"Are you comfortable with Helķne joining us upriver?" he asked. "Between the AnsŌr, bandits, tomb raiders, scorpions, and everything else, it doesn't sound safe for her."

"And does the lady in question get a vote?" Heléne interjected as she stepped into the garden. She wore light canvas trousers, hiking boots, and a long-sleeved khaki shirt with pockets. She looked radiant after last night's encounter, and based on the way Marwa was regarding them it was clear that the mistress of the household had little doubt that the connecting door between their bedrooms had been breached sometime during the night.

Samhi did a mock half-bow as Heléne sat down. "I would not be so brave—or so foolish—as to deny you passage to Luxor."

"And you?" she said to Thomas with a sly smile. "Are you going to stand in the way of my coming along?"

Marwa set Heléne's plate on the table. "Not if he wishes to wake up tomorrow with an intact set of *khisia's*," she said in a motherly tone.

Samhi and Heléne burst into laughter at the remark, while Thomas, who didn't speak Arabic, looked to Samhi for translation. "*Khisias*?" he asked.

The Bedouin guide wiped tears from his eyes and forced himself to stop laughing. Then he slid his chair back and wordlessly pointed to his crotch with the forefingers of both hands, which set him and the ladies laughing again. Thomas blushed, muttered under his breath, and made as if to stand, but Heléne caught his hand and gently pulled him back down.

"You're among family, Thomas. Marwa would not say such a thing if she didn't love you."

Marwa leaned down and kissed his cheek. "I would not really deprive a man of his most important tools," she giggled. Samhi gave her a playful slap as she headed back to the kitchen, still laughing.

"With that settled," Samhi said, "let's plan the day."

"I'm going to the market with Marwa to purchase food supplies for the trip from Cairo to Luxor," said Heléne. "Flour, rice, sugar, dried fruit—enough for five weeks."

"You don't buy those in Cairo?" Thomas asked.

"They charge foreigners double," said Samhi. "And most expeditions pay without complaint."

Thomas nodded. "And for us today?"

"Two things," Samhi replied. "First, I'll take you to a firearms merchant. Then we'll visit the catacombs of *Kom El Shoqafa*."

Heléne was surprised. "The ones that were discovered after the bombardment? But, why? Do they have something to do with my father?"

"They do not," Samhi answered. "But Thomas has never been inside an ancient tomb, and this is the closest thing here that will provide him the experience of being deep underground in confined, poorly lit spaces."

Heléne nodded. "Are you troubled when you are in tunnels, or caves, or other small or dark places?" she asked Thomas.

"To be honest I haven't been in many. I have spent most of my life outdoors, usually on a horse in a wide-open space."

"Then this will be a good experience,"Samhi said. "The catacombs have not yet been opened to anyone but a few government officials and people like me. We will have the place to ourselves, and you, my friend, will learn what it is like to step back centuries into history."

'And I will learn a little more about what kind of man you are,' Samhi thought to himself.

Three hours later a carriage wound its way through rubble-filled streets and deposited Samhi and Thomas outside a fenced enclosure the size of a house. The street was nearly impassable and most of the buildings lay in ruin.

"The bombardment was quite successful," Samhi said as they slung canvas rucksacks over their shoulders and picked their way to the gate through chunks of concrete and piles of dirt. "And the British governor-general has forbidden clean up or rebuilding for the present. He wants the good people of Alexandria to remember who their new masters are."

Inside, a drowsy sentry sat under a tent, an old rifle across his lap. He barely stirred until he caught sight of the folded notes in Samhi's hand.

"How may I serve you, Ra?" the guard asked.

"You know who I am?"

"Yes, Ra, I do."

Samhi smiled. "Ra means boss," he whispered to Thomas, slipping the man his bribe.

"No one else here?" Samhi asked.

"Not for over a week."

"Should anyone else come while we are down below, they are not to be allowed entry until we come up. Is that understood?"

The guard nodded, but Thomas noticed he was still holding his hand out. An extra duty, no matter how small, required extra payment. Samhi pressed another bank note into the guard's palm and then led Thomas over to what appeared to be the remains of an old well.

"There is a central shaft going deep into the necropolis," Samhi said, "and some sunlight makes it down, but we'll need lanterns."

The guard returned to his chair while Samhi and Thomas lit their kerosene lanterns and approached the opening.

"The bombardment opened this?" Thomas asked.

"Partially. A man walking his donkey here caused the collapse."

"And the donkey?"

Samhi tied a bandana around his mouth. "When I first came, the beast was still rotting. Hopefully only bones remain now."

Thomas followed suit and descended into the gloom. He was surprised to see that the spiral stone steps that began just a few inches below ground level looked like they had just been carved. He also noticed that there was no odor from the carcass of the dead donkey.

The men removed their bandanas and Samhi took the lead, holding his lantern at shoulder height. "We have much to learn about these catacombs," he said as they started down the spiral staircase that wound around a six-foot-wide air shaft. "Our best guess is that they are about 2,000 years old. The central shaft allowed in light and air, and it was probably also used to lower dead bodies straight down into the tombs."

With each step they took the air grew cooler and mustier. "How did you determine the age of this place?" Thomas asked.

"Mostly from the wall paintings and statues. They are a blend of Roman, Greek, and Egyptian art, and speak to a time when Alexandria was a hub of trade and cultural exchange."

"Will it be open to the public someday?"

"Years from now, would be my guess. Archeologists must complete their studies, and the place must be made safe."

"Safe?"

"There are drop offs everywhere that lead hundreds of feet into the earth. Walking around loosens rocks and sets off mini-avalanches, and doing something as simple as leaning against a carved wall frieze can send a few hundred pounds of the sculpture down on your head."

A few minutes later they reached the base of the stairs and stepped into the main chamber. In the golden light of the lanterns Thomas could make out stone carvings and reliefs showing familiar Egyptian gods and figures, but as Samhi had noted, most were dressed in Greek or Roman attire. They moved slowly into the main burial hall where bodies were once laid to rest in rectangular recesses called *loculi* that were cut into the stone wall. The hall had a high ceiling supported by heavy columns adorned with carvings that showed scenes of everyday life, religious ceremonies, and mythical creatures whose job was to protect the dead in the afterlife.

Beyond the main chamber was the *Triclinium*, where family members would gather to hold feasts in honor of their departed relatives next to their sarcophagi. A narrow door carved through the rock led to a long passage into the dining hall, and Samhi told Thomas to wait while he went ahead with an extra lantern to set on the floor. "It is blacker than black in there," the guide said. "I've been in, and I know where to step to avoid places where the floor has given way. I'll leave one lantern in there and come back for you."

With that, Samhi squeezed through the door and carefully made his way down the passage until Thomas could faintly hear his steps but no longer see the light from his lanterns.

He was alone, 200 feet underground in a vaulted room carved from solid stone 2,000 years ago in a nation so ancient it was difficult to comprehend. He set his lantern down on a step next to a burial sarcophagus whose painted scenes were still fresh and wondered once again what he had gotten himself into.

Suddenly, he heard what sounded like pebbles brushing across stone. He could not tell where the noise came from, but from the way sounds echoed and bounced off the stone walls and ceilings down here, it could be coming from anywhere, even from the surface high above. As he bent to retrieve the lantern so he could explore the room, he heard a rush of air, and then something heavy slammed into the back of his head. He stumbled to one knee and fought to keep from collapsing, but the object struck a second time, and he crumpled to the floor next to a sarcophagus.

Thomas had no idea how long he had been laying on the cold tile floor. All he knew for certain when he began to stir was that his head was throbbing, and his vision was clouded. He ran his hand down the back of his skull; there was no blood, but that was the only positive thing he could say about his circumstance.

Whoever had hit him was gone, and they took both of his lanterns with them. Had they gone through the passage after Samhi? Were they coming back to finish the job? It was so dark in the hall that he could almost feel the absence of light. He couldn't go back, there were too many twists and turns in the maze of corridors, and, of course, there were the drop offs into the abyss that Samhi had warned him of. On the other hand, trying to find his way back up might be the only hope he had of staying alive. And Samhi? Had the attacker gone after him, too? Who was it, a common thief following what he hoped was a rich European, or could Henri Lavalle have struck again? He sat up and ran his hands through his hair again, straining to focus. The truth was that whoever was after them was less important right now than figuring a way to get the hell out of this mess.

He pressed his hands against his temples in an effort to reduce the pounding that was racking his head and concentrated on finding a way out of the pitch-black passage. First, he had to get to Samhi. They'd figure a way out of this together.

He got unsteadily to his feet and stretched both arms out with his palms facing forward. Feeling his way around the chamber wall until he came to the passage opening wasn't much of a plan, but it was all he had. He took four paces forward and made contact with the wall. Then he began walking slowly to the left, keeping his palms flat against the cold stone. At one point he yanked his hands back when something cold and wet slithered across them, but he pushed the thought of what it might have been from his mind and kept working along the wall.

It seemed like forever before his left hand suddenly slipped into open space. He reached his arms out to the side and realized he had made it to a door. With his arms pressed lightly against the sides of the narrow passageway he started to walk slowly ahead. When his right leg started to slip into a gravelly hole, he jumped to the left to avoid sliding down into the depths.

He slowed his pace and began using his feet to sweep slowly ahead, inch by inch. Then the corridor took a turn to the right and began to slope down. Hadn't Samhi said the corridor went straight into the next chamber?

Had he missed a turn? He stopped for a moment to gather his thoughts. Going back made no sense, he decided. If he was going to die underground in this damned tomb, he was going to be upright and walking when it happened.

Then, in the darkness 50 yards ahead he saw a faint pinprick of light. It wasn't moving, which meant a lantern had been set on a stair or stone table. He drew his Colt and kept walking towards the light, which grew a bit larger with each step he took. Then, voices:

"...your companion is dead, Samhi Al-Katib," an unfamiliar voice was saying, "and my reasons for letting you live are growing fewer by the minute."

Thomas heard a man spit, and then a voice he recognized spoke. "You are camel offal, the son of the village whore, and your backside has been ridden by more men than there are hairs in the beard of the Prophet," Samhi said.

He was nearly to the dimly lit chamber, and he grinned at hearing his friend curse their attacker. With his back pressed flat against the wall he kept his revolver at the ready and slid steadily forward.

Samhi was in a small antechamber decorated with paintings of a warrior wrestling a bull, slumped on a stone couch used by diners on feast days. The front of his cotton robe was stained with fresh blood, and a cut was open above his right eye. The attacker was standing, pointing a .36 caliber pocket revolver at Samhi's head. That might be a lady's pistol, Thomas thought, but at that range it would still take off a big piece of Samhi's skull.

He was about 20 paces from them, but the corridor was so dark that he was still hidden from sight. When the attacker turned slightly to the right, Thomas recognized him as one of the men who had ransacked Heléne's hotel room in Constantinople. Henri Lavalle was still very much in the game.

"Our conversation is done," the attacker said to Samhi. "You either tell me where to find Bovet's journals, or I will splatter your brains across the wall and leave your stinking corpse to the spiders."

As Thomas pulled the hammer back on his Colt and took three more steps towards the chamber, Samhi said, "I prefer the company of spiders to the presence of a pile of goat dung like you. Shoot your little pistol…I am tired of listening to your voice."

When the man pointed and prepared to fire, Thomas shouted, "Enough! Put it down!" Searching for the only word he knew in Arabic, Thomas added, "Or I will blow off your *khisias* and feed them to the dogs!"

The attacker whipped around. The startled look on his face told Thomas two things: the man was astonished that Thomas was still alive, and, who in the hell would threaten to shoot off a man's testicles?

His surprise lasted only a fraction of a second. He raised his pistol and fired at Thomas, but he missed, and the bullet careened harmlessly down the corridor.

Thomas did not miss. He aimed for the center of the attacker's chest and pulled the trigger one time. The .45 caliber slug tore through his heart and made a fist-sized hole as it exited his back.

The retorts of the two guns boomed like cannon fire in the enclosed space. Samhi flinched and then watched as his attacker's body slid to the floor and lay still.

"Were you shot?" Thomas asked.

"Stabbed," Samhi answered with a groan. "In my shoulder, thank God. The man could not aim his blade any better than his bullet. Are you alright?"

Thomas rubbed the back of his head. "No worse than a tequila hangover."

"Tequila?"

Thomas managed a smile. "Mexican cactus juice. I'll tell you someday. Can you get up? I don't know if the guard heard the shots, but we'd better get out of here. There could be more where he came from."

Samhi pushed himself up and shuffled across the chamber. He was a little wobbly, but he could walk. Thomas pulled the top of his friend's robe down and examined the knife wound. "Straight in and out," he said. "Missed anything vital, but you won't be playing piano for a while. We'll cauterize it back at your home. That and a shot of brandy should do it."

"Make it a bottle," Samhi answered with a grimace.

Thomas looked down at the attacker. "What about him?"

"Oh, I have just the resting place," replied Samhi.

Three minutes later their assailant's body lay at the edge of a drop-off in the outer corridor. Thomas gave him a farewell shove with his boot, and they waited in the quiet as the body slammed from side to side of the deep hole until a dull thud echoed up when it hit bottom.

"He'll stink the place up, you know," Thomas said as they began the trek back to the main chamber and the stairs leading up to daylight.

Samhi laughed. "And I will tell them that damn donkey is taking his own sweet time decaying!"

The man who bribed the guard told him that neither the American or his Bedouin companion would be coming up out of the tombs, and so he was dozing off when Thomas' head popped up above the ground. The guard threw down his rifle, raced out of the compound, and disappeared down the rock- and-garbage- littered road.

Thomas climbed out of the tomb opening and pulled Samhi up beside him, "That man has a long run ahead," the guide said. "Either I get to him, or the authorities fire him or Lavalle has him killed."

Thomas smiled, "Or maybe all three?"

He took his friend by the arm and guided him to the waiting carriage. It was midday, and it had grown hot since they went into the tombs. He leaned Samhi back in the seat and motioned for the driver to take them home.

Heléne and Marwa would take care of them.

~FIFTEEN~

On board the paddle steamship Luxor

The banks of the Nile River formed the greenest stretch of land Thomas had ever seen. Towering date palms cast long shadows across the lush, geometrically aligned farm plots in the afternoon light, where men and boys in loose fitting trousers and oversized shirts worked their fields beneath the afternoon sun. Farmers slogged through the muddy river soil behind their oxen, pulling hook-shaped plows, while others drove animals to trample grain or turn great wheels to draw water into irrigation ditches. Beyond the narrow strip of lush green, the desert waited—stretching south into the endless heart of Africa.

Northward, almost lost in the river's gentle curves, stood the Giza Necropolis, where the Great Pyramid and the tombs of Khafre and Menkaure had gazed silently upon the earth for 4,000 years.

He was seated at a small table on the stern deck with a bottle of brandy at his elbow and a pencil and pad of paper close by. A cooling breeze blew across the river, carrying the scent of cook fires and massed vegetation. He had been trying to work on the next letter to Andrew Whitton at the San Francisco Chronicle about his search for the internationally renowned archeologist Professor Édouard Bovet but was so caught up in the exotic sights that he hadn't picked up the pencil.

It had been the same during their days in Cairo, particularly when Heléne had roused him before dawn to join her and Samhi for a camel ride to the pyramids. She enchanted him with stories of the history and culture of ancient Egypt while Samhi poured out the details of the pyramid's construction—the size and weight of the massive stone blocks, the labor required, the staggering scale of the undertaking.

The war brewing in the south had dampened Egypt's growing tourist trade, leaving only a handful of sunburned Europeans and

Americans clinging to their Baedeker Guides, dutifully climbing a few levels up Khufu's pyramid for photographs. Thomas laughed as Heléne pointed out how local guides unfurled their turbans and wrapped them around the waists of the delicate women tourists to haul them up the steep steps.

By day's end, Thomas had drawn two conclusions: the ancients possessed genius beyond anything he'd imagined, and camels—despite their romantic reputation as "ships of the desert"—were foul, snarling, miserable beasts.

Samhi, who shared little more affection for the animals, had twisted the knife further at dinner. "Except for the little ones, the hashi," he said "They're quite tender and sweet. In fact," he said, pointing to a platter of appetizers on the table, "you are eating one right now."

As Samhi and Heléne laughed, Thomas spit his mouthful back onto the plate.

They made the 12- hour train ride from Alexandria to Cairo overnight. Heléne retired early while Thomas and Samhi shared a half bottle of cognac in the smoking car and plotted their next moves. They had agreed not to tell Heléne about the encounter with Henri Lavalle's man in the catacombs, or about dumping his corpse deep into the shaft beneath the tombs.

"Lavalle will send more men," Samhi said when they settled into two worn leather chairs. "He's convinced that the treasure of Amenhotep is real, and quite probably the single richest find in history."

"Based on what?" Thomas asked. "Bovet has not found the tomb, Lavalle hasn't read his journals, and from what Heléne says there's nothing in the scientific literature going back over a century. Lavalle must be a fool."

Sami refilled their glasses. "He is no fool, Thomas, I can assure you of that. But he lives in a world of shadows and rumors and mystical revelations. The legend of Amenhotep's treasure has only grown over the years, and since no artifacts from his tomb have shown up in the antiquities markets, the one thing we all agree on is that the tomb has yet to be discovered. As for the journals…" he paused and set down his glass.

"Yes?"

"I read them the night before we entered the catacombs."

Thomas was startled. "And you chose not to tell me."

Samhi picked his glass up and took a long sip. "I did not know you, then. Who you were…or what you were."

"And now? Why did you change your mind?"

"You came after me in that pitch black tomb. You could have left me down there to rot and protected your own hide."

Thomas smiled. "And be left to face Lavalle and Heléne's anger on my own? I don't think so, my friend. My hide was much better served by going after Lavalle's hired man. In any event, when he does not report back to his master, Lavalle will know that we are not the easy targets he thought we would be."

Samhi raised his glass, and they toasted in silence. Then he unfurled a map of Luxor and the Valley of the Kings, and for the next two hours they planned.

As twilight deepened, Thomas prepared to return to his cabin. Just as he stood, he saw Samhi approaching from the stern of the paddle wheeler, accompanied by a tall, well-dressed man in his forties. The newcomer walked with a limp and wore a sling on one arm. His dark eyes regarded Thomas with keen interest.

Samhi motioned for Thomas to sit. When the waiter arrived, he ordered a bottle of Spanish wine.

"Colonel Thomas Scoundrel," Samhi began, "allow me to introduce Major Dámaso Berenguer, nephew of King Alfonso XIII of Spain and, most recently, soldier of fortune in the service of the Khedive against the Mahdi."

Thomas shook the Spaniard's outstretched hand. Was there anyone in Egypt whom Samhi did not know?

As the waiter poured, Berenguer deftly rolled a cigarette one-handed. The men toasted, and Berenguer emptied his glass with a single drink. "My friends, this is heaven," he said with a sigh. "And a Rioja Tempranillo, no less. Five months I have languished in the Sudan without so much as a sniff of wine or brandy. The Muslim prohibition on alcohol is barbaric—they know not what they forgo."

Samhi smiled and emptied his glass. "That is not true of all my people, Major."

Berenguer refilled their wine. "Colonel Scoundrel," he said, "I first learned of your exploits during your War of Rebellion when I was attached to the Spanish Embassy in Washington in '76. I had hoped to meet you but your War Department informed me that you had been recalled to duty against the Sioux and the Cheyenne with General Crook during the Battle of the Rosebud, and then, of course, the terrible business with Custer. Tragic."

Thomas nodded, his voice low. "Years of tragedies, Major. My deployment ended after the Battle of Wolf Mountain in January of '77 when Crazy Horse surrendered."

"I cannot imagine what it must have been like to do battle on the Great Plains in the winter," Berenguer said, "especially after spending two years in the inferno that is North Africa, where no snow has fallen in generations."

Thomas thought back on the ferocious Montana blizzards, with gusts of glass-sharp snowflakes knifing through his uniform, his lungs filling with icy air, frozen rivers cracking under the weight of artillery pieces and sucking men and horses under, the howling wind drowning out the sound of his rifle.

He saw a Sioux war party appear out of a wall of snow and surround him when he got separated from his command, and he remembered the crunch of frozen snow when he dropped his empty pistol and crumpled to his knees, bleeding from a shoulder wound. He was helpless as the Sioux warriors rode over to him, and their leader prepared to take the final shot.

Then, from a snowbank, a dark shape emerged and loped toward the combatants—a massive gray wolf, its fur silvered with frost, its breath steaming in the frigid air. The wolf passed silently between Thomas and the warriors, paused before their leader, swung its head from Thomas to the Sioux, then turned and vanished into the storm.

Neither the Sioux nor Thomas understood why the wolf had appeared, but all sensed its mystical weight. The Sioux leader slid his rifle into its scabbard, drew a skin-wrapped coup stick tipped with stone, rode up to Thomas, and struck him sharply on the uninjured shoulder.

Then, pulling back the fur from his brow, he smiled, wheeled his horse, and vanished into the swirling snow with the others.

Thomas shook off the memory and looked into the Spanish major's eyes and quietly said, "It was…a difficult time."

"And the war against the Mahdi? What is the news? "asked Samhi.

Berenguer rolled another cigarette. """Something of a stalemate—though entirely on the Mahdi's terms. He commands 100,000 men who are scattered in a great circle around Khartoum. The city is under a partial siege, but Gordon controls the Nile with a flotilla of armor-plated gunboats, and he has constructed an elaborate system of trenches, with makeshift *Fougasse* land mines, and wire entanglements. For the moment at least he can bring supplies into the city while continuing to evacuate civilians."

"Why does the Mahdi hesitate?" Thomas asked. "He has the men, and the momentum, and he claims that God has appointed him for this task. It makes no military sense for him to stand down."

"And London does nothing," Samhi added.

Berenguer exhaled a stream of smoke. "It makes little military sense. But the Mahdi's mind isn't governed by such calculations. Rumors suggest his attention has turned to finding and destroying some ancient treasure. He has dispatched agents across the Ottoman world seeking it. His obsession is interfering with his ability to conduct war."

"But why destroy treasure?" asked Thomas. "Mystic or not, weapons and men cost money. Why not use the money to build his army?"

Berenguer shrugged. "Such are the ways of the Sufi. The man is also celibate, he will not allow a drop of this…" he took a deep drink of the excellent Rioja… "anywhere near his encampments, and he eats only bread, soup, and honey." A slight smile spread across his face. "Imagine, my friends, a life without drink, without meat, and without a warm ass to keep the chill off your *zubb* when winter descends on your camp in the Sahara."

"*Zubb*?" Thomas mouthed to Samhi.

"Later," the Bedouin guide whispered in reply.

The river current was so smooth that they could almost have been seated in a quiet hotel restaurant in Cairo. "I do know this," Berenguer said as a deckhand appeared with an oil lantern and hung it on a hook next to their table. "Pray that your search for Professor Bovet does not lead you anywhere near Khartoum."

"Why would people such as us have anything to fear from the Mahdists?" Samhi asked.

Berenguer looked grim. "In his eyes you are a traitor to your faith, Samhi al Katib. Thomas is a senior military officer of a nation he knows well and whose strength and worldwide intentions he no doubt fears, and for whom the Mahdi may believe Thomas is spying."

"And Heléne?" Thomas asked in a low voice.

"He fears her the most, Colonel."

Thomas looked perplexed.

Berenguer drained his glass and set it on the table. Then he pushed back his chair and stood up.

"She and her father are constant reminders of an ancient past that terrifies him. Heed my words, gentlemen. If you wish to keep a head on your shoulders, stay clear of the Mahdi."

~SIXTEEN~

Marseilles, France, June

Crina Cazacu followed her escort up the wooden steps of the cavernous warehouse. Their carriage had come directly from the train depot near the port, up La Canebière—the historic high street of old Marseille—and through the affluent Réformés quarter to the warehouse district.

What she glimpsed of the city from the carriage was impressive: classical architecture, colorful facades, clean sidewalks lined with shops. Crina was no student of history, but she knew money when she saw it. Whoever her client was, he moved in rarefied circles. The fact that he had paid for her three-day, 1,300-mile journey from Bucharest, offering six months' worth of wages for a single engagement, confirmed it.

Crina would turn 30 next month, and, while she was still in demand with Romanian businessmen and local politicians, she was a realist. As she aged and her beauty faded, her rates would have to go down. In a few years her 'manager' would move her out of his stable, and she would be faced with two equally unappealing choices; marry one of the paunchy, middle-aged customers who had become enamored with her over the years and wanted a permanent arrangement, or find a lower-end brothel in a working section of the city and resign herself to servicing five or 10 men per day instead of just one man as she did now—but at the same daily rate of pay. The road from a brothel—where at least she would be safe and warm—to doing one-minute stand ups against brick walls in dirty alley ways for a few copper leu would be her only choice a few years later. After that? She had yet to meet a woman over 40 in her line of work.

Inside the warehouse two guards roamed the floor where hundreds of crates were stacked floor to ceiling, each labeled and numbered. After a brief word with her escort, one guard pointed toward a flight of wooden stairs leading to a bank of windows above.

At the landing, her escort rapped on a door. A short, sturdy woman with graying hair and a no-nonsense expression admitted them. The reception area was plain but tidy: two desks, wood filing cabinets, a worn couch, and walls lined with books, rolled maps, and bundles of documents tied with string.

The woman studied Crina, then gestured toward a washroom and offered her tea. When she returned the secretary summoned the escort and handed him a thick brown envelope—his reward for discovering me, Crina thought. After a brief farewell, he was gone.

Now the secretary beckoned for Crina to follow her through the carved walnut doors into a lavish office. Oak-paneled walls, copper-tiled ceilings, Persian rugs, and, everywhere, Egyptian treasures: gold and gemstone necklaces, bas-relief statuettes, gilded tables, alabaster jars, jade carvings, swords and shields, gold candlesticks, even wicker baskets brimming with pearls.

Crina blinked. Her mysterious client wasn't just a man of substance—he was fantastically wealthy. Her eyes darted around the room until two things came into focus that brought her to a standstill. The first was the man seated behind the oversized desk. He was leaning forward with his palms flat on the surface, staring at her with a mix of wonder and delight. As for his appearance—she fought to hold back a shudder. He was tall, with eyes as black as his hair, his face clean shaven. He was also enormous; three hundred and fifty pounds, or more. Even his face was obese; his puffy cheeks looked like they were filled with marbles, his jowls hung below his jaw line, and his massive head hid the contours of his neck. He was seated several feet back from the edge of the desk, no doubt as a necessary accommodation to the pendulous stomach that seemed to jut out from just below his chin to below the top of the desk. Crina had known big men, but this fellow was in a class all his own.

Her encounters with fat customers had been in equal measure sickeningly repulsive and mercifully short. She had insisted on mounting them rather than risk having her ribs broken if they were on top of her, and also as a precaution against the man having a heart attack mid-coitus, leaving her trapped beneath hundreds of pounds of smelly, greasy, sweat-slick fat.

The second remarkable object in the room was mounted on the wall directly behind him; a gold-framed, 4' x 6' oil painting of a woman and a boy. The woman was about 30, simply dressed, with her hair piled in a bun. One hand lay on the shoulder of a boy—probably her son, Crina thought—of about 11 or 12, while the other hand rested gently on the top of a mounted world globe. No different than what countless wealthy men would have in their offices or homes, she thought. Except for one thing: the woman in the painting was Crina's exact likeness. Same hair, eyes, facial structure—an eerily exact duplicate of what Crina saw each time she looked into a mirror.

When she realized she hadn't breathed for half a minute, she tore her gaze from the portrait and looked back at the man behind the desk. He, in turn, was examining her closely with curiosity and some other emotion she did not recognize at first.

"Do you speak French?" he finally asked in a voice that was surprisingly feminine.

"*Oui, un peu*," she replied, "but just a little."

"*Bien, merci*. We have much to discuss. Now, could I ask you to please turn around, slowly?"

Crina held her arms at her side and began to turn.

"Slower, if you please," the man said.

She stopped for a moment, and then began to turn very slowly.

"Perfect," he said. And then, "Again, if you please."

As she made her second turn, Crina heard a sigh escape the man's lips. She had heard men do that many times, especially those who paid her to disrobe and then turn around and around in the nude. Sometimes they lowered their trousers and pleasured themselves; other times they just sat, stared, and sighed. Their behavior was of no concern to her; she had no emotional investment in the act, only a financial one. If the end result of her modeling was that the man finished himself off without so much as touching her, another benefit was that she would not have to clean herself up before she took on the next customer.

The man signaled with his hand for her to keep turning. As she did, she observed that he was keeping his hands on the desk, not on his crotch. It was no coincidence that the woman in the portrait looked exactly like her, she realized. That's why the agent in Bucharest had approached her at the hotel, and it also explained the small hand-drawn sketch he had pulled from his pocket and examined closely before he asked her into the restaurant and proposed that she accompany him to France.

The wealthy man at the desk was looking for…

"Yes," he said softly, "my mother. I was 12, just on the cusp of manhood, when the painting was commissioned by my father. She was 31, and unbeknownst to any of us, she was already dying of a cancer."

The room seemed colder now, and she understood why she had been summoned from across the continent. The boy in the painting, 'on the cusp of manhood,' as the gentleman said, had been sexually attracted to his mother, and when she was taken from him while he was struggling with his monstrous Oedipus complex, he became fixated on the idea of having relations with her.

The man continued speaking. "But forgive my manners, my dear. Please sit down."

Crina took a chair and accepted a glass of sherry.

"It appears you have some idea of why you are here."

She nodded.

"First, an introduction. I am Henri Lavalle, a collector and dealer in art and antiquities.

Please know that my intentions are, while clearly not entirely, how shall we say, honorable…"

'To say the least,' Crina thought.

"…are none the less, entirely harmless. You have nothing to fear, and in a few days, we will put you on the train to your homeland with a full purse."

She finished her sherry and nodded.

"I have agents around the world looking for rare art objects, especially Egyptian treasures like the ones here in my office. A select few of these men have been offered great rewards to locate and deliver women with your appearance."

"You mean your mother's," Crina added in a flat tone.

"Yes, of course, with hers. Several women have made the climb up my stairs in the past 10 years, but, my dear, my dear, none has even remotely looked like her. Until you."

He sat back and was quiet, but as Crina watched, his hands slid off the desk and into his lap. When his arms began to move slowly and rhythmically back and forth, she knew that the conversational part of their encounter was about to end. Then, to her surprise he put his hands back on the desk. "The dress and undergarments on the rack in my personal washroom are for you," he said. "You will also find a box of hair pins, and a bottle of perfume. Please dab behind your ears, on your breasts, and…" his voice slowed and lowered, "…on your buttocks and between your thighs. Unbutton the dress enough that the tops of your breasts are visible, and then come back to me."

As she stood, Lavalle asked, "Can you read?"

"Of course."

He slid a book across the desk to her. "I would like you to sit on the edge of my desk and read the third story in this book to me. As you read, I want you to slowly unbutton your dress to your navel until your breasts are fully exposed."

Crina nodded and watched as a shiver of anticipation coursed through Lavalle's corpulent body.

"Remember…slowly," he added. "But when you notice I am staring right at them I want you to close your top and slap my face. Hard. Do you understand?"

Crina looked up at the painting. 'What did you do to your son?' she wondered.

The dress hanging in the washroom was an exact match for the one in the painting. Crina removed her own clothing and slipped it on. Then she went to the mirror and arranged her hair as Lavalle had requested. Finally, she applied perfume to her face and body. When she was satisfied that she had done her best, she walked to the door and put her hand on the knob.

"St. Nicholas, Holy Protector of prostitutes, watch over me," she whispered as she swung it open and waited for Lavalle to motion her forward.

~SEVENTEEN~

The Valley of the Kings, June

The porters led the donkeys uphill, their loads swaying beneath packs of supplies, while the horses were tethered beneath the shelter of an ancient limestone overhang that had shaded royal tomb diggers for more than two thousand years. As the animals settled, Thomas again thought back to his initial unease when he first saw the compact Arabians—so small compared to his Morgan-Thoroughbred cross. But after two hours riding from their Nile scow to the entrance of the Valley, his doubts had evaporated. The jet-black stallion was sure-footed, responsive, and balanced across the uneven ground.

"*Saher* will outlast your Morgan cross," Samhi said when Thomas first swung up into the saddle. "He requires less water, and he can tolerate greater heat. Those smaller hooves are perfect for traversing rocky landscapes, and his sense of balance is superb."

"Sa-her?" Thomas asked.

"It is pronounced 'Sar,'" Samhi answered. "It means vigilant. His line has been unbroken for over 3,000 years. So treasured are these horses that many Bedouin bring them inside the tent at night to sleep beside them."

Thomas chuckled. "I have heard the tales about Bedouins and female goats, my friend, but this is the first I knew they were also attracted to horses."

Samhi laughed and flicked a small pebble at Thomas. "The day may come when your life depends upon Saher being able to take just one more step, Colonel. Pray that day does not arrive, but if it should, think on this moment and ready your apology."

The fire crackled under a black sky littered with stars. The cook prepared lentil soup, falafel, cheeses, fresh bread, figs, and dates. Heléne emerged from the canvas tent carrying two bottles of wine and three glasses, pulling a stool up beside them. She wore canvas trousers, boots, and a man's loose shirt, and Thomas wondered if he might find a way to slip across the partition tonight.

They had stolen time together on the four-day steamship journey from Cairo, and he had no doubt that Samhi was fully aware of their tryst, but his old-fashioned sense of decorum—a gift from his Irish Catholic mother—was just strong enough to hold his decidedly indecorous impulses at bay.

Heléne had been a marvelous guide over eight days since Cairo. Few tourists braved the Egyptian heat after April, and fewer still were visiting this season as the war between the Mahdists and the Egyptians continued to boil. They spent a day walking the vast temple complex at Karnak, near Luxor, and two days rambling around the Memorial Temple of Ramses II at *Medinet Habu*. The immense above-ground Theban necropolis with its sprawling complex of temples, tombs, and mortuary structures dedicated to the pharaohs and their afterlife was a sharp contrast to the subterranean tombs in the Valley of the Kings a mile to the south.

The narrow, rock-strewn ravines that cut through the weathered limestone hills encircling the valley reminded him of the Texas arroyos where he had battled Chief Lone Wolf's Kiowa warriors during the Red River War in '74. But where the monumental temples and sculptures of Karnak and Ramses were massive and awe-inspiring, the small tomb entrances dotting the ravine walls that had been exposed by centuries of tomb robbers and European scientists offered no clues about the warrens of passages and chambers that had been hewn out of the solid rock with crude chisels and wooden mallets.

In the two days they had been camped, they had ventured into three of the most recently excavated tombs. The architecture and wall paintings were impressive, but every single artifact of any value had been carted away, leaving the ravine littered with piles of broken vases, mounds of rubble that had once been magnificently decorated pillars and funerary urns, and bits and pieces of broken wooden tables that workers had tossed into heaps rather than try to sell for a few copper coins.

"The workers know what's valuable," Heléne said as they sipped their wine. "They smuggle smaller gold and jewelry pieces out of the burial chambers in their rectums, because the overseers have a legal right to execute thieves on the spot. The items that are too large to sneak out are catalogued by the Master of the Dig, who routinely makes copies of the lists to send on to Henri Lavalle. He often knows what is being pulled out of a given tomb before the expedition's leaders do."

Thomas shook his head. "And this has been going on for…?"

"Thousands of years," Samhi replied. "Every age has had its Lavalle."

Thomas stirred the fire with a stick, sending orange sparks into the sky.

"This is where your father was working?"

Heléne pointed toward a jagged ridge. "He was working his way to the base of the cliff, looking for a clue to the location of the entrance of Amenhotep's tomb. A wall painting, hieroglyph…something clear and tangible."

"But you don't know if he found anything," Thomas said.

"No one does," Samhi said. "But his chief digger later told a German archeologist that Professor Bovet rushed past him early the next morning, his face flushed, his hands shaking with excitement. He had worked by lantern light through the night."

"He found something important," Thomas said.

"I am certain of it" replied Heléne.

Thomas refilled their glasses. "And then he simply…"

"Vanished," said Samhi. "With three pack camels."

"And the camels explain why so many people believe he found the treasure and carried off as much as he could by himself."

The cry of an owl echoed down the ravine, and the moon settled on top of the hills across the Nile. "There is something I don't understand," said Thomas. "Your father had a spotless reputation. Why did the world turn on him so quickly?"

Heléne looked into the fire. "*Die Verlockung des Schatzes kann Heilige verführen,*" she said in a soft voice.

"I'm sorry?"said Thomas.

"An old German saying," said Samhi with a chuckle. "It means that even a saint can be seduced by treasure."

"My father is not a saint,"Heléne continued. "But he is no thief, either."

It was cold when they finished the second bottle of wine, and the cook brought them small tin cups of thick black coffee sweetened with honey.

"Remind me again why we are waiting here instead of in the village or up in Luxor," Thomas said to Samhi. "It's been two days, and no one has come."

"Had we stayed in Luxor every con man in the region would have attempted to talk us out of the reward we are offering for information about Edouard," Samhi answered. "Now we are five hours from Luxor and two hours from the village–only serious people will make the trek."

"How long do we wait?"

Samhi asked the cook for another coffee and pulled a cloak around his shoulders. "One more day. Then we will return to Luxor, and I will speak to every shop owner, hotel manager, dry goods dealer, and government official. Someone must know something. A man and three camels do not simply disappear into the wind."

He pulled a notebook and pencil from his robe and added, "I am going to stay here by the fire for an hour or so and make a list. You two needn't stay up."

Thomas suppressed a grin and stole a glance at Heléne. An hour…

She flashed a sly half-smile in return. He waited for her to slip inside the tent, then quietly rose, bid Samhi goodnight, and followed, forcing himself not to break into a run.

At daybreak they were sharing coffee around the fire when a giant young man in a black cotton shirt and trousers rounded a boulder and strode up the ravine towards them. He halted 50 yards away and waited for permission to approach. In the desert one did not simply walk into a stranger's camp uninvited. In the desert, entering a man's camp unbidden could warrant a sword across the belly.

When Samhi motioned to the man to come ahead, Thomas stepped to Heléne's side, his right hand drifting to his Colt. The visitor acknowledged the invitation and then turned sideways to show them the cargo strapped to his back. Heléne clapped one hand over her mouth, and Thomas held back a laugh.

The leather straps attached to the front of the giant's belt went over his shoulders to a woven reed chair on which sat a small, grizzled old man with tangled hair and a matted beard. The young man drew near to Samhi, went down to his knees, and waited as his passenger slid off the chair and shook Samhi's outstretched hand.

"Would you please unhook the chair?" the younger man asked. Heléne freed the chair from the straps and helped the old man sit down. A moment later the cook appeared with fresh coffee and a plate of figs and warm bread for their guests, and everyone pulled their stools close to the fire against the last of the morning chill.

Samhi turned to the old man. "I know you. Or, rather, I know of you. In my visits to the Valley of the Kings over the years I have heard stories of a Sufi mystic who lives like a hermit. The village elders come to him for advice and guidance, it is said, and the families of the sick and dying come for counsel. This is you?"

The old man nodded. His eyes were clouded over with a skin of greyish-yellow, and his hands trembled, but when he spoke his voice was clear and strong.

"It is," he replied. "And for 80 floods I have watched as his people"–he bent his head in Thomas' direction–"have desecrated these holy grounds in the search for the treasures of the Pharaohs."

"And for science," Heléne replied in a firm voice.

"Grave robbers are not scientists," replied the old man. "Of what value to the world are the possessions even the bodies–of the departed?"

"They are a window into a past we do not fully understand," Heléne answered.

"And you will not gain that understanding by combing through their tombs any more than the bluebird who stole a silver chain from my table this morning will gain insight into my life."

"A bird has no way to comprehend the human experience," Thomas cut in,

"But we are members of the same species as the pharaohs. We are very much alike."

"You have been inside the tombs?" asked the old man. "You have seen the paintings, the furnishings, the pylons, and the pyramids?"

"I have."

"Then you should appreciate how very different the ancients were from…" he hesitated a moment, and then leaned forward. "Forgive me, but my vision has faded to almost nothing these past few months. Do I know you? What I can make out of your face is very familiar, but I cannot place you."

Thomas shook his head. "This is my first time in Egypt. We have not met."

The old man sipped at his coffee. He was clearly troubled by something.

"And so, you have come to see us," Samhi said. "Do you have word of Professor Bovet?"

Before he answered the mystic popped a dried fig into his mouth and slowly chewed. "I do," he answered. "And yet…and yet…" He looked across the campfire at Thomas, straining to see through the opaque film covering his eyes. Then he turned and leaned forward towards Heléne, but when his vision was focused enough to take in her features a look of horror and realization spread across his face. He uttered a moan and slumped forward to the ground, where he rolled onto his side with his palms pressed over his eyes.

The young man leapt to his feet. "*Mudaris*-teacher!" he cried. "What is it?"

Thomas, Heléne, and Samhi got to their feet and formed a circle around the elderly Sufi as the young man helped him to sit up.

"Teacher, please," the young man pleaded. "Tell us …"

Instead of replying the old man began to chant while scooping dirt into his hands and rubbing it into his hair and across his face.

"What is happening?" Heléne asked.

"He has seen something, a terrible vision," the young man whispered. "It came over him when he looked into your face…and yours," he added, looking at Thomas. "The dirt is to protect him from demons."

Samhi knelt and placed a hand on the mystic's shoulder. "Talk to me, my friend. What did you see?"

"The resting place of Amenhotep," the Sufi answered in a trembling voice. "And them." He pointed at Thomas and Heléne. "A past that is impossible and a future that cannot be, lest our world and everything in it be turned to dust."

"I don't understand," Samhi said. "What do you mean you saw my friends?"

"Darius," said the old man, "We must return to the village—now."

The young man went to his knees and Thomas connected the shoulder straps and helped the old man climb on board.

"But my father," said Heléne as the young man stood up with his passenger. "Please, what do you know about him? Is he safe?"

The Sufi tapped Darius on the shoulder and the young man swung around so that the old man was facing them.

"Your father is being held prisoner somewhere outside Khartoum by a chieftain loyal to the Mahdi. In fact, he was taken from this exact spot."

"But the story of him fleeing with three pack camels?" asked Thomas.

"Just a story, probably intended to throw anyone searching for him off the trail."

Heléne was in tears. "But why Khartoum, and why the Mahdi?"

The mystic looked down from his perch. "The Mahdi has seen what I have seen, but only he can make sense of it. He took your father when he learned he was close to finding the location of Amenhotep's tomb, because that is something he could not allow to happen."

"Then we will go to the Mahdi," Thomas said.

"No!" cried the Sufi. "That you must not do. You all will die, and then…" his voice trailed off "…something even more dreadful will happen."

"More dreadful than our deaths?" asked Samhi.

The old man chuckled grimly. "Do not fear death, Samhi. There are things far more awful than the dying of the light." Then he tapped

Darius on the shoulder and the young man began to walk away from the camp.

"Wait, tell us the name of the chieftain who has my father," Heléne cried after him. "Please, for the love of God."

Darius did not halt. "God would say that your father is safer where he is," the old man called out. "Go home. Do not go to Khartoum. Do not search for your father, and especially, do not attempt to find the Mahdi. This entire business is *maleun*."

Thomas shot a questioning glance at Samhi. "It means cursed by the gods," he said.

They stood quietly as Darius picked up speed and navigated the rocky path out of the valley in the direction of the cool green banks of the Nile.

"*Maleun*," Thomas repeated in a whispery voice. Then, as a warm wind blew across the great river and up into the Valley of the Kings, he realized that his friends had stopped talking. Heléne was holding both her father's and Samhi's hands, and they were watching him, as if waiting to hear something only he could say.

He knew what they wanted to know.

"How far is Khartoum?" he asked with a smile.

A grin creased Samhi's face and Heléne rushed into Thomas' arms.

"Eight hundred miles and two weeks, God willing," said the Bedouin guide.

"The steamer leaves Luxor in three days."

~EIGHTEEN~

In the shadow of the Red Sea Hills, Sudan, July 1884

Lieutenant Harold Desmond of the Royal Highlanders Black Watch infantry regiment doffed his cork pith helmet and set it on an upended ammunition crate.

"And just what in the hell is a United States Army officer doing out here in the bloody middle of nowhere in the bloody middle of this damnable little war?" he demanded to know. "Here to join our little party, are you?"

Thomas smiled. He had just been introduced to the compact, red-bearded Scotsman in the lightweight khaki tunic and trousers with a Webley revolver tucked into a holster attached to his Sam Browne belt, but he liked the man already.

"I am not here on the instructions or at the request of my government, Lieutenant," he answered. "I left my friends at a portside hotel in Suakin three days ago and have come to ask a favor of the British Army. A professional courtesy, if you will."

Desmond looked at Thomas as if he were an inmate in a lunatic asylum. "A favor? Colonel, with all due respect, do you know what is waiting for us in the ravine behind those hills?"

He pointed across the scrub brush and rock-covered plain to a low ridge a mile to the west. "The *Beja*. You call them dervishes. Probably 5,000 of the black buggers to our combined force of 1,200. They're an ancient Nubian people, Colonel, been here since before the pyramids, and they are true warriors, every one of them. They run at you at the speed of a cheetah with a throwing stick in one hand and an eight-foot spear in the other—or, rather they used to, before they captured a cache of several thousand .43 caliber Remington rolling block rifles from us a few months ago."

Desmond lifted a canteen from the crate and poured water over his neck, then passed it to Thomas, who did the same. Though still mid-morning, the heat shimmered in waves off the parched ground.

"And damn it all to hell, the *Beja* captured our machine gun battery yesterday. Stabbed and chopped four gun crews to bits and even slaughtered the mules that carry ammunition."

Thomas looked towards the ridge. Any soldiers attempting to make it up those hills would be caught in a withering field of fire. It would be suicide. "Is the battery still operational?"

"It is, but thank God the boys were able to remove the sights and lock the guns down before they were overwhelmed. They'll do the *Beja* no bloody good."

"Do you have more Gatlings?" Thomas asked.

"None. We have a dozen nine-pounders and plenty of balls, but we've got to take that hill and Gatlings back now or turn tail and run, and I can tell you these boys aren't a bit keen on running away."

Thomas looked around the dusty compound at the knots of Bluejackets, York & Lancs, Marines, and Black Watch soldiers who were cleaning weapons, playing cards, or eating cold stew under the sweltering pale-yellow sky. They had lost nearly 100 of their fellow soldiers in yesterday's offensive, and it was revenge, not retreat that they were focused on.

"I've sent my batman to General Graham's camp, and also to my regiment commander, Colonel Green, to advise them that you are here," Desmond said. He sloshed the water in his canteen and added, "They won't be happy to hear the news, you understand. We aren't in the business of entertaining guests."

"I have been in battle, Lieutenant, and I understand military protocol," Thomas replied. "I'll say my piece and be gone, no entertainment necessary."

Desmond called for an Egyptian camp boy to bring more water and then motioned to a wooden bench. They sat in the shade of a canvas tent awning. and Thomas explained how he and Heléne and Samhi had traveled from Luxor across to the port of Safaga on the Red Sea and then south by steamer to Suakin so that Heléne could seek an audience with Brevet Major Herbert Lord Kitchener, who had been placed in command of the Egyptian contingent fighting with the British.

Kitchener knew Professor Bovet, and if there had been any sightings of the archeologist, the British commander would be aware of them.

But after sitting for two days on the terrace of the white-washed coral-rock building that served as the town's only hotel, he had grown bored and requested Kitchener's permission to ride out into the eastern desert to view the ruins of an ancient Roman city.

He wandered the broken walls and battlements of the settlement 15 miles west of Suakin and camped under the spectacular Sudan sky for two nights. On the third morning he was intercepted by a British patrol and taken to Desmond's compound 10 miles to the south.

"And now you want to enlist our help to find your scientist friend?" Desmond asked.

Before Thomas could answer a whistle blasted, followed an instant later by a second and then a third call to arms. The camp exploded into activity as 73 men slung gear on their shoulders, stamped out campfires, and bolted down the last spoonfuls of stew.

A messenger flew off his horse and raced across the compound.

"Yes, Private?" the Lieutenant said.

The soldier took a breath. "The wogs are coming from three directions, sir. They'll be over the western ridge soon, and the others are coming in two pincer formations out of the north and the south. Thousands, sir."

The boy looked more bewildered than frightened; Thomas thought. He could not have been over 15.

"Has Colonel Green been notified?"

"He has, sir. You are ordered to push due west, summit the ridge and take back the gatling guns. Whitson and Clark will sweep around the oncoming *Beja* and squeeze them from behind while Green meets them head on with his four companies. The plan is to push them back to the base of the ridge where you can rain hell down on the lot of 'em with the gatling guns. Pardon the language, sir, them was the colonel's words."

"The summit which we will of course have taken by the time they arrive," Desmond observed dryly.

Thomas set down his canteen and considered his options; military protocol provided that a non-combatant, foreign military officer could observe hostilities, but he could not take direct part or offer strategic advice.

On the other hand, he wasn't going to sit back and let events unfold around him without doing something to help.

Desmond resolved his dilemma. As he filled the cartridge pouch at his waist he said, "Thomas, my new American friend, I'm afraid our conversation will have to wait. Unfortunately, so will the rules of military conduct. You won't make it back to Souakin, and you can't act as a neutral observer because the Dervishes don't recognize such niceties. No, it's a fight you are in for, colonel, whether you like it or not."

He checked his side arm and slung his rifle over his shoulder as his men finished assembling in three rows. Then he pointed to Thomas's Winchester, leaning against a rock.

"How many rounds do you have?" Desmond asked.

"One hundred."

"You'll burn 1,000 before this day is done." He turned to a giant, bearded sergeant with red muttonchop whiskers and an imposing handlebar moustache. "Wilkes, get this man a proper rifle and 200 rounds."

"Follow close, Colonel Scoundrel. The fact that you are a white man who is not wearing a uniform will be a signal to the *Bejas* that you are someone important, and…" before he could finish another rider raced into the compound, waving a paper. Desmond trotted over to meet him.

"Important…"? Thomas heard himself mutter.

"To these godless heathens, yes, colonel darlin,'" grinned the sergeant. "You'll be more popular than a half penny whore the night before payday."

Wilkes trotted over to the quartermaster tent, chuckling at his own joke. He returned a moment later with a new Martini-Henry breechloading rifle.

"Fires a .45," the sergeant said. "You eject the cartridge with this lever under the trigger…" he turned the rifle so Thomas could see, "… and the lever also cocks the striker for the next shot by opening the breach for the next round. They're smokey bastards, and the recoil's like to tear your shoulder off, and they don't like dust, but by St. Andrew 's pink arse you only need to crease a wog anywhere on his body and he'll spin in circles, and if you hit him in the gut or the head, you'll decorate the desert around him for 50 yards."

Thomas nodded and smiled grimly as he swung up onto Saher's back. "Another thing, Colonel," the sergeant added. "The *Beja* will come at your hands and arms with spears so you can't hold onto your rifle or your reins, and that's after they take down your horse. You see a swarm coming, you dismount and send your horse back to camp."

With that admonition the sergeant joined his men, and Lieutenant Desmond returned. "How much ammunition do you have for your Colt sidearm?"

"Fifty."

"Change that count to 49, Colonel."

Thomas raised his eyebrows. Change the count?

"We can't resupply you, so save one round in your shirt pocket and make sure you don't fire it. If you find yourself surrounded and no help is on the way to help, use that last bullet on yourself. What the *Beja* do to the few prisoners they take alive beggars description, Thomas, especially what they do to the officers. Better to get it over with quickly."

With that, Desmond swung his horse around, rode to the front of the infantry ranks, and led them out of camp in the direction of the arid brown hills.

Thomas slipped the Winchester beneath his bedroll and laid the Martini-Henry across his lap. Falling in at the rear of the column, he moved through the rising dust at the pace of the infantry. The irreverent banter of camp was gone now, replaced by the grim silence of men who had marched into battle too many times to pretend otherwise. Some would not return tonight. Each man's fate rested on his skill, his nerve, the unseen hand of providence, and the countless decisions–small and sudden–that his commanders would make before the day was through.

He wheeled Saher around a stand of thorn bushes and watched the regimental flag flutter in the parching sirocco wind that blew north to the Mediterranean Sea. It had been seven years since he had been to war, but the wind blowing off the prairie that morning was nothing like the furnace blasts sweeping out of the Sahara. Montana Territory was bitterly cold, with piercing wind gusts that cut through his heavy woolen coat. The ground beneath his boots and Cornwall's hooves was hard-frozen, and the landscape around his position overlooking the Tongue River valley was a treacherous combination of slick ice patches and uneven snow drifts, making every step into an ordeal as they navigated over icy ridges and through snow-packed gullies.

The army's campaign against the Lakota Sioux and Northern Cheyenne had stretched into its sixth month, two months longer than the War Department assured him he would be needed when they dispatched a rider from Jefferson Barracks to collect him from the Mississippi riverboat where he was working as a faro dealer. On the morning of the battle, he looked up onto the slopes of Wolf Mountain, glistening in ice and snow under a low, leaden sky, and wondered where the Lakota and Cheyenne warriors were entrenched among the rocky bluffs.

Dawn should have found him asleep on the riverboat in the arms of *Mlle* Duchamp, entertainer extraordinaire, expert gambler, and the friskiest lover he had ever known. Instead, he found himself pulling his greatcoat tighter against the cold and reining Cornwall over beside his second-in-command to issue the day's orders. By now the acrobatically talented, stupendously shaped singer would be performing her favorite stunts with some other lucky gambler. Such were the fortunes of wars and circuses, he mused.

Brigadier General Nelson A. Miles had devised a strategy to flush Chiefs Crazy Horse and Two Moons out, which included having Thomas take command of 436 men from the 5th Infantry Regiment to track down and defeat 500 Indian fighters. Miles had ordered their artillery–small mountain howitzers–to open fire upon the enemy positions at first light in an attempt to dislodge and scatter them.

Thomas had waited impatiently in the pre-dawn darkness until streaks of light began to filter through the heavy clouds and cannon fire finally began to shatter the winter stillness. Shell bursts sent up showers of snow, rock, and dark brown earth less than 100 yards in front of his position. Then, as quickly as it had begun, the artillery barrage ended, and he rode to the head of the column and signaled for his men to move out.

That winter battle would prove General Miles wrong on at least one count; the enemy was not going to be flushed out into the open like September quail in a field of wheat stubble. They would fight to the last man, which meant that the 5th was going to lose its share of soldiers, too. George Custer learned that hard lesson six months earlier up along the Little Big Horn, but Thomas wasn't sure that the army had learned theirs.

Now, as he rode out to do battle alongside British forces on the rocky Sudanese plain at Tamai, he wondered if the British knew their Mahdist enemy better than the U.S. Army had known the Sioux. He wiped a bead of sweat from his forehead and turned in his saddle to ask that question of Sergeant Wilkes when a sound spilling out of the wadis 500 yards ahead brought all conversation in the column to a halt. At first it was no more than a faint murmur on the horizon, like the whisper of an approaching storm, but it quickly swelled into a blend of high-pitched, rhythmic cries, rising and falling in waves that were both chaotic and mesmerizing.

The regimental trumpeter replied with a blast of his own, and Desmond shouted for his men to group into a defensive formation. "We'll be havin' company for dinner, colonel darlin',"" shouted Wilkes as he bolted forward to take command of his section.

Thomas halted Saher, slid the British rifle into his saddle scabbard, and withdrew his Winchester. One hundred rounds or not, he was going to begin this fight with a weapon he knew. As he cocked the lever to advance a round into the chamber, 1,000 screaming *Beja* warriors swarmed out from behind dozens of rocky mounds and bushes and rushed towards Desmond's small contingent. Some were dressed in flowing white robes with bright-colored patches, but most wore simple cotton loincloths. Most were barefoot, and wore their dark, greased hair in great brushy crowns that had earned them the nick name 'Fuzzy-Wuzzies.'

Sunlight glinted off their rifles, eight-foot spears and throwing sticks, but Desmond waited until the enemy closed to within 300 yards to order his two nine-pound cannons to open up. Several heartbeats later he commanded his soldiers to let fly with their first volley of gunfire.

The piercing, collective wails of the charging dervishes echoed with an intensity Thomas thought beyond human capacity, rising to an eerie, unearthly pitch as the nine-pounders tore gaps in their oncoming ranks.

He steadied his Winchester, drew a slow breath, and trained his sights on a dervish sprinting at the heart of the line, clutching a red-and-green banner. He held his fire until the man narrowed the distance by another 50 yards, then pulled the trigger. The dervish staggered and collapsed, but before the flag could touch the sand, another *Beja* snatched it mid-fall and charged onward toward the small British column without breaking stride. Thomas narrowed his eyes against the glaring sun and fired again, striking the new standard-bearer square in the chest.

Out of the corner of his eye, Thomas saw Wilkes wave at him and smile.

'The Yank can fight,' the Sergeant thought. Then a dervish bullet caught his horse in the throat, and he was flung into a thicket of desert tamarisk.

~NINETEEN~

There was no time to check on Wilkes. He cocked his rifle for the next shot and let out a soft whistle; the Beja were swarming across the field at a ferocious pace, their ten-foot spears and throwing sticks at the ready and their Remington rifles slung across their backs. The way the wave of warriors flowed across the rocky ground reminded him of a stampede of thousands of pronghorn antelope he once witnessed in eastern Oregon.

There was order behind this chaos.

Classic British army tactics when being attacked by a fast-moving force included the use of a defensive square, in which multiple companies or an entire battalion of up to 1,000 men arranged into a hollow rectangular or square shape. The soldiers stood shoulder-to-shoulder in two or three ranks, with each side of the square facing outward. Officers and non-combatants, such as stretcher-bearers and ammunition carriers, were positioned inside the square, along with supplies, wounded soldiers, and any artillery pieces they had, including Gatling guns.

The organization of a square was as much about discipline as geometry. Every soldier had a precise place, and the success of the formation depended on their ability to hold ranks under pressure. When a charge was imminent, officers shouted commands and soldiers swiftly pivoted to form the square, their movements drilled through relentless training. The square's greatest strength was its firepower. Soldiers armed with Martini-Henry rifles could unleash devastating volleys at attacking enemies, while bayonets deterred any who managed to get close. Artillery, positioned in the center or at the corners of the square, provided additional firepower to break up massed charges.

But Desmond had only 73 men, too few to form a proper square. No, Thomas thought, this fight was going to be more like the brutal hand-to-hand clashes between the Greeks and King Priam on the dusty plains of Troy 2,000 years ago than any modern battle he was familiar with.

He wiped sweat from his brow, flinching as a throwing stick whipped past his head. The sudden motion startled Saher, but the stallion recovered instantly, pressing forward as Thomas chambered a fresh round and shot down the *Beja* who had hurled the weapon. Ahead, half a dozen warriors charged toward him, spears flashing. As Wilkes had warned, two of them began slashing their blades back and forth, cutting closer to Saher's flank.

Thomas dropped the reins, slung the Winchester, and drew his Colt. Guiding Saher with his knees, he fanned the hammer, sending two rounds into the chest of the nearest man and a third into the forehead of another. He yanked the reins hard, and Saher leapt sideways just as another spear sliced harmlessly through empty air. The attacker stumbled; Thomas shot him twice as he tried to flee, then wheeled Saher atop a rocky rise to reload.

Desmond's men were everywhere, fighting with pistols, sabers, rifles, and bayonets. A Black Watch guard fell beside him, gutted by a *Beja* spear. Thomas fired his Colt as the warrior struggled to free his blade, and the bullet tore through the man's throat and dropped the fighter behind him. Then an iron ball from a nearby nine-pounder exploded, showering him with dirt, shattered branches, and bloody fragments of human flesh.

The barrage of cannon blasts was ripping holes in the *Beja* line, and Thomas had to smile when a green and red dervish flag waved in a circle and the pace of their attack slowed to a slow walk. He watched the Mahdi's warriors spread out until there was at least 50-feet separating one warrior from the next, their way of dampening the effects of the cannon blasts. Thomas seized the momentary lull and spun Saher around to survey the battlefield. All around the stony plain British squads were coalescing into tight, disciplined groups under the watch of battle-hardened command sergeants, and a moment later four soldiers from the York Regiment emerged from the scrub and formed up behind him, waiting for orders.

Thomas pointed and shouted, "Follow me to the top of that rise. Two of you take cover behind the boulder—the other two, up top in prone positions. Move!"

The soldiers flew up the rise. They took their positions, and at Thomas' command began firing steadily into the line of advancing *Beja*. That's when he spotted three more squads of soldiers who had been separated from their units. He waved them over but before he could organize them into firing teams, he saw that the main body of *Beja* had begun to turn and was heading right for his position.

The enemy may have slowed their advance to a fast walk to lessen the carnage from the murderous cannon fire, but he could see hundreds more pouring off the distant ridges. It would only be a few minutes until their numbers grew large enough to overwhelm Desmond's command; cannons or no cannons.

Seventeen soldiers awaited Thomas' orders. He moved them into five separate firing positions, three facing the advancing Beja, and two looking back towards Colonel Green's advancing battalion of 500 men who were now 10 minutes away–a lifetime in their current situation. The Beja would attempt to surround them, and Thomas wanted Martini-Henry rifles and bayonets covering a full circle around the rise. Some of his men would stand, some would kneel on one knee, and four would open fire from atop the boulder.

"How far can they throw their spears with any effect?" he asked the most senior corporal present.

"Thirty, maybe 40 yards, sir," came the reply. "At 20 yards the spear will pass all the way through your body."

Thomas went over to two of the men who were lying in prone positions at the base of the largest boulder. "You will focus only on the Beja whose spear arms are cocked and ready behind their shoulders. Only them. Understood?" The men nodded, and Thomas moved around the rise giving instructions to each of the other teams. When to shoot, where to shoot, who to shoot. One specific target type for each team. He put the youngest soldier in charge of the ammunition cart with directions to make sure each man had at least 200 fresh rounds.

The next wave of *Beja* warriors was stretched out in a dry wash just 75 yards from the rise, pumping their spears in the air as they cried to their god. Thomas decided to wait for the next cannon salvo to hit the line before he gave his teams the order to fire as planned, and he swung Saher behind the boulder, dismounted, and changed his Winchester out for a Martini-Henry,

Saher stood firm, lowering his head once as Thomas stepped around to the front of the rock. "He'll hold," he assured the soldiers tasked with laying down suppressive fire on any *Beja* attempting to flank them. A heartbeat later, two cannonballs slammed into the dry wash and detonated, cutting down four of the advancing warriors. Yet the *Beja*, emboldened by the certainty that Green's artillery wouldn't risk further barrages so close to Thomas's men, pressed forward with fierce cries, brandishing weapons and hurling a storm of sticks and spears. Thirteen British rifles answered in unison and their sharp reports were followed by the swift clatter of reloading. A dozen *Beja* crumpled onto the sunbaked earth, but dozens more charged on, undeterred.

He stiffened in his saddle when 10 warriors came out of nowhere and raced around behind the rise, but when he heard rapid firing from 6 Martini-Henry's , he knew the first assault would be beaten back.

He could hear Green's bugler now, which meant the relief column was only minutes away. The *Beja* could see the approaching force too, but the imminent arrival of as many as 800 men against their 70 or 80 did not deter their advance. They fought for their god and their Mahdi, and no earthly power was going to stop them.

Something flew over Thomas' head, and he ducked as a throwing stick–knockberries the lads called them–smashed into the boulder and fell harmlessly in front of him. The next stick, though, found its mark and one of the soldiers on top of the boulder rolled off and crashed onto the ground next to him, his skull split nearly in half.

Wilkes had told him that a competent soldier could fire the Martini-Henry once every five seconds, and as he dipped again and again into the canvas ammo pouch at his waist he agreed that was a fair assessment. His men were firing at a ferocious pace, and *Beja* bodies were piling up all around their position, but the fanatical warriors continued to pour across the wash and up the rise.

Three *Beja* escaped the volleys and made it up to the soldiers kneeling in front of Thomas, their spears slashing wildly at the hands and arms of the Black Watch regulars. Thomas dropped his rifle and drew his Colt, hitting one of the *Bejas* in the face just as the warrior's spear thrust deep into a British soldier's neck. The *Beja* collapsed on top of his foe as the other Black Watch soldiers jumped forward with their bayonets, impaling the dervish and then stabbing him again and again until Thomas commanded them to halt.

He understood the blind fury that could overcome a soldier in the thick of battle, and that was doubly true in this hellish landscape. The heat was suffocating, and the desert flies were everywhere —in the eyes, nostrils, mouths, and wounds. He cursed softly and pushed the body of the attacker off the mound with his boot. The warrior's partially disemboweled body rolled down the rise, spilling a trail of entrails onto the dirt before it came to a stop against the bank of the dry wash.

Three minutes later an advance guard from Colonel Green's command swept across the broiling sand and up to the boulder where Thomas and his men had finally forced the Beja to break off their assault.

"They'll be back before lunch," growled Sargeant Wilkes as he rode over beside Thomas. He surveyed the carnage around the rise. "Four?"

Thomas nodded and unclipped his canteen. "Brave lads," Sergeant," he said as he took a drink. "I don't know how you do after-battle reports, but I would be happy to add my commendation."

"And so you will," an unfamiliar, high-pitched voice said. Colonel Green had climbed the rise. He was tall, thin and angular, a perfect complement to his voice.

"Corporal McIvers counts 42 dead *Beja* inside your field of fire, Colonel Scoundrel…" Green began.

"Make that 43, sir," piped in the corporal, pointing to the contorted body of a dervish that was almost hidden from sight inside the thorny branches of a tamarisk bush.

Green climbed off his horse and handed the reins to an aide. His battalion was forming into two squares, each bristling with rifles, cannon, and bayonets. Did he plan on fighting a defensive battle, Thomas wondered? If there really were another 4,000 *Beja* waiting in the hills on the shimmering brown horizon, that might be the best tactic.

Four stretcher bearers appeared and began loading the bodies of the English dead to be taken across the wash. They joined another burial detail who were reverently setting down the bodies of 28 more soldiers for whom war was over forever.

Colonel Green motioned for Thomas and Sergeant Wilkes to take seats on a flat rock.

"We don't have much time, Scoundrel," the colonel began. "The buggers you just sent packing were only a feint to measure our strength and resolve. The whole bloody pack will pour down that ridge within the hour."

"Aye, and we'll send them right to hell when they hit the squares," Wilkes said in a determined voice.

Green removed his pith helmet and wiped his sleeve across his face. "We will hit them, Sergeant, but not from here. We are too exposed, and we don't have enough mounted infantry. No, will be on the move in a few minutes."

"But the squares, sir?" asked Wilkes.

"Gives the men a bit of confidence, and frankly, something to do."

Green looked across at Thomas. "You might be both the best and the worst thing that has happened to me today, Mr. Scoundrel."

Thomas could not suppress a smile. He could only imagine the number of laws, rules of engagement, and principles of military protocol he had broken that morning when he took command of the men on the rise. Not to mention the diplomatic firestorm it would ignite in London and Washington. There were no circumstances in international law under which a senior American military officer was authorized to lead foreign troops in battle without explicit permission from his government and a formal invitation from the host army.

He preempted Green's next remark. "I did not anticipate this happening, sir, or desire it, or encourage it." He shook his head and grinned sheepishly. "The moment called for it, Colonel Green. That's all."

The British Colonel's expression was non-committal. He took a long drink from his canteen and said, "We'll get to that soon enough.

First, though, tell me something: the way you took command and then set up and directed the firing positions so quickly. Did you learn that in your Civil War?"

Thomas shrugged. "Actually no. In the Indian Wars against the Cheyenne and the Sioux on the Plains, and the Comanche in the Southwest."

"Good fighters?"

"Some of the best, sir. The Comanche are the best mounted warriors in the world. Their bodies are painted in streaks of red and black, their faces are covered in patterns that almost warp and twist in the sunlight, and they move as one with their horses like no other riders I have seen. As they fly towards you, they dart in and out of rifle range with remarkable precision, firing arrows from beneath their horses' necks as they gallop low to the ground. They don't quit, they don't yield, they don't take prisoners alive, and they show no mercy, not even to women and children." He paused a moment. "And damned if they don't scream and yelp all the while like the devil himself."

An aide stepped up to Green and handed him a note. The colonel scanned the message and scribbled something on it with a pencil. "I only have a minute, Scoundrel, and what I am about to propose might be a river you cannot cross."

Thomas looked Green in the eyes. "I understand, sir."

"Desmond is dead," said the colonel. "His body was riddled with wog spears, at least a dozen of them. Looks like he was standing as they hit him."

Thomas grimaced. He couldn't imagine the strength it took for the lieutenant to remain upright as he was being impaled like that.

"His mission was to get to the top of that ridge…" Green pointed to the hill a mile away, "take back the four gatling guns from the *Beja*, and pour fire down on their heads when my men push them to the base of the hills. His company includes the only men in the regiment who can quickly bring those guns back to life. Wilkes is one of them."

Sergeant Wilkes nodded.

"So," Green continued, "Wilkes and that squad must make it to the summit, unlock the guns and reset the sights, and then pin the bloody wogs to the ground from above while I push them into their fire from below."

"What can I do, sir?" Thomas asked.

"I can't order you or ask you to do anything, you understand," replied the colonel. "It's not in the book. But I need every officer and sergeant I have to flank the *Beja* and turn them back to the ridge."

"Can't order, can't ask," he said. "But I can tell you that should you have a hankering to take a pleasant ride in that general direction"—he pointed to the hills— "in the company of the good sergeant here, I would not be averse to you making the excursion. And should you feel inclined to perhaps make a mild suggestion or two to the sergeant as you make your way, that, too, would be fine."

Thomas glanced over at Wilkes, who was trying to conceal a smile. Then Green shook Thomas' hand and put his boot into a stirrup. He settled onto the saddle and said, "For the record, Sergeant, I cannot order you to ask for or heed Colonel Scoundrel's, ahem…advice. That decision is yours alone. I can send 25 good men to join your company. I hope it is enough. God speed."

Green reined his horse and began to trot away. "Thank you, sir," the giant Welshman called after him. "We'll see you on the ridge."

"So, it's to be a picnic we're having, then, colonel darlin'," said Wilkes with a grin. He slapped Thomas on the back and added, "Shall we be telling the boys?"

~TWENTY~

Tamai Ridge

Six weeks earlier, the 25 bluejackets assigned by Colonel Green to Thomas and Sergeant Wilkes to join the remnants of Desmond's company had been berthed off Alexandria on the HMS Dryad, a four-gun Amazon class screw sloop. The naval brigade of 150 seamen and 400 Royal Marines had been assigned to Green's command and were already battle-scarred veterans of the battles of El Teb and Sinkat.

The chief responsibility of the men now gathered around Wilkes had been to setup, operate and defend the four gatling guns on Tamai Ridge that the dervishes had taken the day before, at the cost of three officers and seven men killed. The bluejackets wanted victory, and they wanted revenge.

"Lads," Wilkes said in a booming voice when all 100 men in the newly formed company had assembled in a circle around him, "we've been given quite the job this bright morning. Them four gatlings are waiting for you on top of the ridge. As far as we know all the ammunition is there, as well. You boys locked them down and removed the sights before the retreat, so the wogs have had no use for them."

"Except to roll 'em down on our heads when we run up that damn ridge," a bluejacket called out to the laughter of his mates.

"Aye, and don't be thinking such a thing ain't possible," Wilkes replied. "Most of the 4,000 or so Beja still up there are about to swarm down onto this plain. They want to end it now. But they won't be leaving the guns unprotected, so it ain't exactly a tea at your auntie's you'll be walking into."

"There's 100 of us," said a lance corporal. "And 4,000 of them about to tear down that ridge? How the hell are we supposed to get through them and up the hill?"

"Colonel Green's plan is for us to march a mile due east while his 800 men form a half circle and invite the Fuzziie-Wuzzies in.

Then they'll open up with artillery and mounted infantry and begin to sweep the bastards back to the base of the ridge, where you lads will roll out a four gatling-gun welcome from above. The wogs will be trapped against the base of the hill, nowhere to go."

"And while they're 'sweeping'?" asked the corporal.

"We're racing out of sight to the east and then angling back to the ridge. The main body of the enemy will have passed us by on their way to attack Green, and we can begin our climb."

"And what about the Yank? He here on holiday?" continued the corporal, asking the question that was on everyone's mind about the tall American in civilian clothes sitting on his horse outside the circle. These men had survived a month of brutal fighting sure in the knowledge that each one there had his back. They weren't inclined to give a stranger the benefit of the doubt.

"That man there is Colonel Thomas Scoundrel, of the U.S. Army, corporal," said Wilkes, "and he was fighting the gray coats in their War of Rebellion while you was still latched onto your mum's teat. Fought red savages out West, too, face to face, and them buggers are every bit the fighters that the Beja are. You boyos listen to me and him, and you just might make it home to a soft teat or two yourselves."

The men laughed, and a voice from the ranks called out, "That Yank just helped a handful of us hold off 100 blacks around this rock. Sent 43 of the bastards straight to paradise. I'll share a canteen with him any day."

The ragtag company of men, some in navy blue, some in marine red and others in dusty khaki, turned towards Thomas. They expected him to say something. Holding Saher's reins in one hand and cradling his Winchester in the other, he looked into the faces of the men he was about to lead into battle. Colonel Green knew when he told Thomas that he 'might' make a suggestion to Wilkes and the men now and then was simply a way for Green to skirt international law and military protocol. He removed his hat and wiped his forehead with his sleeve. This was his command now.

"Sergeant Wilkes…gentlemen," he began. "There is a lot I don't know about you, your training or your command structure. But I do know that there is no more highly motivated and prepared group of professional fighters in the world than you members of the Queen's own military."

One hundred heads nodded under the blazing sun, and a corporal shouted out, "That's bloody right, Yank!" to the cheers of his fellows.

"I also understand something of the tactics and strategy of our enemy. They are expert with spear and throwing sticks, not so good with rifles. They do not work in teams, which means that no matter how brave they are as individuals—and they sure as hell are—the fact that they outnumber us five to one is far less important than they think, because a squad of three of you firing and re-loading together is easily worth 20 of them…"

"Make that 50, Colonel," shouted a Black Watch corporal.

Thomas smiled. "I'm fine with that."

Two signal flags from Green's command fluttered and dipped in sequence 200 yards to the west.

"It's time, lads," barked Sergeant Wilkes. "Two columns, ammunition carts in the center, stretchers at the rear. Alans and Clark, take the scout. Corporal Standish, mind there are no laggards. Steady under pressure, men. No wasted powder."

Green's squares dissolved and then re-formed into three columns of mounted infantry to begin the trek through the scrub brush and boulders, each with its own medical wagons, ammunition carts, and cannons bringing up the rear. When they engaged the Beja, the mounted infantry would dismount from their horses and fight on foot, a tactic that Thomas had always thought to be counterintuitive.

Wilkes was about to say something when Thomas spotted what looked like swarms of ants streaming down the ridge a mile to the west. The sound of thousands of voices joined in the Beja war cry roiled the superheated air, and he calculated that by the time his company began angling towards the ridge Green and the dervishes would be fully engaged.

The battalion's massed cannons opened up with a deafening roar, pounding the advancing Beja lines with volley after volley. A few minutes later Wilkes ordered the signal team to notify Green their company was about to turn east for the ascent up the ridge to the gatling guns. Thomas watched as Green's men split into three separate columns. The left and right columns began to curve around the flanks of the advancing Beja while the center column finally did dismount and form up for firing.

Then Wilkes shouted, "Spread out," and the two columns formed a single line standing shoulder to shoulder at the base of the ridge. The scouts scrambled down through the brush and rocks a moment later and gave their report to Wilkes and Thomas.

"The gatling stations are intact," said one. "All four. And the ammunition cases are right where they should be, too."

"How many defenders?" Thomas asked.

"I'd say 300," replied the other scout. "Maybe a few more. Most are resting on mats on the ground or eating. Doesn't look like they are expecting visitors."

"Sentries?" asked Wilkes.

"One about every 50 yards," the scout answered.

"They'll know company is coming soon enough," Thomas said.

"Gatling crews!" shouted Wilkes.

Twenty men sprinted over and stood at attention. Each gatling gun had a crew of four; a gunner, a loader, an ammunition handler, and a spotter. Martini-Henry .577/450 caliber metallic cartridges were fed into the gun from a hopper or a drum magazine, and God help anyone who wandered into the six-barreled gun's field of fire as it spat out 200 rounds per minute.

Wilkes turned in his saddle. "Ideas, sir?"

"We'll need to minimize our exposure," Thomas answered, "make this damn terrain work for us, and coordinate our fire." Wilkes simply nodded in reply.

It really is up to me, then, Thomas thought to himself. "Divide 75 of the men into squads of five each, Sergeant," he finally said, "and begin the advance in staggered waves. Harder targets that way. As each following squad advances another 50 yards they will halt and provide cover fire to the squad above them. And place a dozen of your best sharpshooters in a line here at the base behind rocks or bushes. They'll provide suppressing fire up to the top as the men advance.

"Each time the squads advance to the next position they will move up into the gap. When we are 20 yards from the top, the squads will disperse to form a single line across the lip and we will go over together, with each man firing straight ahead in a three-bullet arc; one bullet to the left, one to the center, and one to the right. Do that no matter where the Beja are standing. We'll create a solid field of fire that will take them all down."

"And the gatling crews?" Wilkes asked.

"They come up last, just ahead of the sharpshooters, right through the center. When we go over the top, you will have a squad of 10 men surround each of the four teams and lead them to their guns. The rest of the men hold off any Beja still standing."

Thomas looked at Wilkes. "Acceptable?"

The bearded giant smiled. "Best suggestion I've heard all morning, sir." Then he called over four corporals and gave them their orders. Five minutes later the squads were formed, the sharpshooters were in place, and they were ready to storm the ridge.

Nineteen years earlier, on a sunny April morning, Thomas woke up as a 17-year-old cook's assistant with the Ninth Ohio Federal Regiment in the mountains outside Washington DC. By the time the sun went down he was a severely wounded full colonel who had successfully assaulted a Confederate position at the top of Pebble Creek Ridge by himself. He became one of the last and greatest heroes of the Civil War for a battle he had stumbled into and was celebrated for acts of heroism that fell upon him by accident.

Now, at 36, those events were a distant memory, shrouded in a fog of pain and regret. He had wandered the world since the war, never settling in one place for long, but always hopeful that he would eventually find a purpose and meaning for his life. Instead, he lost everything the morning his beloved Keani paddled out across the reef on the South Seas Island of Moorea. From that day on he was determined to never again fall in love. His growing feelings for Heléne were complicating that resolve, and he had decisions to make.

But not today.

He swung down from his saddle and handed Saher's reins to a camp boy, who would take the horse to a makeshift corral behind the battle lines. Then he mopped his brow and pulled his sweat-soaked cotton shirt away from his chest. The weight of the Winchester felt good in his hands, and with the anticipation of what was waiting on the other side of the ridge he sucked in a deep breath and then slowly released it.

This was the first hill he had been ordered to take since the battle at Pebble Creek, but this time was different. This time, he felt ready.

The 15 squads of British fighters spread out in little knots at the base of the rocky embankment, waiting for Thomas's command to begin the advance up the hill. When he raised his rifle into the air and pointed to the top of the ridge the first five squads advanced 25 yards, kneeled into firing position, and waited for the next five squads to trot past them and take their positions. Thomas and Sergeant Wilkes positioned themselves in the middle of the advancing squads and stayed even with each new squad as it took the lead.

The sky was the color of yellow lead, and thin wisps of gray-brown smoke from Green's unceasing barrage on the Beja drifted over their heads. Thomas did not have to look back to know that Green's outriders and the enemy had made contact several hundred yards from where he was climbing the hill; he heard dervish war cries, the sharp crack of massed Martini-Henry's, and the muffled thunder of hundreds of horses storming across the plain.

His focus was straight ahead and up; he was confident that Green could turn the Beja back towards the ridge, just as Green was relying on Thomas and Wilkes to take the gatling guns back by the time the Beja were on the run to what they would expect to be a safe haven at the top.

The sentries spotted them when they were 75 yards from the lip of the ridge. They began firing down on the advancing British soldiers and as the squads took cover behind boulders and thick brush more than a 100 more Beja appeared in a line above them.

"Spears!" shouted Wilkes.

"What's that?" Thomas yelled back.

"Only the sentries have rifles. The Dervishes must have used most of their Remingtons for the attack on Green. The rest of 'em up there at the top just have spears."

Had he not seen how deadly accurate their spears could be, Thomas would have been cheered by that news. Still, he figured he would rather face a hand-thrown spear at 80 feet than a large caliber rifle from 300 yards.

Wilkes shouted to the squad leader nearest him to pass the word, and in less than a minute each of the men clinging to the face of Tamai ridge understood what he was facing. They were in the death business, and so was their enemy. It wasn't up to them to choose how their own ends might come, but no soldier relished the thought of a 12-inch blade tearing through his uniform and into his gut. Better a bullet through the brain and let it be over.

Thomas waved to Wilkes. "Spread the sharpshooters out and pour everything they've got onto the sentries," he shouted. "Ignore the others for now…we're out of spear range. Tell the rest of the men to dig in and save their ammunition."

Wilkes waved back and sent a runner to give the order to the sharpshooters and the squads. The Beja on the ridge continued to shriek and wave their spears and throwing sticks, but as Thomas observed, they knew their weapons were useless at that distance. The question now was whether the enemy sentries would remain exposed or pull back and wait for the British to launch an assault.

A moment later the sharpshooters let loose, and the question was answered. The sentries stood fast and continued to fire down the hill, but their bullets only hit dirt and rock. The British sharpshooters, however, did not miss their marks when they returned fire. A 75-yard shot was child's play, and in a matter of seconds the sentries began toppling down the hill, their rifles still cradled in their arms.

Wilkes looked across at Thomas and grinned.

"Now, the hard bit," Thomas yelled above the din of gunfire and the thunder of Green's cannon. "We've got to move up quickly. I'll take the five outside squads and the two center squads and begin the climb. You move the other eight squads to the middle and concentrate your fire on every Beja who pokes his head above the rim. When we get within 10 yards of the top, you move up and join us for the final push."

Wilkes shook his head. "Beggin' your pardon, colonel darlin,' and with all respect to your rank, but that's the first bad idea you've had this morning. I'll take the lead squads; you and the sharpshooters take charge of the cover fire. The ammunition carts will follow behind you." Thomas shot a questioning look at the Welshman. "The boys don't know you yet, colonel," Wilkes explained, "and none of 'em speaks American army lingo. Won't need no translators with me."

Thomas could not fault that logic, and there was no time to spare. Green should be turning the Beja back towards the ridge by now, but if they did not re-take the gatlings quickly, the element of surprise would be lost and their plan to press the enemy force against the base of the ridge under a hail of bullets from the machine guns would also fail. Green would become the retreating force, not the *Beja*, who would simply regroup and mount another even more ferocious frontal attack on the smaller British contingent.

~TWENTY ONE~

Wilkes sent three corporals across the slope to pass the plan down the line. As soon as the sergeant and his 35 men began their uphill charge, Thomas and his 40 infantry opened fire alongside the sharpshooters, raking the ridge with blistering volleys to pin down anything that moved.

The Beja didn't pull back. Though most of their riflemen lay dead after the first volley, another 50 dervishes surged over the ridge and unleashed a storm of spears. A second wave followed instantly, and the air thickened with steel—dozens of blades slicing through the desert sky like the wind itself was being torn apart.

Wilkes' squads advanced at a steady trot, firing and reloading as they climbed. Thomas waited for them to gain 40 yards, then waved his men forward and took the lead. As they moved, the first wave of spears struck home. Six of Wilkes' men fell, impaled and sent tumbling lifeless down the rocky slope.

Thomas didn't need to give the next order. His men opened fire on the silhouettes above, cutting down a dozen Beja in sharp bursts of Martini-Henry fire. But the defenders didn't flinch. Even as comrades dropped and bodies rolled down the slope, more dervishes surged forward, hurling fresh spears with fanatical precision. The British fixed bayonets and stabbed at any who tumbled into reach, pinning corpses against boulders and thorns.

Wilkes' men were just yards from the summit now. As Thomas and his line closed to 20 yards, another barrage of spears struck. Four more infantrymen collapsed. A blade flashed beside Thomas, and a long spear punched through the neck of the young bluejacket running at his side, dropping him instantly. His comrade stopped to render aid.

"Leave him!" Thomas shouted, his voice raw. A second spear slammed into the helper's shoulder, pitching him onto the rocks.

There was no time for mercy. Thomas pressed on and prayed one of the medics could reach the boy later.

Then, at last, the 87 soldiers who had survived the fight up the hill broke over the ridge. They fired point-blank, bayonets thrusting mercilessly into the tangle of Beja warriors packed along the crest. Ahead, spread in a wide arc, stood the four Gatling gun emplacements—the prize—but between them lay over 100 fanatical defenders, their spear blades and swords flashing in the desert sun.

The Beja advanced with renewed fury, undeterred, their faith in the Mahdi unbroken. And the British answered with the same cold rage—revenge for their fallen mates driving them forward. The fight dissolved into raw, animal brutality. Bayonets clashed with spears, curved knives sliced at British hands reaching for sidearms, and dozens of pairs of men wrestled on the ground until one gained the upper hand, or an enemy stopped the struggle with a quick spear slice or bayonet thrust.

The screams, curses, and death-cries merged into a single inhuman roar that rolled across the hilltop like a storm.

Thomas saw Wilkes push past two Beja and make it to one of the gatling guns. The giant Sergeant dispatched one dervish with his pistol, and the second with his bayonet, but his luck ran out when another warrior raced up behind him. Just as the man pulled back his spear to strike a killing blow into Wilke's back, he tripped on a spike designed to keep the heavy gun from rolling while being fired, and his spear missed its mark. Instead of ripping through the Sergeant's back and out his abdomen the spear caught Wilkes behind the thigh. Thomas pulled his Colt and shot the Beja in the chest, but not before the entire 12-inch length of the blade pierced all the way through Wilke's leg. The impact of the blow spun the sergeant around; he fell back over the gatling gun with his arms splayed across the barrel.

"I'm alive, damn 'em all to hell," Wilkes was able to call out. "It's you and the boys now."

Thomas climbed onto an overturned ammunition box and shouted to the senior corporal, who was yanking his bayonet blade out of the gut of a fallen Beja. "Signal the men to form up here with me."

The corporal pulled a brass whistle from his shirt and blew three piercing blasts. This was the signal for the British soldiers to begin fighting back towards their commander's position. They moved shoulder to shoulder in a tight, practiced formation, fending off any of the warriors foolish enough to rush the line of steel bayonets and rifles.

As Thomas fired over his men's heads into the scrum of screaming dervishes, he saw their spears take down two more soldiers, and then he watched, sickened, as the Beja stabbed at their prone bodies over and over.

When his men began to form up around him, Thomas shouted, "Front line kneel, rear line prepare to fire," and watched the highly trained soldiers immediately go into the classic firing formation the British army had perfected around the world for over 200 years.

"See to your intervals Lance Corporal," Thomas shouted. "Tighten that right flank."

From behind him he heard Wilkes pipe in: "Their center is thin lads; we can break them if we hold the line. When they close, give 'em cold steel."

As soon as the front line dropped to one knee with their bayonets pointed up towards the enemy, Thomas yelled, "Fire!" and the rear line pulled their triggers as one, taking down more than a dozen dervishes. In a heartbeat the standing soldiers went to their knees to reload and prepare bayonets, and the front line stood up, took three paces back behind the kneeling line, and fired at Thomas' command.

The rest of the Beja came to a halt, stopped both by the growing pile of their dead comrade's bodies as well as the brutal accuracy of the rifle fire being directed at them. To prevent them from breaking off the frontal assault and charging around his flanks, Thomas ordered the corporal to signal the first line of men to stand, spread out, and fire at will, while the second line was to form semi-circles at each end of their position and fire on any warrior who tried to run around them.

When he turned his head towards No. 4 gun, he saw that Wilkes was down, lying on his side in the dirt with the spear through his thigh. He leapt down from the ammo box and shouted for a blue jacket and a medic to follow him. He looked down the hill as he ran and saw that Green's pincer movement was in motion; the body of the dervish army was encircled, and they were being pushed back towards the base of the ridge.

Thomas knew the Mahdist commander would not be overly worried about making the strategic retreat. He believed that his army would be protected by rifle fire and spears from the defenders on top of the hill, and so the day's battle would end up in a stalemate to be carried on tomorrow. If they could not get the guns working and pin down the Beja, though, it would not simply end up being a rout for Green; it would also mean death for him and his men when those 2,000 dervishes came boiling up the hill unopposed and found the handful of British infantry who had fought their way to the top.

When the medic knelt down with his kit Thomas made brief eye contact with Wilkes. The Sergeant simply nodded towards the ongoing fight in the compound, and Thomas headed back into the fray, firing his Colt with each step he took. The relentless British rifle fire was having its effect; dozens of Beja lay wounded or dead around the compound.

As he paused to reload, a tall, white-robed warrior with a red turban clambered onto a boulder in the center of the compound, waved a curved sword in a circle above his head and called out something to his fighters. Thomas and his men watched in disbelief as the dervish war cries went still and the warriors turned from the fight and began trotting towards the hills and ravines to the west, chanting an Arabic verse that he did not understand. They knew there were too few British to follow, and they brandished their spears to the sky to promise they would return.

The speed at which the bloody combat came to a halt was startling. Around the compound exhausted soldiers tended to the dead and wounded, refilled their ammunition pouches, and drank deeply from canteens to soothe throats parched by heat and dust and greasy battle smoke.

Thomas took a moment to look around for the first time since flying over the top of the ridge. The canvas tents, smoldering cook fires, and shade-cloth lean-tos the British gun crews were using when they had been forced to retreat yesterday were just as they had left them.

The senior corporal approached, limping from a bleeding wound in his calf. "Orders, sir?" the corporal asked.

"Get the gun crews at their stations and tell them I will be around to speak with them. Then get your leg looked at."

The corporal saluted. "First time I ever saw a Yank in the thick of things, sir," he said. "An honor."

Thomas returned the salute and started across the compound to check on Sergeant Wilkes. As he pressed through the crowd of dust-caked, bone-weary, bloody soldiers each one doffed his cap or saluted.

The honor is all mine, Thomas thought.

Over at No. 4 gun a medic holding a bone saw was kneeling beside Wilkes. Thomas winced. He had seen battlefield amputations in the war and knew that a skilled surgeon could cut through flesh and bone in under two minutes—the faster the better to prevent excess blood loss and infection. It was a damn shame that the Welsh Sergeant had to lose a limb.

Wilkes was lying on his right side, with six feet of spear shaft protruding from the back of his left thigh. He looked up and gave Thomas a half smile. "Fine bit of a scrap you pulled off here, Colonel Scoundrel. We are much obliged," he said through clenched teeth.

"Your men are superbly trained, Wilkes. The fact that we are alive is your doing, my friend, not mine." He hesitated and then added. "I'm sorry you've got to lose the leg."

Wilkes snorted. "And that would be the second time today that you were wrong, colonel darlin'. I ain't losing anything."

Thomas looked down at the medic as he straightened Wilkes wounded leg on a clean blanket. "But the bone saw," he said.

"It's to cut the shaft of the spear, not his leg," said the blue jacketed doc. "Hold his boot steady, would you?"

Thomas took hold of the sergeant's boot with both hands and held it firmly as the medic wrapped his left hand tightly around the spear shaft where it entered his leg. "I've got to pull the blade out from the front," the medic said, "or risk clipping an artery." Then he said, "Ready Sergeant?"

"As I'll ever be, lad," said Wilkes, "Let's get this dance over with."

The medic raised the bone saw in his right hand, bore down on the spear shaft, and cut it off as close to Wilke's leg as he could. Then he wrapped a cotton cloth around his left hand, reached around the front of Wilke's leg and grabbed the shaft that protruded out the front of his thigh.

"You won't like this, Sergeant," he said in a low voice.

"Dammit, boy, let's have it then," Wilkes responded with a grim chuckle.

The medic pulled the spear shaft and blade out of Wilke's leg in one swift motion and dropped it on the ground. Wilkes let out the breath he had been holding as the medic doused the wound with carbolic acid and wrapped a clean bandage around it.

"Colonel Green?" Wilkes asked Thomas in a surprisingly strong voice.

"I'll see," Thomas replied. He went over to the low brick wall that protected the guns at the edge of the cliff and looked down. A half mile below, Green's mounted infantry was pushing against both flanks of the dervish army while the rest of his troops and artillery were pushing the Beja back from the center towards the ridge and the waiting gatling guns.

"Ten, maybe 15 minutes before the Beja have to decide whether to mount a counterattack against Colonel Green or retreat up this hill," he informed Wilkes. "I don't know how the dervish commander thinks, but he still has at least three times as many men as Green. Maybe he'll want to fight it out now."

Two men helped the sergeant sit up with his back against the medical cart. He took a long drink from his canteen before replying. "I don't think he fights today. Between Green's cannon and the Martini-Henrys, it's a pretty even situation now. I say he comes up the hill."

The senior corporal broke away from a knot of men and limped over to them. He smiled when he saw that his Sergeant was still alive, and in possession of both of his legs.

"The gun crews have unlocked all four gatlings and mounted the sights," he said. "They were already positioned to fire at any force coming up from the plain, and all the ammunition boxes are full. We've got over 100,000 rounds to share with those bloody wogs."

Wilkes nodded his approval. "And you have signaled the colonel that we are here?"

"As planned, we waved the red and green Beja flag four times, and we got a response from our own signalman," the corporal said. "The wogs below won't know it's not their men welcoming them home."

"What about our losses?" Thomas asked in a somber voice.

"Nineteen dead, 26 wounded," the corporal replied.

"Damn shame," Wilkes muttered. Then he raised his head. "Anything else, Colonel?"

Thomas thought a moment. "Have some men strip the robes from enough of the Beja so that each gun crew member can put one on before he takes his station," he told the corporal. "The Beja won't know it's us until they are almost to the top. Then make sure all our men hold well back of the edge of the hill so that they can't be seen by the dervishes when they begin their climb."

The corporal smiled again and began to walk away. "A minute, Corporal," Thomas called after him. "Find a robe for me, too, and if there is a Beja as big as the Sergeant out there, get one for him, too. We'll prop him up in the back of a wagon by the wall, so he won't miss a minute of the show."

Despite the pain, Wilkes grinned from ear to ear.

A few minutes later Thomas was dressed in a flowing white and red robe that was decorated in the center of the chest with a bullet hole. He went to the supply wagon Wilkes had been lifted in to and handed him a pair of field glasses.

"Their commander has made his decision, Sergeant Wilkes. They're about to climb the hill. All four gatling crews are sighted in and ready."

Wilkes shook the hem of his dervish robe and laughed. "Up the hill and into the arms of their friends," he said, "or so they're thinking."

Thomas walked to the rock wall and looked down. The main body of the Beja army, more than 2,000 men, had begun the climb. Green's forces kept up a steady rifle fire, but stopped the cannonade when the dervishes were halfway to the top for fear they might hit Thomas and Wilkes.

If all went as planned the enemy were about to find themselves trapped between a storm of gatling gun fire from the top of the ridge and a formidable array of mounted infantry, cannon, and massed Martini-Henry rifles on the plain.

Thomas looked up and down the line of gatling stations and made eye contact with each gun commander. The guns' hoppers were filled, the spotters were ready to tell the crew where to turn the barrel and how to angle it, and the loaders were standing by with full boxes of cartridges.

There was only one decision left to make. Thomas took another look down the embankment at the hundreds of men scrambling through the brush and rocks towards what they believed was a safe refuge.

One decision.

When.

The sun peaked above the parched Sahara landscape, and the fiery wind that had bathed them in the smell of gun powder and blood faded to a whisper.

He raised his hand, cleared his throat, and gave the command.

"*Fire!*"

~TWENTY TWO~

Suakin, Sudan, July

The raiders waited in darkness as Major Kitchener's mounted infantry marched out of Suakin to search for Mahdist rebels. As the dust from the column receded on the horizon and the first rays of dawn spilled across the Red Sea the black-robed warriors mounted their horses. They swept through the crumbling city gates and wove their way through the warren of narrow streets to the wealthy residential quarter along the waterfront.

Suakin was once a mighty trading center and important port, but it had been in decline for more than a century. The leader of the raiding party had been here many times, and the mingled smell of salt air, camel dung, and cook fires sparked memories of his life before the wars began, and his service to the Mahdi dominated his life.

His commitment to help his master throw the British and Egyptians out of Sudan and establish a new Caliphate was total and unwavering. Even so, he had been baffled when he was ordered to kidnap a Bedouin guide and the French woman who employed him from the home of the British counsel. The guide was to be taken to the prison camp outside Wad Madani and the woman was to be delivered to the Shukriya leader Sheikh Ahmed Abu Sinn at his encampment three days north of Khartoum.

Neither captive was to be harmed. Any hand that touched the French woman in anger would be cut off, the Mahdi decreed, and any man who attempted liberties with her would be disemboweled and have his entrails thrown to the jackals.

When they arrived outside the counsel's two-story bayside home, the leader signaled to his men to dismount. They tore through the iron gate that secured the coral fence around the compound and a minute later they strode into the landscaped garden behind their leader.

Samhi heard the commotion from his upstairs bedroom as he was tying a belt around his robe. He slipped into his sandals and went to the open window, where he saw the Mahdi's men spread out across the courtyard. He started for his revolver but thought better of it. Even if he took down one or two of the raiders before he was killed, what would become of Heléne? He had no doubt the men were there for her but given the rules and traditions around kidnapping that most of the tribes in North Africa had followed for 1,000 years, he knew that she would probably not face any physical harm. The kidnappers would be seeking a ransom.

He moved swiftly through the hall and down the steps to the garden where the band's leader was splashing water from the mosaic-tiled fountain onto the back of his neck.

"I am Samhi Al-Katib," he said to the bearded man, taking note of the rifle slung behind his back and the bandolier of ammunition across his shoulders. "By whose authority have you trespassed onto this property?"

"By the authority of my Mahdi," the leader replied in a calm, deep voice, "and through him, by the authority of Allah himself."

Samhi knew better than to ask more questions. With several dozen heavily armed warriors ready to jump to his bidding, the man needn't answer anyone's questions. Whatever he was here for, he was going to get.

"And you want …" Samhi began.

"You, guide, and the French woman who employs you. You will each pack a single bag and be prepared to leave with us in five minutes."

"And what of your ransom demand?" Samhi asked. "Will you leave a letter here for the counsel to share with my mistress' people?"

The warrior leader was offended. "Do I look like a common criminal, Al Katib?" he snorted. "No ransom is asked for, and none will be accepted. It is the will of the Mahdi that you be taken, and that is enough."

Samhi was genuinely surprised. What reason other than money would anyone—especially a powerful leader like the Mahdi who had to raise vast sums to pay for his war—have for taking Heléne?

The leader sensed Samhi's confusion. "*Bi Sharafi*–by my honor–neither you nor the woman shall be harmed. Go now and prepare her for the journey."

Samhi looked the man in the eye. Personal honor and obedience to Allah were the most sacred tenets of Bedouin leadership. In any event, there was nothing he could do to stop what was about to happen. He nodded and went up the stairs to get Heléne.

She was waiting for him beside an open window, still wearing her night clothing, and clutching her .32 caliber pistol.

"I heard him, Samhi," she said. "Why are they taking us? Where?"

He placed a hand on her forearm. "I do not know, child. But he is Bedouin and has given his sacred word that no harm will come to you. I believe him."

"Could it be Henri Lavalle again?" she wondered.

"His reach is far, and his purse is deep," Samhi answered. "So, yes, it could be Lavalle."

"When will he understand that I do not know anything about Amenhotep's treasure, or his tomb's location?" she asked. "Oh, how I wish Thomas was here with us."

"There you are wrong," Samhi answered in a gentle voice. "He is an American soldier who does not know the customs of the Bedouin. He would try to stop these men, and he would fail. No, Thomas is better off where he is. When he returns and learns what has happened, he will come after us. You can be sure of that."

Heléne's eyes glistened as she fought back a tear. "Yes, I know," she whispered.

"Even so," he replied, "keep the revolver close by."

A few minutes later, the Mahdi's warriors mounted their horses and thundered away from the counsel's home. Samhi rode his own horse, while Heléne sat behind the leader with her arms wrapped loosely around his waist.

The household staff watched from the windows of the white coral house as the warrior band and their captives galloped down the alley, swung around a bend, and disappeared.

~TWENTY THREE~

The Gash River Basin, Sudan

Corporal Marquant had not stopped talking since Colonel Green ordered him to deliver Thomas to General Gordon's headquarters in Khartoum, a 17-day journey from the battlefield. But, as sundown approached and they broke camp outside the market town of Kassala, Thomas had to admit that the corporal's non-stop chatter had been a blessing in disguise. 2,600 Beja and 500 British and Egyptians died at Tamai, and while the battle was a victory for the British, there was little for him to celebrate.

The battle had gone as Green planned; his men pushed the Beja up against the base of the ridge, and the gatling guns poured heavy fire down upon the unsuspecting dervishes who thought they were climbing the hill to safety. Green had commended Thomas' leadership and offered to help him return to Suakin to rejoin the effort to find Heléne's father, but that changed the next morning when a rider delivered a dispatch from Khartoum.

The British commander called Thomas to his tent at midday. Across the plain, special details were burying British and Egyptian soldiers in shallow graves and piling up Beja corpses to be burned when night fell. The stench of bodies bloating in the blistering heat mixed with the cries of thousands of griffon vultures tearing at the flesh of the dead.

Green had a kerchief wrapped around his mouth and nose against the smell, and Thomas pressed a bandana against his face.

He handed Thomas a glass of brandy and invited him to sit. "We'll move camp away from this corner of hell later today," Green began.

"The Mahdists have been cutting the telegraph lines to Khartoum since March. Gordon has squads on constant repair duty, of course, but with over 300 miles of line to check he will lose that battle soon, and his headquarters will be cut off from the world. Before the end of the year the Mahdi will be able to lay siege the city."

"Is your government sending a relief force?" Thomas asked.

"They're playing politics," Green answered "The lot of 'em, Gordon included. His orders were to evacuate, but he chose to hang tight. The people want an army sent to his aid, but Gladstone is in no hurry." He picked up a telegraph cable from the field desk. "Which brings us to this."

"I was able to send a telegram to Gordon yesterday and he has just replied. Congratulates me on the victory, and orders that you be escorted to Khartoum immediately."

Thomas finished his brandy and slipped the bandana back into his pocket. "But, why? This isn't my war, Colonel Green. I am needed elsewhere."

"Be that as it may, Thomas, you have made this your war, and probably caused an international incident, to boot, by taking command of Desmond's company yesterday. Not your fault, lad, and I am immensely grateful for your service, but…"

"Politics," Thomas answered dryly.

"The primacy of the Empire, which must at all costs be maintained, to be more exact," Green replied. "General Gordon will be called onto the carpet when the full story of yesterday's battle is made public, and with everything else he has to deal with right now he won't have any choice but to hang you out to dry."

"And I've got to travel 450 miles across this damn desert in the middle of July so he can do that? A telegram won't do?"

Green refilled their glasses. "The unwritten rules of bureaucratic ass-covering, my boy," he said with a half-smile. "His report to the PM will certify that he gave your backside a proper chewing out before ordering you out of Sudan forever."

An aide came into the tent and handed Green a pile of dispatches.

"It seems I have no choice in the matter," Thomas said.

Green looked up from the paper he was reading. "I am sorry, Colonel Scoundrel. For the good of the service and all that, I'm afraid."

"Then I won't make it back to Suakin for at least a month," Thomas replied. "I fear for my friends."

Green stood and the men ducked out of the tent. The British commander placed a hand on his shoulder and said, "You were instrumental in securing our victory yesterday, and your exploits on that ridge will go down in regimental history. You should be proud."

Thomas shook Green's hand and headed towards the field hospital to say goodbye to Sergeant Wilkes. All around the shrub-and-rock-covered plain, the bodies of the dead lay festering under the smoldering yellow sky.

When he stepped over a canvas tarp outside the hospital tent on which lay a boyish-faced soldier who had just had his leg amputated above the knee, Green's final word faded to a plaintive echo in his mind: 'Proud.'

Seven marines and three native bearers accompanied Thomas on the long trip to Khartoum. He and the marines rode on horseback; the bearers loped along on dromedary camels and led two pack camels loaded with 400 pounds of water and supplies. When they reached Berber, they would transfer to one of Gordon's Nile gun boats for the final 90-mile leg of the journey. It was the beginning of the rainy season, which in Sudan meant that a paltry 10-12 inches would fall between July and September. Even so, they took care not to pitch camp in dry washes or gulleys for fear of flash flooding.

They traveled at night and slept in the shade of rock outcroppings or under canvas lean-tos during the day. Their diet consisted of porridge made with dura, dry flatbread and biscuits, dates, dried jerky, lentils and goat cheese. The locations of water wells and springs were predictable along the way, courtesy of the rains that fell every five or six days. Corporal Marquant had traveled this route in both the dry season and the rainy season, and he assured Thomas that despite the oppressive heat, this was the best time of year to follow the trails south and west from the Red Sea to Khartoum.

Marquant fancied himself an amateur naturalist, and he delighted in describing the varieties of flies, venomous scorpions, snakes, spiders, and lizards that confronted Saharan travelers day and night.

"Now the Nubian spitting cobra, there's a delightful little rock-dweller you don't want to meet," he would say as they rode along under the starry night sky, "but he's no match for the Boomslang snake; that bugger will loop down out of a tree and sink its fangs into your leg faster than a two shilling whore on high street. But it's the puff adder, though, who'll really help you meet old St. Peter in a hurry; had a mate once who saw one sleeping under a log and thought he'd have a little fun poking it with a stick. The boy was dead before he hit the ground."

And so it went, night after night; death stalker and fat-tailed scorpions, blister beetles and camel spiders, tsetse flies and horned vipers. By Thomas' count at least a dozen of Marquant's mates had met their ends after encountering one deadly creature or another. From the gates of Kassala to the boat docks at Berber, however, Thomas' only non-human nemesis along the 220-mile trail turned out to be the lowly sandflies who infested every inch of dirt they rode across.

Each time Saher's hooves bit into parched soil, a puff of flies rose up to torment both horse and rider. The bearers claimed that the best deterrent was a cream fashioned with fresh camel dung and urine that you spread liberally on your face, hands, and any other exposed skin several times a day. Of course, the stench from that concoction was so appalling that even Saher recoiled in disgust any time a bearer wearing the potion came close. Thomas grit his teeth, kept a kerchief wrapped around his lower face, and made the best of it until they reached the cool green waters of the Nile.

General Charles Gordon was both more and less than what Thomas had expected. Green had warned him that the General was a strict teetotaler who did not permit any of his men to drink in his presence, and an ascetic diner who seemed to live on little more than tea and biscuits. On the other hand, Thomas discovered that the general had a lively and quick wit and was well-versed in American history.

"I know your story, of course," Gordon said when Thomas was ushered into his office on the second floor of the vast mud brick headquarters complex that sat above the Blue Nile. From the metal shuttered windows to the sandbag barricades and heavily manned gun-emplacements, the building topped with British and Egyptian flags reminded Thomas of a medieval fortress.

Gordon was of medium height and build, with piercing blue-grey eyes, a thick, well-kept moustache and curly, light brown hair streaked with gray. He wore a simple blue tunic with gold-braid over loose fitting trousers, and atop his head sat a red Turkish fez. When Gordon motioned for him to sit, Thomas noticed that his left hand was trembling.

"Read about your derring-do at Pebble Creek Ridge at the end of your nation's War of Rebellion, and I had the pleasure of hearing President Grant speak about your encounters with the red savages during the Plains Wars when I dined with him in Washington."

A servant came into the office with a pitcher of water. He poured two glasses, added lemon slices, and left.

"My government would like nothing better than for you to disappear into the dunes and be done with the hornet's nest you stirred up when you took command of your company and captured that ridge at Tamai. Understandable sentiment for a bloody politician, but men in our profession know better. When Green invited you to give a little advice to Sergeant Wilkes when the attack began, he knew damn well you'd end up in charge. Green and I both can thank you in private, Colonel Scoundrel, but it would mean the end of our careers if we congratulated you publicly."

"I understand, sir."

Gordon fiddled with a brass paper weight. "I've been told about your friends, Scoundrel. I know Professor Bovet. Good man, top-notch scholar. Pity he has disappeared."

Thomas was mystified. Was that all the scolding or punishment he was going to get? Had he been marched halfway across the Sahara in the middle of summer for that mild hand slap?

Gordon looked somber. "There is more news that I do not believe you have been told about. I myself only learned a few days ago. It's about your other friends."

Thomas' head snapped up as Gordon pulled a sheet of paper from the pile on his desk.

"Miss Bovet, and the Bedouin guide, Samhi. Seems they were taken from Souakin on the orders of the Mahdi." He handed the yellowed telegram to Thomas, who scanned it and put it back on the desk.

He sucked in his breath. Heléne taken.

"There is not much information here, General," he began.

"And as far as I know there have been no ransom demands," Gordon cut in. "I do not think this is an ordinary kidnapping."

"Then what? Are they safe?"

"Kidnaping for ransom has been a routine feature of life in Egypt and Sudan since the pyramids were built, Thomas." Gordon finished his water and rang a bell for the boy to bring more. "But there are unwritten rules about how the kidnapped are to be treated, especially the women. I cannot say the same for her guide, but I am certain that Miss Bovet is unharmed."

"It makes no sense," Thomas said. Every fiber in his body wanted to rush to the door, get Saher from the stable and begin the journey back to Souakin. He would start there and not rest until Heléne and Samhi were safe.

"To us, no, it does not," the general answered. "But to the Mahdi? Given his complete focus on defeating us and throwing us out of Sudan, his reasons for taking Miss Bovet must be monumental. You do know that he is obsessed with finding the tomb of Amenhotep? Absolutely mad on the subject, no one knows why."

Thomas shook his head. "That is the same tomb that Professor Bovet has been searching for for years," he said. "And we already have the antiquities dealer Henri Lavalle sending men after Heléne for any information she may have."

The boy refilled their glasses, and Gordon went over and cracked the metal shutters on the window. He motioned for Thomas to join him. "More than 15,000 Mahdist warriors surround us. We can't hold them back forever."

Gordon looked off into the distance. "In fact, Colonel, I expect they will be knocking at our gates by the middle of September."

"What about the relief force from England?" Thomas asked.

Gordon clasped his hands.

"Indeed," is all he said.

"They will not arrive?"

Gordon sighed. "Not in time."

They sat in silence for a moment. Then Gordon chuckled. "But what you want to know is why I had you dragged 500 miles across the desert."

"With due respect, yes sir, that is exactly what I'd like to know."

"Do you play hunches, Thomas?"

"I'm a gambler, sir. I play them all the time."

"I thought so. Don't approve of gambling myself, but when it comes to hunches, I believe in them, and I pay attention."

What hunch could the most senior British general in North Africa have that would involve Heléne, he wondered?

Gordon sat back and slid the paper weight he had been fidgeting with across the desk. "My hunch is two-fold, Thomas. First, I believe there is a connection between the Mahdi's preoccupation with a pharaoh who has been dead for 3,000 years and the Bovets. That would seem to be likely. Mahdi wants to find the tomb as much as does Professor Bovet, though, I would dare say, for very different reasons."

"I agree," Thomas replied.

"My second hunch is that the Mahdi hasn't been able to get the information he wants from the good Professor and so has taken the step of kidnapping his daughter and her guide. Had you been with them in Souakin you also would have been taken, and probably summarily shot since you have none of the information that the professor and his daughter possess."

"Doesn't speak so highly of my value does it," Thomas answered with a wry smile.

"Don't count your blessings quite yet, Colonel. This place is abuzz with spies, and I'd wager that before the sun goes down tonight the Mahdi will know you are here and have spoken with me. He will see you as additional leverage against Miss Bovet, and his men will be on your trail by daybreak."

'Leverage?' Thomas thought. Why would Gordon think in those terms unless he knew…

"Henri Lavalle has been a thorn in my side for years," Gordon said with a knowing smile. "If the man did not own so many politicians and judges here and in Britain I could have dealt with him properly long ago.

On the other hand, the Mahdi is not the only one with a network of informants in the region."

Thomas grinned.

"I was told about Lavalle's attempts on your life. I knew you were coming here almost the moment you sailed from Constantinople, and, knowing as I do of both your…" Gordon cleared his throat… "ahem, your reputation and Miss Bovet's beauty, I surmised you had accompanied her here from France for, shall we say, reasons of the heart?"

Thomas nodded. Touché, he thought.

Gordon lay his palms flat on the desk and leaned forward. "And what I know, the Mahdi knows, or soon will."

"Which means the reason you brought me here was not to clap me in irons or expel me from the continent…"

"But to find the most expedient way to bring you close to where Miss Bovet and her guide are being held, while at the same time protecting my backside from the hyenas in Parliament who would have my scalp had I not dealt with you in person before your role at Tamai blossomed into an embarrassing international incident."

Gordon looked pleased with himself. In the midst of war, a growing siege, political backstabbing, and the daily litany of death and disaster that was swirling around Khartoum, he had pulled off something of a diplomatic tour de force.

'And if no relief sails from England soon, it will be the last victory of its kind he will ever know,' Thomas thought.

Gordon handed Thomas over to an Irish captain who led him down the outside walkway and into a long, well-lit room whose walls were covered with maps and charts. Several clerks were making notations on the maps, while others were diligently copying the hundreds of orders and records necessary for managing thousands of troops spread across hundreds of miles of desert, plains, and mountains.

"The Mahdi has stationed men in more than two dozen camps along this 30-mile circle," the captain began as he ran his finger in an oval shape around the largest hand drawn map in the room.

Thomas stepped closer and studied the map.

"Some camps have as few as 50 warriors, others have 1,000 or more," the captain continued. He pointed to a spot on the map that was encircled with black grease pencil. "This camp is near a spring about 15 miles north of here. The size of the circle around it corresponds to the number of dervishes who are there. This is one of the largest; we believe there are upwards of 3,000 of the bastards there waiting for the order to pour down to our gates."

Thomas' heart sank; dozens of camps, thousands of warriors. It would be like searching for yesterday's wind.

The captain saw Thomas' expression and grinned. "It might not be that bad, though, Colonel. The Mahdi's men follow tradition and the old ways in almost everything they do. They do not take kidnapped civilians to their headquarters or main encampments, too many prying eyes. Your friends would be taken to a small camp, a place where secrets can be kept. There are just eight or 10 that fit that description." He began pointing to the smallest circles on the map. "They still wrap around Khartoum, but it will make your search easier—and safer. How many will be going with you?"

"Just me," Thomas replied in a near whisper.

The captain let out a low whistle. "Just you? Man, are you daft?"

Thomas replied with a question. "The camps are laid out in a 30-mile circle around Khartoum; how many miles will I have to ride to cover that entire distance?"

A clerk sitting close to them raised his head from a ledger. "That's a simple circumference problem, Colonel. You know, pi multiplied by diameter."

Math was not Thomas' strong suit, but the clerk solved the calculation in a few seconds. "94.25 miles in all, sir," the clerk said when he lay down his pencil.

"And why, might I ask, is that important?" asked the captain.

"Planning for supplies," Thomas answered. "If this was going to take under a week, I would carry all my supplies on my horse. This may take 10 days or more, so I will need to take a pack camel along."

"Colonel," the captain said, "with respect, sir, do you intend to reconnoiter these camps by yourself? You'd need a full company of 100 men and a good month to do that properly. Again, and begging your pardon, but what the bloody hell can you do even if you find them? God's wounds, man, the dervishes don't take prisoners in battle. You'll have to kill every damn one you encounter."

"Yes, I will," was Thomas' only reply.

At dawn the next morning he walked the battlements of Gordon's fortress headquarters. Looking down on the peaceful, green-brushed landscape and the placid waters of the Blue Nile, it was difficult to believe that the hellish battle he had come from three weeks earlier was headed this way.

He could make out farmers in white loin cloths and reed sandals slogging through the mud behind their oxen along the narrow strip of land near the river that was covered with dark, fertile soil, as they had done for thousands of years.

How many conquering armies had this land seen, how many pharaohs and Roman legions, kings, and bandit princes had rallied their forces and fought over this brown, barren landscape that flowered only briefly each year?

Somewhere beyond the barricades and army encampments, Heléne and Samhi were prisoners. Whether it had been done at Henri Lavalle's bidding or the Mahdi's was of no consequence; he was going to track them, find them, kill their captors, and bring them home.

~TWENTY FOUR~

Omdurman Hinterland, 30 miles west of Khartoum

Sheikh Ahmed Abu Sinn was reclining on cushions in front of an ochre and royal blue curtain that separated the main room of his tent from the servant's quarters and the bedrooms shared by his four wives. When the ample tribal leader clapped his hands, servants scurried into the tent and set platters of roasted lamb stew, rice flavored with saffron and nuts, warm flatbreads, mint tea, and honey-soaked pastries on low ebony wood tables inlaid with mother of pearl.

Outside the tent a gust of wind shook the wooden poles that held the tightly woven goat hair structure upright, but the thick ropes and anchor pegs held firm, and the wind passed into the great emptiness without doing any damage. A dozen prime dromedary camels, their humps fat with reserves, shifted nervously on their tethers when the wind blew past, and the Sheikh's prized Saluki hunting hounds raced in circles inside their brush-walled enclosure, but other than the soft fireside conversations and muted laughter from the Sheikh's personal guards rising up into the cold, starry night, the desert was still.

There were no villages in this part of the flat, scrubby plain that stretched westward out of Khartoum, which was both a curse and a blessing to Abu Sinn. The Shukriya chieftain enjoyed company, camel races, music, and he especially loved traditional Bedouin poetry read aloud by wandering troubadours who crisscrossed the desert to entertain wealthy patrons in exchange for a fine meal and lodging for a night.

He was bored, and even the tantalizing lengths to which his wives would go to arouse and delight his every physical desire was not enough to quash his growing frustration with this situation. But his Mahdi had requested a favor, and with a war raging, trade caravans diminishing, and centuries old tribal squabbles re-igniting in the absence of a firm

British or Egyptian military presence to keep the peace, Abu Sinn had no choice but to do his master's bidding.

The war would end someday, and no matter who emerged as the winner, his fate would once again be in someone else's hands. He preferred the laissez-faire attitude of the British, who ruled from afar and mostly left the Sheikh's alone. That viewpoint, of course, would earn him a beheading by sword if the Mahdi heard of it, and so here he sat in a desolate corner of the Sahara, biding his time and honoring the Mahdi's request.

Heléne caught the Sheikh's eye and sensed that he was thinking about her. She had been his 'guest' for two weeks, and even though her prison cell was luxurious, and the elaborate meals would have pleased even a connoisseur of good food like Thomas, she was consumed with the idea of escape. There were no bars or walls or iron gates around the Sheikh's compound, only the limitless expanse of the unforgiving desert.

Her captors had traveled at night on the 14-day journey from Suakin to this place, but they kept her head covered with a hood, so she had no idea what direction they were moving in, or about any landmarks or trail markers along the route. She could be anywhere.

She became so restless doing nothing the first few days at the compound that she asked permission to help with daily chores. The Sheikh agreed, and she knew it amused him to watch as she fetched water and firewood, tended to the animals, mended clothing, and helped prepare meals.

The guards grew used to her walking up to the top of the rise behind the encampment, and they did not think it suspicious that she spent so much time grooming and working with the Sheikh's favorite Arabian stallion. They even allowed her to saddle the horse and ride it around the area under their watchful eyes.

But all she could see from the rise was miles of scrub-brush, ravines, and boulders baking under the brutal summer sun. Even if she could sneak out of the tent in the middle of the night, unhobble and saddle the horse, what then? She knew enough about the position of the stars to tell north from south, but if she bolted out of the camp and rode off without knowing how to find and follow the few trails that were dotted with water holes at two- or three-day intervals, she would either die of thirst and heat exhaustion, or be captured and carried off by some other tribal leader, one who would not be bound by the Mahdi's decree that she not be touched or harmed in any way.

Better to bide my time for now, she thought as a servant put a plate of food before her. She acknowledged a nod from the Sheikh and sipped at her tea. Thomas had told her that should a day like this ever come, he would find her. That promise and the small revolver hidden in her waistband were her only hope now.

Samhi's desert prison offered none of the luxuries Heléne was enjoying at the Sheikh's encampment 125 miles to the northwest. His captors had not forced him to wear a hood on the journey from Suakin, and when he first caught sight of the compact cluster of low, flat-roofed mud-brick houses with walls weathered by the sun against the backdrop of the Blue Nile, he recognized it as the small provincial trading center of Wad Madani.

He rode with his guards through narrow, dusty lanes crowded with people in flowing robes—men in jellabiyas and turbans, women balancing water jars or baskets of produce on their heads and listened to the chatter of Arabic and local dialects that filled the air, alongside the bleating of goats and the creak of ox-driven carts.

To his surprise, they did not stop in the town and instead rode east for two more days. They passed through scrubby plains dotted with acacia trees and the occasional baobab until they reached a tiny settlement of mud huts and goat pens sandwiched between two rows of hills cut by ancient rivers that had dried up 1,000 years before the first pyramids were built.

The good news—if he could call it that—was that his abductors had not killed him as soon as they rode out of Suakin. That they had been traveling for 15 days suggested that the Mahdi believed him to be important, but for reasons he did not understand.

The leader of the guards rode alone down to the largest brick structure in the village while Samhi and the others waited on a low rise.

When the leader returned a few minutes later, he was accompanied by three tall, strong-looking young men. One took Samhi's horse by the bridle and the four of them walked down the rubble-covered hill while the guards rode back towards Wad Madani without saying a word.

Samhi's hands had not been bound during the journey, and he gave a brief thought to slapping his horse's flanks and making a run for it, but he had no food, water, firewood, or weapons. He would not have made it far. The only thing he was certain of is that he had been kept alive for a reason. Perhaps the answer lay in this godforsaken scattering of crumbling mud buildings and reeking goat pens.

He was led to the center of the settlement and ordered to dismount. One of the men walked his horse to a corral, while the other two took him by his arms through a low wooden gate and left him standing in the center of a small penned-in space dotted with gobs of dark dried blood and goat hair. The slaughtering pen, Samhi thought as his guards walked away. How fitting.

It was midday, and the late July sun beat down like a furnace. He needed to find water. Then a movement caught his eye, and a ragged curtain parted at the front of a small hut in the corner of the pen.

An old man stepped out. His hair and beard were long and wild, and he was leaning on a tree branch that had been fashioned into a crude walking stick.

Samhi squinted in the bright sunlight, straining to make out the man's features. Then a familiar voice spoke. "Samhi, my old friend, welcome to hell."

The Bedouin guide felt the breath leave his body, and a tear form in his eye. He stepped forward and embraced the old man.

"Professor Bovet," he said through his tears.

~TWENTY FIVE~

Jebel Aulia region, south of Khartoum, August 1

The sun was peeking above the rim of the eastern desert when Thomas lowered the field glasses given to him by General Gordon and swung Saher around a jumble of boulders. The narrow trail was lightly traveled and would help him remain out of sight of the fisherman and farmers who trekked to the banks of the White Nile at dawn to begin their day's labors.

He carefully picked his way down the steep sandstone hill after which the village of Jebel Aulia was named and untethered the pack camel from the acacia tree under which he had camped. Then he attached the twisted palm-fiber rope that looped through the beast's halter to the pommel of his saddle and set off to find the first enemy camp.

In his saddlebag was a leather tube containing a hand-drawn map prepared by Captain Donaghue at Gordon's headquarters. "Two dozen Mahdist outposts encircle Khartoum," the captain told him, "All within a three-day ride, each manned by 10 to 50 Beja. Most of them are too large to keep secrets about prisoners, and so I have marked the locations of nine smaller camps where Miss Bovet and her guide could be."

Then Donaghue pointed to a spot about 25 miles southeast of Khartoum. "I suggest you begin here, and then…" his finger traced a line from the village of Aulia in the southeast, up north to Tuti Island, then north again to the Sabaloka Gorge. The last potential camp was far to the northwest, in the Omdurman Hinterland.

"God willing, you will find her before you have to make the complete circle."

Donaghue's tone grew serious when he slipped the map back into the tube. "I would never call a man with your experience in war a fool, Thomas, but you are…"

"Addled?" Thomas answered.

The captain grinned. "Something like that. The General was correct when he said the Mahdi will learn that you are here, and what you are doing. Every Beja in every camp will be looking for you. They'll have your balls for breakfast, my friend."

Two hours later Thomas loaded Saher and a pack camel onto a shallow-draft wooden nuggar. The boatman shook his head at the sight of a lone American dressed from head to toe in black and thought that he must be a madman to venture onto the river in the middle of a war. But business had slowed to a trickle, and he had mouths to feed at home. He gladly accepted the handful of coins Thomas dropped into his palm and helped to settle the animals in before pulling up the tattered canvas sail and slipping away from the dock under the watchful eyes of a squad of British marines.

The Nile was wide and sluggish south of Khartoum, flanked by muddy banks and patches of papyrus reeds. Three hours out Thomas saw his first crocodile. The 12-foot reptile slid off the bank, splashed into the calm water, and began to swim lazily alongside the boat. He drew his revolver, uncertain where to aim along the heavily scaled body of the monster, only to have the boatman laugh and motion for him to re-holster his Colt.

"Worry about him when you ride your horse along the riverbanks," the boatman said. "They say crocodiles are attracted to horse sweat. Who knows? A hippo, now, he will attack you at any time for any reason. Watch for them, *sayid*, and do not wait for my permission to fire if one approaches."

Beyond the fertile strip of land that lined the river were arid plains and rocky hills that swept to the horizons. He saw few people and almost no wildlife until dusk, when a humming sound emerged from the reeds that choked the riverbanks and thick clouds of mosquitos swarmed down the river in black waves and forced him to take cover.

The ride from the boat dock to the hills behind Aulia took half the night. He made camp under the sheltering branches of an enormous, bottle-shaped baobab tree, fed Saher and the camel, and pulled cold biscuits, dried meat, and dates out of a saddlebag for his own meal. From here on he would not chance lighting a campfire.

As soon as he wrapped a cloak around his shoulders and leaned against the tree a chorus of high-pitched whooping cackles pierced the darkness. Hyenas. The camel snorted, and Saher stamped and whinnied. Samhi had assured him that hyenas preferred feasting on the flesh of dead animals and would only attack people if they were mad with hunger. He hoped the Bedouin guide was right, but he kept his Colt on his lap and slept fitfully until dawn.

Captain Donaghue estimated that the first Beja camp would be eight to 10 miles due east of Jebel Aulia. The flat, open terrain did not afford much cover, so he rode along the bottom of dry creek beds where he could. He took shelter in a jumble of boulders and napped in their shade until the heat of the day had passed and darkness was settling in.

He checked his gear by starlight, wiped down his rifle and revolver with an oilcloth and filled his ammo pouches. Then he pulled his 9" Sheffield steel Green River Bowie knife from its sheath, spat on the wet stone, and worked the edge to razor sharpness. He had carried the big knife since the Civil War, and he liked everything about it, from its heft to the large clip point with a false edge for stabbing and the black ebony handle and steel guard.

Next, he stood and began working through a series of fighting exercises he learned from a decidedly unorthodox Jesuit priest in New Orleans. He practiced slashing at imaginary faces, throats, and forearms before moving into deadly false-edge back cuts that were accomplished with a quick flick of the wrist to open arteries or sever tendons. Then he leaned into aggressive thrusting, which targeted the stomach, chest, kidneys, and neck. A straight thrust could be a fight-ender, but it was riskier than a slashing move because it required close-in engagement with the enemy.

Finally, when he had worked up a good sweat and was breathing hard, he finished up with a dozen parry-and-deflect exercises and the same number of pass and sidestep moves. The sidestep was a particularly important knife-fighting move; rather than meeting an attack head-on, he had been taught to sidestep, letting his opponents stab or slash before he countered. In a knife fight, the most agile fighter had the advantage.

After an hour of hard practice, he sat on a log and drank from the goat water skin. Then he rested for a half hour until the moonless sky was as dark as black velvet. A few clouds slipped below the stars, but there was no wind, which meant that Beja sentries would not be able to smell him as he approached their camp.

He staked out the camel and gave it food and water and then saddled Saher. He mounted up and patted the Arabian on the neck. "It's just us tonight, boy," he whispered. "I'm counting on you to bring us both back." Then he checked his holster and rifle scabbard and touched his stirrups against Saher's flanks.

He rode in total darkness for a half hour and emerged out of a dry wadi to the glow of campfires 200 yards ahead. He had been much closer to the Beja camp than he thought. It was cold, which meant the warriors would be huddled close to their fires. How many would be there, and would they have sentries posted? He hoped they would; his plan was to scout the perimeter, make a head count of the fighters, and then seek out a sentry and question him about any European prisoners who might be held in camp.

The questioning bit was going to be difficult; he had only a rudimentary knowledge of Arabic, gained mostly during the two and a half weeks he had spent traveling from Tamai to Khartoum. He had been practicing common words, numbers, and phrases over and over aloud as he rode, including "Where is the French woman?"

His Bedouin escorts had been patient instructors, and they heaped praise on his quick command of many of the language basics, but he knew he would not be able to engage in anything like a complete conversation with the Mahdi's men.

He rode through darkness for thirty minutes, emerging from a dry wadi to see campfires glowing 200 yards ahead—closer to the Beja camp than expected. The cold would keep the warriors huddled by their fires. How many were there? Were sentries posted? He hoped so; his plan was to scout the perimeter, count the fighters, and interrogate a sentry about European prisoners.

Questioning would be tough. His basic Arabic, learned over two and a half weeks from Tamai to Khartoum, was limited to practiced words, numbers, and phrases like "Where is the French woman?" His Bedouin escorts had praised his quick grasp of the basics, but a full conversation with the Mahdi's men was beyond him.

'It will have to do,' he thought, approaching the campfires.

If a soldier knew where Heléne was, he'd extract the information and kill him. If the sentry claimed ignorance or refused to talk, he'd die anyway. Thomas would then move to another sentry or ride to the next outpost on Donaghue's map. He was at war, and there was no room for hesitation or sympathy.

He rode slowly over rocky ground, eyes scanning for movement, ears alert for sounds of animals or humans. Saher, sensing the tension, stepped carefully around branches and shale to avoid noise.

At 100 yards, Thomas dismounted, tying Saher to a fallen branch.

A thought struck: what if he didn't return? He fed Saher a handful of grain and molasses from his saddlebag, then untied the rein. If he failed, the stallion could return to Aulia and find a new master.

"I will return," Thomas vowed, walking toward the campfires.

His left hand loosened the strap on his Bowie knife's sheath.

He would return.

~TWENTY SIX~

Beja Camp East of Jebel Aulia

The Beja sentry sat on a flat rock, his head lolling against the upright spear resting between his knees. Fifty yards below his post on the brushy knoll, a scattering of tents were arranged in a semi-circle around two fires. Thomas could see that the man was struggling to stay awake. Not surprising, since no British or Egyptian patrols would ever pass within 20 miles of this tiny outpost, and the only enemies the warrior had to worry about when darkness fell were scorpions and snakes.

He picked his way through the low brush and gravel until he was just a few feet behind the robed warrior and waited, holding his breath and slowly drawing his knife. He was not worried about being seen by anyone in the camp; from his black boots to the black cotton scarf wrapped around his face, he was nearly invisible.

Then, a mass of clouds passed directly overhead, and he heard a high-pitched, wavering howl, followed by another and then another. They started with a series of short, sharp yips that rose into prolonged, eerie wails, carrying far across the desert night. He recognized the distinctive cry of the golden jackal, and slipped forward as their cries broke the stillness and gave him the moment of cover he needed.

He shifted the knife to his right hand, gripped the handle tightly, and lunged forward. His left hand slipped around the sentry's head and cupped his chin as he plunged the knife deep into the man's right side, pulled it out, and plunged it in again. He did not want to hit the spine or any vital organs—yet.

The sentry cried out in shock and instinctively tried to leap up, but Thomas used his third knife thrust to pull the man backwards and into a heap on the hard dirt. The Beja's spear clattered to the ground as

Thomas's knee pressed down in the center of his chest and the point of the Bowie knife blade bit into the skin beneath his chin.

"Samitan wa-illa mut!" –"Quiet or die!"–Thomas barked as he pressed the blade harder and felt it slip another quarter inch into soft flesh. It was one of the Arabic phrases he had practiced for hours on end, and based on the sentry's instantaneous reaction, he had successfully captured the harsh, clipped rhythm of the man's native language.

The warrior's eyes went wide in astonishment, and his arms went limp at his side. Before the man had time to think about fighting back, Thomas pushed his left thumb hard against the man's right eyeball. The message was clear: struggle and you will lose your eye first, and then your life.

Thomas raised his head and looked down into the camp. Eight or nine Beja sat talking and drinking from tin cups on logs around the fire, and he watched as one slipped into a tent. They had heard nothing. It was time to get to business.

"Where is the Frenchwoman?" he asked in Arabic as his eyes bored deep into the sentry's face for any sign of recognition.

"Woman?"coughed the man. "No woman. Beja only."

Thomas was a master at poker. He had been reading bluffs, lies, and tells since he was 10. The man's eyes, plus his voice, told Thomas he was being truthful. He thought for a moment, a hesitation that nearly cost him his life when the man suddenly realized that Thomas' attention had wandered.

The sentry yanked his head back from the tip of the blade, violently arched his back, and twisted to his side so quickly that Thomas was thrown to the ground. The man stretched out his right arm towards the spear lying in the dirt just a foot away and grabbed hold of the shaft. But Thomas moved even faster; he rolled to his knees, raised the Sheffield Bowie above his head with both hands, and thrust it deep into the sentry's side just below his rib cage.

When the warrior tried to use his hands to protect his gut from another stab, Thomas pulled the knife out of his kidney, pushed the man onto his back with his left hand, and shoved all nine inches of his blade under the sentry's rib cage and into his heart.

The Beja warrior exhaled once and then went still.

Despite the cold, Thomas was sweating. He wiped his jacket sleeve across his face, withdrew the knife, and cleaned the blade on the front of the Beja's brown robe. Then he stood and looked down into the camp again. Nothing had changed. The muted chatter and laughter of the warriors drifted up into the clear night sky and was carried away by a soft breeze.

Thomas dropped back to his knees. He had given a lot of thought to this moment, mostly because he knew it would not be enough to simply kill a few of the Mahdi's warriors. With over 15,000 devoted foot soldiers ready to obey his every command, up to and including dying happily for the cause, the deaths of a few dozen or even a few hundred would not be of any concern to their leader.

He needed the Mahdi to believe that kidnapping Heléne had unleashed the desert furies of ancient Arabian legend. As a seer and a visionary, the Mahdi understood the deep mystical and spiritual significance of otherworldly signs and portents, and Thomas was going to make sure the message he left would disturb the Mahdi's sleep far more than the loss of a few of his warriors.

He pulled the dead man's robe open, drew his knife, and with the razor-sharp tip of the blade he etched a quick scarab shape—two curved lines for wings and a "T" for the body—onto the warrior's chest. By the time the corpse was discovered, the blood and dust that settled into it would only make the image appear more prominent. His choice of the scarab had been deliberate.

Heléne and Samhi had spent many hours teaching him about Egyptian culture, art, and religion. The life cycle of the scarab beetle had fascinated ancient Egyptians. It rolls dung into a ball, lays its eggs inside, and the young emerge from what seems like lifeless matter. The ancients saw this as a metaphor for the sun's daily journey–rising anew each morning after disappearing at night and, the god Khepri, depicted as a scarab or a man with a scarab head, embodied this cycle of creation and rebirth, pushing the sun across the sky like the beetle rolled its ball.

The Mahdi could not miss the allusion to the bridge between the living and the dead.

"I am the living," Thomas was saying. "You are the dead."

There was one thing left to add. From his breast pocket he pulled a thin beeswax- and-pigment-infused marking stick that Heléne and her father used to mark pottery shards and other small objects taken from the tombs. It wrote in a bright golden-yellow color, a perfect contrast to the warrior's dark skin. Then he deftly drew the Arabic characters he had practiced 100 times during his long journey to Khartoum in four-inch-high letters just below the scarab carved into the center of the Beja's chest:

لام حبشفا

When he was done, he stood up and examined his handiwork. Even in the darkness the words were clearly visible. The wax pigment would fade in a few days, he knew, but not before the commander of the camp had seen it and shared it with the Beja leaders to whom he reported.

He smiled grimly and recited the words he had just written: "*Alshabah huna* ...... The Ghost is here."

Thomas did not know anything about the protocols that Mahdists armies followed, but he assumed that sentry duty in a Beja camp would not be much different than in a British outpost. The man he had just killed was probably on duty until daylight—still four hours away.

He stooped low and began walking in a circle around the perimeter of the camp. The breeze was picking up into a cold wind, and he was relieved to see the warriors around the fires pull their cloaks tight and scurry towards the warmth of their tents.

When he was halfway around the camp he sighted the other sentry. Unlike his fellow guard, this man was alert. In fact, as Thomas drew within a few feet he realized the tall man had leaned his spear against a rock and was urinating into a bush. Perfect, he thought.

He readied his knife and stepped up just as the sentry was closing the front of his robe. Then his boot crunched on a dried branch, and the man whipped around, pulling a knife from his belt as he spun. Thomas extended his arm outward and stepped to the side, twisting his wrist to a 90-degree angle and slicing upwards to the underside of the man's bicep. Then he swung the knife around in a half circle and cut deep into the wrist tendons on the underside of the soldier's hand.

The sentry's knife flew to the ground, but he was not out of the fight. He swung at Thomas' head with his good fist, but Thomas parried the blow with his left forearm and drove his blade up into the man's armpit. The warrior stumbled back, and Thomas saw that he was about to shout an alarm. He smashed the pommel of his knife into the sentry's mouth, and then a second time onto the bridge of his nose.

A look of surprise crossed the man's face as hot blood gushed down onto his chin and chest, only to be replaced with a look of resignation when Thomas used the knife handle to smash him again and again on the forehead.

The sentry collapsed to his knees, and Thomas pushed him the rest of the way to the ground with his boot. The bicep and wrist cuts were momentarily debilitating, but not fatal. The wound in the armpit was different; judging from the amount of blood flowing onto the ground from under the man's arm Thomas knew he had probably severed the warrior's axillary artery or vein. He had only a few minutes to live.

He hunched down close to the man's head. "Listen to me," he commanded in a low voice. "Where is the Frenchwoman?"

The Beja turned his head to Thomas but said nothing.

"Tell me, and I will send for help," Thomas lied.

The sentry coughed up a thick mass of dark blood, and spat out his last words, "I should have pissed on you."

When he could no longer hear the death gurgles bubbling inside the warrior's body, Thomas felt his neck for a pulse and checked to see that he had stopped breathing. He surveyed the camp a final time, and when he was satisfied that no one was awake he wiped the blood off the man's chest and swiftly carved a scarab into his flesh. Then he carefully applied his message to the Mahdi with the yellow wax pigment and walked back to retrieve Saher.

High above the killing field, blue and grey thunderheads were sweeping north from deep inside the African continent, their jagged peaks swollen with rain from the equator.

~TWENTY SEVEN~

12 Miles Northeast of Jebel Aulia

There wasn't supposed to be a camp here. But as the sun fell below the western hills and stars began to appear, Thomas smelled cookfires on the breeze blowing out of the north. He had been traveling the flat scrubby plain along the eastern bank of the White Nile since dawn and had not encountered man or animal.

So, when he heard faint voices rising out of a wadi a half mile ahead, he knew it must be a Beja outpost. The camp was close to the river, which meant these warriors would be protecting a crossing. If the Mahdi was preparing for the final assault on Khartoum that would make sense.

He drove stakes into the hard dirt between two boulders to tether Saher and the pack camel and then ate a meal of cold hardtack and dried dates. The August heat lingered into the night, and the thick, still air made him long for the cool green river in France where he had lunched with Van Gogh and the farmers.

When it was dark, he checked to see that his Bowie knife was unstrapped, and that the wax marking stick and several lengths of leather strap were in his shoulder pouch. Then he adjusted the black scarf around his face and began picking his way through the thorny bushes and piles of broken shale in the direction of the Beja camp.

He spotted the first sentry–a wiry Mahdist warrior with a spear–pacing near a cluster of thornbushes on the camp's southern edge. Using the scrub for cover he crawled through the sand, his dark clothing blending into the night.

When the sentry turned, he sprang. "Stay quiet or die," he hissed in Arabic as he clamped one hand over the man's mouth and pressed the point of his Bowie against the man's throat.

In a low growl, he asked, "Heléne Bovet-French woman, scientist-where is she?"

He did not know the name, the sentry gasped when Thomas loosened the hand across his mouth, but he did know that a group of prisoners being taken north had passed through this camp several weeks ago.

Suddenly, the man began to struggle. He tried to lurch up, forcing Thomas to drive the nine-inch blade upward through the base of the sentry's skull before he could question him further. The warrior's body slumped noiselessly to the ground, and Thomas quickly carved the scarab-with-a-"T" into his chest.

Then he scrawled "The Ghost Is Here" in red wax pigment across the back of the man's white tunic and stood up.

There were no sounds coming from the camp, now just 75 yards ahead. He began walking around the outpost's perimeter and quickly spotted two more sentries. One was leaning against a wooden tent post; the other was seated on a rock five feet away. They were armed only with swords.

Thomas picked up a fist-sized rock and uncoiled one of the leather straps from his belt. He crept up behind the seated man, looped a leather strap around his neck, and pulled tight. As he tightened his grip, he whispered the command to stay silent and then leaned back as the man flailed and kicked sand.

The sound of the scuffle alerted the other sentry. He raised his sword and took three steps towards Thomas, only to be smashed on the temple with the rock. When the dazed man slumped to the ground Thomas dragged both sentries behind the tent. They were alive, but barely conscious.

He bound their wrists with straps and then kneeled on the chest of the man he had beaten with the rock: "Where is the French woman?" he demanded.

"A woman was at our camp in the Sabaloka Gorge three weeks ago," the man wheezed. "But I did not ask about her name, and I do not know where she is now."

The simple mention of a woman passing through a Beja camp gave him the first feeling of hope he had known in days. Still, he could not risk being discovered; these men would calmly cut his throat if he let them live. They chose to go to war, not me, he thought.

He tightened the straps around the first sentry's neck until the man stopped thrashing and lay still. Then he picked up the stone and slammed it hard on top of the other man's skull. The sentry let out a muffled groan, and as a puddle of blood pooled next to his head, Thomas turned him over and carved the scarab onto his chest.

He did the same with the other sentry before pulling out his wax marking stick and writing his warning to the Mahdi on the back of one man's tunic, and on the sheath of the other man's sword.

Then a shout–the body of the sentry he had silenced with his knife had just been found. He retrieved his leather straps, tightened his scarf, and melted into the darkness.

The two-day ride north along the lush banks of the White Nile to Tuti Island was uneventful. The hard-packed dirt road was heavily traveled by traders and farmers, but no one paid any attention to a lone traveler making his way up the river in the broiling August heat.

Khartoum lay to the island's south, and Omdurman to the west. As he grew close enough to make out the island's crescent-shaped land mass, he was struck by the way it appeared like an emerald jewel rising from the water. The most remarkable sight before him, though, was the way the White and Blue Niles surged together just off the little island's southern tip.

The north-flowing White Nile along which he had been traveling was swollen and muddy from the seasonal rains, while the Blue Nile to the east was filled with rich silt from the Ethiopian highlands. The point where the Blue Nile's darker, soil-rich waters swirled into the lighter colored, slower moving White Nile to form the single great river that wound its way northward was a mesmerizing sight.

Thomas found a corral and stables near a cluster of mud brick huts on the east bank of the river and paid the proprietor to board Saher and the pack camel for the night. He walked to the river's edge where locals were gathered around a pair of wooden docks to fish and trade and asked about the ferries that were the only transportation to and from the island. A half hour and a small handful of copper coins later he was on the deck of a boat operated by the stable owner's son for the ten-minute ride to the dock on Tuti Island.

He could make out rich green grasslands and cultivated fields across the narrow island, where palms and acacia trees dotted the tilled fields. The banks were alive with giant heron and egrets, and when he closed his eyes and listened to the lowing of oxen and the rhythmic splash of the ferrymen's oars, he nearly forgot the purpose of his visit. But only for a moment.

He disembarked the ferry along with two men carrying giant wicker baskets piled high with fresh-baked bread. It was for the Beja garrison they told him, which sat just a few hundred yards away in the middle of the island. He was not concerned with being spotted; a solo traveler dressed like locals moving across the island in the middle of the day was not worthy of anyone's attention.

He fell in with the bakers, struggling to understand their chatter, and doing his best to reply to their questions with simple one-word answers as they followed a well-worn dirt path to the outpost. When they came to a low grass-covered rise above the camp, Thomas bid goodbye to the provisioners and took a seat on a palm tree stump.

The camp was less than 100 yards down the rise. It was compact, functional, and, best of all, unfenced. Seven one-story mud brick structures encircled a square in the center of the compound, and as he watched a handful of Beja came in and out of the buildings, crisscrossing the square as they went about their duties.

Fifty yards to the east a mud brick building sat by itself in the center of a sandy hollow. It had a sloped roof made of sod, no windows, and only one door—a heavy looking timber entry reinforced with steel bands. A small sentry box had been built a few yards away from the building, and Thomas could see movement through the open door.

There was no doubt about the structure's function. No matter where in the world one traveled, a military powder magazine looked the same. Thick walls, no shutters or windows, as few flammable sections as possible, and a location well away from the barracks shouted its purpose. Inside would be a cache of rifles, cases of ammunition, kegs of black powder, cannonballs, and assorted supplies.

He sat beside the withered husk of a fallen baobab tree for three hours, watching the sentries walk their circuits, noting the changing of the guards, calls to prayer and meals, and how people entered and left the compound. With no gate or fence around it, anyone could walk into the camp; getting back out tonight after what he had in mind would probably be a bit more difficult.

He estimated there were 100 to 150 Beja in the camp. He also saw that the sentries did not man posts or patrol the perimeters alone. They worked in pairs of two and three.

He smiled when a realization hit him: the doubled-up sentries were his own damn fault. Word of the Ghost-with his blood-soaked trail of corpses and ancient scarabs carved into lifeless flesh-was probably spreading like wildfire through the Mahdist camps.

When he was satisfied that he had committed the location of each building and shack in the camp to memory, Thomas walked back to the ferry dock. The Nile shimmered green and blue in the afternoon sunshine, and a cooling breeze lifted off the water and drifted across the island. Then a feeling of optimism washed through him, and almost without thinking, he began to whistle a lively shanty he learned years ago while scrubbing the decks of a German warship anchored off the coast of Hawai'i. He had been a stowaway, and his capture and punishment–including being tossed 30 feet down from the deck of the ship into waters filled with razor sharp corals and man-eating sharks–was severe.

Why had the memory of that day brought out a song? Perhaps because he had at least been given a chance; make it safely to shore and you can live out your days. Capture here on Tuti Island would mean only a swift and brutal death, and even if he survived to find Heléne and make it home, this was not a time he was going to remember in song.

Late that afternoon the ferry took him back across the river; he was hungry, and there was work to do before night fell. When he turned down the red dirt path that led to the stables the shanty faded from his lips, and his memory.

The ferryman's family welcomed Thomas for dinner in their simple home with steaming bowls of lamb stew and warm bread, their silence as generous as their hospitality. They didn't question why he needed a private ferry to the island under the cover of darkness, nor did they ask why he insisted on returning before dawn. The gold coin he placed on the table after the meal-along with the promise of another upon his return-was a fortune, more than they could hope to earn in an entire season.

After dinner he went into the stable and stuffed a black cotton sack with rope, candles, a tin of coal oil, and matches from his saddlebag. As he checked over his weapons he looked out the door and through the window of the ferryman's house, where the family was celebrating its windfall. Had he given them enough to buy their silence? Or just enough to make them a target? If the Beja discovered what the ferryman had done, they would kill him, scuttle his boat, burn his house to the ground, and leave nothing but ashes in the sand.

When he started out to find Heléne he chose to go alone. He did not want anyone else to share his fate should he be discovered. Now, watching the ferryman laugh and embrace his wife, he remembered what Herman Melville said when they talked about Ahab and his quest for the great white whale:

"No man is an island."

He waited in the lamp-lit stable for four hours, passing the time by penning letters to Heléne, Bill Cody, Diego and Rosalillia, and his editor at the Chronicle. He sealed them in an envelope addressed to the United States Counsel in Cairo and added a few coins for the post. He did not have much confidence that they would be delivered if something happened to him, but he could not bear the thought of not saying goodbye to the people who were so important in his life. He placed the letter to Cody in the envelope addressed to his editor in San Francisco. Bill would be traveling with his new Wild West show and be hard to find, but Andrew Whitton would see to it that the showman got the letter somehow, someday.

It was after 3 AM when the ferryman came for him. He fed a handful of dried dates to the camel and gave Saher a ration of oats and molasses. Then he checked his gear a final time, slung the bag over his shoulder and walked in silence to the dock alongside the ferry operator, where two of the man's sons were waiting. Thomas hopped into the ferry and stood at the railing as the three men dipped their oars into the placid water and began pulling for the opposite shore. Above them, anvil-shaped blue-black thunderheads piled up as a cold wind began streaming down the river.

No one said a word when Thomas climbed off the ferry and onto the Tuti Island dock a few minutes later. He did not know these men, but he instinctively liked them, and he had no doubt they would be waiting for him to return. When he turned and looked back after he had walked a few yards he saw that they had already settled under blankets on the deck.

Ten minutes later he reached the rise overlooking the Beja camp. Lamplight spilled out of front windows from three of the barracks, which told him that the other buildings were probably deserted. Each occupied barrack was guarded by a single warrior. Two sat on the steps with their heads resting on their knees, while the third leaned against the spear he held upright between his legs.

He passed them by and made his way quietly to the front of the powder magazine, where he knelt behind a hitching post. It looked to be unguarded, and the tiny watch shack was empty, as well. He was just pulling his pack from his shoulder when everything changed: two sentries appeared out of the darkness behind the storehouse carrying tin mugs of tea they had brewed at their campfire 50 yards away.

One of the men set his mug on an upended log, pulled a scrap of white cotton material from his belt and walked towards the brush line behind the magazine. Thomas doubted there was a latrine structure out there, which meant the man would have to dig a hole to get his business done. That meant he had several minutes to deal with the other sentry.

He watched the man lower himself onto a small boulder and slurp at his tea before shouting something at his companion and laughing. Soldier's bathroom humor was the same everywhere, Thomas thought as he stepped quietly up behind the man and garroted him with a length of sisal rope.

When the sentry went still, he dragged the body behind a rock, bent down, and tore open the man's robe. It took only a moment to carve the scarab, but he held off using the wax marker to write his message to the Mahdi.

Instead, he rummaged through a small pile of discarded lumber behind the magazine and pulled out a smooth, light-colored plank. He wrote "The Ghost Is Here" in large, thick red letters and leaned the plank against a boulder. No matter what happened in the next few minutes the plank would eventually be found, and the Mahdi would be informed that the ghostly apparition had once again visited his wrath upon the Beja.

When the roiling mass of clouds that had been building for hours smothered the last glimmer of starlight he slipped behind the powder magazine and opened his bag. Before he could reach for anything, though, a torrent of rain exploded out of the clouds and slammed into the camp—sheets of black water, slanting like daggers in the wind, hammering the ground and buildings. It swept in undulating waves across the compound, drowning torches, seeping into every crevice, and turning the hard-packed earth into a sea of slippery mud.

Rain would not change his plan, but it was going to make things more complicated. First, he had to find the other sentry before the man discovered his comrade's body and raised the alarm. That might not be easy; the dark was absolute, and the thundering rain and wind would drown out any noise the sentry made when he returned from the brush.

He unsheathed his Bowie, feeling its cold steel against his palm, and edged forward, each step tentative in the rain-slick mud. The wind howled through the compound, tearing at his clothes, and the downpour lashed his face like needle stings. He could barely see, forced to squint against the relentless sheets of black rain, but he pressed on, his instincts guiding him toward where he guessed the sentry would emerge from the brush.

A deafening crack of thunder split the air directly overhead, shaking the ground beneath him. For a fleeting moment, doubt clawed at his resolve-should he abandon the plan, retreat to the boat, and finish this fight another day? Then, a blinding fork of lightning slashed across the sky.

For a single heartbeat, the world ignited in white. A face-a shadowed, rain-streaked visage-loomed just a foot away. Wide eyes. A gasp lost to the storm.

Thomas struck first.

His arm drove forward, the Bowie sinking deep into the sentry's abdomen. The warrior's body jerked, but Thomas was already twisting the blade, wrenching it free and plunging it in again—once, twice, a third time. A wet, choking sound escaped the man's lips. His sword, half-drawn, slipped from his grasp. His weight collapsed against Thomas, warm blood mixing with the cold rain, before he slid lifeless into the mud.

Thomas staggered back, his breath heaving, his pulse a thunder of its own in his ears. The night swallowed the scene as quickly as it had revealed it, leaving only the rain, the wind, and the lifeless shape at his feet. He had to move. Now.

Then, as quickly as it had begun, the rain and wind melted into a whisper and then disappeared. The stars re-emerged, and he was able to see the area around the powder magazine again. How long would it be before the sentries he killed were due to be relieved by others? Every second counted now.

He sprinted to the magazine, his breath sharp in his throat, and took the three dirt-carved steps in a single bound. The door was a heavy slab of timber, built to withstand blasts, but its iron hinges were crusted with rust, clinging to the frame with little more than brittle nails. He jammed the back edge of his knife against the first hinge, wrenching it loose with a metallic screech. The second hinge gave way with a crack, and the door dropped forward, slamming to the ground with a dull thud.

The air inside was thick with the scent of powder and aged wood. The faint starlight trickling in revealed rows of stacked rifles, iron-banded ammunition crates, and dozens of 50-pound powder kegs. Cannonballs lay in deliberate piles, their dull surfaces gleaming like malignant eyes in the gloom.

He moved swiftly. From his cotton bag, he pulled a coiled five-foot length of rope, fraying its strands with practiced fingers before dousing them liberally in lamp oil from his pack. The liquid darkened the fibers, glistening in the dim light. He jammed his blade into the nearest keg, twisting hard until black powder spilled onto the dirt floor in a fine, deadly cascade.

With deliberate precision, he arranged loose cartridges in the center of the cluster of kegs, wedging a cannonball against them-an added burst of iron and fire for the carnage to come.

One end of the oil-soaked rope nestled in the spilled powder: the other stretched like a snake toward the doorway. He reached for his matches, then froze. His jaw tightened. He had forgotten something.

He bolted outside, his boots splashing in the soupy mud as he rounded the back of the magazine. The two sentries lay sprawled in the wet dirt where he had drug them. He grabbed the last one and flipped the limp body onto its back. His knife flashed in the starlight as he yanked up the dead man's tunic and carved the scarab deep into his flesh.

Finished, he stepped back to the door and fished a box of wooden matches from his bag. He knelt and struck one against the side of the box–*fshht*–a sudden, flickering glow ignited in his cupped hands. He touched it to the oiled rope and the fuse caught fire with a hissing whisper as a slow crawl of embers began to consume the twisted strands.

He lingered just long enough to ensure the fire had taken hold before rising to his feet and moving out. The compound lay in eerie stillness behind him. That would change before this night's work was done.

The walk from the ferry dock to the outpost had taken 10 minutes. At a fast trot, he figured he could cut that to seven, maybe eight. He was 100 yards from the ferry when the night split open.

The explosion tore through the air with a concussive force that sent a tremor through the ground beneath his feet. He spun, his eyes narrowing against the blinding eruption of fire and smoke. A massive fireball bloomed into the sky, its core a churning inferno of reds and oranges, its edges curling into black smoke. Even from this distance, he saw rifles, shattered wood, and heavy iron spheres catapulted skyward, silhouetted for a brief instant before gravity reclaimed them.

Then came the chaos. Shockwaves rippled outward, rattling the compound, shattering windows, collapsing makeshift shelters. Thousands of rounds of ammunition began cooking off in erratic bursts, snapping and popping like a battlefield caught in an endless, echoing crossfire. He could imagine the panic-men staggering from their barracks, shouting, and scrambling for weapons that had already been reduced to splinters and flames.

Thomas turned his back on the wreckage and sped up his pace. By the time the Beja realized what had happened, he would be nothing but a ghost in the dark.

~TWENTY EIGHT~

Desert West of Khartoum

When the Bedouin poet paused to sip his glass of mint tea, Heléne quietly excused herself and slipped out of Sheikh Abu Sinn's opulent tent. A week earlier, the Sheikh would have insisted that a bodyguard escort her up the rise and stand watch outside the privy. But after days of walking the camp's perimeter alone and lending a hand with chores, she had become a familiar, almost invisible presence.

No one in the Sheikh's entourage gave her movements a second glance. After all, where could the Frenchwoman go? For 30 miles in all directions there was only sand, dirt, rocks, and thorn bushes.

Heléne's insistence on going out into the cold night to use the bathroom amused the Sheikh's wives. They were content to use the ceramic chamber pots under their beds and had no qualms about other women being present when they relieved themselves. The servants, of course, had to hike out into the brush to do their business, while the Sheikh enjoyed a luxurious blanket-lined enclosure with a raised wooden seat, warm water, scented candles, and a bucket of ashes to sprinkle into the deep hole after each use.

It wasn't modesty that drew Heléne to hike to the far edge of the encampment to use the Sheikh's privy-it was distance. She wanted the guards to be at ease with her absences to the point where they didn't even look up when she walked past them and vanished from view. When the time came to slip away for good, she would have a long head start.

Beneath her bed a canvas bag was slowly filling with the slivers of dried meat and fruit she snuck from the table. And each morning before the sun burned the dunes gold, she slipped into the paddock to work with the Sheikh's black-blooded stallion. She also passed her hours working with his Saluki hunting hounds-creatures with the slender grace of aristocrats and the instincts of assassins, bred for the chase and the kill.

Now, one of them, a broad-chested male with eyes like molten amber, padded silently at her side as she climbed the hill. Above her, the sky hung black and endless, jeweled with a thousand sharp stars. When she reached the privy and drew back the embroidered curtain, the hound lay down outside without command.

A candle burned on a shelf, its flame flickering in the draft that slipped through the seams of the woolen fabric. Beside a basin of warm, lavender-scented water sat a tin of soap, the steam curling gently into the cool night air. From the main tent below, she heard the voice of the poet—the Sheikh's guest this week—rising in a measured, melodic cadence. He recited in Arabic Heléne could only partly understand, recounting the ancient sea battle in which his Bedouin ancestors had stood against Rome two thousand years ago.

She had begun to pick up fragments of the language-words for hunger, water, light-but the meanings that shimmered beneath the poet's performance eluded her. The audience murmured with quiet reverence; each turn of phrase met with nods and knowing glances.

When she stood to wash her hands, her fingers hovering above the basin, she heard the low, guttural growl of the Saluki.

Then came the sound of tearing fabric.

The privy curtain ripped open, and the candle's flame jumped wildly as a figure stepped inside, silhouetted against the star-pricked sky. He was tall and sharp-featured. A heavy beard cloaked his face in shadows and his chest heaved with heavy breaths.

Below the waist, he wore nothing. He was fully aroused.

Heléne froze, her pulse thundering in her ears.

She stepped back, instinctively searching for shelter in the tiny space, but there was nowhere to go. Her revolver was under her bed, useless now. She reached for anything, anything—and threw the water basin at his head. It clipped his cheek, spraying lavender-scented water across the embroidered curtains. He laughed-a short, jagged sound.

Then he reached for her. One hand found her shoulder, the other groped at her breast. She shoved her palm against his cheek and raked her fingernails down his face, drawing hot lines of blood.

He snarled, and then his fist cracked against her jaw, once-then again in the stomach. The air vanished from her lungs.

I can't go to the ground, she thought, teeth clenched against the black haze closing in. This is not going to happen.

He seized her robe and began to rip it open. She struck him again-both hands slamming against his ears. He only laughed, louder this time, and tugged harder at the fabric.

She fought with everything-slaps, punches, scratches-but none of it mattered. Her blows landed like feathers on stone. Who is he? she wondered in a haze of pain and panic.

Then she realized: the Saluki hadn't stopped barking.

A heartbeat later, the dog was inside-a blur of speed and muscle and white-hot fury. The hound launched at the man's leg, teeth sinking deep into flesh. There was a terrible, wet sound as the dog shook its head, tearing into him. The man screamed and tried to kick the animal off, but it held fast, low growls vibrating through the cramped space.

Heléne pressed herself against the back wall of the tent, breathing in shallow gasps, the air thick with sweat and blood and lavender. She prayed the man would tear free and flee, that this would end in flight, not more pain.

But then-a shout.

Boots. Yells. Movement. And then the entire privy tent was yanked free from its pegs and flung aside like kindling. Moonlight poured in as four of the Sheikh's guards stormed forward.

In the chaos, hands grabbed the hound, dragged it back, while others tackled the attacker to the ground.

The man screamed again-less like a predator now and more like prey.

Heléne stood motionless, her chest rising and falling, her limbs trembling. Her robe hung in tatters, and one cheek was already swelling where the blow had landed. As she took a deep breath for the first time in several minutes, she noticed that between the dog bites and the violent take-down by the guards, her attacker's aroused condition had melted away. She had no doubt that the desert justice that was about to be meted out on the man would ensure that he never enjoyed that condition again.

She inhaled fully-for the first time in minutes-and let the breath go slowly, her fingers still curled into fists. The Saluki turned once to look at her, blood coating its muzzle. Then it sat at her feet, its flank rising and falling with the effort of battle.

She reached down and touched its head.

"You waited," she whispered. And then, thinking of Thomas, she allowed herself to cry.

The sky melted into hues of deep indigo and burnt rose, casting long violet shadows across the sand as the Mahdi paced the rocky banks of the wadi. The seasonal river, swollen by rains, churned below him with a restless current, as though the earth itself murmured secrets he was not meant to hear. Thirty-five miles to the northeast, the Frenchwoman remained a prisoner-but until an hour ago, he'd felt no urgency to decide her fate.

Then came the rider. Dust-caked, breathless, and pale beneath his orange turban, the man had dismounted without a word and knelt. He presented three items with trembling hands: a white robe, a blood-smeared leather sheath, and a plank of painted wood. Only after the Mahdi lifted the parchment did the messenger speak, his voice hoarse: "From the Beja commander at Tuti Island, sayyid. May God protect you."

The words in the letter cut deep. Twelve of his men gone. Seven had been knifed, garroted, or crushed with stones. The remaining five had vanished in the fireball that consumed the garrison's powder magazine. But it was not the deaths that set the Mahdi's stomach to churning. He had long since ceased to mourn individual warriors. Thousands had already found their way to Paradise beneath his black banners.

No, it was how they died-and what had been left behind.

The commander's sketch showed it clearly: scarabs carved into the flesh of the dead. The phrase "The Ghost is Here" scrawled in colored wax and blood-on chests, robes, the sheath of a fallen sword, and again on the wooden plank now lying at the Mahdi's feet. The handwriting was slow, deliberate. Ritualistic.

He bent, picked up a stick, and cast it into the stream. It was carried away at once, disappearing into reeds already pale with the season's end.

Soon the rains would stop, and the wadi would dry-just another ghost of what had briefly flourished.

But this ghost... this one would not pass so easily.

A tall figure in black had been seen walking away from Tuti moments before the explosion. A man, perhaps. But the Mahdi was not quick to dismiss the supernatural. Not in this land. Not now. Whoever-or whatever-had left those marks understood too well the sacred power of symbols. The scarab was no random choice. It was transformation. Resurrection. Judgment. Only the year before he had laid a scarab amulet over his own dead father's heart to guide him safely into the afterlife.

And now someone was using that same symbol to speak to him.

The Mahdi turned slowly, as if expecting eyes behind the stones. The desert had always belonged to shadows-but this? This was different.

It could not be the British. None of their soldiers would know how to invoke such magic. Nor was it the work of any Arab tribe. No devout soul-Muslim or pagan-would risk inviting such wrath upon themselves. Unless, of course, it wasn't a man at all.

His thoughts slipped into older truths and tales of the jinn-the beings of smokeless fire, unseen, ancient, and terrible. In the villages along the Nile, no one poured boiling water at night without uttering a prayer. No one walked into the brush to relieve themselves without first whispering a blessing, lest they offend one of the hidden ones. Could this Ghost be one of them? Or something worse?

Was there a connection between these events and the Frenchwoman and her archeologist father who were being held prisoner on his behalf? And was it possible that his quest to find an explanation for the extraordinary painting on the wall of Amenhotep's burial chamber that presaged his own death might also have something to do with the Ghost? He did not believe in coincidence; the Ghost and the tomb were somehow intertwined.

The first stars blinked into the darkening sky. The moon, thin and yellow, cast trembling silver across the water. Behind him, in the camp, 5,000 seasoned warriors stood ready. Hundreds of horses. Cannon. Camels. No army on this continent could touch him.

But the Ghost had touched him.

Man, demon, or jinn-this enemy had entered sacred ground, and challenged him on a level no British general ever could.

The Mahdi stared into the shadows that gathered along the riverbank.

Soon, they would meet. And one of them would be cast into the black pit of eternity.

~TWENTY NINE~

Near Sabaloka Gorge, the 6th Cataract

Thomas fled north from Tuti Island, traveling two nights along the Nile, skirting small villages and lush banana plantations. Now, the fertile river plain yielded to stark scrublands and dry wadis, guiding him toward the gorge and the Beja camp beyond.

Saher and the pack camel moved with deliberate care, their hooves stirring the loose gravel at the base of the volcanic hills. The silhouettes of the towering rocks loomed like dark sentinels as the narrow throat of the Sabaloka Gorge rose before him.

The night air was cooler now, but still heavy with humidity. He welcomed the relief from the relentless sun, but the silence gnawed at him. There was no voice to answer his thoughts, no idle conversation to distract him. Alone with Saher, the only sound was the soft jangle of the camel's harness and the occasional clatter of dislodged stones.

It was not the desert that unnerved him. Thomas had learned to endure the dangers of these lands-the possibility of an ambush, the sudden glare of a rifle barrel from the shadows. No, it was the unbidden thoughts that plagued him. He had spent much of his life outrunning such reflections, filling the quiet with laughter, beautiful women, drink, cards, and the clamor of cities. But here, the desert allowed no escape. The wind tugged at his coat like a restless spirit, and the stars above burned with a cold, distant fire.

Moby-Dick. The name floated to the surface of his mind, unshakable. He had read Melville's tale twice since their meeting four months ago, and images of the storm-lashed deck of the Nantucket whaling ship

Pequod, and the relentless captain's gaze fixed on the pale leviathan-a pursuit that consumed all reason–kept appearing before him. Captain Ahab's single-minded vengeance had dragged his crew into the abyss, where the white whale loomed as both a beast and a symbol, a reflection of the man's own monstrous fixation.

And what of him? Thomas could not deny the echo of Ahab's obsession in his own present circumstance. His search for Helène had become its own unrelenting pursuit. Every step through the desert, every risk, every life he had taken-they all formed the path he now followed. Ahab's ghost seemed to ride with him, whispering the question he dared not contemplate: was it truly love that guided him, or something darker?

Ahead, the gorge narrowed, its jagged walls closing in around him. Moon-cast shadows moved with the wind, flickering across the stone like waves on the shore. Thomas clenched the reins and focused on the danger ahead. The Beja camp could not be far from here. He would find Helène. He would tear apart the sands and face whatever lay ahead. But the fear gnawed at him still-when the pursuit was over, what would remain of the man who had begun it?

He recalled Ahab's words: *"All my means are sane; my motive and my objective are mad."* Thomas felt the parallel to his own circumstance like a knife's edge. The captain had chased Moby Dick to prove something-to himself, to God, to the void. What was Thomas trying to prove?

Then Saher stumbled on a stone, jarring him back to the present. He'd read Melville's words about the whale's "inscrutable malice," and now he saw it mirrored in the desert's vast indifference and in the Mahdi's unyielding zeal. Heléne was out there, somewhere beyond the gorge, and he'd ride to the ends of the earth for her. Yet, as the night deepened and the stars glittered like ice crystals across the dome of the heavens, Thomas Scoundrel feared he was becoming his own Ahab-driven, yes, but perhaps doomed by the very fire that propelled him forward.

Saher's ears flicked at some distant sound, but Thomas took no notice. The night wore on, but the stars offered no comfort, only their cold, eternal witness.

He slept restlessly until noon in the shade of a granite outcrop, 100 yards from a reed-filled water hole. Leading his animals to drink, he saw a man in a tattered cloak approach, guiding a donkey carrying a woman with a baby. Bedouin tradition forbade violence near water, with beheading as the penalty for defiance. Thirst spared no one, rich or poor.

Thomas welcomed the couple with a nod and stood quietly as the man helped his wife down and then filled two gourds with water from the spring. Judging from their gaunt appearances, these two had been struggling for some time. He went to his pack camel and filled several canvas bags with dried dates, sorghum flour to make porridge, several pounds of pemmican and hard tack biscuits, dried goat cheese, ground coffee and sugar, and a week's ration of chickpeas and lentils for soup.

The man shook his head when Thomas set the bags at his feet.

"*Shkran lak*, thank you, but I have no money to purchase your food," he said. "We are only a few days from my family's village and will make do with what we have."

Thomas saw hunger and pain etched on the woman's face. If she wasn't eating, she wasn't producing milk for the baby. A few days would be too long.

He understood Bedouin pride. No man could accept a gift without providing something of equal value in return. He smiled and said, "I am a stranger here, and this is my thanks to your family for allowing me passage through your lands."

He watched the woman's pleading eyes search her husband's face, and when he signaled acceptance of the gift, she tore into the bags and pulled out a handful of dates and several biscuits and pieces of cheese for herself and her husband. When Thomas settled onto a rock beside her husband at the edge of the water, she pressed the baby to her breast and began to feed it.

"Where do you journey to?" the man asked as he ate.

"To the camp of the Beja," replied Thomas.

The man looked startled. "But you are English, no? Do you seek your death?"

"I am an American, and what I seek is information about the whereabouts of my friend, a Frenchwoman named Heléne Bovet. She was taken on the order of the Mahdi, and I wish to bring her back."

The man let out a low whistle. "The Mahdi. A man of great power."

Thomas knew the Bedouin people had no love for the Mahdi, who had brought only death and destruction to their doors since he began the revolt against British and Egyptian rule.

"A man of great evil," he answered.

"I know where the Beja are encamped," the man said when he finished eating. "Three, maybe four hundred. A half day's ride to the north. Turn east at the red shale escarpment and follow the stream that feeds the Nile from the mountains."

"Are sentries posted?"

"Yes, and quite cleverly. As we passed two of them openly guarding the trail into the camp, I saw a glint of steel and looked up to see two more hiding on a hillside behind a pile of rocks and brush. They can see anyone coming up from the river."

"Are there trails in the hills above them?" asked Thomas.

The man nodded. "Yes, but only a goat trail, too narrow for your horse and camel. You will see the trailhead beside the stump of an acacia tree on which three rocks have been piled as a sign to other Beja coming into the camp. It winds into the hills above and behind the sentries in the rocks. They will not see you."

When Thomas rose to leave, he went over to Saher and dug into his saddlebag. Then he went back to the man and pressed a gold coin into his hand.

"But this is a fortune," said the man, "Enough to buy three sheep and a goat. I cannot accept this."

Thomas swung up into the saddle. "You can," he said, "for your wife and child."

As the man shook his head in wonderment and his wife beamed up at him, Thomas looped the camel's reins around the back of his saddle and rode off in the direction of the Beja camp.

Moonlight bathed the desert in silver. Thomas staked out Saher and the camel in a tangle of acacia trees and began the climb up the narrow goat trail that coiled upward into the jagged hills. The Bedouin at the water hole had been right-the path was treacherous. At its narrowest, it was scarcely wider than his boot, and a single misplaced step would send him tumbling down several hundred yards of loose volcanic rubble onto the jagged rocks below.

After an hour of hard climbing he reached the summit and looked down on a camp that stretched for 100 yards along the river, alight with dozens of campfires. Below him, a lone cloaked sentry stood, his spear casting a long shadow in the bright moonlight.

Thomas uncoiled a length of leather strapping from his pack. He moved across the volcanic rubble in silence and whipped the strap around the sentry's neck, yanking it tight. The sentry's body convulsed, his hands clawing at the leather. They staggered backward, then toppled to the earth. Thomas dropped his weight on the thrashing form, pinning him. The knife gleamed beneath the moon, its tip pressing just below the warrior's chin.

"Quiet," Thomas commanded.

Moonlight caught the sentry's face when Thomas pulled back his hood. Wide eyes. Soft cheeks. He was no older than 12 or 13.

"Damn," Thomas muttered under his breath. A child.

He slid off the boy and motioned for him to sit up against a large rock. Then he used the leather strap to tie the boy's wrists together behind his back and used another strap to bind his ankles together.

The young sentry was trembling, and tears were forming in his eyes.

"Are you alone up here?" Thomas asked.

The boy shook his head. "Another is with me, just below. He stands watch in front of a row of bushes."

"And is he also just a boy?"

"No, master…he is an officer."

Thomas thought a moment. "Do you know anything of a Frenchwoman who came through this camp under escort three or four weeks ago?"

"*Naeam*, yes, I do. I saw them take her from a camel and walk her to a tent. She was gone the next day."

"Do you know where they were taking her?"

"I do not, master," the boy answered in a quivering voice.

"And the officer below. Might he know?"

"He would know more than I."

Thomas pulled a strip of cotton fabric from his pouch and stuffed it into the boy's mouth so he could not call out for help. It would only take him a few minutes to work it loose, but by then the Ghost would be gone.

He stood and slipped his knife back into its sheath. A well-worn path pointed downhill, where the officer would be on watch. Whatever the man did or did not know, Thomas was buoyed by the news that he was getting closer to finding Heléne.

As he stepped onto the path he looked back at the boy whose life he had spared. Perhaps there was less of Ahab in his soul than he had feared.

It was odd that the campfires in the Beja garrison had not been banked for the night. They were either preparing to march out soon to join the main Mahdist forces assembling around Khartoum or they might be anticipating an attack from the flotilla of iron-clad British gunboats that patrolled the Nile in search of enemy outposts to shell.

It only took a few minutes to move stealthily down to the officer's position. The man was seated on a log, gazing down towards the river. Something was going on, Thomas thought. A short sword lay close by, and a rifle rested against the trunk of a gnarled tree within easy reaching distance.

He wished the moon was not so bright, or at least that some cloud cover could form and help hide what he was about to do from prying eyes in the camp below. Men were moving about in small knots and organizing into separate formations of 10 or 12 warriors each. They were moving out…

He drew his Bowie knife and stepped to within five feet of the officer. One more round of questions, one more death, one more scarab carved into flesh, and he would be on his way to the next Beja camp. He hoped this man knew something.

Then, movement. Two forms appeared out of the brush and came to a halt in front of the officer. Before Thomas could react, a dozen more shapes materialized out of the darkness and formed up into a semi-circle around the them. The Beja warriors were armed, and they were staring right at him.

Thomas' hand went to his revolver even as his brain told him that was a futile gesture, but the moonlight bathing the hill answered another question: he could now see the first people who had stepped out from the brush; it was the couple he had met at the watering hole. A warrior was pressing a spear into the man's back from behind, and when the Bedouin made eye contact with Thomas, he shook his head in sorrow. His wife was beside him, clutching her baby tight against her breast. She looked terrified.

Thomas froze. He had no doubt that the Beja would have killed these two and their baby had they not given up his plans. Then the officer stood and turned towards him.

"Torch," he called out, and a man rushed forward carrying a blazing pitch torch. The officer held it high, searching Thomas' features.

"Tahiaati sadiqi, greetings my friend," the officer finally said in a low voice tinged with sarcasm. The dozen warriors who had melted out of the brush kept moving until they formed a circle completely around Thomas.

"Shall I address you as Colonel Scoundrel, or do you prefer to be called 'The Ghost?' "

Thomas shook his head and almost chuckled. "Son of a bi…" he began. He let the words fade away.

"Hundreds of the Mahdi's best men have been searching across the great desert to find this ghost," said the officer. "Ironic, is it not, that it would be a goat herder and his woman who finally brought the chase to an end."

The man Thomas had helped at the watering hole bit his lip and clenched his fists. To Thomas' surprise the man's wife looked into his eyes and mouthed, "God bless and keep you."

The officer stepped over in front of Thomas.

"I ask you in the name of your God not to harm these people," Thomas said. "They have done your Mahdi no wrong."

The officer smiled. "Despite what you may have heard, Colonel, we people of the deserts are not barbarians. These two shall be allowed to pass, and they shall keep the gifts you gave to them."

Thomas nodded. "God's praise on you," he said quietly.

The officer acknowledged the traditional Bedouin complement with a dip of his head, and then replied, "Unfortunately, Colonel, my God's protection does not extend to you."

He raised one hand, and something heavy struck Thomas on the back of the head.

His knees buckled, and the heavens went black.

~THIRTY~

Headquarters of the Mahdi, 40 miles SW of Khartoum

The raven-tressed young woman wheeling the cart into the dining room was stunning. Her low-cut, form-fitting royal purple dress was adorned with hundreds of silver and gold sequins, and her cheeks and lips were masterfully highlighted in subtle shades of sunset red.

That would have been an extraordinary sight anywhere in the world, but this was the headquarters of the Mahdist forces in Sudan, not an elegant restaurant in the heart of New York City. And how to account for the three other equally beautiful young women seated at the long oak table? They were engaged in lively banter with a trio of prosperous looking older European gentlemen while their host looked on from his seat at the head of the table with a fatherly smile.

The woman with the cart paused as a thin Frenchman stepped forward. He was impeccably dressed in formal evening wear, his waxed mustache curled to perfect symmetry. Around his neck, a slender gold chain bore a shallow silver cup-a tastevin, the mark of a master sommelier. Thomas recognized it instantly, a symbol of connoisseurship from the world's most exclusive dining rooms.

The Frenchman cleared his throat, commanding the room with a subtle flourish of his white-gloved hand. The chatter dimmed, and the guests turned their attention to him.

"*Mesdames et messieurs,*" he began, his voice smooth and practiced. "It is my profound pleasure to introduce the wines that will accompany your meal this evening. Each selection has been chosen to reflect the finest traditions of the table, inspired by the culinary artistry of my esteemed countryman, the great Auguste Escoffier. Indeed, your courses shall be served in the elegant style that has dazzled the patrons of the Ritz in Paris and the Carlton in London."

With reverence, he reached down to the cart, lifting a slender green bottle. The foil caught the candlelight, gleaming like a precious jewel.

"Let me first present to you a Louis Roederer Brut, 1877," he declared, his voice lilting with pride. "A champagne of rare finesse, its golden bubbles promise a beginning as magnificent as the evening itself."

The room murmured its approval, glasses clinking softly. Yet even as the sommelier spoke, Thomas could not shake his sense of bewilderment at a display of such opulence and elegance while outside the dining room doors tens of thousands of soldiers spread across a landscape larger than France and Britain combined were engaging in ferocious combat.

It had been a week of such contradictions and revelations. After his capture at Sabaloka Gorge he had traveled under heavy escort for two days to the Mahdi's headquarters southwest of Khartoum where one- and two-story mud-brick buildings were scattered along the banks of a dry riverbed that only filled with water during the fleeting rains. At first glance, the place was unimposing. But when his gaze shifted eastward, he estimated that there were at least 5,000 warriors encamped among the brush and boulders. Beyond them, hundreds more manned cannons on the low hills, the black iron mouths trained toward Gordon's beleaguered forces at Khartoum.

When they arrived in late afternoon, Saher was led away to the stables and Thomas was taken to a small room with whitewashed walls and a single window overlooking an enclosed garden, where slender palms swayed against the sun-bleached sky. Beyond the garden, the river traced a dull, silver line along its rocky banks. The guards remained outside his door.

An hour later a servant arrived with a flagon of warm water and a wash basin. She also brought his saddlebags, which had been stripped of everything but his clothing and toiletries. Someone would fetch him for dinner soon, she informed him, and suggested he change into clean attire. His dust-streaked khakis would be laundered and returned by morning.

As the afternoon began to fade to twilight, the searing August heat was softened by a breeze that slipped off the river, stirring the air and rustling the garden leaves. Thomas bathed, shaved, and pulled on his best shirt and trousers. Just as the light outside began its descent into gold and violet, the guards came for him. Without saying a word, they led him through the garden, and along a smooth, well-worn flagstone path where shadows were gathering beneath arched beams.

When they came to a set of heavy oak doors the guards swung them open and gestured for him to enter.

Thomas found himself in a cool, whitewashed anteroom. The walls were adorned with oil landscapes, which he recognized as the refined brushstrokes of the French Academy, depicting green pastoral scenes far removed from the parched earth outside. Chinese ceramic vases sat on low pedestals, their glazes catching the fading light. But it was the Japanese bonsai in a jade container that held his gaze—a magnificent tree, more than three feet high, its gnarled branches coaxed over many years into a patient, deliberate form.

Before he could take in more, the door across the room opened. A servant waited, head bowed, motioning for him to proceed.

The room had a tall ceiling, and a bank of windows high along the wall above the river were open to catch the evening breeze. Light from oil lamps on the sideboards and the massive oak dining table reflected off the ornate, gilded mirrors spaced artfully around the walls, bathing the room in soft golden light.

The other guests had already gathered, glasses of sherry in hand, their laughter mingling with the lyrical voices of their Bedouin companions. Thomas observed them with curiosity. European businessmen, perhaps? They would hardly be diplomats or politicians—diplomacy had long since crumbled beneath the weight of war. No negotiation could bridge the chasm between the Mahdists and the Empire now.

A servant guided him to a seat at the foot of the table. The placement was deliberate. Close enough to hear the hum of conversation, but distant enough to mark him as an outsider. A glass of sherry appeared before him, along with a pitcher of cold water. None of the other guests acknowledged him. He was simply a presence to be tolerated but not seen.

Then the door at the far end of the room swung open. A tall figure strode in, clad in indigo robes edged with gold. His step was unhurried, yet every movement carried the weight of command. The chatter at the table hushed. The man paused at the head of the table, his gaze sweeping over the gathering—first to his European guests, then, with a slight, almost unreadable nod, to Thomas.

Thomas raised his glass, the rim brushing his lips. Then he realized that the man who had just acknowledged him could only be one person: The Mahdi. The powerful mystic, the self-proclaimed redeemer, the leader who had summoned 100,000 men to arms and who dreamed of expelling the foreign powers and establishing his own caliphate.

Thomas put his glass down so quickly that a few drops of sherry spilled onto the starched linen tablecloth and then watched in disbelief as the Mahdi reached for his own glass of sherry, lifted it to his lips, and downed it in one steady gulp. He extended the empty glass to a waiting servant, who dutifully refilled it.

This was the Mahdi?

The fabled ascetic-the man whispered about in every market stall and around every warrior's campfire as a prophet who had renounced indulgence, embraced hardship, and devoted his soul to prayer, fasting, and self-denial? The same Mahdi who, it was said, refused the touch of women, survived on a monkish diet of gruel, dates, and coarse bread, and who thundered against the decadence of the West? The Mahdi who had outlawed music, burned paintings, and decreed death for anyone caught with so much as a European or American novel.

Thomas's mind spun. The man before him was no starved mystic wrapped in rags of righteousness. No desert-worn prophet hollowed by faith. He was something else entirely-something stranger, more dangerous. A desert paradox in silks and wine.

When the sommelier uncorked the first bottle of champagne, the three European gentlemen applauded lightly. Their crystal stems were soon filled, each glass catching the flickering light like liquid gold. Then Mahdi raised his own glass: "To the gods of wine and food," he declared in flawless French, his voice rich and deliberate. "May they bless our meal and sanctify our business."

Thomas blinked. Business?

He didn't mask his confusion quickly enough. The Mahdi caught the look, his eyes glittering with amusement. With a subtle nod, he summoned another bottle of the brut to be opened. As the cork popped and fresh flutes were poured, the Mahdi gestured toward Thomas.

"I believe introductions are in order," he said. "Gentlemen, ladies, allow me to present Colonel Thomas Scoundrel-American officer, intrepid newspaper correspondent, and, most recently..."

He let the moment linger, tasting the silence.

"How shall I describe his current profession?" he mused aloud, his smile edged with mischief. "Despoiler of ancient tombs? Wandering spirit of the dunes?"

He set his glass down and leaned forward.

"Or perhaps... an avenging ghost?"

His gaze locked with Thomas's, and for an instant, everything else fell away. Laughter, candlelight, the gleam of crystal and silk-all faded beneath the quiet, piercing recognition that passed between them. Not just a host and his guest. Not just enemies across a table. Something older, and more elemental. Prophet and unbeliever. Two men in the eye of a gathering storm.

"Ah, but where are my manners," the Mahdi said, his voice velvet-smooth, carrying a practiced charm. "Colonel Scoundrel has yet to be introduced to my business associates. Forgive us, Colonel. As you can well imagine, international dealings such as mine require the utmost discretion. War has a curious way of distorting political sympathies-and I dare say Prime Minister Gladstone would take a dim view of the nations with whom I have, let us say, mutually advantageous arrangements.

The three gentlemen down the table nodded, and one raised his glass and said, "Here here."

The Mahdi turned back to Thomas. "You may be aware that Nicholas III of Russia believes salvation lies in severing ties with the corrupting influence of Western Europe, particularly Germany and England. France, wisely, has chosen to stand beside Russia. Their vision aligns quite comfortably with my own."

"You mean to extend your Caliphate to England?" Thomas asked, dryly.

The Mahdi chuckled, swirling his champagne. "No, Colonel. I merely wish to be left alone to shape my world without foreign interference. Sudan, Egypt, perhaps what remains of the Ottoman Empire. My ambitions are hardly as global as yours. These gentlemen," he gestured with his flute, "represent munitions manufacturers from Russia and France. Tonight's meal is their generous gift. Can you believe they chartered a ship to deliver an entire French kitchen, chef, and staff to this desert outpost?"

As if summoned by cue, the tall double doors creaked open behind Thomas. A middle-aged man in impeccable chef's whites entered with theatrical precision. He bowed slightly, then began to recite the menu in lyrical French-accented English, pausing just long enough to tantalize.

"We begin with *Huîtres au Champagne* –oysters served raw on the half-shell with a sabayon of champagne, egg yolk, lemon, and a touch of caviar."

"Accompanied," the sommelier interjected smoothly, "by the Louis Roederer Brut, a vintage first presented to Tsar Alexander II himself. It is mature yet crisp at seven years old, and you will feel effervescence cutting through the oysters' brininess."

Two of the European men raised their glasses at the mention of the Tsar, as much in respect as to indicate that their glasses were empty.

Thomas sat unmoving, his thoughts spiraling. This entire affair was surreal: the Mahdi-his sworn enemy, the scourge of British Sudan-was wining and dining arms dealers while offering his American prisoner a seat at the table. Every man here was playing with fire. The British Empire would never tolerate such treachery. And yet-here they were, sampling oysters and fine wine in the heart of rebellion.

"The cream of carrot soup will be paired with a Savennières, Château de Chamboureau, '81," the sommelier continued. "Followed by Turbot with Mussels and Cider Sauce served with Chablis Grand Cru Les Clos, Domaine Vincent Dauvissat, '79."

The chef nodded. "A creamy sauce of Normandy cider and shallots, finished with calvados. A delicate puff pastry to garnish."

As the litany of delicacies unfolded-beef tenderloin *en croûte*, roast pheasant with grapes, and a procession of exquisite wines-Thomas found his gaze locked on the Mahdi. He saw not a religious visionary, but a cold-eyed tactician playing host to death itself. This man had kidnapped Samhi, Helène, and her father. He had drenched Sudan in blood at Tamai, where British soldiers-his comrades-had died by the hundreds.

Ahmad bin Abdullah. Not a prophet. A fraud. A butcher in borrowed robes.

The Mahdi caught his stare. As servants wheeled in the oysters and steaming bowls of soup, he addressed Thomas without shifting his gaze.

"Does this offend you?" he asked softly, gesturing to the feast.

Thomas said nothing.

The Mahdi smiled. "My father was a wealthy merchant. He insisted I study the world. I lived in Paris for three years. London for one. As you can see, I developed certain...appreciations."

"Was mass murder, the destruction of a nation, kidnapping, and wholesale theft part of that education?" Thomas asked. He doubted he'd live to see the morning and so had no qualms about confronting the great man who could–with a wave of his hand–have him impaled with a spear before the filet was served.

The Europeans were occupied with the procession of extraordinary food and the attentions being lavished on them by their beautiful companions and paid scant attention to the skirmish going on between their host and the American Colonel.

"You're quick to condemn," said the Mahdi. "May I call you Thomas? How many men have you killed since your quest to aid Miss Bovet and her father began? From the man you threw out of your hotel window in Constantinople to the assassin in the Alexandria catacombs-yes, Thomas, I know about that one, too, you yourself have committed murder after murder."

"Self-defense is not murder, Ahmad."

The Mahdi was not surprised that Scoundrel knew his real name. "And the Beja fighters you helped to massacre with gatling guns at Tamai, and the sentries and warriors in my camps whose lives you took without provocation? Were those murders justified?"

The sommelier was at his elbow now, pouring a deep ruby stream of Château Lafite Rothschild, Pauillac, '70 to accompany the pastry-wrapped beef tenderloin. The wine caught the candlelight like blood, and the master of wines waited expectantly as Thomas took a deep drink and set down his glass. He couldn't help but chuckle at the thought that this superb and complex Cabernet Sauvignon would be the last wine he ever tasted.

He thanked the wine steward and then looked back at Ahmad. "You declared war on England. On Egypt. On my friends, and on me. The men I killed would have slit my throat without hesitation. I chose to survive."

The Mahdi studied him, then gave a slow nod. "But I have been ignoring my other guests," he finally said. "We shall continue this discussion later."

As Ahmad began speaking with the arms merchants, Thomas slid the bottle of Lafite closer and topped off his glass.

~THIRTY ONE~

A breeze stirred the reeds, carrying with it the smell of wet earth and morning smoke from distant cookpots where meals were being prepared for thousands of warriors. The Mahdi's sandals whispered through the sand as he walked along the riverbank, swollen with water from last night's torrential rain. His hands were clasped behind his back, his robes billowing in the river breeze. Thomas strode beside him in silence, his boots crunching grit, his jaw clenched tight. Three guards walked a few paces behind them, watching the American for any sign that he might make a move to harm their leader.

"You have rivers of blood on your hands," Thomas said after they had been walking for several minutes. "Men, women, children, all slaughtered like cattle. Was it worth it, all this death?"

"You call it slaughter, Colonel," the Mahdi said after a long pause, his eyes fixed on the slow, glinting roll of the water. "I call it purification. And was it worth it?" he repeated, his tone soft yet unyielding, like a prayer spoken over a grave. "Thomas, you see only the flesh that falls, not the spirit that rises. These deaths are not an end; they are a gate. Through it, we pass into a world cleansed of tyranny, a caliphate where God's law reigns supreme."

Thomas kicked a stone into the river, watching it vanish beneath the murk. "A gate paved with corpses. That's a steep toll for your paradise."

The Mahdi stopped, turning to face him fully. "A toll, yes, but a small one when weighed against the sin of submission. The British, the Egyptians-they chain us to their greed, their godless rule. Every soul lost in this fight is a martyr, a seed planted in the earth of our freedom. Do you not see? The infidel's yoke is broken only by the sword, and the sword demands blood."

"Empires bleed the land, inch by inch, Colonel. Coins in one hand, guns in the other. But this struggle is a holy fire. It burns away what is rotten. The Turks, the English, even the Egyptian pashas in their silken arrogance-they must go, all of them. And if death is the price of rebirth, so be it. A caliphate born from ash and blood can still be holy."

He continued, his voice soft but firm. "The Prophet, peace be upon him, cast out the idols from the Kaaba. I will cast out the foreigner from Sudan. This is the will of God, Colonel. I am merely His servant."

Thomas stopped walking. His voice came low and sharp.

"You're no prophet. You're a butcher with delusions of grandeur."

The Mahdi didn't flinch. "Do you not see, Colonel?" he replied. "The feast you attended last night, the arms merchants you dined beside-they are not signs of hypocrisy. They are the instruments of liberation. France and Russia understand what England does not–that this land will no longer kneel."

Thomas stopped. "And so you think your cause justifies this madness? Twenty-five thousand dead. Cities starved. Villages razed. Children-" he bit the word, "slaughtered. All for some imagined purity?"

"I saw your feast. I saw the wine, the silk, the laughter. You wear the mask of a holy man, but you dine like a king and deal in death like a banker. You say the dead are martyrs. That they died for some holy cleansing. But I saw the fields at Tamai, the boys torn apart by Gatling guns. I saw the villages burned in the name of righteousness. You call that purification?"

He stepped closer to Ahmad.

"You kidnapped a woman. You put a blade to her father's throat. You have your meals served on French china and your battles fed by Russian steel-and still you speak of purity. What are you cleansing, Ahmad? The stain of foreign boots? Or the memory of the man you were before you crowned yourself divine?"

The Mahdi's expression shifted briefly, a flicker of something beneath the mask. Then his calm returned.

"And yet, here you are, Thomas Scoundrel. Fighting through the desert. Killing my men without hesitation. For what? For your woman? For glory? For someone else's Queen?"

"For a promise," Thomas snapped. "One I made to the people you hurt. To Heléne. To myself."

He pointed to the river.

"You think God speaks to you, Ahmad? Then maybe He'll be kind enough to explain how many more must drown in that water before your kingdom is satisfied."

The Mahdi stared at the river a long moment, then turned back toward the distant lights of his stronghold.

"History is not written by the man with the cleanest hands, Colonel. Only by the one who still holds the pen."

Thomas stood still, his fists balled at his sides.

"Please answer a question, Ahmad," Thomas said quietly. "Why am I still alive?"

The Mahdi halted mid-step and turned to face him. His dark eyes studied Thomas, unreadable. "I will," he said at last, "but first you will answer mine."

Thomas gave a single nod.

"Why do you seek the tomb of Amenhotep?" the Mahdi asked. "Are you a thief? A seeker of gold and forgotten gods?"

Thomas blinked, genuinely thrown. "I couldn't care less about Amenhotep's tomb. I made a promise to Heléne Bovet. Her father vanished while pursuing that tomb, and she believes he's still alive. That's why I came. I find him, I bring her home. Then I leave this place for good."

The Mahdi's gaze didn't waver. "And you know nothing of the prophecies tied to that tomb?"

Thomas shook his head. "I'm not here for scrolls or stories. I came after you to find Heléne. When I find her-and I will-we'll finish what we started. Her father, then home. If he's alive, he comes with us. If not, we bury him."

"You disappoint me in the most satisfying way, Colonel Scoundrel." The Mahdi allowed himself a faint smile. "Of course, only the man whose exploits are spoken of in Cairo and Constantinople, and even whispered about in the salons of Paris, would imagine he could simply walk away from all this and back into the ordinary world."

Thomas returned the smile with a wry one of his own.

"A man has to move forward, Ahmad. No matter what the world throws at him."

The Mahdi motioned to the guards to hold back and stepped closer to the river's edge. He stooped, picked up a flat stone, and skipped it across the water. The ripples widened and faded.

"You asked why I let you live," he said at last. "It's not an easy answer to give. Had you told me you were here in search of Amenhotep's tomb, I would have had your severed head drifting past fishing boats by now."

Thomas did not reply.

"I am a mystic, Thomas," the Mahdi continued. "Not a conjurer, not a prophet, but a man touched by the divine. My visions are not dreams. They are truths veiled in symbols. And you, whether you understand it or not, are part of something far older and far larger than yourself. So is Miss Bovet."

Thomas let out a short, incredulous laugh. "I'm just a soldier, Ahmad. A worn-out American with sand in his boots. Whatever you think you saw, it wasn't me."

But the Mahdi was unmoved. "We both know that's not true. You are no ordinary man. Nor is she an ordinary woman. There are forces at work in this world you have yet to understand. And for now, you must remain alive. That much is clear."

He picked up another rock and flung it far. It struck the water with a sharp plunk and vanished.

"You have a part to play, Thomas. A purpose you may not yet see. But you will." He paused. "Think on it. Your fate is no accident."

Then he looked Thomas directly in the eyes as if he were struggling with a difficult decision and said, "My men will escort you to a place three days south of here. There, you'll begin to understand what this is, what you are now a part of."

With that, the Mahdi turned and walked back toward the mud brick buildings that crowned the ridge, his robes catching the morning light like smoke rising from the earth.

Thomas waited with the guards at the river's edge for the Mahdi to disappear over the rise. For the first time since arriving in Sudan, he didn't know whether to laugh, curse, or run.

~THIRTY TWO~

Near Wad Madani, 100 miles SE of Khartoum

Samhi emerged from the ramshackle hut where he and Professor Bovet had been confined for the past three weeks. The crude structure, pieced together from scrap wood and tattered cloth, sat within a fly-ridden goat pen circled by jagged fence posts. He lugged a reeking slop pail to the pen's edge, dug a shallow hole in the hard ground with a wooden shovel, and held his breath as he emptied the foul contents.

The stench clawed at his throat, triggering a cough so violent it bent him double. He clutched his ribs, wheezing. The sickness was tightening its grip, knotting in his lungs and stealing his sleep. A parting gift, he thought bitterly, from wading ankle-deep in goat urine and droppings day after day.

Bovet was faring worse. The professor barely stirred now, fevered and frail, burning with the same hacking cough but weaker, as if each breath might be his last. They subsisted on thin soup and stale bread, barely enough to keep them alive. Only the guards' constant bickering punctuated the slow grind of the days. Shouts about women and money would erupt into sudden, vicious fights with stools flung and gourds shattered before melting back into the drone of oppressive heat and the infernal buzzing of thick swarms of flies.

The brothers worked four-hour shifts around the clock, lounging on a reed chair under a canvas lean-to. They ate roasted meat and dates in the shade, traded jokes with the goat keeper's daughters when they passed by, and paid little attention to their charges.

Now and then, one of them would erupt wild-eyed and senseless into sudden violence. No warning. No cause. A goat would be kicked, a sheep struck with a cudgel. Sometimes it was Samhi or Bovet who bore the brunt of the outburst. Samhi's cheek still throbbed, swollen and purple from the blow he had received last night from one of the brothers.

He thought of escape constantly. Had he been alone, he would have slipped into the night already, vanishing into the dunes with nothing but the stars and silence. Better to die beneath the vast sky of his beloved desert than rot here in this steaming pit of waste and cruelty. But he would not leave Bovet until he devised a way to get them both out. That would also mean stealing at least one camel and supplies for several days.

The sun blazed overhead and cast hard shadows as Samhi covered the slop hole with dirt and leaned against the brittle fence. Flies buzzed around his face, undeterred by his weak swats. Across from the pen, his jailor dozed in the hot sun, his head tilted back, his mouth agape.

It would be so easy, Samhi thought. So easy to slip through the fence and between the warped slats before circling behind the snoring brute, and… and what?

Garrote a man half his age, twice his strength? With what—bare hands, diseased lungs, and starvation-ravaged limbs? Perhaps find a stone or splintered plank to bash his skull in? Then what? The others would be close, no doubt. The goat keeper and his family too. He couldn't fight them all. Not like this.

He swallowed a curse. Heléne… and her father. His worry for them gnawed more viciously than hunger ever had. For now, all he could do was hope and plan. He turned to go back into the hut and check on Bovet when movement on the ridge caught his eye.

Atop the brushy rise, 100 yards off, four riders were silhouetted against the pale sky. They began to descend, and Samhi squinted to try and make them out. Three wore the flowing dark robes of Mahdist warriors, rifles slung across their backs. But the fourth—

The fourth rode in the center and wore khaki trousers and a dust-covered shirt. His head hung low. Even from a distance, Samhi could see his hands were bound to the saddle's pommel. A prisoner.

Samhi's breath caught. He stepped closer to the fence, gripping the top rail with trembling fingers.

Above them, a high, gauzy cloud slid across the sun, muting the heat for a fleeting moment. The guard stirred in his chair, rubbed his eyes, and stood. Moments later, drawn by the sound of hooves, the other two guards appeared around the corner and all three walked to the edge of the compound to receive the new arrival.

The riders came closer. Fifty yards out, the prisoner lifted his head.

Samhi's heart surged against his ribs like a drumbeat of hope.

Thomas.

It was Thomas.

The robed warriors dragged Thomas down from Saher's back and pushed him toward the guards without ceremony. Samhi watched them closely, noting the flicker in their eyes—not from fear exactly, but caution. The American was tall, broad-shouldered, and clearly no stranger to violence. He would not be an easy man to keep in chains.

As the guards seized his arms and began leading him toward the pen, the goatkeeper stepped from the shade of his house, wiping his hands on a rag. One of the Mahdist riders handed him a small pouch that clinked with coin, followed by Saher's reins. Payment, Samhi thought bitterly. Blood money for housing one more captive.

Thomas lifted his head when they reached the pen's gate. For a heartbeat, confusion clouded his face, but then his gaze found Samhi through the mess of beard and grime, and recognition broke like sunlight. He said nothing, just tightened his jaw as the guards shoved him through the gate and slammed it shut behind him.

When two of the brothers wandered off around the side of the goatkeeper's mud-brick house and the third settled beneath the lean-to for his watch, Samhi crossed the pen with quick, quiet steps. He threw his arms around Thomas, holding him close.

"Ah, my friend," he whispered. "My friend. Even in this stink hole, it is so good to see you."

Thomas was about to quip that the stink might be mutual when a ragged figure shuffled out of the hut, leaning heavily on a stick. He moved unsteadily in the heat, skeletal and slow.

Samhi gave a small nod.

"Yes," he murmured. "This is Heléne's father."

The figure approached. His eyes were cloudy, his skin stretched thin over the bones of his face. He studied Thomas a moment, then smiled faintly and extended a trembling hand.

"Colonel Scoundrel," he rasped in a brittle voice. "Samhi speaks of you often. I'm damned sorry to meet you in a place like this."

He swatted at a fly attempting to settle on an open sore on his cheek, sighed, and began to sway. Thomas lunged forward, catching the old man before he collapsed and easing him onto a battered stool near the hut's entrance.

"Hell of a way to greet our first guest, eh Samhi?" Bovet wheezed, the trace of a grin playing at his mouth. "Samhi told me you once claimed wine could be made from almost anything."

Thomas gave a cautious nod, unsure where this was going.

Bovet's eyes twinkled faintly. "As you can see, we have no shortage of goat merde. Think you can do something with that?"

A grin tugged at Thomas' lips. That Heléne's father could joke in this filth, in this ruin—he admired him already.

"That's a miracle not even the old gods could manage," he said. "But if I get desperate enough, I'll give it a try."

Samhi retrieved the only other stool and gestured for Thomas to sit. Then he fetched a gourd of water and handed it over.

"It won't kill you," he said, "but you'll have the runs until your stomach makes peace with the devils that live in it."

Thomas declined the water, and Samhi handed it to the professor. Bovet sipped and asked, "My daughter, Thomas. Heléne. What news?"

Thomas's expression turned grave. "Only that she is held under the protection of one of the Mahdi's allies. I was told no harm would come to her."

Bovet placed a hand on Thomas' arm. "Bless you," he whispered. "Samhi believed she might be safe. But I needed to hear it from someone who had seen her. My last wish on this earth is to see her again."

Thomas's gaze swept the pen. The filth. The stench. The sagging, fevered man beside him. And Samhi, doubled over in the grip of another violent cough. Neither of them would last much longer in this place.

Beyond the fence, the compound was quiet, and the windows of the goat keeper's mud home were dark. Only one of the guards was visible, lounging beneath the lean-to close to where Saher's saddle rested atop the fence post.

"You'll see her sooner than you think, Edouard," Thomas said quietly.

Samhi looked at him sharply, his brows lifting. See her soon? Was Thomas simply feeding hope to a dying man?

"The guards will bring you a mat," Samhi said, shaking his head. "One tin cup, one spoon between the three of us. No soap. No coffee or tea. Not quite what you're used to, I'm afraid."

Thomas didn't reply. His eyes followed another one of the guards as the man rounded the house, slung a burlap sack over his shoulder, and began walking toward the ridge.

"You'd be surprised what I can get used to," he murmured, almost to himself. "Do you know where he's going?"

Samhi nodded, still coughing. "Two of these pigs share a woman in a village a few miles from here. He won't return until morning."

"And the goat keeper—does he ever stand watch?"

"No. When one leaves, the other two double up. There's always at least one on duty."

Thomas looked at Bovet again. The old man was slumped on his stool, head sagging forward, breath shallow. Then he turned to Samhi, who had braced his hands on his knees, body wracked by another coughing fit that left him shaking.

There was no time left. If they waited, this place would consume them all.

He stepped close to Samhi, lowering his voice. "Is there anything of value left in the hut?"

Samhi blinked, confused. "Nothing. The goat keeper took everything we had. He likely has your things, too. Why?"

Thomas locked eyes with him. "Because Samhi al Katib, master of the desert and my loyal brother, we are not dying here."

He took a slow breath, then said it again, low and certain:

"The three of us are leaving this place… tonight."

~THIRTY THREE~

An hour after nightfall Thomas left the hut and moved stealthily across the goat pen. In the light of the half-moon he could see that the guard was asleep on his chair in front of the lean-to, his rifle resting across his lap. In fact, he heard the watcher's snores before he saw him. Samhi thought that the second guard would be sleeping on a cot in the stable for another two or three hours.

Thomas walked swiftly, and without breaking his stride circled behind the sleeping guard. Then, in one fluid motion, he stepped forward, his boots muffled against the dirt. His right arm snaked around the guard's neck; his forearm pressed hard against the man's throat. The guard's eyes snapped open, wide with shock, but Thomas tightened his grip, his bicep flexing as he locked the chokehold in place. The guard's hands flailed, clawing at Thomas's arm, his legs kicking weakly against the chair. A choked gasp escaped him, but the sound was stifled by the pressure cutting off his air.

Moonlight glinted off the guard's bulging eyes as they darted in panic, his face reddening, then purpling. His struggles grew frantic but weaker and his body jerked against the chair, which creaked under the strain. Thomas's jaw clenched, his own breath ragged but controlled, his left hand gripping his right wrist to reinforce the hold. The guard's movements slowed, his hands dropped limply to his sides and his rifle clattered to the ground. Thomas maintained the choke for a few seconds longer and only released his grip when he was sure the job was done.

He scanned the darkness, but nothing stirred—no shadows moving, no footsteps on the hard-packed dirt, no voices raised in alarm. The only sound in the cold night air was the whisper of wind through the thorn bushes beyond the compound fence.

He gave a low whistle—the signal he and Samhi had agreed upon.

A moment later, the Bedouin emerged from the corral and joined Thomas. A flicker of grim satisfaction crossed his face when he looked at the crumpled body of the guard on the ground. He nodded at Thomas and they trotted silently to the stables.

Inside, the air was thick with the scent of dust and animal sweat. A single oil lamp burned low on the far wall, casting the space in deep, shifting shadows. Three horses stood in their stalls, flicking their tails at the flies. Saher lifted his head and snorted softly at the sound of their approach. Outside the open rear door, two camels knelt motionless in the dirt.

According to their plan the second guard was meant for Thomas's blade. But as they crept toward the cot where the man lay sprawled in sleep; Samhi touched Thomas's arm and shook his head. This was his justice to deliver.

No words were necessary. Thomas saw the resolve in his friend's eyes and handed him the long-bladed knife. Samhi and Bovet had endured too much at this guard's hands for there to be any question about his punishment.

Thomas stepped outside to watch for movement around the compound. The goat keeper's home loomed nearby, dark and silent, and a dog barked in the distance, but nothing moved in the yard. Then he heard a muffled groan, followed by the dull, lifeless thud of a body collapsing to the ground.

Samhi emerged a moment later, blood smeared across the blade, his breathing steady. He handed the knife to Thomas with a nod, and they hurried through the gloom toward the hut in the goat pen.

Samhi peeled back the ragged blanket that hung in the doorway and slipped inside. "Professor," he whispered.

Bovet stirred and looked up, blinking through fevered eyes.

"Are we… truly leaving this place?"

Thomas came in and crouched beside him. "Can you walk?"

The old man grinned. "My friends, tonight I feel like I could fly."

"Sunrise is in six hours," Samhi said. "There is much to do before the other guard returns."

They armed themselves with the dead guard's rifles and knives, then crossed the open yard to the goat keeper's house in the center of the compound. The wooden door was bolted, but Thomas stepped back, lowered his shoulder, and drove into it. The latch shattered with a crack like a pistol shot, and the door swung open.

"Stay here until we call," Thomas told Bovet.

Then he vanished inside with Samhi on his heels.

The interior of the house was dim, thick with the smell of cooking smoke and old bedding. In the corner, the goat keeper and his wife were rising groggily from their straw-stuffed mattress near a clay stove, blinking at the shadowy figures who had burst into their home.

They couldn't see the faces—just the barrel of the rifle that Thomas leveled directly at their heads.

"Don't move," he said in a low voice. "We don't want to harm you. But if you try to stop us, we will shoot you."

The goat keeper's voice trembled. "The guards…?"

"They've gone to paradise," Samhi answered from across the room where he was lighting an oil lamp.

The flame caught and flared, throwing golden light across the cluttered room. Pots and baskets, sacks of grain, a broken lute. The goat keeper and his wife sat with their backs against the wall, eyes wide, limbs frozen.

Thomas moved slowly around the room; his rifle still trained on the couple in their bed. "We will take what we need. Then we will go."

Samhi nodded. "And if anyone follows—they will join the guards."

A moment later Samhi stepped outside and helped Professor Bovet into the house. He sat the old man on a chair at the table and then went over beside the bed.

"Do you have any dried thyme?" He asked the woman.

She nodded. It was a common ingredient of teas used for coughs and fevers.

"Honey and laudanum?" She nodded again.

"I want you to make tea for this man and add a spoon of honey and one of laudanum to it. Make another cup for me without the opiate. Quickly!"

Without a word, the woman swung out of bed and added sticks to the low fire that flickered in the clay stove, stoking it back to life. Her hands trembled as she opened a cupboard and pulled down jars of herbs and vials in dusty glass.

While Samhi kept a watchful eye on the couple, Thomas finished his sweep of the room. He turned to the goat keeper. "Do you have a storehouse?"

A shaky finger pointed to a small shack just across from the front door. Thomas slipped outside, boots silent on the hard ground. Inside the shed, he lit a lantern, looked over the shelves, and then began filling his arms.

Clay jars of lentils, dried beans, and salt. Baskets of dates, cured meats, sacks of wheat. Coffee, oil, even a few bricks of sugar. When he returned, arms heavy with supplies, the tea was ready.

He handed one cup to Bovet, who drank with eagerness. Another went to Samhi before he poured his own.

"Do you have any bread?" he asked the woman.

She pulled several small loaves from a wooden box near the stove. Thomas tore them open, slathered them with honey and watched with a smile as Bovet and Samhi devoured them.

His eyes swept the room one last time. "Where is the money?"

The man's face collapsed into a mask of innocence. "I have no money, *yutkin*. I am but a poor goat herder. As God is my witness—"

"I am not your master," Thomas cut in coldly. "And God may be your witness, but he's about to witness your death. You were paid to imprison us, and you stole from my friends. You have the money, and I won't ask again."

Something in Thomas's voice—steel sharpened on rage—cut through the man's protest. He slid out of bed, bent low, and drew a chamber pot from beneath the mattress. Thomas motioned him back and lifted the lid.

Inside, nestled beneath the reek of old piss, was a small fortune in gold and copper coins.

Samhi chuckled under his breath.

"Get bags," Thomas ordered the woman. "Canvas, as many as you have. Pack the food and the medicines. The laudanum, too. The herbs. All of it."

She moved quickly as Thomas turned to the husband. "Do you have pack frames for the camels? Saddlebags for the horses?"

"I do, but please, you cannot take them. They are all I have left."

Thomas stepped closer, his eyes like glass. "Wrong. Your life is all you have left, but that can change."

Samhi remained inside as Thomas carried the first full bags out to the stable. He fitted the pack frames on one camel and tied on the bags. Then he saddled Saher and two of the goat keeper's horses. When he returned, the woman had finished packing. "Now put those sacks in the saddlebags," he told her. "Fill three water skins and get three bedrolls together. Quickly."

He turned to Samhi. "Once that's done, we tie them up."

Samhi tilted his head, a wicked gleam in his eye. "Do we really want to tie them up in here in this nice, warm little nest they kept for themselves? Or…"

Thomas smiled. "The pen."

Bovet let out a hoarse chuckle. "A fitting change of residence."

They grabbed rope from the stable wall and marched the couple outside. The air was thick with the ripe stink of ammonia and filth. The goat pen was still slick with the waste they'd been forced to live in. Sloshing through it, they forced the couple down, back-to-back, into the deepest mire.

The wife gagged. Then retched.

Samhi bound their wrists and ankles with quick, practiced knots.

Bovet leaned down to them, his voice gentle but edged with threat. "Don't worry," he said with a smile. "When the sun comes up, it will be much, much worse."

They rode through the endless hush of desert night, the silence broken only by the steady rhythm of hooves and the soft creak of saddles. Overhead, the stars burned like cold fire, and by the time the first blush of dawn lit the eastern hills, the heat was already beginning to rise.

They pushed forward for six hours. Professor Bovet, against all odds, remained upright in his saddle, swaying like a broken reed but somehow clinging to his mount. Thomas and Samhi exchanged glances—they knew the professor had nothing left.

They sheltered in the thin shadows that pooled at the base of a jagged pile of boulders. Thomas helped Bovet down and eased him against the stone. The professor exhaled shakily and closed his eyes. The pack camel knelt nearby, groaning as it folded its limbs beneath it.

"I'll find us a place to sleep the day," Samhi said quietly, swinging into his saddle without waiting for a reply. He rode east, into the growing light.

He returned an hour later, dust rising in spirals behind him.

"There's a seasonal spring just ahead," he said. "Brush thick enough to hide the animals. The water tastes clean."

They made their way there slowly and arrived as the sun crowned the sky. The grove was sparse, but enough to shelter in, with low acacias, thorny tamarisks, and a pocket of green where the spring whispered softly from a cleft in the rocks.

They watered the horses and camels, staked them in the shade, and Samhi set about preparing a simple and hearty meal: a soup of lentils and beans with onions boiled over a small fire, hard biscuits softened with broth, and a scattering of dried dates.

Bovet ate like a man who hadn't tasted food in weeks. "The finest feast I've ever had," he declared, licking honey from his fingers.

They spread their bedrolls close to the spring, where the ground was cool and damp. Before long, the desert heat deepened into stillness, and they slept. When night fell, the temperature dropped quickly, bringing with it a hush broken only by the soft crackle of fire and the sighing of wind through the brush. Thomas sat on a rock beside his two companions, staring into the flames. Shadows danced across his face, drawing lines of fatigue and resolve.

"We're nine days' ride from Suakin," he said. "Kitchener's camp on the Red Sea. For you two, at least."

Samhi gave a slow nod, unsurprised. "You will go for Heléne, then."

"Yes. And we will make our way to Luxor and meet you there in six weeks."

Bovet looked up sharply, brows furrowing. "Luxor? Wouldn't it make more sense to go north to Alexandria and return to France from there?"

Thomas turned his gaze on him. "You won't be going home just yet. The Mahdi is obsessed with your work, Edouard. Fixated on the legends of Pharaoh Amenhotep. He believes Helène and I are somehow part of that story. It's the only reason I'm still breathing. I don't understand his mystical talk, but I know this much: until we see the inside of that tomb, none of us are safe. We meet in Luxor. And this time, my friend, you're going to find him."

Bovet's expression changed, a quiet light blooming in his eyes. He raised his tin cup in salute but found himself too choked with emotion to speak.

Samhi, ever practical, broke the silence. "Thomas, I will guide you there, of course. But we've searched the Valley many times. What makes you believe we can find the tomb now?"

Thomas poked at the fire with a stick, watching a flurry of sparks swirl upward into the velvet night.

"Because this time," he said softly, "it feels like the gods want us to."

Samhi raised an eyebrow. "And do the gods plan to show you where Helène is, too? Sudan is a vast sea of sand. Six hundred thousand square miles of it. What signs will you follow?"

"One of the Beja who brought me to Wad Madani is an officer. Close to the Mahdi. I believe he knows where she's being held."

Bovet looked up, cupping his tea with both hands. "But he left almost two days before us. You'll have to catch him."

"He's not in a hurry," Thomas said. "I'd wager he's stopped at some village along the way. Resting, maybe even sampling the pleasures of a camp full of your legendary dancing girls."

Bovet chuckled. "I can almost guarantee it."

Samhi leaned forward, arms resting on his knees. His voice was low, cautious. "So, you find him. And what then? Extract the information, somehow. But Thomas, you're one man. Wherever she is, there will be guards. Perhaps many. How do you get to her?"

Thomas didn't answer right away. He looked across the fire at Heléne's father, whose eyes shone with something more than firelight—

hope, fear, memory. Tears trembled on his lashes as he took a slow sip of tea.

Then Thomas leaned back, his voice quiet and steady.

"Gentlemen…have you heard the story of the Ghost of Khartoum?"

~THIRTY FOUR~

Across the desert

The first two days out of Wad Madani had gone better than Thomas expected. The rains had eased, though the air still hung with a sodden weight, and the camel—dun-colored and stubborn—kept pace without complaint. He had left behind the slow green of the Blue Nile basin and turned northwest across country that smelled of wet dust and wild acacia. Saher moved easily, his hooves striking a dry rhythm over red earth veined with the tracks of water.

He had avoided the caravan routes. Mahdist patrols were out scouting, foraging, and conscripting, and a lone rider with a pack camel would raise questions. So, he cut a diagonal through thorny scrubland and shallow wadis, threading between rain-swollen creeks and baked hillocks the color of rusted iron. At night he rolled himself in a woven blanket beneath the ghostly shade of acacia trees and fell asleep to the high cry of hawks circling invisible in the dark.

By dawn of the second day, a shimmering haze blanketed the land. The sky had gone flat and pale, and the horizon lost its edge. He gave Saher the lead rope, trusting the stallion's instincts. The camel followed behind, ears twitching at unseen insects. The ground rose gently westward, becoming stonier and fractured, with slopes of crumbling shale and sudden fissures like scars in the earth.

It was around midday—with the heat climbing, the shadows short and sharp—when they came to a break in the plateau. A narrow defile opened between two low ridges of pitted rock, a natural choke point where winds had scoured the stone clean of soil. Thomas dismounted and walked Saher carefully along the edge, his eyes focused on the path. The camel, slower and less precise, lagged a few paces behind.

Then came the sound, a sudden, dull slide of gravel and a panicked grunt.

Thomas turned.

The camel, loaded with canvas-wrapped bundles of supplies and sacks of food, had stepped too close to the edge of a shallow ravine. Its front leg buckled as the loose earth gave way. For a moment, it twisted sideways, trying to shift its weight. Then the entire mass of the animal lurched forward and disappeared in a violent cascade of stone and dust.

He ran to the edge.

The ravine dropped more than 45 feet and was steep-sided, narrow, and choked with brush. At the bottom, sprawled awkwardly among shattered rock, lay the camel. One rear leg twitched once, then was still. His supplies—canvas bags of food, three water skins, a small brass cook pot, and a sack of dates—were strewn across the debris.

He knelt and called softly, then louder. There was no response. The beast's neck was twisted at an unnatural angle, and a dark pool spread slowly from beneath its flank.

He swore once, quietly.

There was no safe way down. The sides were too steep, the rock too brittle. If he attempted it, he might join the animal. He tied Saher to a shrub and circled the ravine twice, looking for an angle or foothold. Nothing.

Finally, he stood above the wreckage, hat in his hands, and made the mental inventory. Three days of water. Most of his food. Half his cartridges. His bedding. All gone.

He was alone now. Just him, the stallion, and what he carried in his saddle bags. The silence stretched around him, broken only by the whisper of dry leaves and the buzz of insects.

That night he rode another hour and made a small fire beneath a thorn bush, carefully shielded. The stallion drank sparingly, and Thomas ate the last of a flatbread and a few dried figs, then wrapped himself in his coat and leaned against a rock, cradling the rifle across his knees.

The moon was a dull smudge behind high clouds, and the stars flickered as if shivering. He dreamed of cool green Ohio rivers, of distant thunder, and of Heléne's voice echoing through empty chambers.

The third day opened under a lid of low clouds and a pale wind that moved nothing. The trail westward had grown faint, reduced to scattered hoofprints and the worn paths walked by tribesmen and smugglers. The stallion moved steadily, his black coat streaked with dust and dried sweat. Thomas drank sparingly from his flask, his tongue thick, his jaw aching with desert grit. The loss of the camel was now more than a burden; it was a ticking clock.

The sole lump of barley cake that had survived the camel's fall had gone sour in its oilcloth and so he ate nothing that morning. He chewed on raw acacia pods that afternoon, spitting out the fibers, and kept moving. To stop was to die.

By noon the land had begun to harden. The acacia groves thinned. What little green there had been now faded to gray-brown and beige. Here and there, skeletal trees clawed at the sky, bark peeling like old parchment. Buzzards wheeled high above, and a pair of them followed his progress at a steady distance.

Once, he thought he glimpsed movement in the rocks, perhaps a jackal or a man. He unslung the rifle, scanned the low ridgelines, then pushed Saher onward. His focus narrowed: one mile, another, then the next.

He passed a rock outcropping near sunset and considered sleeping in its shade. But the scorpions liked places like that, a still rock, windless dust, cool shadows. He kept riding.

By the fourth day, his tongue was cracked and swollen, and his flask was near empty. He found a shallow pool inside a wadi and recognized it as a remnant of a flash flood, but the water was fouled by insects and animal dung. He strained it through cloth, gagged at the taste, but drank anyway.

Saher lipped the mud at the edges and then stood still, sides heaving. Thomas ran a hand along the stallion's neck and spoke softly to him. The horse had become quieter in recent days; they were both conserving strength.

That night, Thomas dreamed of Heléne. She was not in chains or in flight, but seated beside a cool spring. Her voice echoed softly in French and Arabic, calling him to drink. He awoke with the rifle beside him, the sky bruised with early light. His throat burned, and his legs trembled as he stood.

Late that day, as he crossed a field of weathered stone, the scorpion struck.

He had stopped to rest in a sliver of shade beneath a sun-split boulder. He removed his boot to massage his heel and reached blindly for the water bag. Pain lanced through his hand like fire. He yelped and flung it backward, his heart hammering.

There it was: no larger than his thumb, black-bodied with a pale stinger curled above its back. It skittered across the stone and vanished beneath a crevice.

Thomas fell to his knees, panting.

The sting bloomed rapidly. His palm swelled and a numb heat crept up his forearm. Sweat broke across his face, and his thoughts began to slip; they became unanchored, abstract. He forced himself to wrap the hand in cloth, but the fingers wouldn't close. His breath rasped; his legs shook.

He tried to stand but stumbled. Saher shifted, ears forward, then looked back at him and stamped once.

Thomas knew he couldn't hold the reins or trust his legs to stay firm. He removed his belt, looped it through the saddle's forward rings, and tied the other end to his chest. Then he leaned forward, pressing his cheek against Saher's neck.

"Take me there," he whispered. "Wherever there is."

Then he blacked out.

What followed came in pieces.

The burning sun on his face. The rhythmic sway of the horse. Shadows sliding across his vision like ships beneath glass. At one point he saw a line of camels drifting across the plain, but if they were real or imagined, he couldn't say. Later, he heard voices of men chanting near a fire, but when he opened his eyes, only silence answered.

Somewhere in that blur, his belt broke. He slipped sideways and felt himself falling. Then Saher turned, snorted, and lowered himself gently. Thomas rolled limply from the saddle and his body struck something soft; mud, water, cool earth. The shock of it made him cough.

He lay there, face half-submerged in a shallow basin, as the world snapped back into place. It was a pool of real water. Saher nudged his shoulder, and with a groan, he pulled himself free of the saddle blanket and dragged his upper body toward the pool. He drank like a man who hadn't tasted water in weeks. Then he vomited, then drank again.

Time passed in fragments. Saher stayed beside him, unmoving, as if guarding some sacred ground.

By nightfall, Thomas was dry but breathing. The fever had begun to ebb. His hand throbbed but could move. He took a mouthful of water, then rolled onto his back as the stars came out. They came slowly at first, one by one, as if summoned, and then all at once, flooding the heavens with a brilliance that stilled the breath. No fire, no city, no tent ever made could compete with the vast cathedral above him.

He saw constellations unfamiliar to his boyhood Ohio sky: bold slashes of stars etched across the black, clustered like tribes around a celestial fire. The Milky Way arched overhead like a smoke trail from God's own pipe.

He sat up, cradling his arm. The night was perfectly silent. Even the wind had hushed. Somewhere far off, a jackal called once, then no more. The pool shimmered faintly, catching starlight in its dark mirror. Saher nickered quietly, still watching.

Thomas drew in a slow breath and exhaled. This was not the end, he realized. It was the middle of something ancient and strange and utterly real. He had lost everything, and he had nearly died. And yet the stars above remained unmoved, eternal.

He lay back down, folding one arm beneath his head, and watched the night sky stretch across the world like a map too vast to read.

~THIRTY FIVE~

Camp of Sheikh Abu Sinn

The spring saved him. For three days Thomas lay beneath a battered canvas tarp propped with brush, sipping slowly from the water hole Saher had led him to. His body fought the scorpion poison, and his thoughts slowly recovered from feeling like thick molasses. The sting on his hand had turned a dark shade of plum, but the fever broke on the second night. By dawn, the world had taken shape again, and he knew he was going to live.

The sun had worked its way deep into his skin which was dry and cracking, but the spring water was fresh and cool, and Saher never strayed far. He owed that horse everything.

On the fourth day, a merchant caravan with seven camels and three traders passed by. At first, they greeted Thomas with slow nods and wary eyes. He must have looked half-dead: tattered clothes, sunken cheeks, a man weathered raw by the desert. But an ancient courtesy older than the pyramids required that they share their meal of flatbread and lentils with crushed garlic, warm dates, and something spicy wrapped in cloth that he could not identify. Thomas thanked them and ate heartily.

That night, under stars stitched into the sky like silver embroidery, one of the merchants leaned close to the fire and addressed him.

"We go west in the morning," he said, "ten miles. To the camp of Sheikh Abu Sinn. You've heard the name?"

Thomas said nothing, but his attention sharpened.

"He is rich, this one," the man continued. "Loves music, poetry, women, and the sound of his own voice. And he is devout. The Mahdi favors him. I bring gifts. Spices, cloth, a fine mirror. And sometimes," the man laughed low in his throat, "I bring him women. For pleasure, if they please him. If they don't, I take them back to Suakin. But this time…"

He paused for effect. "This time the Sheikh has no appetite. The Mahdi gave him a gift he cannot touch."

"A woman?" Thomas asked.

The merchant grinned. "Not the usual frightened creature. This one, she is exceedingly clever. A Frenchwoman. Pale, smart, beautiful. The Mahdi sent her to Abu Sinn for safekeeping. The Sheikh's wives gossip that he sleeps in another tent, for fear of the Mahdi's wrath should he let his desire for this foreigner take hold of his mind. Poor Abu Sinn, may Allah pity him, can't so much as lick a date in her presence. Not if he wants to keep his manhood intact. A terrible fate, yes?" He chuckled and sipped his tea.

Laughter rolled around the fire. But Thomas was already somewhere else. He felt the heat of the fire on his face and something colder along his spine. The ache in his body vanished. His path was clear again.

Heléne.

"She's still there?" he asked quietly.

"For now," the merchant said. "Though what the Mahdi plans, who can say? War makes strange promises."

Thomas lay awake long after the fire burned low. In the morning, when the merchants left, his saddlebags were full: bread, dates, water skins, and a pouch of grain. They also gave him the precise location of Abu Sinn's camp. "Follow the broken ridge," a merchant said. "Past the lone acacia. You'll smell the camels before you see the tents."

Thomas and Saher rested one more night at the spring. He cleaned his weapons, mended what he could of his shredded clothing, and rubbed the horse down until the black sheen returned to its coat. He spoke little to Saher, but the horse seemed to understand.

That evening, with the last light draining from the sky, he mounted up and rode into the west.

The moon was high when he smelled the camels on a light breeze and saw the flicker of lamps as he rode along a rise. He circled wide, moving silently, watching the terrain. The camp was just as the merchant described; half buried in the open desert like a mirage. A great black tent shimmered under starlight, framed by the rise of dry hills and the silhouettes of drowsy camels. He made a complete circle, finding only one guard, half-asleep on a flat rock with his sword in his lap. Thomas crept forward on foot, the leather garrote looped and ready. He moved like a shadow over sand and stone, wrapped the strap around the man's neck, and pulled until the desert took him without a sound.

Saher was tied out of sight near the rocks when he crossed the corral. He paused briefly to admire the Sheikh's black stallion and then slipped through the ochre and blue curtains that fluttered at the entrance.

Inside, the lamplight flickered on walls of draped silk and thick carpets. Scents of rosewater and roasted lamb lingered. The Sheikh's bed sat on a raised platform, draped in embroidered cushions. The man himself was round, bearded, and shirtless, and he snored lightly, with one arm flung across his chest.

No sign of Heléne, and no reason to wait, he thought. He drew his Colt and fired two shots straight up through the tent roof. The roar shattered the silence, and smoke curled into the lamplight. The Sheikh jerked upright, shrieking. From the side, a guard burst in, sword raised. Thomas fired once more. The man's body collapsed onto the thick lambswool rug, his blood dark against the white.

From the back of the tent came a flash of movement. A curtain parted, and Heléne stepped through, revolver raised.

She froze.

For a moment, the world narrowed to just her. She was never more beautiful, Thomas thought. Her hair tousled, her eyes defiant, and her pistol cocked. She froze, and her mouth fell open. Then she ran to him.

Thomas caught her in one arm, the other still holding his Colt. She buried her face in his chest and let out a laugh that was half-sob, half-joy.

"You found me," she whispered.

"I said I would," he murmured into her hair. "Now, go and fetch his wives."

The Sheikh leaned forward on the bed and screamed again, sputtering orders to guards who weren't coming. "Who are you?" the Sheikh demanded. "Do you know what you've done? I am under the Mahdi's protection, and he will hear of this! He will have your entrails for breakfast!"

Thomas didn't even look at him. "We've already dined, the Mahdi and I," he said dryly. "But I don't think he will be inviting me again. What you are going to do now is fill a bag with gold and silver coins and jewelry to compensate Miss Bovet for the inconvenience you have caused her. Do that this instant and you may yet live to see the next sunrise."

Something in Thomas' tone told the obese sheikh that this was not a time for argument or negotiation. He rolled out of bed, tugged on a shirt, and huffed across the room, where he took a key from his necklace and opened a wooden and steel strong box. Thomas watched as the sheikh took a small handful of coins and places them in a tiny cotton bag.

Thomas shook his head. "More?" the sheikh asks.

Thomas nodded. "All of it."

"But that will leave me destitute," the sheikh said as he began to sob.

"Better to be poor and alive than dead and rich, my friend," Thomas answered.

The sheikh fetched a heavy canvas bag from across the room and began to empty the strongbox as Heléne returned with the Sheikh's four wives.

"The servants ran off into the hills when the shooting started," she said, barely able to suppress a giggle.

"Then these women are going to have to do some work," Thomas replied. "Tell them to pack enough food and water to last for a week. Cooking pots, coffee, everything. Can any of them saddle a horse or pack a camel?"

"They all can," Heléne answered.

"Good. Have them saddle the Sheikh's stallion and fill his saddle bags with whatever supplies you think we will need. Bedrolls, too. Mine was lost. Then pack the food and water bags on one of the camels…does the sheikh have any guns?"

"Yes," Heléne said. "In a chest in the guard's room.

"You should get those," Thomas said, "in case the ladies decide to get brave."

Heléne took the women outside and gave then their instructions and then went off to collect the sheikh's firearms. Twenty minutes later, Thomas assembled everyone outside the tent. He had fetched Saher, and now the horses were saddled, the camel was packed, and the sheikh's treasure was safe inside Heléne's saddlebags.

"And what of me," raged the sheikh as a cloud scuttered across the face of the moon and a breeze picked up out of the desert. "I am an important man, you cannot simply rob me, kill my guards, and then ride off into the night."

"You're right, you know," Thomas answered. "I can't do that…I can do more."

He told Heléne to keep her revolver trained on the sheikh and then went back into the tent where he took two lamps down from their posts. Back outside he smashed their glass panels and tossed the burning wicks into the tent, setting it on fire almost instantly.

Then he went to the corral and chased the remaining horses and camels out into the night where they rushed to the top of the rise and disappeared into the vast darkness beyond.

"And now?" demanded the sheikh, his eyes bulging in anger. "What are we to do without food or water or shelter?"

Thomas nodded for Heléne to get on her horse. Then he took the long rein of the pack camel, tied it to the back of his saddle and swung up on Saher.

"You will walk, oh mighty Sheikh," he said with a smile. "And pray that your wives do not become so hungry on the journey that they turn on you for food."

They rode up the rise together. Below them the tent was fully engulfed in flames, casting orange light across the sand. When they reached the crest, Heléne pulled her horse alongside his and leaned close for a long kiss.

When she pulled back, a troubled look crossed her face. Thomas raised his eyebrows.

"I've forgotten something," she said, turning her horse back towards the camp.

"The tent is gone, Heléne," Thomas replied. "You can't go inside."

"I don't need to…this will only take a moment." With that she trotted down the rise and disappeared behind a stand of tall brush. When she emerged from the thicket a moment later, Thomas saw a lean, broad-chested hunting dog loping beside her.

When she brought her horse to a halt, the dog sat without being commanded.

"A friend?" Thomas asked.

Heléne gazed down at the dog with a look of respect and admiration. "Oh, yes, and in your absence, my protector."

"Then we have both been blessed with good friends," Thomas said as he leaned forward and patted Saher's neck. "Four hours until sunrise. It's time to go."

"Where now, my darling?"

"We ride north for three days. There's a wharf outside Khartoum where General Gordon's boats leave for patrol along the Nile. They sail twice a week, and we will be on the first one to Luxor."

"Three days? But you had his wives pack for seven…why so much?"

"We have food, water, bedrolls–and a lot to talk about. I'm in no hurry."

Heléne rested a hand on Thomas' knee. "But I am. I need news of my father."

Thomas smiled and tapped his boot against Saher's flank.

"And that's the first thing we are going to talk about."

The moon arced slowly across the desert sky and the stars illuminated the path towards Khartoum as they rode side by side into the night.

~THIRTY SIX~

Luxor, Egypt, September 1884

Relaxing in the bathtub of his suite at the Luxor Grand Hotel, with a bottle of iced champagne nestled in a bucket beside the tub and a cool breeze blowing through the open window off the Nile, was akin to a religious experience, Thomas decided. It had been nearly three months since he had bathed with anything more than a strip of cotton cloth and a slosh of water from a battered canteen.

He smiled as he heard Heléne humming a tune in the dressing area next to the bath, her voice light and clear, weaving through the warm evening air. When he thought about the dinner awaiting them in the hotel's elegantly appointed restaurant, his smile widened further. Civilization, for all its flaws, had never seemed so glorious.

After rescuing her from the desert encampment of Sheikh Abu Sinn, they had begun their escape in the dead of night, riding hard across the scrubland with a single pack camel trailing behind. For two days they rode northward in a broad arc, using shallow wadis and wind-carved dunes to conceal their movements and skirting Khartoum by more than 20 miles. Thomas navigated by instinct sharpened through hard experience, ever watchful for Mahdist scouts or the telltale dust plumes of riders on the horizon. The terrain was merciless, yet Heléne clung to her saddle with quiet, unyielding strength, calling down encouragement now and then to the dog trotting loyally beside her horse.

On the third morning, they reached the Nile's western bank at a discreet rendezvous point known only to river traders and sympathizers of General Gordon. There, hidden among reeds and sycamore roots, lay one of Gordon's remaining armored steamers, a squat, iron-plated vessel with a Gatling gun mounted at its prow. The captain, a wiry man with sun-scorched skin and a pistol tucked into his sash, waved them aboard with urgency. Thomas paid him a handsome sum from the treasure they had "liberated" from Abu Sinn, and just before dawn, the steamer's paddle wheels churned into the muddy waters, pushing them northward against the Nile's steady pull.

The voyage to Luxor took 29 days, the steamer moving mostly at night under a shroud of darkness. Mahdist patrols prowled the eastern banks, while the western shore teemed with brigands and desperate men. By day, the crew moored the vessel beneath overhanging trees or behind small islands, camouflaging the hull with mud to blend into the riverbanks. Heléne spent long hours under the shade of a canvas awning, resting and recovering, while Thomas kept watch on the deck, his rifle across his knees and his eyes constantly scanning the banks for movement.

At night, after the watch changed, Thomas and Heléne would climb atop the cabin roof or sit near the boiler stack, gazing up at the stars mirrored in the black waters of the Nile. At first, their words came haltingly, as though spoken across a great distance, but gradually, the river seemed to carry them back to one another. Heléne spoke of her captivity and the stubborn flame of hope she had nursed through long, bitter days. Thomas told her of the scorpion sting that nearly claimed his life, of desert mirages, and the moment he thought he would never see her again.

As they passed familiar stretches near Dongola and Wadi Halfa, the nights grew warmer, and their conversations deepened. They dined with the steamer's crew on salted meats, hard biscuits, and strong black tea brewed over a soot-streaked kettle. Heléne, regaining her strength, began sketching again, tearing pages from Thomas's battered field journal to capture quick studies of riverbanks, camels, and crewmen. Her hands, once trembling, were steady again; her blue eyes sparkled with renewed curiosity.

By the time the spires and columns of Luxor shimmered into view through the haze, their bond had deepened beyond words. As they disembarked onto the bustling pier, Professor Bovet and Samhi were waiting, their faces alight with a mixture of astonishment and joy. Their new search for the tomb of Amenhotep would begin soon enough. But when Thomas helped Heléne down the gangplank, both of them paused, knowing that their journey—like the Nile itself—still had miles to go.

That evening, they dined beneath a linen awning on the hotel's riverfront terrace. The Nile glittered in the early evening sun, and across the river, the temple complex of Luxor rose in solemn majesty, its grand pylons and solemn obelisks casting long shadows toward the Avenue of Sphinxes that stretched to Karnak.

Heléne was radiant in a form-fitting gown of soft rose chiffon. Her father had regained at least fifteen pounds since Thomas had last seen him outside the prison camp at Wad Madani; the professor's limp remained pronounced, a permanent souvenir of his ordeal, but his spirit seemed undiminished.

Samhi could not stop smiling. He clapped his hands sharply for more champagne and lifted his glass high.

"To life!" he cried, "And adventure!"

"To be honest," the professor said dryly, "I would prefer a bit more of the former, and rather less of the latter."

Heléne squeezed her father's hand. In a more serious voice she said, "Amenhotep has been sleeping for 3,000 years, Father. He can slumber a few more if we decide to go home and return another day."

Thomas and Samhi exchanged a glance but said nothing. This decision was not theirs to make.

Professor Bovet looked thoughtfully into his champagne flute for a long moment before replying.

"No," he said quietly. "We aren't going home just yet." His gaze swept across the river to the ancient ruins silhouetted against the fading sky. "This will be my last expedition. The pyramids may endure forever, but I, alas, will not."

A hush fell over the table. The sun had dipped below the horizon, and a faint coolness crept into the air. Distantly, from across the river, the faint cry of a heron echoed.

At that moment, two white-jacketed waiters arrived with rolling carts laden with steaming tureens of soup and delicate plates of local delicacies. The scent of spiced lentils and roasted lamb wafted over the table, but for a moment, no one reached for their forks.

Samhi leaned forward, studying Bovet carefully. "Tell me, my friend, why not savor your victories? There is no shame in recognizing that you are no longer 20."

"Or even 60," Bovet said with a rueful chuckle. "No, it is something Thomas said when I asked why he was so confident we could find Amenhotep's tomb now, after all these years of searching."

He turned to Thomas, a faint smile playing at his lips.

"'Because the gods want us to,'" Bovet quoted. "That was his answer. And somehow, I believe he's right. I feel it in my bones. Our timing is perfect."

A shadow crossed Samhi's face.

"I fear that Henri Lavalle and the Mahdi share your revelation, old friend," he said gravely. "Each for his own reasons believes this to be his moment as well. But unlike you, they are willing to do whatever it takes to reach the tomb first. Lavalle, for the treasure. The Mahdi...for something more profound."

"And that would be?" Bovet asked.

Thomas finished his glass, set it down with a quiet finality, and spoke in a low voice that carried in the gathering darkness.

"The key to eternity."

Two thousand miles away, in Marseilles, Henri Lavalle sat brooding in his office above the antiquities-packed warehouse on the waterfront.

From the opulence of his paneled study, with its silk curtains and ivory-inlaid desk, he had spent the past months dispatching orders to a network of spies stretching from North Africa to the Ottoman ports. The intelligence they gathered both heartened and unnerved him. Professor Bovet had been liberated from a desolate prison enclosure east of Khartoum, and with him, the Bedouin guide Samhi Al Katib. That they had been rescued by the American adventurer, Thomas Scoundrel, was of little concern. If anything, it was a blessing. Lavalle was certain that Bovet would now resume his pursuit of Amenhotep's tomb with renewed urgency.

But it was troubling that the Mahdi himself had ordered Bovet's imprisonment. The rebel leader's interest in the tomb suggested something more dangerous than Lavalle had first assumed. Spiritual, perhaps. Or apocalyptic.

Only days earlier, Lavalle's spy had reported that Bovet and Samhi were at the Grand Hotel in Luxor, awaiting companions. That could only mean Heléne Bovet and Colonel Scoundrel, further proof that Bovet was close to his goal.

That morning, Lavalle had given new orders to his most trusted lieutenant: recruit a dozen men from Cairo and Luxor–ruthless, experienced, and discreet.

"Find them. Hold them. Interrogate them. Kill them one by one if you must," he had said. "But get the tomb's location before the last breath leaves the last survivor. As for the woman," he said, his mouth twisting into a grotesque smile, "you may keep her for yourselves but see to it that she does not live beyond her usefulness."

Now, alone in his office, Lavalle gazed up at the oil portrait of his mother hanging behind his desk. Her pale, severe features seemed to watch him with approval.

A familiar warmth stirred low in his belly. Reaching into a drawer, he withdrew the last vial of her perfume, dabbing a few drops onto his groin. The heavy floral scent thickened the air.

Ringing a small silver bell, Lavalle barked for his assistant to fetch the Romanian girl from the adjoining apartments.

Soon, the final pieces would be in place. He would claim all that the ancient king had left behind–for himself alone.

He looked at his mother again.

It would only be a minute now.

~THIRTY SEVEN~

Valley of the Kings

The old mystic's hair and skin were matted with dirt and his clothing was little more than a bundle of rags. Not surprising, Thomas thought, given that the man had been living in a rock-strewn cave above an excavated tomb for the past year.

Heléne, her father, and Samhi were seated on flat rocks outside the cave while a team of porters from the village set up their camp. Only two tents were going up, Thomas noted with a private smile. Professor Bovet had made no comment when Samhi ordered supplies, nor when it became clear that he and Heléne would be sharing one of the tents. Bovet had given up any pretense about Thomas' relationship with his daughter.

They knew that Henri Lavalle's watchers had probably been spying on them since they arrived in Luxor, so they bought supplies quietly for the trip through a trusted middleman and had them packed to the Valley of the Kings four miles away in the dead of night.

The travelers left the Luxor Grand before dawn. The Nile was still cloaked in morning mist as they crossed by boat, the first rays of sun gilding the water like polished gold. On the west bank, they mounted their horses and began the slow, deliberate ride through the Necropolis. At Gurna, the village that had supplied laborers for tomb expeditions for centuries, the crumbling mud brick homes stared out with hollow windows. Curious children watched from the shadows as they passed, but no one spoke.

Beyond the village, the desert opened wide and wind-scoured, the ground cracked and pale beneath hooves that stirred small clouds of dust. The colossal statues of Amenhotep III rose in the distance, fractured but defiant, and as they passed between them, a silence settled over the group. The road narrowed into winding trails flanked by ancient ruins, including the broken pillars of the Ramesseum, sun-blasted and leaning like tired sentinels, and the low walls of Deir el-Medina farther south, half-swallowed by the sand.

As they climbed toward the entrance to the Valley, sheer limestone cliffs pressed in from both sides. Jagged, eroded, their pale faces glowed beneath the morning sun. No birds called. No wind stirred. Even the horses stepped lighter, as though mindful of where they walked.

They all knew this road, Professor Bovet most of all. He had spent years wandering these tomb-lined ravines. But today felt different. Their pace was purposeful, their silence heavy. Somewhere among the rocks, Lavalle's eyes were watching. And perhaps something far older was watching, too.

The old man's cave was situated on a limestone hill behind the tomb of Seti I in the East Valley, the main branch of the Valley of the Kings. The valley itself was a winding, V-shaped gorge formed by erosion, with a flat, gravelly floor that narrowed in places. Sheer cliffs provided natural concealment for tomb entrances, and the cliffs were jagged and eroded, with loose scree piled up at their bases.

The mystic had refused to come out when Samhi called for him, nor did he respond to Thomas or Heléne's pleas to join them. Professor Bovet solved the impasse when he went to the cave entrance and shouted, "Old friend, show yourself now or I will personally blow the entrance to your abode to hell with a sack of dynamite!"

A moment later a thin figure appeared at the entrance, and when he was satisfied that it really was Bovet, the old man hobbled forward as fast as he could and embraced the professor.

The camp cook arrived with tea and flatbread drizzled in honey, and the group settled on stones beneath the shadow of the cliffs.

"The villagers say you've gone mad," Bovet said, eyeing his old friend. "Your cave and appearance don't exactly refute the claim."

The mystic devoured another piece of bread before replying. His speech, when it came, was surprisingly lucid and measured, even elegant.

"Ah, yes," he said, wiping crumbs from his chin. "But were I thought rational, I would have been killed long ago. Sanity is a liability these days."

"Killed by who?" Samhi asked.

The old man looked around the camp as if he was being watched by unseen eyes.

"The Mahdi," he said in a hushed voice.

The name fell like a stone. Thomas and his friends were astonished at the old man's reply, and for a moment no one spoke. Then Heléne said, "He knows you?"

"More than that," the mystic replied. "He came here. Six months ago, in March. In secret. With only a handful of men."

Professor Bovet's voice was low, wary. "Why would a man of such power travel 800 miles across hostile territory just to see you?"

"It wasn't me he sought," the mystic said. "It was what I found. Or rather… what a shepherd boy found and shared with me."

Bovet stared. "Amenhotep."

The old man nodded. Samhi exhaled sharply, and Heléne instinctively reached for Thomas's hand.

"The boy was chasing a kid goat," the mystic continued. "It had fallen into a crevice. He made a rope of thorn branches and climbed down into a buried chamber. There wasn't much light, but enough to see furniture, a chariot, strong boxes. Statues."

Bovet leaned forward, his face lined with dread. "And he came to you? Why?"

"He told his parents. They beat him for lying. So, he came to me."

Bovet nodded slowly. "Go on."

"I brought a rope ladder and a lantern. The boy led me to a slope near two large boulders. Between them, a narrow fissure had opened, likely from one of the recent tremors. I climbed down, 10 feet at most. And when I raised the lantern, I saw the cartouches. The name. The face. It was him. Amenhotep."

"Did you take anything to prove you had been there?" Thomas asked.

The mystic shook his head. "No. And then I made a mistake. After I hid the entrance and swore the boy to silence, I sought out your chief digger, Edouard. A man we trusted."

Bovet nodded his head in agreement.

"The digger left almost immediately to find the professor, who we understood was on his way from Alexandria."

"He never found me," said Bovet.

"No, Edouard, but it seems the man was also a braggart with a loose tongue, and he shared the information with a fellow traveler, who, as it happens, was one of the Mahdi's most trusted lieutenants. The soldier killed the poor fool and hastened to the Mahdi with the news."

"But why?" Heléne asked. "The Mahdi is waging a war. Why would a pharaoh's tomb matter to him?"

Thomas opened his mouth to speak, but the mystic raised a hand.

"That is… difficult to explain. I can only tell you part of the answer now. To tell you more, you would have to see the tomb for yourselves."

"We must," Bovet said. "Immediately."

The old man was quiet. His eyes, clouded with age, were still penetrating. He looked from Heléne to Thomas, as though weighing something unspeakable.

"All things in time," said the old man. "First, as to the reason the Mahdi cared enough about the discovery of the tomb to leave his headquarters outside Khartoum and journey all the way to the Valley of the Kings…"

He went quiet, gathering his thoughts and selecting his next words with great care. Before he spoke, he looked hard into Heléne's face, and then into Thomas'.

"Inside the tomb, on a wall opposite Amenhotep's burial sarcophagus, is something so terrifying, so astounding, and so…I'm sorry, I cannot think of any other word…so supernatural, that the Mahdi had no choice but to rush here as quickly as he could."

"Something that important is painted on the wall of a 3,000-year-old tomb?" Bovet asked. "I'm sorry my friend, but that is very hard for me to believe. What kind of painting could be of such significance that a leader as important as the Mahdi would step aside from his duties for weeks simply to look at?"

The old man smiled softly. "One that portrays the moment and method of his death." He turned his gaze to Thomas. "And the one who will kill him."

~THIRTY EIGHT~

Valley of the Kings – Dawn

No one slept that night. Heléne crawled into Thomas' cot, and they lay together for hours, talking about everything except the dangers that awaited them with the rising sun. Their whispers mingled with the desert's stillness, and when faint rustlings outside signaled the waking camp, they dressed and stepped out into the cool predawn air.

At the fire, Samhi had already brewed a pot of strong coffee. The flames flickered low, casting long shadows across the limestone walls. Professor Bovet was awake as well, rubbing warmth into his hands as he chewed on a dried fig. When the old mystic descended the rise from his cave, he was almost unrecognizable. His face was freshly shaven, his hair washed and combed, a clean robe cinched at the waist with a braided sash.

"Yes, they may yet kill me," he said, smiling crookedly at Heléne's approving whistle, "but I will die a clean man."

Gear had been piled near the fire: ropes, pitch torches, candle lanterns, and sticks of dynamite wrapped in cotton batting.

"Dynamite?" Heléne asked, raising an eyebrow.

Thomas nodded as he tightened the straps on the canvas bag. "Twelve sticks. Carefully bundled."

"Why the cotton?"

"To prevent sweating," he said.

"Dynamite sweats?" she asked, chuckling nervously.

"It does. And that sweat is nitroglycerin. If you're lucky, it just makes the stick useless. If you're not..." He mimed a small explosion with his hands and gave her a wink.

Heléne slipped her sketchbook into her rucksack and slung it over her shoulder. She leaned in and kissed his cheek. "I'll try to remember that."

The eastern hills were turning pearl-blue when Thomas checked the cylinder of his revolver and gave a sharp nod to Samhi.

"Are we ready?" Samhi asked.

Professor Bovet squeezed his daughter's hand and waited for her to answer for them both.

"We are," she said.

"Then let's climb."

The mystic lifted his lantern and led them along a narrow footpath into the hills. The climb was slow, the path stony and choked with brush. As the sun broke over the cliffs behind them, the shadows shrank, and the stones around them faded to the color of sand.

After 15 minutes, they reached a low shoulder in the limestone. The mystic halted beside a cluster of medium-sized boulders and tangled branches.

"This is where the entrance once was," he said quietly. "Where the boy brought me that first day."

Professor Bovet frowned. "But where is it now?"

The mystic's eyes clouded. "The Mahdi came with three of his men, two hired laborers, and me. I took them to the main burial chamber. When he saw what you are about to see..." he turned pale and silent. "Then he gave orders."

"What kind of orders?" Heléne asked.

"To kill the laborers once they had served their purpose. They were waiting above the chamber. No one who knew of the tomb could be allowed to live."

Heléne's voice dropped. "And you? And the boy?"

He lowered his head. "The boy, his parents, the digger who helped me... all gone. I was spared only because I was believed mad. No one listens to a lunatic."

"All this for a painting?" Bovet said, almost to himself.

The mystic looked up sharply. "This is about far more than a painting, Professor. The gods themselves have moved in this tomb. The Mahdi is not just curious; I'm sure he is terrified. He would order the deaths of 10,000 to understand its secret."

"But he didn't kill Edouard," Thomas said. "Or me. Or Heléne. That doesn't make sense."

"He couldn't. The prophecy forbade it. To violate it would be to undo its power. The Mahdi feared that more than he feared you."

Professor Bovet's voice grew sharper. "Prophecy? You speak in riddles and myth. Enough of this! If there is something written about my daughter, about Thomas, or about me, I want to know it now."

The old man sank onto a stone. The morning was growing hot already, the rock beneath their feet beginning to radiate heat.

"The Mahdi had this outcropping dynamited," he said, gesturing toward a blast-scarred cliff face just ahead. "He ordered it sealed beneath four feet of rubble. But I believe he meant to return. With the three of you."

He paused, his eyes sweeping across them.

"Thomas has disrupted that plan."

"Then is there another way in?" asked Bovet, straining forward.

The mystic pointed to a patch of earth 50 yards up the hill, partially obscured by brush.

"I found another entrance a few weeks ago. A split in the rock from a recent tremor. I've left it untouched. I thought it only right that you be the first to enter."

Bovet stepped forward and, in an uncharacteristic burst of emotion, embraced his old friend.

"Forgive me," he said, his voice breaking. "I've waited 40 years for this. And in my impatience, I forgot myself."

The old man laid a hand on his shoulder.

"Ah, but Edouard, my friend... this moment has waited for you for 30 centuries."

They stood together in silence, four figures framed by rising sunlight and crumbling rock. Somewhere below them, beneath layers of dust and secrecy, the answers they had chased across continents and decades waited, patient, silent, and ancient.

None of them said it aloud, but each of them knew whatever they found in that tomb, their lives would be changed forever.

Thomas and Samhi pulled the brush away from the fissure where the old man had discovered the new entrance to the tomb. Behind them, Heléne and Professor Bovet unfurled the ladder and lit the wicks of four oil lanterns. A knapsack was already packed with pitch torches in case they needed stronger light once they reached the inner chambers.

When everything was ready, they staked the ladder ends into the hard-packed ground and carefully unrolled it into the opening. It disappeared into shadow with a soft rattle of iron rungs.

Thomas dropped to his knees beside the fissure, holding a lantern low into the gap. A cool, mineral-scented draft rose from the darkness. He studied the shadows, listening. Nothing but the faint creak of the ladder and the heartbeat in his ears.

"I can't see much from here," he said, standing. "But the ladder touches the floor. We're good to go."

The old man stepped to the edge, peering into the gloom. "This entrance should place us about 100 feet from where I entered with the Mahdi. That puts us just inside the antechamber, outside the burial chamber itself. There's a corridor ahead, sloping down steeply for about 50 feet. Then a low door. And after that..."

He hesitated.

"Yes?" asked Professor Bovet.

"A wide set of steps–four, if I recall correctly–that lead down into the main chamber."

"The sarcophagus," Bovet asked, "it's surrounded by statues, yes?"

The old man nodded slowly. "Monumental ones. Guardians, perhaps. On the side walls are scenes of harvest festivals and the turning of the Nile seasons. The ceiling shows Amenhotep receiving the gods in procession."

"And the mural?" Heléne asked quietly. "The one that terrified the Mahdi?"

The mystic turned to her. "It's at the far end. About 20 feet past the sarcophagus. You can't see it until you're nearly upon it. There are two steps that rise to it. It's meant to be seen… up close."

"We'll tread carefully," Bovet said. "We know how to spot the robber traps that drop into the abyss."

"And scorpions," Samhi added dryly, brushing the back of his neck. Thomas shuddered. One sting in a lifetime was enough.

The mystic shook his head. "Those are temporal dangers," he said, his voice rough with warning. "What waits down there cannot be explained by your modern science. And for reasons I cannot fathom, the old gods have summoned all of us to this moment."

Heléne stepped beside him and laid an arm gently around his shoulders. "Then we'll face them together, old friend. There's strength in our numbers…"

"And in our explosives," Thomas added with a grin, hefting the sack of dynamite.

The mystic's tone sharpened. "Hear me…and heed this: This is not another tidy expedition from your European academies. Your weapons are of no use in the world below. Your education won't shield you from what you'll see. And your prayers will not reach the gods who dwell beneath this hill."

A hush followed. Even the wind stilled.

"So, what do you suggest?" Samhi said softly. "That we leave now, pretend this place never existed, and spend the rest of our lives wondering what lay beneath our feet?"

The old man lowered his eyes, staring into the sand. Far below them, the Nile shimmered with bands of emerald and blue. A hawk cried high above, and a small cloud passed across the sun, scattering shadows over the tomb mouth.

"That would be the wise thing," he said at last. "The gods of Egypt were abandoned 2,000 years ago. But in places like this, their power lingers."

Professor Bovet adjusted his hat and picked up a lantern. "And yet, we've come. If they summoned us here, why would they want us to turn back now?" He turned to the mystic, voice quiet but firm. "You've given more than enough. If you'd rather not go further, we'll take it from here."

The old man didn't answer. Instead, he bent down, took up his own lantern, and smiled.

The five of them formed a loose circle around the opening. Silence fell again. Then all eyes turned to Bovet. He had been exploring tombs since before Thomas or Heléne were born. Whatever lay below, this was his expedition now.

"I'll go first," he said. "Then Heléne, followed by Samhi." He looked to the mystic. "You're with us?"

The old man nodded solemnly.

"Good," said Bovet. "You last, Thomas. Hold your lanterns high when you reach the floor. Let's get our bearings before we move."

He stepped to the edge, took a breath, and climbed down into the darkness.

Heléne turned to Thomas, gave him a small, quiet smile, and followed her father down the ladder, the lantern glowing above her head.

Samhi uttered something under his breath–probably a prayer–then pulled his pack across his shoulders and descended after her.

Thomas helped steady the mystic, holding the shoulder of his robe as he stepped onto the ladder. A moment later, Samhi reached up and took the old man's hand, guiding him safely down.

Thomas lingered a moment, taking one last look across the broken limestone hills, down to the green thread of the Nile. The dynamite sat shaded beneath a nearby outcrop, alongside the extra supplies they'd staged for later.

He picked up his lantern, then hesitated.

His mother's voice came to him, unbidden: "Saint Michael the Archangel, defend us in battle. Be our protection against the wickedness and snares of the devil." She'd been a fatalist, hardened by the Great Irish Famine and forever preparing for the worst.

Thomas smiled. "Thank you, mom."

And then he turned, gripped the ladder, and lowered himself into the deep.

The stone-floored antechamber was cool and thick with the dust of centuries and the golden light from their lanterns spilled across the floor and up the walls–the first real illumination this room had seen in 3,301 years. The five travelers from across time stood motionless, the silence broken only by the soft crackle of oil wicks and the sound of them breathing.

A shaft of morning sunlight slanted through the opening above, cutting into the gloom and setting the ancient dust to dance like gold thread in a loom.

Thomas turned slowly, lantern raised, his eyes moving across the chamber walls. A procession of life-sized warriors encircled the space, each painted in vivid, undimmed hues of crimson, cobalt, and ochre. They stood poised, spears in hand, gazes fixed eternally forward.

"Protectors?" Samhi whispered.

The professor shook his head. "Escorts to the next world. A mighty king does not journey alone. Not even in death."

Heléne tilted her head, studying the painted faces. "And they believed these images would protect him?"

"Count them," Bovet said quietly.

Samhi swept the room with his eyes. "Thirty-six."

Bovet stepped forward and pointed to a section of wall where the plaster and brickwork bore subtle signs of tampering—stone replaced with care but not perfection.

"Behind that wall," he said, "you'll find the remains of 36 soldiers. Pharaoh's personal guard. Entombed with him. Each in ceremonial armor. Each with his shield."

Thomas felt a chill that had nothing to do with the cool air. "They went willingly?"

Bovet's voice was soft. "They did. They knelt, holding sword and spear. And the priests slit their throats, one by one."

Heléne stared at the floor. "You said remains. Not mummies?"

"Mummification was for preservation," Bovet explained. "But Pharaoh needed warriors for his journey—not relics. A mummified man can't rise when summoned."

A hush followed. Then Thomas cleared his throat. "What now?"

"We light two torches and proceed to the burial chamber," said Bovet.

Thomas and Samhi moved toward the knapsack, but the professor raised a hand. Instead, he walked to the low doorway that opened into the sloping corridor beyond. He paused there, lantern outstretched, the flame throwing shadows into the stone throat ahead.

"My life has been devoted to scientific truth," he said. "To peeling back the layers of history and myth in search of fact. My Christian faith steadies me, but it does not guide my research."

He glanced into the darkness beyond the doorway.

"And yet," he continued, his voice tight with conviction, "what waits for us may not be subject to the rules I have trusted all my life. It may not be understood—only witnessed."

He turned to the old mystic. "We may look to you for meaning."

The mystic gave a silent nod.

They lit the torches and the smell of burning pitch filled the chamber. Then, one by one, they stepped into the sloping passage in the same order they had climbed down the ladder.

The corridor was narrow and choked with centuries of stale air. The ceiling pressed low, and Thomas moved with his shoulders hunched, one hand on the wall, which was damp and veined with white mineral lines and smelled of old moss.

And then it opened.

Thomas stepped out last. He rose to his full height and looked up into the vastness of the burial chamber—the Hall in Which One Rests. The others were already gathered in a hush before one of six massive stone sentinels who stood watch over Pharaoh's sarcophagus. The torchlight threw slow-drifting shadows across their faces.

The vault above rose into darkness. The combined glow of lanterns and torches barely reached beyond the platform, leaving the outer corners of the chamber shrouded in gloom.

But beyond that—just past the sarcophagus, across the dark floor, beyond the reach of light—stood the far wall.

Thomas could feel it. The mural was there. He knew it was waiting.

And though every part of him longed to rush across the floor and lay eyes on the thing that had haunted his dreams, he held back. So did they all. Because the air itself was different now.

He could feel it shift.

They approached the far wall in silence. The vaulted chamber echoed with the sound of their footsteps, muffled and uncertain, as if they were intruders walking on sacred ground. Their torches stretched long shadows across the stone floor, and above them, painted gods watched from the ceiling, their faces frozen in mid-gesture.

Then the light found it.

A wall-sized panel, broad and tall, emerged from the gloom like something waking from a dream. The mural had been painted in unmistakable Egyptian style with stiff-limbed figures, deep reds, blacks, ochres, and turquoise–but what stopped them was the realism. The center figures were unlike anything ever found in a tomb of this period.

They were alive.

A man and a woman stood side by side, rendered in colors as fresh as if the brushes had been laid down that morning. Their garments were unfamiliar, neither linen wraps nor priestly robes but layered tunics and tailored trousers. Their faces were forward, eyes direct, unsmiling but calm. The man's forest-green eyes held a fierce clarity. The woman's pale blue gaze was softer, but no less steady. They stood not as servants or gods or scribes, but as witnesses. Equals. Outsiders.

Thomas couldn't breathe. He felt his torch tremble in his grip.

"That's–"

He stopped. He didn't finish. He couldn't.

Beside him, Heléne stepped forward with wide eyes. Her breath caught as she lifted her lantern. "It's us," she whispered. "It's us."

The painting surrounded them. Behind the central figures was the Valley of the Kings, shown not in glory, but in ruin. Collapsed tombs, shattered statues, the desert choked with debris. In the distance, a figure was pinned to a wall by a wooden pole, his robes swirling, his face obscured. But, from the ring of gold around his head, there was no mistaking who it was.

"The Mahdi," Samhi said, quiet and certain.

And in the foreground: the man, a figure who looked like Thomas, pushed the pole against the other man's abdomen with both hands.

Professor Bovet dropped his torch.

The clatter rang off the walls like a trumpet blast, but no one flinched. He didn't stoop to retrieve it. He just stared, his eyes wide, his mouth slightly open, as if something inside him had broken loose.

"My God," he said.

Thomas took a step backward. The air felt thick. Too heavy to breathe.

He turned to Heléne, and for the first time since entering the tomb, he saw fear in her. Not panic or dread. Something deeper. She wasn't looking at the mural anymore; she was looking at him.

Samhi bowed his head. He muttered something in Arabic and touched his hand to his chest.

The old mystic took a long breath, as though the mural itself exhaled through him. "It is as I told you," he said softly, almost with reverence. "The painting is not a prophecy. It is a memory." His eyes glistened. "Time does not move forward in this place. It surrounds."

Bovet finally stepped back from the painting and turned toward his daughter. "Heléne, I…"

He stopped. Words failed him.

They stood together–five souls who had crossed deserts, survived violence, endured visions–and yet nothing had prepared them for this.

The mural did not answer their questions. It erased them.

Then a sound, faint and echoing, followed by voices.

"I'm telling you; they came this way…," an unfamiliar voice said.

Thomas's head snapped up. He grabbed Samhi's arm. "Lavalle's men," he said.

Heléne extinguished her torch as Samhi pulled Bovet back from the mural and motioned towards the sounds in the corridor.

The mural faded into darkness.

After all they had gone through, they had seen it.

And now they had to leave it behind.

~THIRTY NINE~

"Get down behind the sarcophagus," Thomas whispered, urgent and low. "One lamp stays lit–snuff the rest."

The tomb plunged into near darkness, with the lone flame flickering softly. He reached for Heléne's arm. "You have your revolver?"

She nodded, already drawing the .32 caliber Navy pistol from her belt.

"If anyone enters without a word, shoot," Thomas said.

"Wait," she whispered. "What are you going to do?"

"We can't wait for them to come to us. They won't stop until they reach this chamber." He looked over at Samhi, who was crouched beside him. "We go to them."

Samhi nodded without hesitation. Words were unnecessary now.

"And then what?" asked Professor Bovet in a low, hoarse voice.

There was no time to answer. Thomas held Heléne's gaze a moment longer, sharing a silent promise. Then he tapped Samhi's shoulder. Together, revolvers drawn, they moved soundlessly up the steps to the low doorway leading into the corridor.

A faint glow bobbed in the distance.

"They're coming," Thomas murmured. "We can't both go in," he added. "Too narrow. And when the shooting starts, nowhere to dodge."

Samhi answered with his eyes. He would follow.

More voices echoed from the tunnel.

"They've stopped talking," said one of Lavalle's men.

"Means they know we're close," said another.

The lantern's dancing light went still.

Thomas reached for the wall and found it by touch. "I'll draw them to me. I'll shoot three times. You wait. When they fire back and then go quiet, you step out and return fire. Three shots."

He didn't wait for an answer. He slid two steps to the left, steadied himself and squeezed the trigger three times. The explosion of the .45 Colt was deafening in the stone tunnel.

A startled voice howled from the darkness. Then came return fire from two pistols. Bullets chipped the limestone beside Thomas's face, spraying his cheek with slivers of rock.

He ducked just as Samhi took the center position and fired off three shots.

One shot struck the attacker's lantern; the glass shattered, and the light tumbled to the floor. Another scream, and a body crumpled in shadow.

Were there two left? Three?

Thomas didn't wait to find out. He stepped into the corridor and advanced fast, firing three more times as he moved.

Another muzzle flashed in reply and Thomas felt heat near his scalp as a bullet zipped past and cracked into the wall behind. He pulled the trigger again but heard only the click on an empty cylinder.

Samhi tapped his back and Thomas stepped aside, reloading in the darkness as the Bedouin swept forward and continued firing.

There was silence, and then footsteps and the sound of feet scuffling backward in retreat. The attackers were pulling back into the antechamber.

Thomas shoved the final round into the cylinder, snapped it shut, and surged forward. Samhi followed behind him, reloading on the run.

Then a man launched from the shadows and slammed into Samhi. They went down hard, their weapons scattering, and the sound of their fists and grunts echoing through the passage.

Thomas didn't stop. He ducked and barreled into the antechamber. Light from the fissure above poured down in shafts of gold where two of Lavalle's men had retreated. One lay writhing, bleeding on the floor. The other was reloading fast.

Thomas' shot caught the man clean in the chest. The impact of the bullet sent him tumbling back, where he struck a pillar and collapsed, sending his burning torch clattering across the floor.

Thomas grabbed it, turned, and hurled it down the corridor.

It spun end-over-end and landed where Samhi was still wrestling with his attacker. Samhi pushed away and lunged to pick up the torch. He slammed the burning end against his attacker's body and a moment later, the man's hair and shirt erupted in flame.

Thomas couldn't stop to watch because the wounded man on the ground had drawn a curved blade and was struggling to his feet. Thomas kicked the sword away, knelt, and drove his Bowie knife deep into the man's throat.

When he stood and turned to check on Samhi, the corridor was ablaze, not just with fire, but with a man on fire.

Samhi backed away, the torch still in his hand. The flaming attacker staggered, arms flailing, mouth open in a soundless scream. His feet found no escape, only one of the tomb-builder's deadly thief-traps: a gaping shaft in the stone floor.

He dropped, flailing and shrieking until his body hit bottom, where a dozen sharp spear tips embedded in stone by priests 3,000 years ago tore through his flesh and brought his agony to an end.

Samhi bent over to catch his breath, his chest heaving, sweat gleaming on his face. Thomas grabbed his shoulder.

"You alright?"

The Bedouin nodded. "That one won't have much to tell Lavalle."

Thomas looked to the opening in the rock and dirt above them. "There are more up there," he said. "At least two. They haven't followed yet, they're waiting to see who comes back."

Samhi nodded again. "They'll know soon enough."

"We can't fight another battle down here," Thomas added. "We need to get everyone to the surface and find out what's next."

He looked up to where sunlight streamed through the fissure in the bedrock. He could not see anyone near the opening or hear conversation or footsteps.

"I've got to take a look," he told Samhi. "Bring the others here and wait for me."

He holstered his revolver and took a deep breath. Then he climbed slowly up the ladder until his head was just below the opening. Still no sound or movement. He peeked just above the rim and swung his head around. There was no one in sight.

The heat slammed him as he climbed out of the antechamber, but he paid it no attention. He quickly scanned the brush and boulders surrounding the tomb entry, but no one was here. Then he walked over to the edge of the hill and looked down into the valley below. There they were–three men on horseback, riding swiftly in the direction of the narrow limestone cleft that led out to the plain and the Nile beyond. Lavalle's men were retreating. But why?

Professor Bovet came up from the antechamber last and marched over to Thomas, who had one arm wrapped around Heléne's shoulder. The shock of seeing the mural, combined with her fear for Thomas and Samhi's safety as they battled Lavalle's men had left her numb.

"We must return to the burial chamber. Now," the professor insisted. It was not a request.

Thomas shook his head. Then he walked Heléne over to a flat rock and sat her down beside the old mystic, who was mumbling a prayer under his breath.

"That isn't going to happen, at least not until tomorrow morning," Thomas answered. "Lavalle's men might have turned to run for home, or they might be meeting up with reinforcements. Until we know, we stay right here on this hill where we can see who is coming and going into the valley. If they haven't returned by an hour after sunrise we can go back inside the chamber. But not until then."

Bovet turned to Samhi,who nodded his head. "Thomas is right, Edouard. We can hold off attackers up here. We wouldn't stand a chance down at the camp."

The Professor sighed in resignation. The greatest moment of his long and distinguished career had to wait. "I'll need my notebooks from camp, and I'm sure Heléne wants to sketch from memory while it is still fresh."

Thomas looked over the edge of the cliff to their campsite 200 yards below. "Samhi and Heléne and I will go down and fetch whatever we all need," he said. "We'll pack food and water, bedrolls, and wood for a fire up on the horses. The dog, too. We can get by for one night without tents."

An hour later their supplies were unloaded, and the horses were tethered in the shade of a rock outcropping. The sun was at its peak directly above them, and the green ribbon of the Nile teased them from a distance with its promise of cool water and refreshing breezes.

The professor found a comfortable log to sit on and was soon filling the pages of a notebook with thoughts on today's remarkable findings, while Heléne struggled to calm her emotions enough to begin sketching the wall mural in the burial chamber from memory. The old man volunteered to make dinner and Thomas and Samhi traded watch at the edge of the hill. No one would be able to come into the valley without them seeing.

And when they did, especially if they came in force? Thomas didn't want to think about that. For now, he was content to sit in silence next to Heléne, watchful, his Winchester across his lap. After what they had seen in the tomb, what could either of them possibly say?

That night after dinner, as a blanket of gleaming stars greeted the new moon and the temperature dropped 50 degrees, they gathered by the fire. Thomas passed a bottle of brandy around to fortify the coffee, and he was pleased to see that even the old man poured himself a slug. Each of them wanted to speak, but no one knew how to express the cascade of emotions that had overwhelmed their senses the moment the light from Thomas' lantern illuminated the mural in Amenhotep's tomb.

It fell upon the professor to break the silence. "I cannot pretend that I understand what we witnessed today," he began as Thomas added another log to the fire, sending sparks streaming up into the darkness. "In fact, until we can go back and make a thorough study of the mural, I can't even say for certain that we saw anything."

"What do you mean, professor?" asked Samhi. "Are you suggesting we did not see what we know we did? I'm sorry, but that's crazy. I saw something… unreal. We all did."

"You make my point for me, my friend," said Bovet. "You acknowledge that what we saw was 'unreal.' Follow the logic: it is physically impossible to witness unreality. A thing either exists in reality, or it does not. There is no middle ground."

"You're suggesting we did not see Thomas and me in that mural?" asked Heléne. "But that is madness, father. You saw it, I did, we all saw it. It was no phantasm."

The old mystic couldn't hold back. He broke out in laughter, long and loud and so infectious that Thomas and Samhi couldn't help but join him.

The professor was not amused. "You said this morning that I should not try to explain what we might find in the tomb through the language of science," he said sternly. "But I tell you this, old friend, your mystic mumbo-jumbo can't explain it, either. At least I can define the situation in scientific terms and then seek out the most plausible explanations for the phenomena. Can your runes and incantations do that?"

The old man had stopped laughing, but he was still grinning from ear to ear. "Look up, Edouard," he said, pointing high into the night sky. "What do you see?"

"Alright, I'll play along," the professor answered. "I see stars, and a new moon."

"Can you name the stars?"

"A few of them."

Then the old man traced a line across the heavens with one boney finger. "And how many might there be?" he asked. "Thousands, millions, millions of millions?"

"Impossible to say," the professor replied. "We don't have any way to count them all."

"All created by your god?"

"Yes, I believe that to be true."

"And for what purpose did your god create these points of light?" the mystic continued.

"Not having had a conversation with the Almighty on the topic, I could not say," answered Bovet.

"So, then, now you have told me, with no absence of certitude or scientific confidence, that not only do you not know how many stars are in the heavens, but that you also have no clue as to what purpose–if any–they may serve."

"I will submit that many things in heaven and even here on earth have yet to be understood, my friend," said Edouard with a smile. He knew where the old man was headed.

"And are there some things that we may never understand, no matter how arduously we apply your vaunted scientific method to the search?"

Professor Bovet chuckled. "I concede your point. However, in defense of science I would also add that the search for explanations is never ending, whether it has to do with stars or murals on a 3,000-year-old tomb wall."

"It is a miracle, you know," Heléne said in a soft voice.

Thomas nodded and stirred the fire with his stick. "My mother would say that the point of a miracle isn't to be explained. It's just to be witnessed.

"And what does her son say?" asked Samhi with a smile.

"He says that 3,000 years ago someone painted that wall expecting us to find it. That's not science. And it's not mysticism either." He looked at Bovet. "It's intention."

The others waited for him to finish his thought. He poured more brandy into his cup. "We saw it. It doesn't matter why. What does matter is what we do next."

Heléne took his hand and for a moment no one spoke.

"Here is what I do know," Thomas continued in a slow, solemn voice. "Some things are true before we understand them. What we saw today is real."

The conversation around the fire died out, and the five friends sat quietly as the orange flames burned down to embers under the endless sky.

~FORTY~

Valley of the Kings Overlook

Heléne's dog smelled the riders before Samhi spotted them through the field glasses. The sun had just broken above the eastern hills, casting long shadows across the desert and bathing the valley in hues of lavender and blue. Professor Bovet had been awake for hours, pacing with the nervous energy of a child on Christmas morning, his canvas kit bag slung over one shoulder.

Thomas and Heléne sat near the last embers of the fire, finishing bowls of porridge the old mystic had prepared. When the dog gave a low growl and went rigid, Thomas rose and joined Samhi at the bluff's edge. Below, their camp lay quiet and abandoned. Beyond it, near the river's edge, the first shards of morning light were catching the slow curve of the Nile.

Thomas handed Samhi a tin cup of coffee. The dog stood beside them now, hackles up, ears pointed toward the wind.

"What is it, boy?" Thomas asked softly.

"Fox, jackal, hyena... take your pick," Samhi said, squinting into the light as he handed over the binoculars. "The only thing it can't be is a scientist. No expeditions this late in the season, and none at all since the war began."

"Hard on your business?" Thomas asked, scanning the valley through the lenses.

Samhi chuckled. "Hard enough that my wife has suggested I become a rug merchant in Alexandria. She says there's a fortune in selling handwoven carpets to British ladies. Can you picture it, Thomas? Me in the bazaar, smiling sweetly while I say, 'Madam, this rug is so plush it will keep your toes warm through the darkest London winter.'"

As he sighed and turned toward the fire, Thomas said, "It's no jackal. There are men riding up from the river."

Samhi took the binoculars back, adjusted the focus, and frowned. "Six of them. Three in front, two behind, and one in the center."

Thomas was already loading his Winchester. "Middle man's important, then."

Samhi nodded. "Likely. They're guarding him."

"I'm sorry, Professor," Thomas said as Bovet appeared with his pack slung and ready. "We have visitors. You'll have to wait before heading back into the tomb."

Bovet's shoulders sagged. He opened his mouth to protest, but Heléne laid a hand on his arm and guided him away to help her feed the horses. The mystic wordlessly resumed tidying up the breakfast pots.

Thomas returned to the ridge. "Anything more?"

"They're dressed in black," Samhi said, his voice lower now. "No turbans. Not Lavalle's men. And those aren't the nags his mercenaries ride. Too fine."

Thomas took another look through the binoculars. The rising sun was behind the riders now, and the glare washed their outlines in gold, making detail difficult. But the number held—six. Six men, riding with purpose.

"How far?" Samhi asked.

"Close to 1,200 yards," Thomas said. "They'll be at the canyon entrance in ten minutes."

"That rifle of yours good at that range?"

Thomas shook his head. "The Model '76 is solid to 300 yards, but past that it drops like a stone. It's chambered in .45-70. Good for buffalo at two-fifty."

Samhi gave him a side glance. "You have noticed that we are a bit short on buffalo in these parts?"

Thomas managed a grin. "Let's figure out who they are before we start knocking anyone off their horse."

Bovet and Heléne returned as the sun rose higher, brightening the limestone canyon below. The ancient tombs that lined the sides of the canyon below were half buried by dust and time and looked like broken teeth. Their own camp lay just past the final bend and was still out of sight from the riders, for now.

"They're about 800 yards," Samhi said. "I can see faces. Don't recognize any of them. But they're armed, and they look disciplined."

Thomas adjusted the field glasses again, sweeping from left to right. The men rode with a smoothness that came from long experience. Their robes were simple and black, unadorned. No banners. No ornament.

When they entered the canyon a few minutes later, the group vanished for a moment behind the rock walls. Then they reemerged, and Thomas's breath caught.

He turned the dials slowly, bringing the central figure into sharp relief. The glare faded. The face came into focus.

Thomas lowered the binoculars and stared at the earth. His chest rose once, deeply, and he could not speak.

Heléne stepped to his side and gently touched his arm. "Thomas?"

He didn't answer right away. Then he looked up at her, at Samhi, at the professor, and at the old man by the fire.

Samhi's voice was quiet. "Who is it, my friend? More of Lavalle's assassins?"

Thomas looked toward the horizon, past the Nile and into memory.

"Not Lavalle," he said, the words like stone. He turned to Heléne, his voice grave. "It's the Mahdi."

Samhi and Bovet stood stunned, speechless.

The Mahdi. The man whose word had imprisoned them, kidnapped Heléne, and thrown half of North Africa into chaos. A man whose name alone turned cities to battlegrounds and inspired tens of thousands to die for his vision of empire and faith.

"He only brought five men?" Heléne asked.

"There could be 5,000 more behind them," Samhi muttered.

"Or 50,000," added Bovet grimly.

The mystic finally spoke. "No. It is as before. He travels in secret. A larger force would provoke too much notice, and perhaps even war with Britain on a new front. He is powerful, but not reckless."

"Then why come?" Samhi asked. "To see the mural again?"

"To fulfill his destiny," the mystic said. "And to challenge the gods of prophecy by killing Thomas."

Heléne's grip tightened on Thomas's arm. Bovet stepped toward the ledge, gazing down at the six black-robed riders approaching their campsite below.

"What of the treasure?" he asked. "The tomb?"

"The Mahdi doesn't care," the old man said softly. "Only what it means. To him, this is a holy place. But only if he destroys it."

Bovet bristled. "Speak plainly, damn you. What does he want?"

"To bury the secret," the mystic replied. "And all of us with it."

Thomas stood straighter and drew his shoulders back. He stepped to the edge of the bluff, his face in full light now, and watched the riders approach. When he turned back, the others saw it in his eyes—the quiet resolve of a man who had faced war before and was ready to face it again.

"The Mahdi is not going to get his wish," he said.

"Not today."

Thomas and his friends watched in silence as the Mahdi and his five riders circled slowly around the empty tents on the narrow canyon floor below. Their black robes trailed behind them like shadows, and the only sound that drifted up to the ledge was the creak of saddles and the dry crunch of gravel beneath the horse's hooves.

"We all know why they've come," Thomas said to the group, "and with those cliff walls surrounding us on three sides, there's no other way out."

Samhi finished his thought. "Except through the riders."

Thomas motioned for Heléne and her father to back up by the old man beside a protective rock outcropping before he crouched beside Samhi to take better stock of their situation. Heat shimmered over the rocks around them and the harsh light of noon washed everything in bone-white glare.

Below them, the riders paused at the edge of the abandoned tents.

"They haven't seen us," Samhi murmured.

"Not yet," Thomas said as he moved into a prone shooting position at the very edge of the bluff. "But they will. No point in waiting…"

He pulled the Winchester up along his cheek and raised the Lyman tang sight with a practiced flick. The sight was a gift from Bill Cody, who had shown him how to account for distance and windage when they hunted buffalo in the Dakotas.

"If you want to hit a man in the chest from 200 yards," the famous army scout told him, "Aim for the top of his hat. And if there is a mild cross wind, also adjust by half a man's width at 150 yards."

The vernier scale glinted faintly as he dialed it to 250 yards, the distance his experience and instinct judged the riders had reached. As he peered through the peep's aperture his world narrowed to a single rider's silhouette, the warrior riding directly in front of the Mahdi. When the front bead settled true just a few inches above the unsuspecting warrior's head, he fired.

The bullet took the man in the left shoulder, spinning him off his saddle and onto the ground. Samhi immediately fired his rifle, but his shot missed. He fired again and dust spat up near the Mahdi's feet. The Bedouin guide's third shot found flesh and a second warrior tumbled to the sand, screaming as he clutched his gut.

Chaos exploded around the camp. The remaining four riders scattered for cover, leaping from their saddles behind rock outcrops and overturned crates.

Heléne and the old man and her father huddled behind a rock column, and her dog stayed low, silent and waiting.

Thomas and Samhi knew they had to stay on the offensive. They stood and moved fast, sliding down the steep embankment in bursts, from boulder to bush, gravel giving way beneath their boots. As they worked their way down, the Mahdi and his warrior's rifles cracked again and again in unison, echoing against the canyon walls and spraying Samhi and Thomas with clumps of brush and shards of gravel. Sweat streamed down Thomas's spine as the sun climbed higher and burned away the last cool breeze of morning. He stopped at a jut of limestone and fired again as a third rider lunged from a tattered canvas lean-to only to catch a bullet clean through the chest. He staggered, pitched forward, and did not move again.

Now three remained: two warriors, and the Mahdi.

Thomas ducked behind a thick bush to reload and was distressed to see Samhi toss aside his rifle, stand straight up and begin firing his revolver as he walked steadily and deliberately down the hill towards the camp. The Mahdi's last remaining protectors returned fire, and Thomas continued to fire and watched as sand erupted around his friend's feet.

Samhi kept walking. Then another shot from his revolver rang out and struck home. A man crouching and firing from in front of the Mahdi collapsed and the great leader and his last remaining bodyguard scurried for protection behind a boulder.

Then came the spit of return fire, and Samhi jerked sideways. He was hit hard and tumbled down the slope into a clutch of thorn bushes, vanishing into the thicket without making a sound.

Thomas froze; his eyes fixed where Samhi had disappeared. He waited for movement, any sign, but there was nothing. Only the wind moved now.

He slid behind a flat boulder and scanned the valley floor. One warrior was left, and the Mahdi was still hidden. They were waiting and watching.

Time passed and the September heat grew unbearable. An hour. Maybe more.

Then, faint and hoarse, he heard a whisper from the brush below.

"Thomas."

Samhi was alive.

Thomas looked up the hill and signaled to Heléne and her father to provide cover fire with their revolvers. Their bullets ricochetted off the canyon floor and threw dust and gravel around the Mahdi's hiding place, allowing Thomas to break cover and sprint down the slope, where he found Samhi dragging himself up the hill.

The Bedouin's side was soaked in blood, but there was no way Thomas could tend to him here. He slung his friend over his shoulder and climbed uphill as fast as he could, as Heléne and her father used the last of their ammunition to keep the Mahdi pinned down. When Thomas got to the top of the bluff, the old man helped pull Samhi off his shoulder and Thomas collapsed in exhaustion.

Heléne and the old mystic worked fast; binding Samhi's wound and pressing cloth to the bleeding. Samhi grimaced and tried to speak, but he had lost a lot of blood and could not find the strength to do anything but lay back with the cool damp cloth Heléne laid on his forehead. She looked across at him, fear and worry etched on her face.

Thomas pulled himself up and went over beside them. He touched Heléne gently on the cheek and then knelt and placed a hand on his friend's shoulder. "I'll see you soon."

When the old man and Professor Bovet joined them a moment later Thomas said, "The Mahdi isn't going to wait, even with just one warrior to help him. We can't fight up here, and so I am going back down to finish this business. No matter what, when you hear the shooting stop you must get off this hill. There are supplies and ammo in the camp. Get them, then leave the old man with Samhi and go to the village for help."

He took Heléne's hand in his. "It won't be long," he said. Her eyes glistened with tears and her lip was trembling, but she nodded in understanding.

Her father stepped forward and lay a hand on Thomas' shoulder. "Thank you for everything," he said.

Thomas stood, slung his rifle over his shoulder and descended the hill once more–this time alone.

~FORTY ONE~

The sky was hard and high and cloudless, and the air turned metallic with heat. Distant birds wheeled over the Nile, a silver thread on the far horizon.

He moved low with his Colt in his outstretched hand, weaving between crumbling mud brick walls and terraces that had been cut into stone 3,000 years ago, until he reached the slope behind the Mahdi's hiding place in a cluster of rocks and wooden shacks built by three generations of European Egyptologists. He flanked left, staying below the line of sight, circling silently.

Then, a rustle in the bushes.

A black-robed figure sprang from the thicket, blade in hand.

Thomas barely turned before the curved knife flashed toward his neck. He caught the man's wrist and twisted hard, but the blade nicked his cheek, and hot blood ran down his face. They struggled–grappling, panting and sliding in the dust. The warrior was young and strong, and he was able to drive Thomas back while slashing his blade back and forth. Thomas stumbled over a wooden post and fell onto his back, his revolver tumbling onto the hard-packed dirt. He raised both arms and immediately formed an 'X' shape with them in an attempt to ward off the killing blow that he knew would come next.

Then–a blur.

A white streak bounded down the slope, spraying dirt and gravel in its wake. It was Heléne's Saluki. The dog launched from a rock ledge six feet above the combatants and landed full force on the warrior's back. The hound's teeth tore into the soft flesh of the man's neck. He screamed, dropped his knife, and tried to roll away, but the dog held fast, swinging his powerful jaws left and right as he ripped deeper into the man's throat. Blood sprayed in pulsing jets from the warrior's neck, drenching the Saluki's white coat as the hound shook its jaws. Moments later, the warrior slumped, dead.

Heléne whistled once from above, and the dog scrambled back up the rocks, vanishing like smoke.

Thomas struggled to catch his breath and pushed himself upright. Now he faced only one man; the Mahdi.

Thomas waited in the shade of a towering thorn bush and wished he'd brought a canteen. The Mahdi was secure in his hiding place among the rocks and unused expedition supply shacks just 50 yards away. Heléne and her father changed watch above him every 15 minutes. They knew that the next exchange of gunfire between Thomas and the Mahdi would be the last of this battle. When the shooting died out, they would honor his final command and come down the hill to face whatever awaited them.

After two hours of waiting, Thomas began to work his way silently towards the cluster of rocks and small wooden structures. When he stepped on a brittle tree branch, the snapping sound alerted the Mahdi that he was on the move.

The Mahdi's voice floated across to him, calm and mocking.

"Colonel Scoundrel, my old friend. Still alive?"

"Unlike your personal guards, Ahmad bin Fahal. Shame they weren't better trained," Thomas called back.

The Mahdi's voice grew stronger. "I give you safe passage, Thomas. Throw down your rifle, gather your friends, and leave this place forever. I will spare your lives."

Thomas raised his head. "I appreciate the offer," he called back. "But I have dinner plans, and my hosts don't like their guests to be late. In any event, you are alone now, and in no position to bargain for anything."

In reply the Mahdi chuckled. "When I do not return to the river within the next hour," he said, "50 men will sweep up into this little valley. You and your friends will be dead before the first owl begins its night song."

Thomas considered what the Mahdi was saying. It was entirely possible that he had traveled with more men than the five warriors who had escorted him into the valley. Or the old man could have been right about the kind of international incident that traveling with a force of that size might bring about.

Ultimately, it didn't matter. One way or another this battle had to end. He thought for a minute and then, in a loud, clear voice, said, "So be it. Enjoy your journey to *hadis*."

The Mahdi answered with a full-throated laugh. "Hell? You have been an excellent student of our language, Thomas Scoundrel. Despite your sincere wishes, though, I suspect we will make that trip together."

As dusk bled across the sky the heat broke, replaced by a dry wind sweeping up from the Nile.

Thomas moved, fast and low, across the canyon mouth. He reached an old excavation ruin of crumbling bricks and limestone blocks abandoned years ago only a few yards from where he believed the Mahdi was holed up.

He crouched, reloaded the Winchester, and stepped around a wall with the rifle at the ready. The Mahdi was there, kneeling behind the canvas tent with his rifle across his knees, watching for Thomas to come from the other direction.

Then, Thomas heard a crunching sound in the gravel behind him. The Mahdi's warriors were all dead. Had Heléne or the professor clambered down the trail to come to his aid? He turned to see, and a rifle stock smashed into his face.

He dropped to one knee, his vision blurred. He shook his head…they hadn't killed all the warriors! But he also saw that the man looming over him with his rifle barrel pointed at his face was unsteady on his feet. He had been wounded, but not gravely.

Thomas lunged forward and grabbed the barrel of the rifle, and the two men began wrestling for control. The warrior shoved him back, raised the weapon and pressed his finger against the trigger.

Then—a single shot.

But it was the warrior who fell dead, not Thomas. He whirled around to see the Mahdi standing behind him, his revolver still smoking.

"This fight is between you and me," said the Mahdi, his eyes blazing. "As the gods foreordained."

Then he tossed aside his revolver and drew a dagger.

Thomas pulled his Bowie knife, and they began to circle, two men marked by prophecy, their shadows long on the sand.

Thomas lunged and the first clash of steel on steel rang out. The Mahdi dodged the thrust, spun around and slashed at Thomas' chest.

Thomas ducked and countered, and the Mahdi grunted as the blade of the Bowie clipped him across the ribs.

Now the Mahdi feinted low with lightning speed and caught Thomas's thigh with a slice.

Thomas stumbled, staggered back, and then surged forward and slammed into him. They rolled through the dust, their knives flailing, their feet kicking wildly.

They broke apart, both gasping for air as the sky above them turned gold, then copper, and then violet.

A few heartbeats later they were on their feet and charging again, their blades clashing, arms locked, and breath ragged. When Thomas suddenly slipped on a pile of excavation rubble and crashed backward, the Mahdi straddled his body and raised his dagger.

Thomas reached to his side and then behind his head, his hands scrabbling for a rock, a shard of pottery, a thorn branch, anything he could use to ward off the next knife thrust.

He stretched his arms our farther behind his head and his fingers made contact with something made of wood. Then he kicked the Mahdi between the legs with all his remaining strength before grasping the pole and pulling it across his chest. The Mahdi grimaced in pain and nearly lost his footing, but he regrouped quickly. That gave Thomas time to see what he had grabbed; a four-foot digging pole that was sharpened to a fine point at one end, flat at the other.

He got up to one knee, slid the flat end of the pole under his arm and tightened his grip with both hands. Then, as the Mahdi flung himself down to finish the battle with a final killing thrust, Thomas drove the pole up into the Mahdi's belly.

The Mahdi gasped and staggered back, his eyes wide in shock and realization more than pain.

Still holding the pole, Thomas scrambled to his feet. He repositioned his hands for better control, lowered his shoulders and then drove forward with everything he had.

The force of his movement slammed the Mahdi back several feet against the door of a wood shack. Then Thomas pushed again, and the sharpened pole drove completely through the Mahdi's abdomen, out his back and into the door.

The Mahdi arched and his mouth opened, but he made no sound.

Then his arms dropped to his sides, and he hung forward like a limp rag doll, impaled beneath a sky of dying light.

Thomas collapsed in a heap just as Heléne and her father raced into the camp. She went to her knees beside him and cradled his head on her lap while her father circled the battlefield with his revolver to make sure no more attackers were waiting in the gathering darkness.

When he was satisfied they were safe, he returned and helped Heléne walk Thomas to his tent, where they lay him on a cot and covered him with a blanket. Then he added wood to the smoldering campfire, mounted the Mahdi's horse and trotted up the hill to check on Samhi and the old man.

The sun disappeared behind the ridge a few minutes later and the first stars blinked into view. Heléne wrapped a shawl around her shoulders and pulled a camp stool close to Thomas' cot.

She took his hand in hers, and when he closed his eyes, they heard the night song of an owl, low, hollow, and haunting, singing to the stars, the stones, and the ghosts who still walked these ancient sands.

~FORTY TWO~

Professor Bovet spent the night on the bluff, helping the old mystic tend to Samhi's wound. The Bedouin guide was rallying, but Bovet knew he would need to be seen by a doctor in Luxor as soon as possible.

At daybreak, he rode down the hill with the other horses in tow, and stopped short when he saw the Mahdi's corpse still hanging from the door of the storage shack. He found a canvas tarp and had just begun to cover the body when Thomas and Heléne emerged from their tent and began restoking the fire.

"Can't leave him like this," Thomas said as he walked across camp and joined the professor. "Or him," he added, nodding towards the warrior he had been fighting until the Mahdi killed his own man with a pistol shot.

"I'll help you move them," said Bovet.

"No. I've done this before, best you don't have to," Thomas answered. "Why don't you help Heléne rustle up some coffee."

Once Bovet left, Thomas wrapped his scarf around his nose and mouth and yanked the tarp off the Mahdi. He braced a boot against the wall and pulled the pole out of the Mahdi's abdomen. There was a stomach-churning sucking sound as the pole exited the front of the body, which collapsed like the carcass of a dead animal onto the hard dirt.

He dragged the Mahdi behind a pile of rubble and pulled the body of the dead warrior over beside him. Clay rubble and dirt were plentiful around the digging sites, and it took only a few minutes to cover both bodies under a foot of debris. Wild animals would still be able to root them out, but by the time these bodies and the corpses of the other four men he and Samhi killed yesterday began to ripen in the heat he and the others would be back in Luxor.

In a valley filled with thousands of the dead, who would be troubled by six new residents?

"Thank you, Thomas," said the professor when he returned to the fire and accepted a cup of coffee from Heléne. "It's one thing to see a prophecy in paint. Quite another to live through it."

Thomas could only nod. No words could describe the flood of emotions that had consumed his mind since they stood in front of that damn mural.

Bovet understood. "We must get Samhi to Luxor," he said, changing the subject, "or bring a doctor here."

"We can have him there in four hours if he can ride," said Heléne. "Sending one of us to fetch a doctor and bring him back would mean at least eight hours until he could be properly cared for. That's too long."

Thomas and the professor shared a glance. She was right.

"We'll leave all of the extra gear here and send porters for it later," Thomas said.

"What about the Mahdi's horses?" asked Heléne. "There are six."

"There's forage and water along the river," Thomas answered. "They'll be fine."

"One more thing," said the professor. "The Mahdi was an important person, the leader of hundreds of thousands of warriors and the architect of the war against Egypt and Britain. Who do we tell? The news must be shared with the world."

Thomas stared at the horizon. "Why? No one knows he came here. Not the British. Not the Egyptians. Khartoum has fallen. Gordon is dead. The war's over. Let it be."

Bovet hesitated. "So, the man who dreamed of ruling a caliphate stretching from Turkey to Spain ends up as worm food behind an abandoned shack?"

Thomas put his foot in a stirrup and swung up onto Saher's back. "I guess that's about the size of it," he said as he tapped the horse's flank.

When Heléne and her father followed him up to the camp a few minutes later her dog trotting close at her heel.

Thomas was with Samhi, pressing a cool cloth to his brow. As Heléne tethered the horses, he knelt beside the cot. "Let me check your wound."

Samhi nodded, then winced as Thomas peeled away the bandage. The bullet had passed through clean, but the edges were darkening. Infection had started. Thomas rinsed the wound with a thimble of brandy, then passed the flask to Samhi, who managed a grin after a sip.

When Heléne returned a minute later her father asked if she had seen the old man. She shook her head.

"Latrine?" Thomas asked.

Samhi coughed and tried to speak but it was clear that talking was just as painful as moving because he had to use his abdominal muscles. But when Thomas laid a hand on his shoulder to urge him to remain quiet, Samhi shook his head back and forth and forced a whisper.

"He's not back?" he managed to ask.

"He is not," answered the professor.

"Left ten minutes ago. Carrying something, I couldn't see what…"

Heléne hurried to the limestone overhang where they had piled the gear they used to go into the tomb. Lanterns, torches, small shovels and pickaxes…all there. Except…

She rushed back to where her father and Thomas were helping Samhi to sit up. If he was to get on a horse with one of them, he had to start here.

"Oh, Thomas," Heléne blurted. "Your dynamite. It's gone!"

The professor's eyes locked with Thomas'. "You don't think the old fool…"

"Did he say anything?" Thomas asked Samhi.

"Nothing," came the answer in a hoarse voice.

"Stay with him," Thomas told the professor. Then he gestured to Heléne, took her hand, and they raced up the hill to the tomb entrance.

They spotted him at once—squatting next to the fissure. The rope ladder had been lowered into the antechamber and the canvas dynamite sack was slung over his shoulder. In the other hand he held a pitch torch.

He saw them and grinned. "I knew you'd come," he called. "But you need to get out of the valley now. I'll give you as much time as I can."

With that he disappeared into the darkness. Thomas sprinted the last few yards to the opening, but before he could follow, the ladder was yanked from its moorings and the iron hooks clattered on the stone floor 20 feet below.

Heléne knelt at the edge, peering down into the dark. There was a rasping sound and the flare of a match.

The torch caught.

"Don't do this," Thomas called down. "For the love of god, throw the hooks up to me."

A chuckle echoed from below, reverberating off the walls of the stone chamber. "For the love of my gods, I must," he called up in reply.

Heléne leaned over the opening. "I beg you, please," she pleaded, "…think of history, of my father's work, the loss to science…your life."

The old man did not reply. They watched as he walked slowly to the end of the antechamber with the torch high above his head and disappeared into the corridor that led to the burial room and the mural.

Then, a muffled laugh floated up. They could barely hear the old man call, "Remember what I told you, Miss Bovet? That I might die, but I would die clean? Let's hope that when this tomb is found again in 1,000 years, they appreciate that!" His last words faded, and then it was silent.

Heléne looked at Thomas. "He's really going to do it?"

In response he took her hand and began walking quickly back to where the professor and Samhi were waiting.

Bovet knew the moment he saw Thomas' face. "How much time do we have?"

"Not much. Get on your horse and Heléne and I will put Samhi on behind you."

When the professor was settled, they half-lifted and half-pushed Samhi up onto the saddle behind him. Thomas cut one of the leather reins with his knife, wrapped it around Samhi's back, and waited as the professor tied it to his pommel.

"It's only 150 yards, mostly downhill, so his weight will be against you. We don't have to worry about him falling backwards."

Thomas swung Saher to the right side of the professor's horse and Heléne went to his left. They each put a hand on one of Samhi's shoulders and began the descent down the steep trail.

When they reached the camp, Thomas told the professor and Heléne to ride to the first tomb nearest the canyon entrance and wait for him.

"Which one?" Bovet asked.

"I know which one he means, dammit, man," Samhi cut in. "Just ride."

Thomas waited for his friends to start down the trail before he leapt off Saher and ducked into a tent to retrieve Heléne's journals. They could replace almost everything else at Luxor, but not those. Then he joined the others behind a mud brick wall close to a tomb that had been excavated a century earlier.

Heléne was rolling up a blanket to put behind Samhi's head and her father was pacing up and down between the tomb entrance and the main trail when Thomas arrived.

"Why does he have to do this?" Bovet muttered over and over as he paced. "Why?"

"Edouard, stop," Samhi finally said. "You are as much a prisoner of your beliefs as that old man is of his, and for that matter, as the Mahdi was."

Bovet halted and leaned down to rest a hand on Samhi's shoulder. There were tears in the professor's eyes.

"I know, old friend, I know," were the only words Samhi could form in reply.

"We should all go inside," Thomas said when he and Heléne returned from moving the horses to the safety of the covered area outside the tomb.

The professor shook his head. "The rock in the valley is unstable," he said. "We don't know what that much dynamite will do in a confined chamber. Perhaps the stone walls will absorb the blast—perhaps not."

"Or perhaps he will change his mind..." Heléne said. "We can hope."

Thomas took her hand, "Yes, that…"

His words were lost in the roar of the explosion. The ground bucked, and the wall beside them collapsed.

Samhi toppled over, and the professor knelt and covered his friend with his body. Within a matter of seconds, thick clouds of red-brown dust were swirling down from the hills, choking and blinding them.

Thomas held Heléne tight and felt her body shake.

They stayed in place for several minutes. When the dust began to settle, Thomas led Heléne and her father out onto the trail. Then they heard thunder and looked up to see the limestone cliff on the upper bluff come apart. Great boulders, some as big as a cabin, broke loose and rolled down the hill, knocking over everything in their path. Behind the boulders came thousands of tons of rock and gravel, sweeping like a tidal wave and burying their camp and the outbuildings around it.

Then the rumbling stopped, and the last of the red dust blew away towards the Nile. Above them, the sky was blue and cloudless. The desert heat reclaimed its place, and an eerie calm suppressed the cry of birds and the rustle of bushes in the wind.

Bovet pointed up to the place where they had camped the night before. The cliff was gone, the overhang had disappeared, and the trail was buried beneath enough debris to fill a long stretch of the Nile.

The professor wiped away the dust that caked his face. "Was this part of the prophecy?" he asked, looking deep up into the hills.

Thomas wrapped an arm around Heléne and began walking her back to the shelter.

'It might not have been a part of prophecy,' he thought to himself, *'but it is a part of life.'*

And the thing about life, he knew, is that it went on.

~FORTY THREE~

Alexandria, Egypt, October

Samhi had not been home in four months. Until Marwa received his telegram from Luxor with news that he was returning with Heléne, Colonel Scoundrel, and Professor Bovet, she had nearly resigned herself to life as a widow.

Instead, she was bustling about her rooftop garden at dusk as the smells of roast chicken, lamb, and spice from the bazaar floated up on the breath of aMediterranean breeze. Samhi sat at the head of the table, still recovering from his wounds but in good enough spirits that his youngest daughter had climbed into his lap, and was shrieking with laughter as he tickled her.

Marwa directed the servants to begin laying out platters beneath the white cotton canopy, checked that the lamps were lit, and confirmed that the wines Thomas had requested were properly chilled. Alexandria was becoming so cosmopolitan, she joked to Heléne, that it had taken only two shops to find the Premier Cru Chardonnay from Puligny-Montrachet and the Joh. Jos. Prüm Mosel Riesling Thomas asked for.

When she finally joined the others at the table, she and Heléne exchanged a private smile. Marwa nearly giggled when she thought of the moment, just the day before, when Samhi had casually informed her she needn't prepare separate rooms for Thomas and Heléne. What a delightful little scandal.

Thomas knew he ought to feel happier. This was his element: special friends, a Mediterranean evening, a rooftop strung with lanterns, and food and wine worthy of any European capital. Heléne looked radiant in a simple white linen dress embroidered with delicate flowers.

Her father held court for the children, retelling tales of pyramids and mummies, and Samhi–alive, strong, laughing–was steadily healing.

Still, something in him resisted the moment.

Heléne turned her head, caught his distant expression, and raised an eyebrow. He smiled quickly in return, a silent reassurance. But she could see the subtle distance in his eyes. His heart and his mind weren't having the same conversation.

Their first night together in a proper bed had been the most tender, most passionate experience they'd shared since they met. She was everything he could have hoped for: intelligent, brave, funny, kind, beautiful.

And yet, if the past five months had taught him anything, it was that only a fool imagined he could chart his own fate. The mural in Amenhotep's tomb proved otherwise. The image had churned through his mind night after night, and he'd spent most of the six-day steamer journey from Luxor pacing the decks, watching the Nile unspool behind him like time.

He'd never been one to dwell on decisions. Each day brought new opportunities, and, he admitted, new temptations. He tried to do what was right, but didn't punish himself when he missed the mark. It wasn't that he had no regrets, it was that he refused to let regret govern his choices. He didn't believe in apologies. It was enough to fix what he had broken, to make amends, and then move forward.

Now, across the table, Heléne smiled at something Marwa had said. The candlelight shimmered in her eyes, which were the same color as the deep blue sea just beyond the rooftops. And Thomas knew: a decision was coming. One he couldn't dodge.

Heléne glanced at him again. This time, she raised her glass and gave a small nod before turning back to Marwa.

Thomas lifted his own glass in return. She knew. Of course she knew.

She understood why he seemed distant. And she loved him enough not to press. Because in her heart, she was having the same thoughts.

After dinner on their fourth night at sea, Heléne and Thomas took their coffee and brandy to a pair of comfortable chairs on the First-Class deck of the SS Sutlej. Heléne wore a light wrap against the early autumn chill, but the sea was smooth, and the breeze no more than a whisper. A half-moon hung high and yellow above the French coast to the north.

Aside from the coaling stop in Malta on their third day out, the voyage had been uneventful. They breakfasted each morning in the salon, lunched and dined in the grand dining room, and spent the afternoons on deck, reading, napping, or talking with Professor Bovet about his plans to rebuild his reputation in the academic circles of London and Paris. Both Thomas and Samhi would assist with written testimony detailing the professor's kidnapping and imprisonment.

At night, as the steamer sliced through long, gentle swells, they made love with a quiet intensity. The boat's rhythm matched their own. But last night had been different; fierce, urgent, and unlike anything they'd known before. Afterward, breathless and exhausted, they had lain in silence for nearly an hour before drifting to sleep.

Thomas hadn't understood what had come over them.

Heléne had.

After a steward passed and offered her a lap blanket, she tucked it over her knees, then turned toward him.

"Which of us is going to broach the subject, my darling?" she asked softly.

He glanced over. "The subject?"

She rested her hand on his and leaned her head on his shoulder.

"Us."

"Ah," he said. "That subject."

"We have to talk about it, my love."

"You mean figure out what the hell we're doing, and where we go from here."

"We're three days out of Marseilles, Thomas. Then two days by train to Paris. Not much time, especially if you still plan to settle things with Henri Lavalle."

"I have to. For your sake, and mine."

"But what can you do? He's rich. Connected. He owns judges, police captains–this isn't like slipping into Abu Sinn's tent under moonlight."

Thomas smiled. "Or maybe it is. But that's a worry for another day. Tonight, we're talking about us."

"And it should be so simple," she said. "We love each other. We've survived something no one else could ever understand."

He kissed the top of her head. "No, they wouldn't."

"In normal times," she went on, "a normal couple would marry, have children, build a life."

"But these aren't normal times," he said, "and I doubt we're what anyone would call a normal couple."

"Really?" she teased. "You mean most young couples don't gallop across the Sahara battling mystical warlords, escape desert prisons, uncover lost tombs, or," her voice dropped, "stand in front of a mural painted three thousand years ago that showed their own faces?"

"Which was then blown to hell," he added, "along with half a mountain."

"And one of the best men we ever knew."

Thomas nodded. "One of the best."

Heléne raised her head, still holding his hand. "Last night… when we made love. Did you feel it?"

He grinned. "I think we both did."

She slapped his wrist, laughing. "Not that, you beast."

Then she leaned in and kissed him–long, slow, and certain.

They felt the ship shift course slightly, angling northeast. Thomas knew they'd passed the halfway mark. A steward lit another lamp near their chairs.

"That's not what you were talking about, was it?" he said at last.

"Oh, my love... our bodies knew. Our hearts knew. And we know, too."

She turned to him, eyes searching. "Don't we."

To his surprise, Thomas didn't flinch. He did love her. He did want her. And after what they'd been through...

And yet. They both knew. Their real lives and their separate worlds waited for them on the wharf in Marseilles. What lay behind them had been a wild, improbable dream. One they'd somehow survived.

But now?

"You'll return to work with your father, I suppose," he said.

Her reply came quickly. "There's so much to do. Years of translating, writing, publishing. He'll go on the lecture circuit in Europe and America."

"And you'll be there," Thomas said gently. "Clearing the way."

Heléne stood and walked to the railing. She looked out over the dark sea, then up at the stars. When she turned, he saw tears in her eyes.

He rose and went to her.

She pressed her head to his chest. Then looked up into his face.

"Please… please just tell me you're going to be alright."

He chuckled. "Tell you what–we've got three more nights on this tub. Let's take up that subject…"

He gave her backside a gentle squeeze.

"Starting now?" she asked, eyes glinting through tears.

"Right now."

They walked arm in arm down the quiet deck toward their cabin, as blue-and-white smoke curled up from the stacks and drifted into the clear October sky.

~FORTY FOUR~

Marseilles, France, October

Thomas asked the doorman to summon a horse-drawn fiacre cab in front of his hotel on the fashionable Boulevard La Canebière, rather than one of the leather-and-velvet-appointed landaus favored by Marseilles' wealthy elite. The shabby, single-passenger cab, with its torn cloth seat, marked him as an ordinary citizen, not a businessman or public official. That was exactly the impression he wanted to make.

It was late afternoon, and the clouds above the city were thick with the promise of rain. As the driver threaded his way through the alleys of the Réformés quarter toward the warehouse district, Thomas leaned back and let his thoughts drift to Heléne.

They had spent their final days aboard the steamer side by side, watching the deep-blue ocean from deck chairs, lingering over meals, and talking late into the night after making love.

When they parted two days ago at the foot of the steamer dock in Marseilles, neither shed a tear. This wasn't the time for sentiment. They knew where their paths diverged, and more importantly, they understood why.

As he watched Heléne and her father pull away in a landau bound for the train station and their journey back to Paris, Thomas felt no sorrow.

Only gratitude.

After checking into the Grand Hôtel Beauvau, Thomas spent his first day in Marseilles tending to unfinished business. He penned a long letter to Andrew Whitton at the Chronicle in San Francisco and delivered it personally to the American Consulate, with a request that it be relayed to the U.S. Embassy in Paris and forwarded to his contact at the War Department in Washington.

He included a second letter addressed to the American military attaché in Paris, requesting payment of the five months of pension he was owed. As a retired senior Army officer, he was entitled to draw it anywhere in the world with an American presence.

His final stop was the Société Générale bank in the heart of the city. The leather satchel he carried through the tall walnut and stained-glass entryway contained half the gold coins and bars he and Heléne had taken from Sheikh Abu Sinn as payment for her captivity.

The bank officer was curious but professional. He converted half of the gold into francs and issued an international letter of credit for the rest.

Later, with most of the cash and letter of credit safely locked in the hotel vault, Thomas took another cab to the warehouse district, where he spent several hours in a café across the street from Lavalle's headquarters, watching.

Only three people passed through the heavy double doors that afternoon. First, a man in a plain blue suit rapped several times before being admitted. Minutes later, a second man in identical dress emerged and walked briskly down the street.

Changing of the guard.

The third was a sturdily built, middle-aged woman. She returned a half hour later carrying a canvas bag, the tops of two loaves of bread poking over the edge.

Lavalle's wife? A housekeeper? He couldn't be sure. He knew little about Henri Lavalle beyond the essentials: his hunger for antiquities, his black-market empire, and his preferred tools of extortion, kidnapping, murder.

Thomas had no qualms about the justice he intended to deliver.

He thought of Bovet and Samhi, locked for months in a squalid desert goat pen outside Wad Madani. Of Heléne, imprisoned by Abu Sinn. Of what he himself had endured being ambushed in Constantinople, nearly killed in the catacombs of Alexandria, caught in the chaos of the Battle of Tamai, and nearly dead from a scorpion's sting in the desert.

No, Thomas would not waste time mustering an ounce of pity.

Not for Lavalle.

He returned to the cafe the next day an hour before the changing of the guard. His Colt was holstered beneath his jacket, and his Bowie knife sat comfortably on his other hip as he sipped a coffee and waited.

When he saw the blue-suited guard from yesterday a block down the street he left a few francs on the table and hurried across the lightly trafficked boulevard. He timed his pace to match that of the guard and met him just as the man rapped on the door for his compatriot.

As the door started to swing open, Thomas pulled his Colt with his right hand and with his left hand shoved the guard who was about to step into the warehouse hard on the back. The two men collided, but before they could pull apart and turn on him Thomas leveled his revolver at them...

"You can end the day dead, or alive, your choice," he said in a steady command voice. "I have no interest in either of you. Do as I say, and you will go home to your wives. Do anything else…" he held the gun higher, right at their faces…"and your widows won't recognize what is left of your heads."

Lavalle's men knew what a .45 could do at close range. They raised their hands and took a step back.

"C'est bien," said Thomas. As his eyes adjusted to the darkened warehouse interior, he spotted a coil of rope hanging on a peg on a nearby post. Thomas leveled the Colt at the two men.

"On the floor," he said, calm but unmistakable. "Now."

They hesitated.

"Try me," he added, cocking the hammer. The sound was enough. They dropped to their knees, then to the floor.

Thomas stepped in closer, keeping the muzzle trained between them.

"You," he said, nodding to the smaller of the two, "tie up your friend. Hands behind his back. Tightly. Like you've done it before."

The man's hands trembled as he reached for the rope Thomas tossed in front of him. He glanced up, but the cold stare in Thomas's eyes told him not to test the limits.

"Make it count," Thomas said. "If he slips out, you take his place."

The man worked quickly. Thomas circled behind them, adjusting his angle to keep the pistol on both as he checked the knots. Satisfied, he gave the tied man a nudge with his boot.

"Lie down. Face to the wall."

Then he turned to the second man, the one who had done the tying.

"Your turn."

He backed the man toward the wall with a flick of the barrel. "Hands behind your back. Crossed."

The man complied. Thomas stepped in close, and, still covering him with the Colt in one hand, he looped the rope with the other. The first pass was quick and rough, and the man flinched.

"Don't move," Thomas said. "I've done this left-handed before."

It took only a minute. The man's breath came shallow and quick as the rope tightened around his wrists, then locked into place with a practiced twist. When Thomas was done, he holstered the Colt and checked both men's bindings. He rolled the second man onto his side and gave a sharp tug on the rope to test it.

"I don't have anything to gag you with," Thomas said once he was satisfied the two men weren't going anywhere. He crouched in front of them and waved the revolver in a slow arc. "But I do have this permanent gag. If either of you so much as burps while I'm upstairs—*comprenez?*"

The men nodded in unison, eyes wide. They understood.

"A question," Thomas said. "Is anyone else in the building besides Lavalle and the woman I saw shopping yesterday?"

"The whore," one of them answered in a shaky voice.

"Whore?"

"Yes. He brought her from Romania. Looks like his mother. Her name is Crina, she has been here for weeks."

Thomas frowned. A whore who resembled Lavalle's mother? What madness was this?

"They won't let her leave," the other added.

"'They' being…?"

"Monsieur Lavalle and his secretary."

"The woman who shops for him?"

"Yes," said the first man. "She also handles his books, correspondence, legal affairs...everything."

"Does she know about the murders he's ordered, the theft, the smuggling? Is she part of it?"

The men exchanged a glance. Under different circumstances, answering that question would've gotten them fired. Now, they were certain silence would get them shot.

"No, *monsieur,*" said the first. "Not the criminal side. She runs the office. We suspect some things, because of what we're asked to do, but she isn't involved."

"I believe you," said Thomas. He stood. "You just saved her life. Tell her that someday."

He looked toward the wide staircase leading to the next floor. "What's up there?"

"Lavalle's office, his apartment, a lavatory," said the second man. "And a small suite where the Romanian girl stays."

"Last question: is he armed?"

Both nodded.

"A revolver. Top drawer of the desk," said one.

Thomas took two steps back. "Remember…no sound."

~FORTY FIVE~

He scanned the dimly lit warehouse. Crates, chests, barrels, and statues loomed in the low light; gods, pharaohs, crocodiles, ibis-headed men. A fortune surrounded him. Most of it stolen.

He moved quickly and quietly up the broad staircase—wide enough for six men to ascend abreast, designed for the movement of treasure. At the landing, a gas lamp burned softly. A hallway ran off into shadow. Directly ahead stood two heavy oak doors trimmed in brass. He turned the knob, revolver ready, and stepped inside.

The outer office was richly appointed: thick oriental rugs, velvet chairs, tall walnut shelves crammed with books and maps. At the center, a massive oak desk lay strewn with journals and correspondence. Lavalle's assistant was a woman in her late thirties. She sat at a Hammond typewriter, her fingers flying across the keys.

Her head snapped up. One hand flew to her mouth.

Thomas raised a finger to his lips. "Quiet. I promise you won't be harmed."

"If you've come to rob us," she whispered, "I assure you, there's no cash in this office."

Of course not, Thomas thought. Just gold, rubies, and stolen history.

"Where's the woman?"

"Crina?"

He nodded.

"She'll be here any moment. This is her usual time."

"To see him?"

"Yes."

"What's your name?"

"René Duval."

"Do exactly as I say and everything will be fine. Scream, reach for anything, and it goes badly. Understand?"

She nodded, eyes wide.

Just then the door opened and Crina stepped inside, wearing the same dress she wore each afternoon for Lavalle's pleasure. She froze. One hand hovered on the doorframe.

Thomas stepped gently to her elbow and guided her beside René.

"Make no sound, Crina. You'll be safe."

Crina looked to René, who gave a helpless shrug.

"Now," said Thomas calmly, "we're going into Lavalle's office. Walk in ahead of me. Stand behind him until I say otherwise."

René shook her head. "Monsieur…we can't."

"Yes, you can."

"No, I mean… he's very large. There's no room behind his desk."

Thomas smiled. "Then stand on either side."

The women nodded. Thomas motioned with his Colt. René smoothed her skirt and straightened her posture before opening the door.

Habit, he thought. Always look your best for the boss.

Lavalle's head was buried in a ledger. At the sound of the door creaking open, he looked up sharply, scowling. No one entered unannounced.

Then he saw Thomas–and the gun.

"What is the meaning of this?" he barked at René.

She said nothing. Her eyes flicked to Thomas.

"We'll get to that," Thomas said evenly. "René, open his top drawer and bring me the pistol. By the barrel."

Lavalle's scowl deepened, but René obeyed. She removed the revolver and handed it to Thomas with shaking hands.

"Who are you?" Lavalle demanded. "How do you know me? And that I keep a weapon?"

"Oh, I know a great deal about you, Henri. As for the rest, we'll get there."

He turned to René. "You prepare legal documents?"

"I do. Frequently." She squared her shoulders. "I'm a certified notary."

"Clean credentials? No lawsuits? No scandal?"

"Impeccable."

"Good." He turned to Crina. "You're from Romania?"

She nodded.

"Would you like to go home?"

Crina's eyes flared. Her whole body seemed to come alive.

"Oh, *monsieur*, yes. With all my heart."

"So, this is why you're here," Lavalle sneered. "To kidnap a whore? You don't know who you're dealing with. Take her, then. She's nothing. But I'll find you. I'll kill you both."

Thomas took in the opulence of the carved shields, alabaster jars, amulets, ruby-encrusted daggers. Then he turned back to Lavalle.

"Crime's been good to you."

"I am a legitimate and respected businessman."

Thomas cut him off. "A businessman who uses kidnapping, murder, extortion, and bribery to make his fortune."

René and Crina stiffened.

"You have no proof of any of that," Lavalle hissed. "This is slander!"

"I have proof, Henri. Documents. Witnesses. Enough for France, Egypt, Britain, in fact, everywhere you've done business."

Recognition flickered across Lavalle's face.

"You… you're the American colonel…"

"Thomas Scoundrel. U.S. Army, retired." He tipped his head to the women. "At your service, ladies."

"Scoundrel," Lavalle spat.

"You know Professor Edouard Bovet and his daughter Heléne. Also, our friend Samhi Al Katib. You arranged their kidnappings. They nearly died."

"Some would say that was the Mahdi's doing."

"They would if the Mahdi weren't dead, rotting behind a rubble pile in the Valey of the Kings."

Lavalle glared down at his desk.

"Now, Henri," Thomas said. "Let's get to business."

"You want money," Lavalle said flatly. "How much?"

"Let's talk about that. René, please come here."

When she approached, he nodded toward her desk. "Sit down. We're going to dictate a will."

"A *Testament authentique*?" she asked cautiously.

"Yes. You're a notary, and Crina and I are the witnesses."

Lavalle exploded. "A will? Dictated to a tourist and a prostitute? This is absurd."

"Witnessed by a decorated senior American Army officer who is a friend of the President of the United States." He smiled at Crina. "And a respected Romanian businesswoman."

"I am not a…" Crina started.

"You are now," Thomas said gently. "Open a dress shop. A bakery. Whatever you like."

Crina could only blink in astonishment.

"René, how many copies are needed?"

"One for each heir, one for the court."

"Make four. Do you have carbon paper?"

She nodded.

"Do you have your seal?"

She began assembling the papers.

Thomas turned toward Lavalle. "This is the final will and testament of Henri Lavalle. Full legal name, address, birth date. First bequest: all real property, including the antiquities in this building, to Professor Edouard Bovet and his daughter, Heléne. Here's their Paris address."

René typed rapidly.

Thomas gestured to the steel safe in the corner.

"How much cash?"

"You will not!" Lavalle thundered.

"He does all his business in cash," René interrupted. "Roughly 100,000 francs."

"All in notes?"

"Yes."

"What's your salary?"

"3,000."

"A living?"

She shrugged.

"Add this: I, Henri Lavalle, bequeath 50,000 francs to my loyal secretary René Duval, and 50,000 francs to my dear friend Crina Cazacu."

Crina sucked in her breath.

"Can you complete the legal language?"

René nodded, smiling faintly. She sealed the signed documents, waxed them, and handed a copy to Thomas.

"One for you," she said, giving Crina her envelope. "One for the court, and I'll keep the last."

"Now then, for the distribution of the assets," Thomas said. "Can you open the safe?"

René smiled and nodded. "He trusts me."

"Fools! Idiots! Thieves!" Lavalle thundered. "You cannot do this…and has it escaped your attention, Colonel Scoundrel, that I am still alive? You cannot register the will of a living man."

His eyes narrowed. "Unless you planned on murdering me, in which case the will is invalid. Your plan is dead in the water, Scoundrel."

Thomas did not respond. He pointed René to the safe, which was five feet tall and three feet wide. It took only a moment for her to dial the tumblers and swing open the foot thick steel door.

"Take out all of the cash," Thomas said. "And divide it into two equal amounts." Then he looked at Crina, who was still wide-eyed in disbelief. "Please get two valises from the front office and fill them up."

A few minutes later the leather valises were filled and snapped shut.

Lavalle ran his hands through his hair and wrung his hands through the ordeal but had nothing left to say.

"Whatever else is in there will become the property of the Bovets," Thomas said to René. "Please write down the combination for me to give them."

When she handed Thomas a slip of paper with the combination he said, "A final legal question, René. Is the will of a person who commits suicide legal in France?"

She smiled and nodded. "Completely."

Lavalle barked out a harsh laugh. "You think I am going to kill myself? You are not just a fool, you are insane. The prefect of police is in my employ. He will round you up and slap you into prison within the hour."

Thomas looked at the women, each of whom was holding her bag of cash. "Go down and wait for me by the door," he said in a calm voice. "I won't be long."

The women scurried out the door and Thomas sat down in the chair in front of Lavalle's desk.

"Your watchers told you that the Mahdi and I spent time together at his camp, and that he also put on a feast for me worthy of an Ottoman emperor, yes?"

Lavalle nodded. "But I have heard nothing of his supposed death."

"You will Henri, you will. You should also know that I earned the confidence of the Mahdi's most trusted lieutenant. That's how I know that the messenger who has been coming here monthly for the past three years to collect payment for the stolen treasure the Mahdi sends you did not come this month."

A light flickered in Lavalle's eyes.

"He won't be coming, Henri. Not this month, or ever again. What will be arriving at the offices of the state prosecutor, however, is a full and complete accounting of every statue, every bauble, every stick of furniture, every piece of jewelry sent to you by the Mahdi in defiance of French law. The list is in my hotel room, signed by the Mahdi's aide. You will be arrested within days, Lavalle. And you will be prosecuted and probably hung."

Lavalle remained expressionless. Thomas believed the man still thought he could bribe his way out of any trouble with the law.

"And should you be able to pay your way out of this mess," Thomas went on. "Something even worse awaits you. The Mahdi's corpse was found two weeks ago. I have sent a letter to his lieutenant explaining that his master's death was done at your bidding because you wanted to keep all the treasure money for yourself. No doubt you thought the British would defeat the Mahdi and stop the uprising, meaning you would not have to honor your obligations."

Thomas watched Lavalle's eyes. "Mahdist forces captured Khartoum a few weeks ago, Henri. They slaughtered Gordon's forces and cut off his head. It's impaled on a pike outside his old headquarters.

"With him dead and the British defeated, the last piece of business for the Mahdi's successor is to hunt down his murderer. How long do you think it will take them to sail here and deal with you?"

Lavalle shifted in his chair. A bead of sweat had broken out on his forehead and was running down the bridge of his nose.

Thomas leaned forward. "Do you want to know how they are going to kill you, Henri? After they flay the skin from that mountainous gut of yours, they will slice off your balls and feed them to the dogs–or maybe force them down your throat and make you chew them up and swallow. Then they'll put a stick in the fire and let it get red hot before they gouge out your eyes and ram it up your ass. The best part? That's just what is going to happen in the first ten minutes. I have seen this torture, Henri, they are expert at it. They will keep you on the edge of death for an entire day, taking you apart one piece at a time."

Thomas stood up. "No, my friend, I would not wish that death upon any man. But I promise that is what waits for you. Unless you wish to confess your crimes to the authorities before the Mahdi's warriors get here. They'll probably hang you, but a clean snap of the neck would be preferable to a slow torture, no?"

Lavalle's eyes were brimming with tears. "I cannot..., "he began. "I don't know how...it can't be..." His voice trailed off.

"There may be another way," Thomas said, "but it is a course for a brave man. Can you be brave for once in your life, Henri?"

Lavalle grasped at this whisper of hope. "Please, please," he blubbered, clasping his hands as if in prayer. "Let there be another way."

Thomas reached over to the bookcase and picked up the pistol from Lavalle's desk. It was small, a .32 caliber, but it would get the job done.

He removed five bullets, and rolled the cylinder to where it would strike the last bullet when the trigger was pulled.

He held the pistol up. "The only other way, Henri. You end it yourself. If you can't, then your only choice is death by slow torture or at the hangman's noose after a long and humiliating trial."

Lavalle wiped his nose and through his tears said, "How can you ask such a thing?"

"Ask? It's not a question you face, Henri. It is a choice."

Lavalle sat back in his chair, bewilderment on his face.

"Pay attention," said Thomas in a stern voice. "Hold the pistol here..." he pressed the barrel against his right temple. "Do not let it slip. If you just wound yourself, it could take hours to bleed out and die. Better to pull the trigger once and be done with the pain."

Thomas set the pistol down on the far edge of the desk. "Slow and painful or fast and easy," he said. "Those are your choices."

He backed out of the office, keeping his revolver pointed at Lavalle until he closed the door.

It didn't take long. He heard weeping, and then Lavalle's voice. "I'm sorry mother…please forgive me." Then the explosion of a single shot and the sound of something hitting the desk.

Thomas went in. Lavalle's head was on the blotter, a pool of dark red blood spilling across the polished walnut. He stood quietly for a moment, not in reverence for a man's death, but in appreciation for justice being delivered.

He was ready to leave, but something compelled him to look around a final time. The treasures on the shelves were enough to make a man rich. But it was not gold or jewels that called to him, or the corpse slumped over the desk. What pulled at him was the oil painting. How many years had Lavalle endured the sight of his mother looking down at his ten-year-old self with such complete indifference?

Thomas walked slowly down the grand staircase. Crina and René stood by the front door, valises tucked under their arms, their eyes questioning.

"Yes," was all he said.

"What do we do now?" Crina asked.

Thomas smiled.

"You live.

~EPILOGUE~

Arles, France October 1884

Thomas slung the cotton sack over his shoulder and grabbed a wooden chair from the porch of the yellow, two-story farmhouse. Inside the sack was the same lunch the farmer's wife had packed every day for the past week: dark wheat bread made with stone-ground flour, smoked sausages with mustard, two apples, a wedge of cheese, and a bottle of wine pressed from the farmer's prized *grenache* grapes.

He carried the chair across the rutted dirt lane that stretched from the Rhône River to the Alpilles mountains. Wheat stubble from the recent harvest covered the land as far as he could see. On the low hills a half mile away, a few orange leaves still clung to the woody vines, remnants of the red grape clusters that had ripened under the summer sun.

Vincent's easel was already set up beside an irrigation ditch, across from an ancient oak whose twisted limbs curled into grotesque angles. Perfect for Van Gogh, Thomas thought, smiling.

The day before he was scheduled to leave for Le Havre to board the steamer to New York, he learned that his friend was painting in Arles, only 50 miles from Marseilles. It had been six months since they'd last seen each other, but when Thomas walked into the stone floored café with the red-tile roof and saw Vincent seated alone with a bottle of vin *ordinaire* and a sketchpad, it felt like home.

Vincent had been delighted, too, not only because he had made few friends in Arles, but because the first words out of Thomas's mouth were: "Innkeeper... a bottle of absinthe and a bowl of fresh stew for my friend."

Late that night, after more drink than conversation, the two men staggered out of the village and back to the farmhouse where Vincent was boarding. Thomas slept on the floor at the foot of his friend's bed that night and moved into a spare room the next morning.

For the next six days their routine was the same: breakfast with the farmer's wife, a walk into the village for pipe tobacco and drawing charcoal, then into the fields or hills until late afternoon, followed by wine and dinner in the café.

Today was different. Thomas was taking the coach to Paris tomorrow, and Vincent had asked him to deliver several rolled canvases and to buy tubes of paint to post back to Arles.

"What colors should I get?" Thomas asked, setting the chair a few feet behind the painter and sipping his black coffee.

"All of them, if you'd be so kind," Vincent said after a long pause, brushing in the soft hues of a fall morning sky.

"I've never seen you use turquoise blue," Thomas said. Vincent looked up, surprised.

"Don't know that anyone uses it, except maybe a few of the British portraitists. One of the problems with turquoise is it fades fast. A year or two and poof–it becomes a robin's egg. Color has to last, my friend."

Thomas chuckled. "Tell that to the Pharaohs."

"What's that?" Vincent asked.

"Pharaohs. The ancient Egyptians. They loved turquoise. I've seen it on tomb walls that were painted 3,000 years ago. They are still vibrant and alive."

Vincent muttered something Thomas couldn't hear and returned to the canvas. Two hours later, he stopped abruptly and turned. Thomas had stretched out in the grass with one of Vincent's sketchbooks.

"You've seen the tombs?" Vincent asked.

"Oh yes."

"Since I last saw you?"

"That's where I've been. Egypt. And the Sudan."

Vincent set down his palette and opened the cotton sack. He poured wine into two pewter mugs, then sat on the grass beside his friend.

"But... wasn't there a war?"

"There was."

"And you, being you…don't tell me you avoided it?"

"I didn't."

Vincent sliced the cheese in half with his penknife, gave Thomas a piece, and wolfed down the rest.

"War. Death. Chaos. Obliteration…"

"All of that," Thomas said. "And more."

Dusk settled around them, and the air grew colder. Vincent refilled their mugs.

"Let me ask you something," Vincent said.

Thomas nodded, knowing it might take time for the artist to gather his words.

As the last orange light filtered through the bare limbs of the great oak, Vincent finally asked, "What did you gain, Thomas?"

Thomas looked down. Then he sighed and raised his head, his eyes fixed on the distant horizon.

"Everything,"

"And what did you lose?"

When Thomas turned to answer, Vincent saw the tear in his eye.

"Everything."

The sun slipped behind the hills in a final kiss of fire. Vincent drained his mug, then stood and began to pack his easel.

When Thomas joined him, Vincent placed a hand on his shoulder.

"Everything gained, and everything lost," he said. "A life in perfect balance."

Van Gogh smiled, slung the easel over his shoulder, and began walking across the field. Dried wheat stalks crunched under his boots.

Everything and nothing, Thomas thought, as he followed his friend back to the yellow farmhouse.

THE END

~About the Author~

B.R. O'Hagan earned undergraduate and graduate degrees at UCLA and wrote for film, television, and as a ghostwriter of twenty-three books for Fortune 100 CEOs, national political figures, and other prominent individuals. He is also the author of the novel *Martin's Way* and the family holiday book *Jonathan Marvel's Christmas Pockets. The Ghost of Khartoum* is the third entry in his six-book Thomas Scoundrel historical adventure series.

B.R. lives with his family in rural Oregon, surrounded by Douglas fir forests and the finest pinot noir vineyards on earth.

~ ACKNOWLEDGMENTS ~

To my wife Lesli, whose patience and faith are boundless, thank you. To Todd Rhine, whose vision, confidence and steadfast support and encouragement have been a rock, many, many thanks. To Anne Marie Levin, great appreciation and thanks for your expertise and enthusiasm. To my daughter Natalie for her love, and to Kai Douglas for bringing such joy to my life every day.

I am a blessed man.

~A Note to Readers~

I appreciate you tremendously, and thank you for coming along with me on the big adventure. As I begin work on the 4th Scoundrel novel, *The Last Wild West*, I would like to invite you to get in touch with me to share your Scoundrel experience. My email is *brad@brohagan.com*, and yes, I read them all.

Also, I would consider it a great favor if you would consider logging on to AMAZON and writing a review for *The Ghost of Khartoum*. Short and to the point is just fine, or pour your complete thoughts out in detail. (And speaking of pouring, if you want to recommend a special wine, that would be greatly appreciated, too!)

A QR code link to the ThomasScoundrel series page is below.

Many thanks!

Wishing you all the best on your own great adventure,

B.R. O'Hagan

www.brohagan.com

Made in United States
Cleveland, OH
19 September 2025

20597353R00184